WILLOW GRACE

CREOVIS

BOOK TWO OF THE VINDICTA SERIES

VENDERA PUBLISHING

Editing by Ramona Mihai

Cover designed by Karisa DeLay

Formatting and interior art by Aubrey Joy Rosales (Jai Design)

ISBN: 978-1-936307-56-2

Published by Vendera Publishing

Dedication

To Paul, who chose to be my father, and to Eric, the dance dad who still tries to go to each and every book signing (even though he had his own book signed within the first month of its release).

BELLUM'S COLOSSEUM

M OF
...NIA

2

FAMES' WASTES

PRONUNCIATION GUIDE

This guide is here for any who wish to use it! This novel is fantastical science fiction, so *of course* you can't pronounce the names. Each word in each category is listed alphabetically. There's both a phonetic spelling of the word and a much easier, simple pronunciation next to it for those who haven't learned the phonetic alphabet (and probably never will).

A note before you begin: An apostrophe in the Delfungaye language denotes a tiny pause when pronouncing a word: a staccato.

Characters

- ☐ **Avenlae** -/ˈɔvɛnl,e/ (AH-vehn-lay)
- ☐ **Darinrain** - /dˈɔrɪnren/ (DAH-rin-rain)
- ☐ **Havyeque** - /hɑv,aɪˈik/ (hahv-EYE-YEEK)
- ☐ **Kaigar** - /kˈaɪgɑr/ (k-EYE-gahr)
- ☐ **Klaecyia** - /klesˈaɪjə/ (klay-SIGH-yah)
- ☐ **Lieneata** -/l,aɪˈɛnitə/ (lie-eh-NEE-tah)
- ☐ **Matri Me'leiv** - /m,ɑtrˈi mɛl,ɛiˈv/ (MAH-tree meh'-leh-EEV)
- ☐ **Notien** - /nˈoʊʃən/ (NO-shun)
- ☐ **Novissime** - /nɑvˈis,ime/ (nah-VEE-SEE-may)
- ☐ **Saetyl** - /sˈetɪl/ (SAY-till)
- ☐ **Sinivir** - /s,mɪvˈir/ (SIN-ih-VEER)
- ☐ **Vindincta** - /v,indˈiktə/ (veen-DEEK-ta)
- ☐ **Xiaye** - /zˈaɪj,e/ (z-EYE-yay)

Cultural Names/Labels:

- ☐ **Audritya** - /ˈaʊdritjə/ (OW-dree-tyah) - Name of the largest river of the Silvacastra forest
- ☐ **Fae'oteek** - /fe,oʊtˈik/ (faye'-OH- TEEK) - Silvacastra's largest

mountain range, divides the plains and Laizuteek forest from the Icelands

- ☐ **Fae'yeerium** - /fej'iriəm/ (faye'-YEE-ree-uhm) - Mother Death
- ☐ **Glae'atii** - /gle'ɑt,i/ (glay'-AH-TEE) - sacred nest of the armorers
- ☐ **Hi'pret** - /h'iprɛt/ (HEE'-pret) - sheet woven from the fireproof core of the deepest jungle trees
- ☐ **Je'quiet** - /ʒɛk'wiɛ/ (JE'-KWEE-eh) - Delfungaye historians. The honor of becoming a Je'quiet is passed down through direct bloodlines
- ☐ **Le'eseia** - /lɛ'isi,ə/ (leh'-EE-see-AH)
- ☐ **Lyceliah** - /l,aɪs'iliə/ (lie-SEE-lee-ah)
- ☐ **Silvacastra** - /s'ilvəkæstr,ə/ (SEEL-vuh-CAS-trah)
- ☐ **Visiocustos** - /v'isiouk,ustoʊs/ (VEE-see-oh-KOO-stohs) - Sloviyankae historians
- ☐ **Wiegt'ri** - /w'igtr,i/ (WEEgt'-ree) - Delfungaye Celebration of the change of Seasons

Food:

- ☐ **A'ta'ya** - /'ɑtɑj,ɑ/ (AH'-tah'-YAH) - Delfungaye wine
- ☐ **Anteel** - /'ɑntil/ (AHN-teel) - Laizuteek tea
- ☐ **Bauete** - /bɔte/ (baw-tay) - fruit from the Laizuteek forest
- ☐ **Graetae** - /grete/ (gray-tay) - Fyr'aeset pastry
- ☐ **J'guaya** - /ʒg'ɔɪjə/ (j'-GOY-yuh) - seed of the cave trees

Creatures

- ☐ **Gueirag** - /g,ɔɪ'iræg/ (goy-EE-rag)
- ☐ **Kreelcur** - /kr'il,ur/ (KREE-LOO-er)
- ☐ **Voxmor** - /v'ɑksmɔr/ (VAHX-more)

Power

- ☐ **Creonex** - /kr'ioʊnɛks/ (KREE-oh-nex)

- **Creovis** - /krˌioʊv'is/ (KREE-oh-VEES)
- **Genepotentia** - /ʒ'ɛnɛpoʊtˌɛnʃiə/ (GEN-uh-poh-TEN-shee-uh)
- **Excitialium** - /ɛksˌiti'aliəm/ (ex-SEE-tee-AHL-lee-uhm) - metal mined from the Fae'oteek mountain range

Tribes

- **Delfungaye** - /dˌɛfluŋg'e/ (DEL-foo-ing-gay) - Name for the winged humanoid species of Silvacastra.
- **Fyr'aeset** - /f'irɛsˌɛt/ (FEAR'-eh-SET) - Known for their golden skin, sleek black wings, navy eyes and platinum blonde hair, these people are the Gliders of Silvacatra's plains.
- **Hopyroque** - /hˌɑpir'oʊk/ (hah-pee-ROWK) - Inhabitants of the Fae'oteek mountain range, these people are known for their vivid copper skin, forest-green hair, and small tusks (instead of the elongated canines found in the majority of the Delfungaye species)
- **Laizuteek** - /l'aɪzˌutik/ (LIE-ZOO-teek) - The Silver People of the Forest: this tribe is the most abundant after the initial slaughter of the Delfungaye. Their skin is snow white, and they have silver feathered wings that brighten their silver eyes. Their canines are the largest in the species, and are flashed as a sign of dominance or aggression.
- **Sloviyankae** - /sloʊˌaɪj'ɔŋke/ (slav-EYE-YONK-aye) - Distant cousin of the Delfungaye species.
- **Y'araye** - /j'ɔrˌe/ (y'-AHR-aye) - Known as the deadliest mercenaries and warriors in all of creation, the Y'araye once ruled the deepest jungles of Silvacastra before the Voxmor invaded. They're incredibly similar to the Laizuteek, except for their more muscular build, prismatic eyes, and stronger instincts.

CHAPTER 1

I awoke to the sound of his strangled scream tearing through the night.

The sound ripped me from sleep so abruptly that it took me a second to realize that I was awake, even though there was no break in the drawn-out cry that scorched Avenlae's throat. My pulse made my fingers tremble as I fumbled with the blankets to try to get to him.

"Avenlae!" I croaked during a short pause in his cry as he sucked in a breath. It wasn't the sound of him awakening from whatever nightmare his mind held him captive in, however, for he screamed again, the sound making my throat constrict as a primal fear froze my veins. Avenlae's vivid night terrors were not unusual. Still, their intensity had recently escalated to a level that made me concerned I might no longer be able to wake him from them.

Finally rid of the covers, I threw my right leg over Avenlae's waist, straddling him to prepare to hold him down as his silver eyes popped open, wide and terrified. If I couldn't get to him the second he started whimpering, he would become dangerous — I had very little time left to bring back the gentle Avenlae I had gone to bed with. I didn't fear for myself. I only feared the look in his eyes when he realized what he'd done.

"Sh, Av, please," I soothed as I wrapped my fingers around his wrists, stabilizing myself and forcing them down on either side of him, "You're okay. Listen to my voice—"

"Don't *touch her!*"he shrieked, his wings beginning to flutter underneath him as he tried to thrash out of my grip.

"No one is in danger, Av. It's just you and me." I took a deep breath and felt my powers lazily buzz down my arms. *This is not the damn time for* you *to wake up sleepily!* I thought angrily as the blue metal filigree of the Creonex finally began to glow around my left hand.

Avenlae's onyx hair plastered across his face as he panted, shaking his head, flashing his canines, sweat building over his tattoos. I sucked in a nervous breath—he was beginning to become defensive. I wouldn't be able to hold him back much longer.

"Avenlae," I urged, trying to force calm through the Creonex and into his body. "I'm safe. You're with me here in the forest, in the tribe. No one is hurting us — the war ended five years ago. Okay? Just listen—"

With a strength born of panic, Avenlae pushed me off of him, sending me skidding across the room as he rolled out of bed, pointed ears pinned back against his temples, and canines fully bared. I scrambled to my feet, ignoring the dull ache in my back from where I had hit the hardwood floor.

"Don't you *dare* make me do this, Avenlae!" I pleaded, pure golden *genepotentia* beginning to arc across my skin and feathers as I prepared for him to charge. No matter how many times I warned him, he always did. At this point, I knew he wasn't thinking clearly enough to control himself, and I knew he always understood I had to act in self-defense, but I still always hated it. I hated that it meant I had to hurt him . . . I had to hurt my already broken warrior, my love.

2

So when the moment finally came, it was with the drop of a tear from my red eye that I allowed a burst of golden energy to push Avenlae back as he rushed towards me, wings extended so that the black claws of his wing joints would've reached me first. With the drop of another tear, this time from my silver eye, I stepped towards where he had fallen against the foot of our bed, gasping, shaking his head. But those tears were dry when I knelt in front of him. I couldn't let him see how much those night terrors also affected me, not because of my pride, but instead for his.

Avenlae's silver eyes rose to meet mine, his pupils dilating the second he became aware of me. His ears moved forward as he studied me, trying to understand why we were on the floor. I had long since stopped explaining the situations to him—in time, he figured it out. I didn't need to exacerbate his humiliation or guilt.

"A-another one?" Avenlae's voice was so feeble yet so filled with pain that it took all of my self-control not to allow more tears to blur my vision. I just nodded, holding his gaze, the rise and fall of his chest indicated only by the glimmer of early morning light across the sweat coating his skin. He lowered his eyes, reliving the previous events in his mind in silence. I wanted to hold him, wanted to press my fingers to his warm brow to show him how safe he was, but I knew better. I needed to wait for his invitation. While the love we'd grown through the *lyceliah* had lasted through the past five years of rebuilding Creation and our own Delfungaye civilization, Avenlae was, first and foremost, a *Y'araye* warrior. There was a pride that ran deep into his psyche that no tender caress from me could break.

Although worse than the previous night terrors, this one didn't differ in resolution. Avenlae, keeping his eyes averted, lifted a shaking hand to rest on mine, whose palm pressed against my knee. Gradually, I shifted so that I was

3

closer to him and could feel the heat of fear radiating off his body. Avenlae's wings stretched from behind his back and folded around us, closing our embrace off from the world. I curled into his lap where he still sat on the floor, placing my left palm against his cheek, and watched as his eyes closed and the tension left his muscles. Memories, all of his favorites, began to transfer to him from where they were stored in the metal filigree Creonex wrapped around my left hand. I folded my wings closely against my back, partially for warmth but mainly for security.

"I cannot escape them, *Le'eseia,*" Avenlae whispered, his eyes cracking open after a few silent moments. The glow of the Creonex deepened the shadows along the scar from his right temple down to the left side of his jaw. A reminder of who I was, what I could've been . . .

"That's why you have me, Av," I said quietly, placing a soft kiss on his forehead where his scar began.

The calluses of his hand were rough against my cheek as Avenlae guided my mouth towards his. There was a delicate tremble in his lips as they pressed into mine, the whisper of his fear salty on my tongue. It may have seemed odd to the outsider—the tender embrace after his previous aggression—but I understood it to be his way of reminding himself of who I was, where he was, and that we were both still alive. This scene had become repetitive, especially in the past few months. Still, I didn't complain when compared to the other reaction Avenlae would sometimes have to the after-effects of his night terrors: forced cold indifference. It had taken me all of the five years since the fall of Sinivir, the Fifth Creator, to convince Avenlae that my eyes remained nonjudgmental as I saw him vulnerable during his nightmares. To me, each kiss he gave me as he calmed from his fight-or-flight response was progress, a small victory, a deeper connection.

"Did I hurt you?" The question was whispered, laced with drops of worry.

"No," I answered simply, the memories fading from the Creonex as I felt Avenlae's pulse slow.

One dark eyebrow arched. Avenlae knew I was lying before I even opened my mouth.

"Not any more than you have in the past."

He lowered his silver eyes again. "They are getting worse."

"I know."

Silence swelled between us. It so often had. So much time had passed, yet both of us could recall parts of the trauma of Creation's War as if it had happened just the week before. Avenlae's memories were much stronger than mine, and I found that often my silence was healing enough when he experienced these flashbacks. He just needed my presence, and I was okay with that. I was never very good at helping someone work through intense emotions, anyway.

"I am sorry," Avenlae murmured, his voice a low growl. The anger behind his words, I knew, was directed at himself. It always was.

"No, Av. Please don't apologize to me." I used a finger to tilt his chin up so he was forced to look at me in the low light of the first rays of suns' rise. "I may not feel these emotions like you do, but it doesn't mean I don't feel them at all. You know I understand. You have done nothing wrong."

Avenlae lifted his head out of my grasp, then nuzzled into my neck as he wrapped his arms around my waist, breathing deeply. "Your empathy is limitless, My Queen. I am undeserving."

"Your attempts at flattery are absolutely ridiculous, *My King*," I responded, allowing him to continue his exploration, "and I don't accept them as an excuse to ignore what I said."

Avenlae chuckled, the warm puffs of air from his mouth sending goosebumps rippling across my skin before he raised his head. "You love me too deeply, Xai."

I smiled down at him, running a hand through the full length of his hair as it fanned over his silver wings. "I love you because you chose to love me."

"That is what I get for choosing an immortal, hm?" Avenlae set his hands on my hips, attempting to move me closer to him as he shifted his wings back, but I put a hand on his chest to stop him.

"Even so, *this* immortal is not immune to being woken up before suns' rise." Avenlae's ears twitched back as his eyes flicked away from mine. "No, none of that. Just find me some coffee. The humans dropped a shipment off with the *Sloviyankae,* and Saetyl should have brought some with her yesterday."

Avenlae scoffed as he straightened, keeping a hand on my hip as I moved away from him so he could stand. *"You* are the only reason the humans have a coffee trade with the Delfungaye, you know."

"I am supporting them as they work to rebuild a global economy and fully enter into the Inter-universal Market," I said in the most autocratic voice I could muster as I rose to my feet, pointing my nose up.

"What a political way to admit an addiction to a human substance," Avenlae grumbled as he threw a light *Laizuteek* tunic over his head, covering the tattoos on his chest and torso that had been misplaced by the ugly scar down the middle of his sternum. I was fascinated nonetheless, for his muscles still rippled with his every movement despite the tightness of that scar. Letting out a huff, I crossed my arms, too distracted to remember what I was supposed to respond to. Avenlae just smiled as he picked up one of his scabbards and placed it across his back, walking towards me with his head bowed, tendrils of hair falling over his shoulders.

"Anything for my *Le'eseia,"* he whispered as he kissed me before heading out the door to a vendor we both knew well, who was also always up before suns' rise because she knew how early I liked to have my cup of coffee. I sighed, realizing Avenlae had kept me distracted long enough to forget to remind him that he no longer needed to travel around the tribe armed. Of course, I couldn't blame him—there were very few within the tribes of Delfungaye that dropped the habit of remaining armed at all times. Their weapons had become smaller, more easily concealed, but still ever-present. I usually left my own rapiers behind in Avenlae and my room when I was out, but I never forgot what kind of weapon the Creonex was, and neither did anyone else.

After throwing on some of the most basic *Laizuteek* robes I owned, I stepped out onto our balcony and leaped into the air, spreading my wings and arcing widely over to the top of the Queen's Nest. The morning air still carried a hint of the cold season in its breeze, yet it held the scent of spring, of new growth. The humidity that had seeped into the forest on Silvacastra was already strong enough to make my skin feel sticky. However, after the frigid last season, I welcomed the oppressive heat.

I landed on a thick branch that stuck out above the Queen's Nest, one that I knew was just above where Avenlae and I stayed, and that I had ordered be left alone. There was something to preventing the Queen's Nest from complete perfection, and, besides, it was where I often liked to sit to watch the suns rise or set. It was far enough removed from the tribe that I felt as if I could breathe on my own, but still close enough that I didn't ignore my responsibilities, no matter how much I sometimes wanted to.

Breathing in the smell of the season changing, I watched more orange and pink rays of suns' light burst out from the horizon. The colors of the forest awoke in the light of the suns, the emerald of the leaves appearing sheer against the colors of the sky, and the trees' white bark turning a blazing orange. My raven hair sparkled with hints of auburn as the warmth of the suns hit my face, and I was sure my red left eye appeared even more menacing than usual. The alien birdsong of the Delfungaye forest hit my ears as the rest of the world began to rise, harmonies and melodies just as sweet to the ears as they had been back on Earth. The air carried a coolness that almost reminded me of autumn — that scent of change I used to love. But here, it smelled of silver bark and wild rain instead, as if the world itself had rewritten the season for me.

I was starting to realize, however, that my memories of Earth were becoming fractured. I knew the sounds I heard were different from those I had grown up hearing, but I couldn't recognize how. I knew the world of Silvacastra was different, like Earth in a glitch, but I couldn't picture the comparisons in my mind. I didn't feel pain at this realization, though, like I had when I realized I could no longer clearly remember my mother. Instead, I felt a release, as if accepting this forest as my home freed me from the weight of the pain Earth held.

I wondered if I would feel the same about my memories of Novissime someday.

I buried the prick of pain I felt as I saw Avenlae gliding through the trees below me. Novissime was one topic we never spoke about. It was too painful for him, and I decided it wasn't a battle I was going to pick. He never asked me about my mother, so I never asked him about his. It was an unspoken agreement that had worked well in our favor.

Avenlae didn't bother looking around for me; he angled his flight straight up the front of the Queen's Nest and beat his wings to slow his momentum as he reached me, blowing my hair back away from my face. He was so powerful, so dangerous, yet almost ethereal when I looked at him with the light of the suns behind him. I didn't hide the smile that bloomed over my face as he landed next to me, two closed crystal cups held in his hands.

"If only my return brought out the same smile as coffee does," Avenlae sighed sarcastically as he held out the cup. I felt the condensation of cold brew as I took the cup from him, excitement building in my chest—our coffee vendor had perfected her craft.

"You know the smile was only for you, Av," I said as I sipped at the drink, rolling my shoulders. A crack sounded next to me, and I looked over to see a proffered half of a *j'guaya* seed, its black interior just as unappetizing as the very first time I had seen it. I grinned as I took it from Avenlae and we ate, sitting together on a branch, watching the suns rise in the same way we had for the almost six years we had known each other. If there was nothing else, there was this constant. This reliance we knew we could have on each other's strength, even if there were times he needed it more than I did.

"I am sorry," Avenlae said softly, keeping his sparkling irises on the suns before us, "for waking you."

"I know." I looked over at him, at the twitch in his ears as he fought to appear unbothered. I raised a hand and rubbed my palm along his shoulders, Avenlae's wings lowering as he leaned into my touch. "There will come a time when your past won't affect you so violently."

"Will there?"

I could hear the touch of anxiety twisting his words, even if he hadn't wanted me to. "Yes. I never thought I'd say it, but this time of peace... It's been more of a transition than a simple relief. But I think as you become more accustomed to it, your nightmares will fade."

"Perhaps." The dismissal was strong in his voice as we both watched the sleek black wings of my closest friend dart through the canopy of the trees, her golden skin burning with the warmth of the suns. Avenlae would never allow anyone but me to know of what he felt were his "weaknesses". Of course, Notien knew, as there was very little in the world that I kept from her, but she was good at hiding it. She never let on that she saw Avenlae as anything other than the well-respected King of the Delfungaye that he had grown into being.

Notien's round navy eyes crinkled into a smile as she swooped up the front of the Queen's Nest to reach us, her platinum bob shining. She had left behind the Delfungaye warrior's garb in exchange for the tightly wrapped white silk bodice and long, flowing black pants that were more traditional for her tribe, the *Fyr'aeset*. I knew, however, that sheaths were still strapped around her thighs. The fresh tattoos that swirled around her collarbones may have chronicled her victories in the Creation's War, but to Notien, they were reminders of what she had survived. I glanced down at my forearms, my fair skin now decorated with the accolades of a Delfungaye warrior. I had broken tradition by getting the mark of each tribe woven into my own warrior's tattoos, but I felt that I needed the reminder placed boldly upon my skin as much as my team, my *friends*, did.

"You are making me miss the days when I would meet you at your nest before training," Notien grinned as she hovered before us, bowing her head once in my direction and once towards Avenlae.

"I missed them this morning," I said, tilting my head down in acknowledgment of her respect, "seeing as *you* never grumbled so much about getting me an early morning drink or food." A low growl rumbled in Avenlae's chest. "And he's *still* grumbling!"

That earned me a look from Avenlae, but Notien just laughed, her melodious voice dancing with the surrounding birdsong. "We have not even started the day yet! Are you sure you will survive meeting with the tribes, My King?"

"It is not *my* ability to survive that you should be worried about," Avenlae scoffed.

Rolling my eyes, I pushed myself to my feet, my cup of coffee drained. I stretched my wings out behind me, not sparing a glance toward Avenlae before saying, "Shall we, then? Something tells me Saetyl will not be waiting very patiently to see you."

A soft smile played along Notien's lips as she lowered her eyes. "I visited her this morning before coming to find you. Three weeks apart really is not as long as it seems."

"Does she agree?" I asked, my eyebrows raised.

"Of course not," Avenlae answered from beside me, jumping into the air and nearly throwing me off balance from the swaying of the branch.

"How exactly have you figured that one out?" I called as I flapped my wings, finding better stability in the air. "I never knew you two were ever close enough for her to discuss these things with you."

Avenlae shrugged. "She does not. But I know what kind of warrior Saetyl is." He twitched his head in Notien's direction. "She will fiercely protect whatever is most important to her. Therefore, three weeks outside of her immediate protection is three weeks too long."

"Be that as it may," Notien pipped up as we began to make our way towards the front of the Queen's Nest, "I think we should find a different topic to discuss, My Queen."

I waited until after we had dove down to the official entrance to the Queen's Nest before responding to her. "First of all, you already know how I feel about the 'My Queen' business." Notien lifted an eyebrow and smirked as we landed on the broad branch that made the front walkway of the Nest. Just before we entered, I stopped and turned to her. "Secondly, these past years haven't changed *that* much. You're allowed to confide in me if you need to."

"You say that, but . . ." Notien turned her eyes on Avenlae as he walked past us, nodding to the *Laizuteek* guards as they bowed their heads and averted their eyes. "Somehow, I feel as if the time that has passed has changed everything."

"It's changed our dynamics, yes," I said, pressing a hand gently to her back as we began to walk forward, "but not who we are. You're still my best friend, and I am yours."

Notien offered me a soft smile, letting her wings drag as we entered the bustle of the Queen's Nest. "Well, Xiaye, as your friend, I should probably warn you."

"Warn me about what?" I asked, stopping in the middle of the central area of the Queen's Nest.

"Kaigar has already ordered that drinks be brought to the meeting room."

I shook my head. "You're joking."

Notien raised an eyebrow and looked off to our right, where a harried member of the waitstaff was trying to rush through the crowd with a tray full of crystal glasses and bottles.

I threw my hands up. "I should've gotten more coffee."

CHAPTER 2

"Ah, Your Majesty! Kicking off the tribal meeting rather nonchalantly, are we not?" Darinrain's voice boomed, causing Avenlae, who had not changed out of his tunic, to stiffen with annoyance. Darinrain's smile was genuine and nearly contagious as he neared with a hand offered forward as if to pat Avenlae on the shoulder.

"If you touch me, I will kill you," Avenlae hissed.

"No can do, my friend. I am a little too important now."

"Do not *ever* refer to me as your friend."

Darinrain's smile became a little tighter as he turned to face me, the tattoos of the *Je'queit* zigzagging up the golden skin of his neck and bare skull. "What dead thing did you feed *him* this morning, Xiaye?"

"You call me 'Your Majesty,' but *she* is just 'Xiaye'?" Avenlae snapped, evidently much more offended than I was by being referred to by my name and not my title.

"Well, you are not my friend!" Darinrain responded with mock offense.

"I see old habits never die." The rasp of Saetyl's voice cut across whatever

retort Avenlae was about to make. Notien couldn't hide her smile as the much larger woman approached. Saetyl's ceremonial *kreeleur* pelts hung down her shoulders and across her upper back, accentuating the rough nature of her black feathers along her curved wings. Although the weather within the forest was warming, she looked much more at home in the thicker garb of the *Hopyroque* mountain tribe than she ever had been in *Laizuteek* dress or the style of the combined Delfungaye tribes during the war. A few tiny white claws hung from braids in her curly forest-green hair, but they remained the only ornamental accessories Saetyl would ever wear.

"The day those two get along will also be the day one dies," I said, shaking my head at the glares Avenlae aimed at Darinrain, who was artfully ignoring his King.

"I do not know, Xiaye," Notien folded her arms over her chest, "I do not think Avenlae will admit to liking Darinrain even with his last breath."

"Should we let them speak about us like that, My King?" Darinrain said, suddenly becoming very serious and moving closer to Avenlae as if they were about to start making a plan.

"I am beginning to think we should not," Avenlae's intense silver gaze met mine, warning me not to take the joke further.

"Well, settle it later," Saetyl said, looking over my shoulder and arranging her expression into that of a diplomat. "The *Sloviyankae* delegation approaches."

"I wonder who Queen Klaecyia has sent this time," I breathed, turning to face the group entering the Nest behind us. I attempted to place a soft, welcoming smile on my lips, knowing that there had always been a touch of tension between the *Sloviyankae* tribe and the rest of the Delfungaye. No matter how good the Defungaye's memory was, the *Sloviyankae's* was sharper.

I let out a quick breath of relief when I saw who the four *Sloviyankae* guards were escorting. The man's black eyes crinkled, and his three nostrils flared from how he beamed at the sight of us. His silver hair was braided tightly to his head, but his skin shimmered opalescent in the light let in from the windows dotted around the height of the Queen's Nest.

"Havyeque!" Darinrain called, stepping forward with his arms outstretched. "It has been too long, Brother!"

"Indeed!" Havyeque agreed joyously, embracing Darinrain without hesitation. When he was released, he bowed deeply towards Avenlae and me. "I have missed my winged brethren greatly. It is truly my honor to be chosen to represent the *Sloviyankae* during this tribal meeting, Red-Eye."

"Don't you think you could call me Xiaye after all this time?" I asked, grinning back at Havyeque as I stepped forward to greet him.

"If it is what you request, My Queen, I will abide." Havyeque kept the bat-like remnants of the *Sloviyankae* wings folded tightly against his shoulders as he bowed his head and grasped my hand. Avenlae dipped his head forward towards Havyeque, but did not move from where he stood next to Saetyl. Havyeque, however, took no offense at Avenlae's lack of enthusiasm as he looked around with a smile, asking, "Will the mighty Vindicta be joining us for this meeting?"

"She should be returning from a mission to aid the *Reecytclous* people in the second universe momentarily," Saetyl responded curtly. She then faced me and continued. "Kaigar arrived after the changing of the Queen's Guard."

I nodded, then said, "Let's move this conversation to a less populated portion of the Queen's Nest, shall we? Vindicta will have no trouble finding us."

With a few sparse words of agreement, the group began to migrate towards the far wall of the nest, where a set of wooden doors sat. Behind them was the unimaginatively named Tribal Meeting Room, the only room large enough within the Nest to house all required to be in attendance for the quarterly meetings of the Delfungaye. Avenlae slowed to walk with me as Darinrain engaged the others in begrudging conversation ahead of us.

"You must make a more concentrated effort to be likable, My King," I said, suppressing a chuckle at Saetyl's uncomfortable stance when Darinrain threw a friendly arm around Notien's shoulders as he dove into the energetic retelling of some *Je'queit* tale of morals.

"The only one required to like me is you, my love," Avenlae said quietly, brushing his fingers against mine while he continued to watch protectively over the group ahead of us.

"Yes, well, the Delfungaye tribes need to respect their king as much as their queen."

"I am respected out of fear. They still know what tribe raised me." A dark tone shadowed Avenlae's tongue as he spoke. His place within the immediate tribe and the Delfungaye civilization as a whole had changed dramatically when he had chosen me as his mate. Still, he didn't forget the years he lived just outside of the central *Laizuteek*, nor the hard, distrusting stares of his fellow tribespeople as he moved through the trees. There were moments when I, too, questioned if their lowered eyes now were out of respect for me instead of respect for Avenlae's new title.

"If that is the aspect of you some Delfungaye choose to fixate on, that is their choice. Ensure, however, that it isn't the only aspect of you that they are allowed to see." I looked him in the eye as I said it, watching as he touched the tips of his ears against his hair, the only sign of annoyance he would show me in front of others. Avenlae tilted his head towards the open doorway of the meeting room, a soft smile spreading his lips as he said, "Consider it done, Xai."

I returned his soft smile as I brushed past him and walked toward the seat I had decided to claim as my own. It was positioned towards the middle of the large, white, and gray marble round table, so that all in attendance could see me and I, them. Large mullion windows circled the room, keeping it well-lit naturally as the suns of Silvacastra poured the full strength of their light over the forest. The slate-grey walls of the room were left bare, save for a few simplistic light fixtures for meetings that could extend long past the setting of the suns.

A few successful *Fyr'aeset* and *Laizuteek* merchants set drinks and a variety of Delfungaye finger foods around the table as Notien, Saetyl, Darinrain, Havyeque, and Avenlae gradually took their seats around me. Kaigar, his metal wing reflecting the suns' light, watched intently as the merchants began to shuffle out, the whirring of the machinery that held his body together like white noise behind echoes of conversation. He nodded his head briefly toward both Avenlae and me, then took a large swig from a mug he had snatched from a merchant's hand as he had passed. I bit down a smile—Avenlae had a very similar-looking mug in front of him that I knew held a finely fermented alcohol from some of the northernmost *Hopyroque* tribes. The General and the King were more alike than they ever cared to admit, and Notien, Saetyl, and I had a running gamble on who would finish their drink faster during the tribal meetings. I always chose Avenlae, since he had so little patience, but the look in Kaigar's eyes told me I would be losing a bet that day.

"Call for Vindicta," Kaigar grumbled.

I nodded wordlessly, catching Notien's eye for a second as a silent communication passed between us—it was going to be a *long* meeting. I shut my eyes and focused inwards, letting my powers curl around the Creonex. There was a golden thread that connected the Creonex to Vindicta's mind, a thread that had been rewoven when I had freed her from the influence of the Fifth Creator. It was this thread that I followed when I needed her, a link between our minds that we were able to access almost effortlessly. She pulled the thread tight, indicating that she was aware I was attempting to reach her. Once the link was activated, I pulled the golden

17

power of *genepotentia* through the Creonex, bringing Vindicta closer as if she were something I had just hooked on a fishing line.

Within moments, the golden tendrils of power that had seeped from my wings and hands to flow into the space behind me began to take the form of Vindicta. She remained crouched, aware that while the room was spacious enough for her to fit, it was not tall enough for her to stand at her full height. The glow of her body dissipated into pale scales, with flattened spines down her black, two-curved, serrated tails, and six prismatic eyes. Her forked tongue flicked around the room, tasting the air as she settled behind me, observing the assembled through multiple senses.

Shall we begin, Creovis? Vindicta's deep voice echoed within my mind, and the nearly imperceptible shift Avenlae made next to me was the only visual sign that he heard her, too. Those around us knew that Vindicta attended the meetings since she controlled the Voxmor, but she served another, ulterior purpose: she could access the minds of those around her without needing to be in physical contact with them. There were no true liars when I held court.

"What do you have to report on the *Reecytclous*?" Kaigar asked gruffly.

Vindicta clicked a few times, ruffling the frill around her neck. *They are grateful for the aid they are receiving. My Voxmor work during the day so as not to disturb the towns when they awake at nightfall. There is a small resistance building in their industrial district to the presence of Voxmor, but it is not entertained by their leaders or the rest of the population. Our work will be done long before the opposition gains any real traction.*

"Ensure that it is. The last thing we need is tension with the *Reecytclous* leaders," Kaigar responded, sipping from his mug.

"Their military is young and weak, but it would not look good to those in the other universes if we had to send in our well-trained warriors to calm an unnecessary uprising," Avenlae agreed.

I will pull that hive out early if needed, Vindicta said, blinking each of her eyes in turn. *Each of the other hives, thus far, has reported nothing but success in their respective missions. Earth, in particular, has experienced the most progression with the three hives placed within the warmer continents of their planet. Very soon, they will no longer need us.*

"Darinrain," I said, making eye contact with him just as he stuffed a blue crustacean into his mouth, "we will have to draw up a treaty with the humans for one hive to stay on Earth."

Darinrain furrowed his brow, chewing quickly before asking, "If the humans can continue without aid from the Voxmor, why keep a hive among them?"

"Enforcement," Avenlae answered.

I nodded. "I don't trust the humans with any kind of power. They will be the first after the Delfungaye to regain stability after the War, and it is all too likely that knowledge will go to their heads."

"Might I make a suggestion, Queen Xiaye?" Havyeque lifted a hand as if to ask for permission to speak. I gestured for him to continue. "I would first like to make it very clear that my Queen Klaecyia agrees wholeheartedly with the continued reminder of interuniversal enforcement with the humans. However, humans can be just as cunning as they are intelligent and resilient. Perhaps it would be better for the *Sloviyankae* to come to an agreement for there to be a base of our own warriors on their planet instead of a Voxmor hive? I think the humans would not see that as being as big a threat as leaving behind the Voxmor after they have already served their purpose, especially since their peaceful relations with my people have lasted decades longer."

"As long as there is a clause in whatever treaty it is you draw up that allows warriors from *all* Delfungaye tribes to take up residence on this base you speak of, I will support it," Kaigar said, raising his cup half an inch off the table towards Havyeque.

"Prepare it then, Darinrain, when the meeting has concluded. And, Havyque, send word to your Queen that I will be sending Darinrain back with you when you meet with the human delegation to finalize and enact the treaty." Both men nodded their understanding.

"A journey through the snow will be quite refreshing as the heat of the forest builds," Darinrain smiled as he looked over at Havyeque.

"You two will have separate quarters during the break in your travels among the *Hopyroque,*" Saetyl said, rolling her golden eyes skyward. Next to me, both Avenlae and Kaigar took another drink.

"No worries, Saetyl. My loyalty remains solely with the King." Darinrain flashed his navy eyes at Avenlae, who bared his canines across the table.

"The *Fyr'aeset* hunters have become quite prolific early in this hunting season," Notien said, breaking the tension before it became too thick as she deftly changed the subject. "The market will soon be saturated with meats from the plains."

"Enough to break into the Interuniversal Trade?" I asked.

"Perhaps, but they would have to be sold at a high price—our hunters refuse to over-hunt the prey animals. There are some that they could begin to farm, but many of the species are too important to their ecosystem to be completely removed from the wild."

"Gather a small team that can determine what can be farmed and what can be considered a Delfungaye delicacy if put into Interuniversal Trade," I said. Notien scratched down a note on a bit of parchment placed before her. "The Delfungaye have more resources than most of the worlds, so we need to offer into trade whatever we can as Creation continues to rebuild."

"The *Hopyroque* mines have introduced Delfungaye metal to the Third and First universe markets," Saetyl said, sucking the juice of a purple fruit off of her fingers. "There are no reports of it being used to make weapons yet."

"I trust you'll ensure it stays that way," I said sharply.

"Safeguarding the Delfungaye weapons against Creation, My Queen?" Kaigar asked, his greying eyebrows raised.

I gave him a stern look. "I will allow Creation access to our weapons in the event of another war, but that is a scenario I am actively attempting to avoid. Delfungaye exports are meant only to support peaceful interuniversal commerce during this rebuilding phase."

"The control of weapons makes me suspect that war is instead something that you are expecting." Kaigar kept his silver and white eye on his mug, but his words alone were enough to cause an uncomfortable silence to settle among the others.

He speaks out only because the prospect of another war is as frightening to him as it is to the others. Vindicta clicked as she shifted behind me, her voice only heard this time by Avenlae and me. *That fear runs too deeply within us to be assuaged by a few years of peace.*

I clenched my jaw, then reached for Avenlae's mug, letting the prickling feeling of the bitter drink calm my nerves as it flowed down my throat. When I lowered the mug to the table with a louder *thunk* than intended, Avenlae looked at me, his silver eyes searching.

"That's a record!" Darinrain said suddenly, a laugh behind his voice. "The Queen was moved to drink in less than fifteen minutes!"

Evening in a peaceful Delfungaye tribe had proven to be more beautiful than I had thought it would be the first time I arrived on Silvacastra. The colors of

21

the suns' set were just as vivid, and the calming whisper of nightfall still rustled through the forest leaves to brush across our cheeks. What was different, however, was the lively interaction of the tribespeople as they moved through their new nightly routine—socialization. I stayed within the limits of the *Laizuteek* tribe, so most of the Delfungaye I saw were those with skin as white as snow, hair the color of coal, eyes colored by the silver of moonlight, and wings glinting with feathers that shone brighter than chrome. But when the suns began to set, the people took on new colors, shapes, and dialects. This was when those who traveled in from the *Hopyroque, Fyr'aeset,* and *Sloviyankae* tribes would arrive, and the dimming light in the forest gave way to the birdsong of the Delfungaye languages as friends welcomed each other into their homes. This, Notien had told me, reflected what life had been like before Creation's War, with each tribe intermingling as they spread news, products, food, and other resources.

The pure silver of Avenlae's irises reflected the glowing patterns of the *Sloviyankae* uniforms as they climbed nimbly across newly erected walkways between the trees, their bat-like remnants of wings as useful as a third pair of limbs. While Notien, Saetyl, Darinrain, and I enjoyed a bottle of *a'ta'ya* together on the front-facing balcony of the Queen's Nest, the King watched the movement of the tribespeople intently, silently. As twilight neared, I knew he would become more restless. He never could thoroughly shake the drops of fear that fell from the shadows.

I passed Avenlae a crystal cup of *a'ta'ya* under the cover of Notien's laugh and Saetyl's snort at the end of Darinrain's recollection of some of their time in training together. Avenlae's eyes moved to the cup, then locked onto mine. His face held a soft, pleading look, silently begging to leave the draining social event.

"Just a bit longer," I assured him under my breath, "Besides, you know them. We fought a war with them."

"I do not judge the King's exhaustion," Saetyl said with a sigh as she toyed with her cup in her hand, "I empathize with it. Those weeks I spend traveling to the *Hopyroque* and *Sloviyankae* are a welcome break from the chattering of this one."

The look Notien sent towards Saetyl could've melted metal. Saetyl cowered. "Of course, the time spent without you also intensifies my appreciation for the love you have for me."

"I never would have guessed that it would be Notien who could train you so well, Saetyl!" Darinrain chuckled as he finished off the last of his drink. I sipped my own, smiling against the sweet liquid as Notien side-eyed me.

"You know I've only ever enjoyed the amusement our friendship has brought us," I said to her with a smile. Notien's navy eyes crinkled as she returned the smile, her platinum bob shimmering with the last of the suns' light before they ducked below the canopy of the trees.

"That, and the information," Notien nodded, recalling how often I had used her as an informant. I couldn't help it—she was a master of manipulation when she wanted to know something. This particular skill was born from the trauma of Creation's War, and I used it to my full advantage. Notien was well aware of her role, and yet she still would accept any invitation of mine for a meal or drinks without hesitation. I shared in the soft laughter that spread through the group. For a moment afterwards, we all stayed silent, our eyes on our empty or near-empty cups.

"I still find it odd sometimes," Darinrain said, his tone unusually sober, "that we can still sit here and laugh over a drink."

"I find it odd I can still watch the suns' rise each morning and not be preparing to train for battle," Notien said, her eyes darting from mine to Darinrain's. The change after Creation's War was good: at least, I thought it was supposed to be. But I felt a deep-seated restlessness in my subconscious, a feeling that something was left undone. It was an anxiety that had become so interwoven throughout my being that I hadn't figured out how to undo the knots for years. Apparently, neither had my friends.

"We are supposed to be reveling in the peace after the War," Darinrain frowned at his cup. "I can joke all I want, smile at everyone, laugh when I am supposed to. But it does not change what has been done or who has been lost."

I stopped myself from reaching out a hand towards Darinrain. Like Avenlae, he would never take it.

"It does not get better," Avenlae said, and all eyes turned to him in surprise that he had bothered to speak up. "It just becomes different." He downed the cup in front of him and stood to leave without looking back. I clenched my jaw, trying to control the sudden frustration I felt. I loved Avenlae, and more than anything, I wished he didn't have to feel the pain the memories of his past brought forth, but he would never let me help him beyond calming his mind before he slept. He would never speak of his inner demons, not with me or anyone else.

"He'll open up one day," Notien said, as if reading my thoughts.

"What day?" I asked in exasperation. "It's been five years, Notien. I can only wait so long."

"Did you ever think he was afraid to tell you?" Saetyl tilted her head to the side so she could see me better as she spoke. "Avenlae's resentment runs much deeper than any of ours ever could. You are probably the only person who has made him feel truly alive and loved. He is probably terrified to lose that."

I knew, out of all of them, that Saetyl would understand her own words the best. She had revealed her darkest secret to me, and it was the mercy we had for each other that had ultimately won us Creation's War. I thought Saetyl probably did understand Avenlae in a unique way none of the rest of us could.

"Do not worry, Xiaye, Notien is right," Darinrain said, and a sly smile began to spread across his face, bringing us out of the macabre mood. "I am sure, in time, I can convince my friend to open more."

CHAPTER 3

*M*y *Queen, the Rider's Ceremony will begin in a few hours.* Vindicta's voice flowed into my mind gently, like a push of a mother's hands against her child.

"Weren't you supposed to wake me up earlier?" I groaned, rolling over and stretching my limbs as I cracked my eyes open.

Indeed, but if you meet me on the balcony, you will see I have brought you and the King food. So, I allowed you a little extra time to sleep.

I smiled softly, checking briefly on Avenlae as he began to stir before throwing back the covers and stepping towards the French doors leading outside our chambers. The suns were already bright that morning, their heat scorching my skin the second I stepped out into the fresh air of the forest. Vindicta stood along the front of the balcony, her pale scales shining as she set a tray of breakfast onto a table. She clicked as I neared, lowering the front half of her body so that her snout was right in front of me.

There is anteel and bauete fruit on the menu this morning, as well as a fresh batch of fish brought in a few hours ago, she said, shutting her prismatic eyes as I ran my hand along the scales across her jaw.

I smiled up at her. "Well, good morning to you, too. We should have the Rider's Ceremony more often if this is how I get to wake up."

Vindicta sniffed, opening her six eyes and looking past me. *Ah, but if this is how I greeted you every morning, you would get too used to it.*

"I suppose," I sighed, settling myself into a chair as I heard the telltale brush of feathers along the wooden floor that signaled Avenlae's entrance onto the balcony. His wings were the only things that made any noise — he allowed them to drag only because it was Vindicta who waited for us. It had taken years, but she had finally won his trust. She became one of the four individuals in Creation Avenlae whom he would let his guard down around.

He sniffed the air as he walked around the back of the second chair across from me, a small smile twisting his lips. "You are too kind, Vindicta. Allowing us to sleep *and* bringing us breakfast?" He sat, taking a long sip from a cup of *anteel*. "What happened this morning to warrant such a kindness?"

It is the day of the Rider's Ceremony. And the Tribal Meeting was... interesting, yesterday. Perhaps, too, an argument could be made that I simply like you two enough to feed you every now and then.

I gave her a sharp look. "Sure, but what happened ***today?***"

Vindicta twisted her head around, suddenly becoming very interested in the trees along the edge of the balcony as she settled onto the floor in front of us. **Oh, nothing of importance.**

"Vindicta," I said, a warning in my voice, before I took a bite of my food.

There are a large number of members from both the Queen's Guard and Night Guard who will be participating in the Ceremony today.

"Kaigar already told me," Avenlae said, his mouth still full as he began to slice off another piece of fish, "how many Voxmor are Bonding?"

Ten from my hive. And, surprisingly, three from Inquiri's hive.

My eyebrows rose. Inquiri ruled as queen over a Voxmor hive nestled in the *Fae'oteek* mountains, near the *Sloviyankae's* southern border. The hive's tunnels extended into the *Sloviyankae's* subterranean city, granting Inquiri's hive the unique ability to aid the Iceland tribe. "Do we have more *Hopyroque* attempting the Ceremony today, then?"

Well... no. Vindicta stared intently at an unremarkable branch. *Queen Klaecyia sent more Sloviyankae.*

Avenlae frowned. "We met with the *Sloviyankae* delegation yesterday. I did not see any extra warriors with Havyeque."

This is because they arrived this morning.

I set my cup of *anteel* down with a clatter. "What?"

Vindicta shook her head, fluttering her frill. *Do not worry, My Queen, Kaigar handled the greeting of the group.*

I tried to breathe evenly. "Did he handle it *well?*"

Vindicta blinked all six of her eyes in succession, tilting her head like a shrug. *Well enough.*

I closed my eyes, dropping my head with a sigh.

All is well, My Queen. No one left the exchange offended — all the niceties were observed.

"Yes, well, remind me again of those *niceties* the next time I receive communication from Queen Klaecyia. I can guarantee it will be *strongly worded.*"

"You stress too much, Xai," Avenlae said, finishing off the last few bites of the *bauete* fruit on his plate, "Queen Klaecyia may be strict about traditions, but she will do no more than scold. You know she would never risk the peace between the Delfungaye and *Sloviyankae* over something so trivial."

Glaring at Avenlae, I stabbed my fork into a slice of fish with a bit more agitation than intended. "I imagine you won't mind at all, then, if you have to be the one to meet with Klaecyia when she calls, given that I will miraculously find myself too busy to be available."

Avenlae's chewing slowed as his silver eyes raised to meet mine. I chomped on my bite of fish, not daring to break eye contact. He swallowed. "Of course, My Queen. And I am sure," he said, lifting the last bite of fish from his plate and waving towards Vindicta, "Vindicta would agree to accompany on such an occasion? Since Queen Klaecyia *loves* the Voxmor."

The Voxmor Queen bristled. *You dare to wave food before me as if I were a pet?*

"You do not want it?"

A momentary silence stretched between Avenlae and Vindicta, each staring intently into the other's eyes. Finally, Vindicta snapped the fish out of his hands, growling, *Of course I do, I never say no to food.*

Avenlae smirked as he took a sip from his *anteel*. "See, Xai? Vindicta and I will handle Queen Klaecyia should she decide to speak up about you being unavailable to greet her warriors the very second they entered the tribe."

"I don't know if I should be grateful or terrified," I mumbled, sitting back in my chair and raising my *anteel* close to my chest.

Vindicta snorted and rose to her feet. *Well, then, if I am no longer needed...* She began to amble over to the other side of the balcony when Avenlae stopped her.

"Vindicta," he called, suddenly sitting up straighter, "will the borders be secure during the Ceremony?"

"Av," I said quietly, "I don't think there's any need —"

Yes, Vindicta said, interrupting and shooting me a quick, sharp look, *I have changed the rotations of the hive's guard to ensure there will be no difference in the numbers around the borders.*

Avenlae nodded once before settling back into his chair, drinking deeply from his still-steaming cup.

It makes him feel safer, Vindicta said, allowing me to hear her voice only. *And so I am willing to do it, even if it may seem like an inconvenience.*

I tilted my head at her in an imperceptible nod, trying to hide that she had said anything at all that Avenlae couldn't hear. She chuffed, then climbed onto the branches that wove around the bulk of the Queen's Nest, heading off to prepare the members of her hive participating in the Rider's Ceremony. Avenlae lowered his cup, his *anteel* nearly finished. "You never know what is still out there, Xai."

"I know," I said softly, "you tell me that all the time."

He lowered his eyes. "Keeping our people safe is still a priority and a job we must undertake."

"I'm not angry with you." I drank from my glass, finishing off the rest of my *anteel* before leaning forward to set my hand on his arm. "I know where your fear comes from. I just... sometimes wish I could find a way to help you let go and relax."

"I will relax when I die," Avenlae said, his silver eyes shining as they met mine. "This is how I have always lived my life, *Le'eseia.* It does not harm me to stay this way."

The suns' light glimmered across the silver feathers of his wings as Avenlae pushed himself out of his chair and headed back into our room. I watched him go, searching through my thoughts for something more to say. But there was nothing. There never really was anything more to say when Avenlae was like that. It didn't matter how many memories and feelings of calm I transferred to him, or how many different ways I found to tell him that he was safe and loved—that protectiveness, that fear of war was ingrained into his being. He'd adapted to life that way, all vigilance and silence, and sometimes it hurt me to see how deeply survival had become his only way of being.

After another moment, I raised myself out of my chair, taking a deep breath and following Avenlae back into our chambers. He had already set out our armor across the bed and was in the process of sorting through different accolades and pieces of beadwork that we would be required to wear for the Rider's Ceremony.

"I'm always reminded how lucky I am that you know how we're supposed to dress," I said, leaning against the foot of the bed as he laid out a small headband of aquamarine beadwork.

He smirked. "I cheated."

"What do you mean?"

"Notien used to tell me what to prepare before each event we had to attend," Avenlae said, taking a moment to check over the ceremonial dress. "And when she was called to stay out in the plains for longer periods, she wrote out directions for me to memorize for when she was gone."

"It's been five years, and I'm only *now* finding out about this?"

Avenlae shrugged. "At first, I thought I had something to prove. I thought I still had to show you I could teach you more about the Delfungaye, and prove my worth as King."

"You thought you'd do that by always knowing how to dress?" I asked, one eyebrow raised.

"That was Notien's idea."

"Of course it was." I grinned, planting a kiss on his cheek.

"Yes, well, I continue it now because I know you would be lost if I did not lay out your clothes," Avenlae said, holding up my armor with all of my accolades already pinned exactly where they were supposed to be.

"Too true. I desperately need my valiant warrior King to be in charge of my wardrobe at all times," I said with a mock flourish, "where would I be without you?"

That was met with stony silence. I rolled my eyes, taking the armor from him as I pulled the straps of my romper off my shoulders. "Killjoy."

Avenlae reached out, snaking an arm around my now bare waist and pulling me forcefully against him. "Is that what I am?" He growled, his eyes moving hungrily over my breasts.

"Sometimes," I whispered, trying to hide the sudden quiver in my voice.

He leaned down, kissing me slowly before flicking his tongue across my lips. "Shall I prove to you how wrong you are?" He purred.

"Perhaps."

In a way, I did end up regretting how easily I allowed him to take control of the situation, as it made us quite unforgivably late. But *damn,* it was worth it.

She will quite literally never let you hear the end of this, I thought as I glided down to the lowest level of the Queen's Nest, where Notien and Saetyl's visiting room was. The Nest was conspicuously quiet and empty, since the rest of the tribe was, well, actually on time for the Rider's Ceremony. Unfortunately, this included Notien, as her room was empty, and I still needed my hair braided in the traditional way. Although Avenlae had become proficient at nearly all the royal styles, he still preferred to send me to Notien anytime she was within residence at the Queen's Nest. I closed my eyes, clenching my jaw as echoes of the scolding I knew I was going to receive bounced around my head.

"My Queen?"

I gasped, whirling around as the Creonex glowed around my left hand, sending a shock of energy through my body. Darinain stood behind me, his gold and black armor in place with beadwork of burning red twisting around his neck. He raised a hand, a gentle, peaceful gesture. I let out a breath, controlling the power that had begun to writhe in my chest. "Darinrain. Aren't you supposed to be at the Rider's Ceremony?"

"I could say the same for you," he responded with a grin. "Your absence is much more obvious than mine."

"Yes, well, I was… preoccupied for longer than expected this morning."

"Ah, is that it?" Darinrain tilted his head at me knowingly.

"Why are you still here?" I snapped.

"Why is your hair still down?" He tsked. "Surely you do not plan on showing up to the Ceremony like *that?*"

"No, I certainly did not, but, seeing as Notien isn't here—"

"Oh, dear me, Xiaye, you do not really think I am *that* useless?" Darinrain waived a hand and pushed past me into Notien's chambers, flicking on the light. "Hurry up and sit. We do not have much time."

"You can braid?" I asked, plopping myself onto the seat before the vanity as Darinrain began to section off my hair.

"Of course I do. Why would I not know how?"

I raised an eyebrow at him through the mirror. "Darinrain, you have no hair."

"Just because I do not braid my own hair does not mean I should not know how to braid others'," he said, beginning the simplest of the royal styles. His hands were steady, careful — the kind of care that came from respect, not vanity. "Besides, Notien would never leave the tribe without ensuring that you always have more than one person to help you with appearances."

I smiled faintly, watching the dark strands twist and coil between his fingers. The movement brought back the ghost of another pair of hands: Novissime's, patient and sure, as she'd once promised to teach me the meaning behind every braid. Each pattern had a purpose: to bind the tribes together, to honor the ancestors, to remind a Queen of the weight she carried.

But she was gone before she could teach me her secrets, and now each morning felt like trying to speak a language I'd only half learned. The braids still formed beneath Darinrain's touch, but I couldn't help wondering what Novissime would have said of them — of me — and whether she'd think I'd earned their pattern yet.

"You all seem to think I'm utterly helpless," I grumbled.

Darinrain paused in his work, meeting my gaze once again through the mirror. "No, I don't need you to say *anything* to that," I said as he began to pin the braids to the back of my head.

"We are lucky this is the first time in years you have needed *me* to come to your aid," Darinrain said with more dramatic flair than was necessary. "Hand me the headpiece."

"I suppose I should arrive at the Ceremony before you?" I asked, trying to move the subject along.

"Is Our King already there?"

"He should be."

"Then you should arrive *with* me," Darinrain said, nodding his head at my hair and stepping to the side, offering his arm. "That way, it will appear as if a meeting with your advisor is your excuse for being late. Should you arrive alone *after* your mate, the people will start *talking.*"

"As if it's really any of their business," I mumbled, stepping around the chair and allowing Darinrain to escort me out of the Queen's Nest.

"There are no wars to be fought now, My Queen," Darinrain said with a grin as we took to the air. "Our people now have the time to be concerned with something as trivial as the gossip about the King and Queen."

"And I'm sure *you* do nothing to encourage this gossip, do you, Darinrain?" I asked, raising an eyebrow at him.

"Oh, now, where is the fun in keeping my own mouth shut?"

I rolled my eyes as we continued on to Vindicta's hive, which was placed within the Fourth Quadrant. She had taken over the skeleton of a hive we had previously vacated towards the end of Creation's War. She simply extended the existing tunnels to run underneath the entire original *Laizuteek* territory. The Voxmor had access to every strategic defensive and offensive position in the forest, making the *Laizuteek* territory a migration point for all tribes in emergency situations.

The massive main funnel entrance to the hive rose to touch the very bottom branches of the trees, and served as the middle of the gathering of the tribes and hive for the Rider's Ceremony. Avenlae, Saetyl, Notien, and Kaigar stood upon a small net stretched between two branches over the funnel, and Vindicta had positioned herself around the trunk behind them. Her frill twitched as her six eyes scanned the crowd, communication passing between herself and the Voxmor that prowled the trees around the gathering. The Queen's and Night guard formed a massive circle in the branches around the funnel, all dressed in their armor and cheering for those of their ranks who had stepped forward to take their chances at being chosen as Riders. Voxmor, who were available for bonding, were perched around the top of the funnel, their heads flicking around as they studied their prospective Riders. It was ultimately the Voxmor's choice on who became their Rider — they could attempt bonding multiple times, but a warrior could only try three times. After that, the mental toll of the Ceremony would be too much for them to survive.

Darinrain and I landed before Avenlae, Kaigar, Saetyl, and Notien, and I smiled at the whoops from the warriors around us. Kaigar bowed his head towards me, and Avenlae stepped forward to greet Darinrain.

"Care to explain why *you* have made her late, Darinrain?" Avenlae asked in an undertone, masking his annoyance with a curt nod as Darinrain bowed deeply, showing his neck.

"It was my duty to ensure her wardrobe was suitable for such an occasion, My King," Darinrain said as he rose from his bow, grinning and turning to wave to the crowd.

"That is *not* your responsibility," Avenlae growled as he took my hand, gazing around at the warriors and clenching his jaw.

"It would be an embarrassment if it were your responsibility, My King," Darinrian responded, spreading his arms wide to the cheers of the people.

"Watch your words, *Je'quiet.* I would take too much pleasure in your punishment."

Darinrain bowed to the crowd, his grin widening as they clapped and whistled while he prepared to open the Rider's Ceremony. My smile tightened as he turned to perform one more bow to Avenlae and me.

"Too bad," he murmured as he rose once more, stepping back to leap from the branch. "My Queen needs me."

Avenlae's hand tightened around mine as Darinrain took to the air. "Forget about it," I whispered as Darinrain began to speak to our people. "He's just trying to get a rise out of you."

Kaigar grunted. "He only does it because Avenlae always responds."

Avenlae curled his lip, flashing a canine at Kaigar. The General took a small step away from the King.

"Men," Saetyl murmured, and Notien tried to hide a snicker. I turned back towards them, grinning, but careful not to say more as a growl rumbled in

35

Avenlae's chest.

Vindicta slithered away from the trunk of the tree just then, shaking her head as she stepped forward. She blinked each of her prismatic eyes at me, waiting for Saetyl and Notien to step aside before she moved into place next to me.

Are you ready, Creovis? She asked.

"Always am," I said, turning back to where the Voxmor and warriors waited. The Voxmor bowed their head, closing their eyes and preparing for the connection. A mixture of fear and determination flashed in the eyes of the warriors, and the forest quieted, the Delfungaye waiting with baited breath. Vindicta raised a tentacle, resting it along the back of my head and spine.

"Prepare yourselves," I called out to the warriors. Taking a deep breath, I focused my power on where Vindicta's tentacle touched my scalp and neck. She opened her frill, her eyes becoming unfocused, and the Creonex glowed as it expanded the reach of Vindicta's mind. A soft hum rose from the circle of Voxmor as they connected with the threads of Vindicta's telepathy, our minds becoming one force. I closed my eyes, able to see the golden web of our consciousness within my mind. With a pulse of energy, streaks of blue exploded out from the web, and I heard a rustle move around the circle of participating warriors as their minds were connected to that of the Voxmor.

With my part done, I opened my eyes to observe the rest of the Ceremony. The warriors were on their knees, their bodies stiff, veins popping along their temples as they fought to cope with the strength of the connection. It wasn't the opening of their minds that was so difficult to survive — it was that ***each*** of the Voxmor before them was able to access the warriors' consciousnesses. It was that ***multiple*** Voxmor were scanning their minds at the same time. Healers made their way through the crowd, positioning themselves behind each warrior, preparing to tend to them as soon as the Ceremony was done. One by one, the Voxmors' heads snapped up, their eyes locking on a warrior, their chosen Rider. That Rider would collapse forward, their body released from the paralyzing hold of Vindicta's connection. They would smile broadly despite the trembling of their limbs, the blood dripping from their noses, and the throbbing of their temples as their Voxmor leaped from the funnel to the branch of their new Rider. The Healers stepped in to treat the damage of creating the bond as each Voxmor held their Rider, using the strength of their minds to heal the consciousness of the warrior.

I took a breath, feeling the cool touch of Vindicta's bond as it soothed the dull ache in my temples. Whoops began to rise from the Guard as they moved forward to celebrate their fellow warriors who had become Riders. Avenlae tensed next to me. I looked up, frowning, trying to follow his intense stare. Both he and Kaigar were frozen, watching movement on the far end of the Ceremonial circle. A *Laizuteek* warrior had collapsed, and a second Healer was fighting his way through the crowd to get to the fallen man. His bonded Voxmor had leapt onto the branch, a hunter with vibrant golden eyes. She extended her tentacles, cradling the warrior's head. A trail of blood dripped from his nose and from the corner of his mouth.

"It is Dya'kia," Saetyl murmured behind me, a crease between her brows.

"Is he okay?" Notien asked, unable to see from her vantage point as well.

"It was his third time trying for the bond." Saetyl kept her voice soft. "It appears he was successful, but I do not know if his mind was able to cope."

I watched silently as the Healers worked, scanning Dya'kia's skull and pulling medications into sleek syringes. His Voxmor remained still, her golden eyes focused on her Rider, but still, he showed no signs of life. Silence gradually began to fall across the Guard and onlookers as they realized not all was well. Avenlae and Kaigar watched on — they always worried about their warriors. They would never admit it, but the Rider's Ceremony was always a tense time for them as they waited to see if the chosen Riders were mentally strong enough to survive it.

There is still life within Dya'kia's mind, Vindicta reported, moving closer to us. *His bondess, Scyr, has not given up.*

Seconds stretched into minutes, and the stillness of those gathered became so complete that we could hear a leaf fall to the underbrush below. Darinrain hovered before us, unmoving, and even the beat of his wings made no sound. Then, finally, Dya'kia's silver eyes flickered open, and he gave Scyr a weak smile.

The entire forest erupted with whistles, shouts, and applause. Darinrain spread his arms wide and turned to us, a grin plastered across his golden face. "And now, we celebrate!"

CHAPTER 4

That night was even more lively than when the tribes had first arrived for the tribal meetings. Beadwork from each tribe was draped across the branches, and the beats of tribal drums echoed far into the forest. Smells of freshly cooked meat, brewed drinks, and baked desserts took over the scent of the underbrush, and the trees were aglow with the kaleidoscopic lights the Delfungaye danced under. Kaigar left our little group early on to join his warriors, and Darinrain was long gone the very second we returned to the central hub of the *Laizuteek* tribe — no one could keep him from the thrill of celebration for long. Saetyl and Notien stayed with Avenlae and me for a while, sharing a meal and drinks before being swept away by members of the Night Guard who'd remained their friends.

The colors of the celebration shone within Avenlae's silver eyes as he looked over the tribe from the highest branch of a bar we were perched upon. I took a sip from the glass of *a'ta'ya* in my hand, enjoying the taste of the last few drops in the glass. Warmth had already washed over me, and the night began to feel heavy on my eyes and limbs. Setting the cup down, I leaned against the back of my chair, watching lights flicker and dance over Avenlae's cheeks and jaw. We were both still in our armor, as the ceremony dictated. Even so, Avenlae was just… a beautiful creature. The way his eyes seemed to glow even brighter than the lights reflected within them. The deep onyx of his hair was darker even than the shadows of the canopy above us. A soft smile pressed his canines into his lower lip as he watched members of the Guard share a drink and a laugh below us.

Mine.

Something moved in the shadows.

My eyes flicked up, a rush of power searing my veins. The sounds of the Delfungaye quieted as I studied the leaves and branches that hid the night sky. **Something** had moved. Something was there. The Creonex warmed around my hand the longer I stared into the canopy, waiting to see the movement again. Nothing but the night breeze rustled the leaves.

"Xiaye."

I flinched, trying to hide a gasp as my eyes shot back down to Avenlae. His brow was furrowed, and he appeared to still be calm, but for the tilt of his wings. He knew I'd seen something: he just didn't know whether to be prepared to fight, or to act unaware. With a final glance up into the empty canopy, I shifted around in my seat, trying to calm my nerves as I gave him a smile. "It's nothing, Av. Your protective nature is rubbing off on me, and I'm seeing things that aren't there in the shadows."

His ears flicked back, listening for sounds behind him as his pupils constricted.

"It's nothing," I repeated, leaning forward to place my hand over his.

It was, perhaps, me coming to meet you, Vindicta said softly as she crawled around the other side of the trunk, settling herself next to our small table.

I sighed, relief relaxing my muscles. "See?" I smiled at Avenlae again, whose

40

ears lowered to their natural position. "I told you. Nothing to be worried about."

I will be better about announcing myself, Vindicta clicked, nuzzling my hand over her snout.

"Approach from the front," Avenlae grunted, throwing back the last gulp of his drink.

"It doesn't help that you've been so on edge," I responded quietly, ducking my gaze as his silver eyes bored into me.

"Delegations from all tribes are here. I am *always* on edge."

Vindicta's six eyes searched mine, her rainbow irises glittering. She then turned to Avenlae, a soft hum echoing up from deep within her chest. *I can help you, My King.*

"No," Avenlae snapped.

Vindicta lowered her hum, an instinctive sound made to soothe. I sighed, exasperated. "Her offer is made out of *kindness,* Avenlae."

He gave me a long look. Finally, he reached out, touching a hand to the side of Vindicta's cheek and lowering his wings. "I know. I will relax in a few days when the delegations leave, and things return to normal."

If you say so, My King, Vindicta hummed, blinking her eyes slowly in the form of a bow. *Be calm tonight. There are no reports from the borders. The night remains peaceful.*

"We should sleep well, then." I scratched Vindicta along her lower jaw. "What about you? Are you staying up for the festivities?"

I have no need to. I have experienced enough festivities in my lifetime.

Avenlae smirked. "Are you saying you are too old for this, now, Vindicta?"

That elicited a growl. *I still have many years left. We live longer than your species, after all. And I must remain well-rested to be ready at* your *beck and call.*

I chuckled, raising myself out of the chair. "Sleep well, Vindicta. Besides, Avenlae has no room to speak — we were about to head back to the Queen's Nest, anyway."

Vindicta snorted at Avenlae, who just grinned and swatted at her nose gently with his wing as he rose to follow me. "I will meet you and Kaigar in the morning. We have new Riders to brief before they leave to join ranks within their tribes."

Vindicta slithered down the trunk of the tree as Avenlae and I leapt from the branch. Glasses were raised to us in salute as we glided past, members of every tribe pausing in their celebration to bow in respect. Even six years later, there was still a part of me that felt as if I didn't really deserve the recognition as their Queen. I hadn't even accepted *myself* as a part of the Delfungaye until after I'd taken the throne, and then it had felt as if I'd done so out of necessity. I'd spent those early days trying to keep one foot on Earth, clinging to the silence of its forests, the loneliness I once mistook for peace. I told myself I could rule them without truly being one of them, but the truth was, I wasn't ready to let go of the world that had broken me. Now, Silvacastra had become my home, the Delfungaye my people, and yet...

"There is sadness in your eyes, *Le'eseia,*" Avenlae murmured as we landed at the entrance to the Queen's Nest.

"I'm just thinking," I said quietly, folding my wings and moving to rest my head against his shoulder as we moved into the darkness of the Nest.

"You have been doing a lot of thinking lately."

"Mhm."

We stayed quiet as we made our way to our chambers, then began to remove our ceremonial armor. My eyes caught the reflection of firelight along the swirled hilts of my rapiers where they hung in honor against the far wall of our room.

"It's just… difficult to settle into normalcy after living my life in war for so long," I said distractedly.

Avenlae paused after removing the undershirt of his armor, turning to look at where his rapiers hung next to mine. "Xai," he said, stepping closer to me and extending his wings forward, "you heard Vindicta. The borders are quiet. They have been quiet for years, now."

He brushed his fingers across my cheek. "I know I remain anxious, but that is only to keep me prepared to protect you and my people. That is what I am meant to do."

I slid my index finger down the raised scar across his face. It remained tight against his skin, the only scar he couldn't easily hide. "Not anymore. You share the responsibility with me."

Avenlae pressed his lips against mine, a gentle kiss as he cupped the back of my head with his calloused hand. "I love you, Xai."

"And I love you, Av. Always have, and always will."

Something moved in the shadows. It was hard to tell if I was conscious or stuck in a twisted lucid dream. But *something* was moving. I could feel the cooling air pulling me out of sleep, the thundering of my heart intensifying as my eyes fell upon two dreary, gray irises that were unfamiliar. Yet Avenlae slept so soundly next to me, even as my limbs thrashed in uncoordinated panic as I ripped the covers off of me and tried to scramble out of the bed. My romper, with its thin material, suddenly felt so pathetic, like an insult. The gray eyes moved in the darkness, and a body formed, its outline hazy in the creeping shadows of the bedroom. It was *real.* My own eyes flicked towards Avenlae's prone figure, first checking that his chest still rose and fell rhythmically, then again as my anxiety rose that he still did not stir.

"He will not wake." The figure spoke with the voice of a thousand whispers, and the sound gripped my spine, paralyzing me where I stood. "He is not aware of us right now."

"What do you want?" My voice crept out of my throat as if it, too, was terrified of the being in the shadows.

Sharpened metal teeth reflected what little starlight twinkled through the windows as the creature smiled. The body that had formed as it stalked closer to me was feminine, but that voice… it had no gender, no identity. "You do not ask who I am first, but instead what I want? Were you expecting me, then?"

"I won't talk in circles," I said, forcing more strength into my words than I felt. "Answer me."

The shadows shifted again, and the creature stood just a foot away from me. It had taken the shape of *Fae'yeerium*, or who the Delfungaye believed Death to be. I could recognize the emerald beadwork along its throat and across its chest and remembered seeing the way its three fingers melted into sharpened metal claws in ancient pictures Darinrain had shown me years ago. "Shouldn't that be obvious?" It hissed, cocking its head to the side the way a bird of prey does before it digs into a meal. "I want the *Creovis.*"

"You have no need of it," I kept my voice low, my mind racing as I struggled to find a way to stall the creature long enough for me to grab one of my rapiers. "I'm told Death already has her own access to *genepotentia.*"

The creature laughed, its voice grinding together like the blades of chainsaws. "I can appear however I wish, *Creovis.* It is one of my more well-known talents. However, I do not seek your access to *genepotentia* — a Creator controls the vast expanses of that power without aid."

44

My blood ran as frigid as the air that stung my skin. *Who will stop my brothers from regaining control over the universes, Creovis? "You*," I hissed, "y-you are—"

"Mors, the Fourth Brother." The creature's body changed as it spoke, the edges of its line thinning into the very blackened shadows that coated the corners of the night. Only its gray, dead eyes remained, focused intently on me. "I thought if I appeared as something familiar, you might be more amenable to my presence."

"I am not amenable to *anyone* in my bedroom at midnight." I lowered my voice to a growl. My rapiers hung *behind* where Mors stalked. *Stall him. Stall him longer.*

"At least grant me permission to explain my predicament." Those metal teeth gleamed as Mors smiled malevolently. "Perhaps then we can reach some form of... *arrangement."*

The way his voice slithered around the word made my skin crawl. I straightened, crossing my arms over my chest and taking a slow step forward as if I were actually considering his words. *Get him to speak. They love to talk.* "I'm listening."

His gray eyes narrowed as the shadow of his body rose. "Your victory against Sinivir did not go unnoticed, *Creovis*. My Brother's ambition was his downfall, as we warned him it would be. He had this foolish idea that Creation should be allowed conscious thought and free will, yet he chose to create *you*, his ultimate weapon, to destroy the very freedom he had bestowed upon the mortals."

"I'm sure you're here to tell me that Creation should instead fall under your rule, correct?" I took another step, inching closer to my rapiers, fighting the urge to glance at their position and give away my intentions.

A long, insidious hiss emanated from the shadows of Mors' body before he responded. "Tell me, *Creovis,* can there be peace without control?"

"There's peace now without your intervention," I snapped.

"Is that why you chose to control the trade of Delfungaye weapons?" It took everything in me to stand my ground and not cower away in terror as the shadow of Mors swelled, the dull gray of his eyes suddenly becoming as sharp as an obsidian knife. "It is time for my brothers and me to finish what we started. With Sinivir gone, there is nothing left to stand between us and Creation."

"Nothing but me," I said, a quiver in my voice.

"Which brings me to my proposition." The First Creator weaved his head back and forth as he spoke, as if such banal movements would put me at ease. "You are not forced to stand in our way. If we had access to your power, we could rewrite the history of Creation to one of pure bliss before the mortals had the chance to feel pain or fear. They would have no memory of their past lives—they will have never known suffering."

"But *I* will know." My knuckles turned white as I clutched at the skin of my arms. "I will remember ***everything.***"

"You would be doing them a service, ***Creovis,***" Mors swirled around me, a hunter circling its prey. "That should calm whatever conscience you have evolved."

"That's where your brother went wrong." I raised my eyes, blinking back the tears that began to swim in my vision. I stepped to the side so that I was facing Mors as I spoke, my wing brushing against the scabbard of one of my rapiers. "You say it was his ambition that finished him off in the end? I say it was his ***arrogance.*** You all think we're just pawns in your game, just pieces you can move across the board and redecorate with no consequences. Those 'mortals' you speak of with such disdain have entire ***lives*** that I ***fought*** for! You think I'll just bow to you and the other Brothers now because you promise superficial bliss?"

"I would prefer to have your cooperation, ***Creovis,***" Mors spread, his darkness swallowing the other side of the room where Avenlae still slept, "but make no mistake, I *do not need it*."

The hazy outline of Mors' body swirled again, twirling around the room as if it were being sucked in multiple directions. I spun and ripped one of my rapiers out of its scabbard, my muscles tensing immediately as I prepared for a fight. When I turned back to face Mors, however, the adrenaline coursing through my veins stalled, and my heart thundered in my ears.

Mors stood over Avenlae, one slender claw hovering over the scar across Avenlae's sternum, restless energy barely suppressed in the subtle tremble of its sharpened tip. "I could do it." Mors pulled back his lips to bare his metal teeth. "In the blink of an eye, I could take *everything* from you."

"It wouldn't change a thing," I spoke, but I couldn't hear the sound of my own voice through the rising panic in my pulse. "It would just make the hunt for you and every last one of your Brothers that much sweeter. It would make your destruction that much more satisfying."

"Careful, *Creovis*," the Fourth Brother growled, his whisper slicing through Avenlae's slumber, "You sound like you want to declare war against the Creators."

Only I noticed the infinitesimal pause in Avenlae's breathing and the way his muscles stiffened. I tightened my grip on my rapier, steadying myself as I said, "As far as I'm concerned, your presence in my bedroom tonight is an act of war. Tell your Brothers to prepare — I will be your reckoning."

As I spoke, golden *genepotentia* began to crackle down my arms and across my blade. The glow of the arcs of power that forked across my skin and through my feathers did nothing to penetrate the darkness of Mors' body, but instead danced in his devious gray eyes.

"So be it." There was half a second's pause before the bedroom exploded into complete chaos. A burst of energy flew from the blade of my rapier as

Mors lifted his claw to plunge it deep into Avenlae's chest. As the Creator was sent stumbling into the wall, Avenlae threw himself to the other side of the bed, wrapping the claw of one of his wing joints around the strap of one of his scabbards as he rolled. I reached back and withdrew my second rapier, the glow of my power growing stronger as I stalked toward the impenetrable shadow of Mors. His grey eyes were wild with belligerence as he clicked his claws together. He made another swipe towards Avenlae. Avenlae deftly parried the attack, but dared not to use his wings as weapons—he knew as well as I did that Mors' claws had to be sharp enough to slice the wings from Avenlae's back in one stroke.

I sent another fork of electrical energy into the shadow of Mors, this time from my wings as I flared them behind me, attempting to make myself appear as the more dangerous opponent. Avenlae wouldn't survive long against the pure ferocity of a direct attack from a Creator. I wasn't sure I really had much of an advantage either, but I was willing to take my chances.

A hiss of animosity tore itself from between Mors' clenched metal teeth as he turned to face me, claws extended. The strength behind each of his attacks as he launched himself at me nearly made my knees buckle, and it took every bit of training I had had over the years to remain just a step ahead of him. Each time my rapiers connected with his claws, my arms were thrown wide, slowing my reaction time. But the crackling *genepotentia* flowing down my blades also kept the Creator at bay, for the sparks against Mors' claws were weakening them bit by bit.

It didn't work fast enough, though, for he finally threw my arms back wide enough for me to lose my balance and fall back against the floor. The clatter of my rapiers rang treacherously in my ears as victory flashed in the Creator's cold, dead eyes, his claws poised to take the final blow. They clanged instead on Avenlae's sword as he thrust it in front of me, pushing the deadly claws into a panel of wood next to me. Mors let out a scream of rage as his shadow twisted violently, focusing in on the now-defenseless Avenlae.

48

I didn't think, I just acted. I threw my left hand up, letting the power within me take complete control. A beam of vindictive red power burst from my palm and thundered into the Fourth Creator's chest, pinning the shadow of his body against the back wall of our bedroom. The scream of a Voxmor queen tore through the night, warping the beam of my power and making even the shadow of Mors tremble. Avenlae stayed standing next to me, his ears forward as he waited for another attack; his pupils contracted so tightly that his eyes were only silver, like two stars plucked from the sky. Mors slid down the wall, his now weakened, black-robed body heaving with shuddering breaths as the energy faded from the Creonex. I pushed myself to my feet, trying to hide the trembling in my muscles as I angled my wings down towards Mors, energy as red as rubies spreading from my wing joints through my feathers. In the distance, trees groaned as Vindicta tore through them.

"Sinivir taught you a few tricks before you disposed of him, *Creovis,*" Mors seethed.

"No. In his arrogance, Sinivir forgot the weapon he created could also *absorb* his power." I took a step closer to the Fourth Creator, keeping my spine straight and tall. "You see, you *cannot* control me. I will *always* fight you, just like I did him."

"Dare you fight us on common ground, then?" Mors' lips parted to reveal his metallic teeth again as his robes began to whip around him as if he were caught in a whirlwind. "I'll be waiting, *Creovis.* We shall soon see just how powerful a weapon you are."

The echo of Mors' final whispered hiss scraped against my ears as his shadow dematerialized from the corner of the room. At the same time, Vindicta crashed through the double doors that led out to our balcony, her eyes wide and two serated tails thrashing. I darkened the power in my wings as I set my rapier against the wall, moving forward to calm Vindicta before she alerted more of the tribe.

He was here! Vindicta's voice cried in our minds as her head darted around the room. *I could sense him!*

"Not anymore," I said, trying to keep my voice calm and my hands steady as I reached up for her snout.

I could sense *him, Xiaye. I could* feel *a Creator!*

"He is gone, now," Avenlae croaked, glancing around the room once more before moving to the wall to grab the sheath for his rapier.

You do not understand, Vindicta hissed, moving further into the room and ruffling her frill. She completely ignored any movement I made to try to calm her. *He was here. The entirety of that Creator was in Creation.*

"Vindicta, there's no one here now—"

He wasn't afraid of you! She snapped, her head whipping around, the flick of her tongue just inches away from my face.

I set a hand over her nose. "It was Mors, the Fourth Brother. He has no reason to fear me, yet."

This was the first time Mors came to Creation in hundreds of years, Vindicta said, her sides heaving as she looked between Avenlae and me, willing us to understand. *And he didn't bother to leave his Essence behind. The part that makes them immortal when the Creators come to Creation. You could have killed him.*

"He was confident enough to make himself mortal the first time he met Xiaye?" Avenlae asked, his ears up and facing Vindicta.

She clicked, stepping even closer as the echo of a panicked shriek rang in my ears. *Mors needed to test your strength, Xiaye. He needed to see what kind of weapon he and the Brothers are up against.*

I felt my eyes widen as I dropped my hand, taking a step back from Vindicta, my throat tightening as she said, *The war never ended. It barely began six years ago.*

CHAPTER 5

Just under an hour later, I was pacing a well-worn path in the clearing Avenlae had first trained me in years ago. A golden glow of firelight danced along the bark of the tree line from flames leaping out of a fire pit next to me. Vindicta sat behind me, her eyes following every movement. Her frill twitched as she communicated with her hive, keeping them calm as units changed and moved around the borders. Some tribe members had awoken to the sound of Vindicta's shriek, but fortunately, not enough to set the entire tribe on high alert.

Wind ruffled the waves of my dark hair as it fanned around my face. I hadn't bothered to try to braid it. Within moments of Vindicta arriving within our chambers, Avenlae and I had changed into the armor we had worn for Creation's War. We sent runners to awaken Darinrain, Notien, and Saetyl. No part of me wanted to tell them why they were being disturbed in the middle of the night, but they deserved to know. My friends deserved to have a choice in whether or not they wanted to fight *this* part of the war with me.

"Why… why are you wearing that?" Notien was the first to arrive at the clearing. Firelight danced in her navy eyes as they widened. Her skin was the purest gold in the warm light, but its opulence didn't disguise the worried arch of her brows. "Why are you both dressed in your armor? Why did I hear Vindicta scream not even an hour ago?"

"It is the Creators, is it not?" Saetyl's rasp came from behind Notien. The larger woman's face, calm in its masculine features, was set, her golden eyes burning. She knew without anyone saying a word. She knew, just as well as I had, when we embraced within the flow of blood the day we had won Creation's War.

It was only the first battle.

Notien looked back and forth between us. "What?"

"Mors, the Fourth Brother, came to me tonight. They want to take Creation back. Reset it. Reset their experiment."

"Any chance you could send someone else to retrieve me next time we must have a clandestine meeting in the middle of the night, Xiaye?" Darinrain called before he landed next to me, stumbling slightly. "That messenger was not very pleasant, and I have a raging headache." When no one responded to him, Darinrain rubbed his eyes petulantly and took another look around. His gaze fell upon Notien's wide eyes, and his eyebrows furrowed questioningly.

"Th-the Creators…" Notien whispered.

Suddenly, all the sleepy humor left Darinrain's face. He turned to Avenlae as he stepped out of Vindicta's shadow. "Already?"

Avenlae only nodded, the shadows from the fire in the middle of our group sharpening his features.

I could sense him, Vindicta said, all of us able to hear her voice. ***There is no question that Mors was here.***

"B-but it is too soon!" Notien seemed barely able to keep the hysteria out of her voice. "We have barely had the time to rebuild from Creation's War.

52

How are we supposed to face this? How are we supposed to face **Creators?"**

"**They** are not as invincible as they seem," I responded, not looking at Notien, but instead staring intently into the fire. To look into the fear that was growing in my friends' eyes was to break my own resolve. "I was able to defeat Sinivir. I'll just have to find a way to defeat the rest of his brothers."

"You defeated Sinivir only **after** he killed off more than half of Creation," Saetyl growled. "I do not doubt in your power, Xiaye, but I do doubt this is something you will be able to pull off by yourself. How many more lives will be lost in collateral?"

"None... beyond our own." A tense silence fell. Vindicta shifted behind me, a whisper of her frill opening and closing. I was asking too much: I knew it. But I couldn't deny what Saetyl said. I refused to pull all of Creation into this new war, refused to make their lives collateral. This would be a fight between me and the Four Brothers, with or without my team beside me.

"You... you want us to help you?" Notien whispered. "You want us to fight another war? After everything we have already done for you?"

"I don't **want** you to." I swallowed hard, working to keep my voice steady, "I don't have a choice but to **ask** you to."

"What could we mortals do to a Creator?" Saetyl scoffed. "It took all of your power to finish off Sinivir. We could hardly land a scratch on him with our weapons."

A soft rustle was all we heard of Avenlae tensing. Saetyl, Notien, and Darinrain lowered their eyes and their wings. They knew better than to test Avenlae, despite how strong their opinions were.

"We cannot hope to touch them if they manifest here," Darinrain said, his voice trailing off.

"Spit it out," Avenlae growled, "I do not have the patience for your dramatic pauses."

"But is that not how all fantastical solutions to impending doom are presented?" Darinrain asked mockingly.

"Out with it, Darinrain," I said sharply, "what do you know?"

"As you wish." He tilted his head forward in a bow he knew was shallow enough to be rude before continuing. "We mortals cannot harm the Creators like you can when they manifest within each of their universes. To us, their manifestations are mere projections of themselves. According to what little I remember from the *Je'quiet* stories, if one were to wield **genepotentia** against a Creator when they manifest, one can send their projection back to wherever their real Essence is kept. Still, you cannot harm them enough to remove their Essence from their creations."

"How is that supposed to help us?" I cursed inwardly at how desperate my voice sounded.

"Because, when Sinivir came to Creation's War, he brought his Essence into this universe." **So did Mors,** I thought as Darirain continued. "That was why you were able to defeat him, Xiaye—he had no fifth universe in which to conceal his Essence. If we can find a way into whatever realm each Creator is hiding their Essence, we can cause far more damage than if we wait for them to come to us."

"Are you suggesting we go to **them** before they get the chance to go after Creation?" Avenlae asked, his voice void of its usual hatred towards Darinrain.

"With how little we truly know about the Four Brothers, I think that is our only option." Darinrain shrugged, making the *Je'quiet* tattoos up his skull appear as if they were slithering with archaic knowledge.

"That is complete madness." Saetyl shook her head. "A suicide mission. You speak of realms we have no real knowledge of, and Creators whose power came too close to destroying everything we have ever known."

"I speak of knowledge from the *Je'quiet,*" Darinrain said softly, "and, if you remember, the last time I did, we discovered the lost tribe of the ***Sloviyankae.***"

"But, Xiaye," Notien pleaded, turning to me, "is this really ***our*** fight? Have we not done enough for Creation already?"

"***Creation*** is where we all live, Notien," I responded. "Creation is our ***home***, the people we love. It ***is*** everything we've ever known."

The fact that we are all standing here, with time to decide whether or not to take action, should tell you all something, Vindicta spoke, lowering her head to the middle of where we stood. *The Creators have not destroyed the universes. They have not come down to kill any of us, yet. Mors didn't destroy Xiaye because he was testing her. Likely, they cannot all agree on what to do with the universes, so they are each on their own. And Mors sees Xiaye as a threat.*

"We would be taking on one Brother at a time," Avenlae said, his silver eyes on me.

"And we know more this time," I said to Notien. "It's not much to go on, but it's more than we had during Creation's War."

Notien's navy eyes stared round and unblinking into mine, her fear the most conspicuous out of all of us.

"You are going to go after them whether or not we go with you, aren't you, Xiaye?" Saetyl asked.

I pulled my gaze from Notien, nodding slowly at her mate. Saetyl sighed, lowering her head. "I do not know why I bothered asking, I already knew the answer."

"I want to bring the fight to ***them***," I said, flashing canines I didn't have. "It's the only way to keep them out of Creation. Keep them busy with us."

"We will need to find a way into the realm of the Creators, then," Darinrain said, rolling his shoulders.

"You'll help me?" I should've tried to hide the surprise in my voice, but

55

I didn't. I couldn't. My guilt over asking them to fight again was too heavy for me to keep faking strength.

"I have to," Darinrain shrugged, uncharacteristically serious, "You are powerful, My Queen, but the Brothers are nearly indestructible. You cannot stop them alone."

"Mercy." I looked over at Saetyl again, whose eyes burned with the light of the fire before us. "I may think you are crazy, but you will always have my loyalty. Shall I prepare new Guard rotations in the morning?"

"I'll send Avenlae to speak with Kaigar in the morning. I don't mean to undermine your authority, but, in this case, he'll respond better to the King than the Voxmor liaison."

You make the right choice, Xiaye, Vindicta said, rising to all four feet, *I will stay near Saetyl until we hear word from the King about the organization of my hive.*

Saetyl merely bowed her head, saying, "As you wish. With your permission, then, I will take my leave. No doubt, tomorrow will be a long day of organizing the Voxmor and the Guard, the very second Kaigar hears of this new threat. I should rest before then."

She looked pointedly at Notien, but said nothing more before turning to fly off into the night. Notien lowered her eyes, but remained where she was as Darinrain stepped forward. "I will meet with you in the morning, My Queen," he said, "There is a lot we must plan before moving forward."

"Should I come with you?" Avenlae growled, his voice a whispered threat.

"I am flattered you want to spend time with me, My King!" Dainrain grinned before I could answer.

"No," I answered through gritted teeth, "I'll need you with Kaigar and Saetyl to prepare the Queen's and Voxmor Guard."

"If you are sure." Avenlae's intense gaze remained on Darinrain. I could feel through the *lyceliah* that his protective instincts had been heightened to an extent that he couldn't override. I just sighed, knowing there was very little I could say or do at that moment to dissuade him from homicidal thoughts about Dainrain.

Dainrain, however, bumped my shoulder and smiled down at me as if we were sharing some kind of inside joke. "He will like me in the end. Do not worry, this is progress in our friendship!"

"Under no circumstances—" Avenlae began, but Darinrain had jumped into the air and was soaring over the trees before another word was said. Avenlae flashed his canines in annoyance at Darinrain's antics, but calmed himself the second our eyes met.

"I guess… I guess we should rest, too," I said to him, although I had no clue how either of us was to fall back asleep. His head tilted ever so slightly to the side as his silver eyes softened, concern flooding the bond between us.

"Xiaye," Notien spoke, her voice soft and unsure. She stood beside us still, her navy eyes trained on the ground as if it held all the answers she was searching for. Vindicta clicked a few times, nudging me towards Notien before she slithered into the shadows of the treeline. Nodding to Avenlae, I stepped closer to Notien, hearing a moment's hesitation before Avenlae left us alone in the clearing, next to the dying embers of the fire.

Without looking up, Notien murmured, "Is this the right thing to do?"

"Is—is what?"

"Going after the Creators," Notien took a breath, then raised worried eyes to mine, "attacking them… is that the right thing to do?"

"What… what else *is* there to do? I'm sure as hell not going to sit here and wait for them to attack." I shook my head in disbelief, even though I'd heard that same question echoing softly in the back of my mind.

"With you gone, searching for the next Brother to confront, will that not entice the other Creators to come here? Would it not make sense for them to try to destroy the stronghold in which you hide? We already know they have access to this universe. Mors appearing before you should frighten you enough into staying and protecting your people."

"Staying here, doing nothing, and mounting only a defense is what… is exactly what led to the Delfungaye nearly being eliminated as a species last time." I felt the pain of Notien's flinch at my words like a jab through my chest. Speaking poorly on the rule of Novissime wasn't a tactic, though—it was simply the truth. "Allowing the Creators time to mount an attack will mean allowing them time to strengthen their power and prepare an army. That's what Sinivir had: centuries to build his army and… and me. I can't allow his brothers the same luxury."

Notien nodded, but averted her eyes, uncertainty adding a distracted twitch to her fingers. I sighed. "You don't have to come with me. You could stay here, protect the people."

"No, I could not." Notien's shoulders dropped. "I already knew Saetyl would follow you. She is too proud of a warrior not to. And I cannot stay here, wondering what is happening to her. Or you." Her gaze met mine again, and tears swam in the depths of her dark eyes. "Do not take my words as disrespect, Xiaye. It is only that I had hoped so fervently that once we brought about peace, it would be a feeling we would become used to as a tribe."

"This fight is so much bigger than our people," I said, crossing my arms over my chest. "I wish I could tell you something more comforting, but I think our struggle is far from over. We're going up against the very powers that made our reality exist."

"And yet, you are not dissuaded," Notien gave me a weak smile. "I may be worried, Xai, but you are easy to follow. In the end, I know it will be your determination alone that will defeat the Brothers. And it will be my honor to be there to witness it for Creation."

Wrapping her in my arms, I took a deep breath, pulling my wings in close to my back. "Don't stop being my voice of reason, okay?" I whispered into her platinum hair. "I'm going to need it now more than ever."

"Because you always have listened so well to my advice." Her eye-roll was evident in her tone, even if I couldn't see it.

"You know, it was so much more fun when you didn't understand what sarcasm was."

Notien laughed softly before stepping back, but she kept her hands on my shoulders. "I know I was questioning you, but you are my best friend. I have to make sure we are doing what is best for us and for our people."

"Don't worry, Notien." I offered her a small smile. "I'm not angry with you. I know everything you say and do comes from a place of love. Besides, we're planning on taking on an insane task. I need someone to fight back on some of my decisions to make sure my judgment doesn't become clouded."

"I can be very good at that," Notien smirked.

"I'm aware," I responded, returning her smirk as we turned, letting our arms drop as we prepared to take off back towards the Queen's Nest.

"And so, everything changes again," Notien said, taking a deep breath as she spread her wings.

"It does. But none of us are alone this time," I called to her, feeling the night air move through my feathers.

Yet, the very fact that I was no longer alone made the threat even more terrifying. A part of me hadn't cared much about whether I lived or died during Creation's War, at least not until the end.

But this time, for this war, it was *so* much worse.

In the gentle light of the moon, Avenlae's form took on a much softer shape. He no longer appeared menacing with the sharpened lines of his muscles accentuated through his tattoos. In the shadows, they swirled across his skin, calming the fire that usually burned in his eyes. I stared a moment too long as I re-entered our bedroom, watching as he removed the scabbards from his back and the armor from around his torso. He seemed to pull his chest in, as if to hide the jagged scar down his sternum from the moonlight that flitted in through the shattered windows behind me. As if I hadn't gotten used to how it disrupted his tattoos, to how it stretched when he moved. As if I wasn't supposed to see the only physical sign of weakness he had.

"Roll your shoulders back," I said quietly, keeping my tone neutral, "your upper back will start aching if you slouch so much."

"I still have years before I have to worry about the pains of an aging body," Avenlae grumbled, but he still straightened his spine.

"You may age differently than I'm used to, but you'll still thank me when you're seventy or eighty, right?" I asked, stepping closer and attempting a smile.

"Perhaps I will, if I get to see that day," Avenlae sighed.

"Don't say that," I snapped, sharper than I meant to.

Running a calloused hand across my cheek, Avenlae tilted my head up as he pulled me closer to him. A rustle flitted behind me as his silver wings closed behind my back. A prick of fear entered my chest, but I couldn't tell if it was my own or what I was feeling through the *lyceliah.* "I can feel your fear, *Le'eseia,*" he murmured, "I am sure you can feel mine."

"Am I making a mistake? Acting too rashly?" My voice was almost a whimper. I couldn't describe it to him, but I needed his assurance, almost as much as I needed the very air I breathed.

For a long moment, a moment full of a silence that seemed to suck the air from my lungs, Avenlae simply looked at me. His moonlight eyes had always been intense, but now they looked right through me. They read all the thoughts swirling through my mind, watched my emotions battle with each other, and bore into my soul. My fingers trembled as I set them across the scar on his chest, trying to ground myself in the steady beat of his heart. Finally, Avenlae spoke. "Time should be the judge of that, Xai, not me. I cannot tell you whether or not to attack the Creators, but I will follow you into battle without hesitation. Besides," his eyes darkened, "staying here, doing nothing while knowing the fate of Creation…" A soft growl rumbled in his throat. "That is not something I can agree to. That would be the act of a coward."

I leaned forward, resting my head on his chest and listening to the thump of his heart. That strong, steady beat, that reminder that he still survived, despite everything we had done and seen. That resilient beat… I needed it to last. Just a bit longer.

Until the end.

CHAPTER 6

The next morning, the suns of Silvacastra rose just the same as they had the previous six years. But the air didn't feel the same. Warmth didn't caress my skin as I left the Queen's Nest. The earthy taste of the breeze didn't tickle my tongue as I flew, nor did the sweetness of the **anteel** I drank force energy into my limbs. Nothing I did that morning calmed the twisting monster of anxiety that bloomed in my chest and settled heavily in my stomach. So much of my energy was expended on forcing my face into an expression of calm confidence that I had already downed a cup of coffee on top of the **anteel** by the time I met with Darinrain.

He wore a ceremonial **Je'quiet** tunic of faded violet, and deep jade beadwork trailed up his neck, rattling as he bowed his head in greeting. "You did not bring my friend with you this morning, My Queen?"

"I really don't know why you insist upon torturing your king, Darinrain," I replied, keeping the reprimand in my voice gentle, "You're fighting a losing battle."

"Ah, that is how it may appear to the outside observer, but fear not,

Xiaye," Darinrain struck a dramatic pose, "I shall prevail against the murderous tendencies of your mate."

I rolled my eyes, then gestured for him to follow me as we headed towards the outer borders of the tribe. Darinrain had insisted we stop first with the *Matri Me'leiv*, but hadn't explained why. A silence fell between us, in which the serene sounds of the lively tribe battered against my ears. They seemed insulting, enraged almost, although not a soul beyond my inner circle knew of the impending threat to Creation. The smiles and bows of those we passed ripped holes in my resolve and fed my guilt. Was my choice to act upon the appearance of Mors in Creation one that would lead the Delfungaye into an unnecessary war?

"You cannot question yourself now, My Queen." Darinrain's voice startled me. It was soft, low, and assured. Different enough that I stopped, hovered where I was, and stared at the jagged tattoos that wound their way up his bare scalp. He didn't look back at me at first. His shoulders heaved as he took a deep breath before turning around. "Your silence is loud. I know your thoughts because I, and the others, share them."

I lowered my eyes, a shocking move for a queen. "Then why haven't you stopped me?"

For the first time since I had met him nearly six years previously, Darinrain's gaze became intense. "There is nothing else in Creation that can stand against a Creator. The Brothers make their threats because they believe that their power makes them untouchable. But I watched you *destroy* Sinivir. I witnessed the impossible become reality. So there is nothing in Creation that could stop *me* from following My Queen into battle for the liberation of my people. The Creators' weakness is their arrogance, and it will be their downfall."

"Is that what has happened, then?" The deep, demure voice startled both Darinrain and me enough that our hands flew to the hilts of our weapons.

A sweet breeze caressed our cheeks from the gentle movement of the *Matri*

Me'liev's onyx wings. She hovered just behind us, just far enough away to be polite as her navy eyes narrowed on me. "Our Creator has approached you, then?"

"Could you sense it?" Darinrain asked before I could speak. I flashed a glare in his direction, for his voice had been a bit too direct for the *Matri Me'liev* to mistake it as simple surprise.

The old woman's eyes shifted to Darinrain. Beadwork clicked ominously down her shock of pure white hair, and her silence was deafening.

"It is time. You have to tell us everything you know."

"Darirain," I hissed. Turning back to the *Matri Me'liev,* I dipped my head quickly out of respect, saying, "I'm sorry. He insisted we come to see you before doing anything else to prepare for this new threat. Unfortunately, you are right—Mors, the Fourth Creator, came into Creation last night."

The *Matri Me'liev's* gaze softened when she looked at me. "I am sorry, My Queen, but there is little more I can offer you than spiritual guidance. The only pertinent advice I have is to be cautious about causing panic within the tribes. They have only just started to live peacefully on their own, and there is no need to hurt them if they are not to be a part of this fight."

"How do you know whether or not all of Creation is again at war with the Creators?" Darinrain asked, his voice sharp. "We said nothing of what kind of battle we are up against."

"There has been no official announcement," the old woman shot back, "Therefore, it is safe for me to assume Our Queen does not want to involve the people unless she must."

"She's correct, *Darinrain,*" I responded, glaring over at him. "I suggest you explain the reason you wanted to come speak with the *Matri Me'liev* and watch your tongue."

"She knows more than she is letting on," Darinrain said, moving closer to where the spiritual leader hovered. "We need to know what she does. She has the key to defeating the Brothers."

I looked between the two of them. "*She* has the key? Darinrain, I know she's an integral part of the Delfungaye culture, but just because she is a spiritual leader doesn't mean—"

"She is not," Darinrain snapped, narrowing his eyes at the *Matri Me'liev,* "she is an Oracle."

My eyes widened, and I stared longer at Darinrain, unable to speak. The *Matri Me'liev* just hovered, and stared so deeply at Darinrain I half expected holes to begin smoking where his eyes were. Then, fast enough that I had to take a second to understand what had happened, Darinrain's knife had plunged hilt-deep into the old woman's chest, and her crimson blood was dripping down his closed fist. I didn't know what to do. I didn't know what to say. I just froze and watched as a drop of blood began to make its way down the corner of the *Matri Me'liev's* wrinkled mouth. In the secluded outer borders of the tribe, there was no one else around to witness her death, no one to rush forward and yank Darinrain back.

But there was me. And yet… something about the look in Darinrain's eyes told me to wait. Even as my hands shook and violet flames exploded down my wings, I did not move.

An odd, almost psychotic smile inked its way across the *Matri Me'liev's* face. "How long have you known, boy?"

And then we were falling. Darinrain and I were tumbling through shadow, our wings gone, our lungs spasming in terrified gasps and shrieks. Something stopped our fall—something plush that absorbed the impact so we felt no pain. But when I tried to stand, I felt no ground beneath my feet. It was as if I were simply floating in a space of absolute nothingness.

"Darinrain?" I called out cautiously.

"Behind you, My Queen," his voice came floating to me, "I think. I may be next to you… Or above you?"

"Do not panic, young mortals," the melodic voice of the **Matri Me'liev** reverberated through the darkness before me, and within one blink of my eyes, the shadows had taken form. First, a current curled the darkness—a ripple of faint violet beneath my feet that glimmered and spun. From there, radiant filaments of light and shadow bled upwards, entwining like root and vine. They folded over one another, splitting into fractal branches that curled and grew. As they did, they gathered pigment from memory: the bleed of dusk along riverbanks, the soft glow of bioluminescent mosses, the gold-limned blue of distant nebulae seen only in dreams. I had the sense not of confinement, but of being inside a living engine built from color and emotion. The boundaries of the room stretched away as if the walls were only an afterimage burnt behind the eyes. "You are in Somnia. Nothing can harm you here."

"We're… what?" I asked in awe as I spun on the spot, marveling at the stained glass designs of the high-arching windows around us and the Gothic twists of the elaborate metalwork that adorned the walls where they met the ceiling. Pillars of burning amber, encased in swirling vines of deep navy, stood between each window, casting the room in an ethereal, unnatural glow.

"Xiaye, your wings!" Darinrain gasped behind me. His golden skin almost glowed in the room's light, but his fear was just as radiant. His own black sparrow-like wings were gone, and so were his weapons.

A spike of fear dove down my spine as a soft hiss emanated from beside me. Groping for knives I already knew I didn't have, I stepped in front of Darinrain as wisps of white smoke began to take form before us. "This is Somnia, the Dream Realm," the creature said in the **Matri Me'liev's** voice as it materialized, "Everything you had that gave you an advantage in Creation is gone here. Your weapons, too, are not necessary within this realm. You exist in your simplest form, that is all."

What stood before us was a creature unlike anything I had ever seen. She had no eyes, no nose, just a mouth twirled up into a soft smile. Her head extended up into a fan that was almost crystalline, and from the back of it fell a waterfall of delicate silver hair, shimmering as if woven from the moonlight itself. Swaths of cloth in hues of violet, indigo, and the purest golds wrapped themselves graciously across her willowy body, flowing out around her as if she were beneath the water. Hands the color of night extended out from beneath her robes with thin fingers longer than her arms. They weren't claws, though—simply peaceful extensions. Her skin glowed with the light of thousands of tiny stars and galaxies that seemed to breathe with every graceful movement she made.

"*This* is your 'simplest form'?" Darinrain said with very little tact.

What used to be the **Matri Me'liev** laughed, and the sound seemed to pull every bit of happiness I had ever felt to the forefront of my mind. "I am an Oracle, one of the Pillars of Somnia. My powers remain unchanged, only because they are derived from the very essence of the Dream Realm."

"*You?* You're *the* Oracle?" I stuttered. My mind was reeling as it tried to comprehend what had happened in mere seconds. "As in… the Prophecy of the Daughter of War? The Oracle of Delf?"

"What I would like to know," the Oracle said, completely ignoring me, "is how *you* discovered me, Story Teller."

Darinrain shrugged. "You had not died yet."

That statement was met with a moment of silence. "Is that all?"

"Well, my brother told me his suspicions before he died," Darinrain continued, "I just confirmed them."

"How interesting," the Oracle smiled, "that I would forget something as mortal as dying. That's what happens when you become too involved in the mortal world—you forget what you are, and how to keep up appearances."

"Darinrain," I said through gritted teeth, wishing so desperately that I had wings I could light on fire, "Exactly *when* were you going to bother explaining any of this to me?"

"When it became relevant," Darinrain grinned. "It did just now!"

I raised my eyebrows.

He gestured excitedly as he began to tell his story. "My Queen, I remember my brother once saying that he believed the Oracle of Delf was still alive. According to his theory, the Oracle was not a mere mortal, but rather a powerful being. He had his suspicions about the *Matri Me'liev*, but I thought it was just because he admired her control over the tribe. The only way to confirm his theory would be to release her from her physical form."

"Which means killing her?" I asked hesitantly.

"Surprisingly, he is correct," the Oracle said, as if she were praising an exceptionally bright student.

"And what if you weren't?" I scolded. "What if you had just murdered the *Matri Me'liev* because your hunch was wrong?"

"Well," Darinrain's smile faltered at the corners. "I was right, was I not? There is no need to worry about what *could* have happened, Your Highness."

"You do not call her by her name, here," the Oracle interrupted before I had the chance to continue, "Yet, I have heard you speak her given name in conversation before I brought you to Somnia." Her head swiveled to face me. "You do not demand respect from the Story Teller, *Creovis*?"

I fought back the flinch I wanted to make at her referring to me as *Creovis*. "He was my friend, first. All those in my inner circle call me by my name periodically. I had to earn their trust as much as they earned mine, and

I rule over the Delfungaye only because I have their help. Therefore, I have no right to remind them of my power."

"Ah," Darinrain sighed, "I am always proud to serve by your side, Xiaye, but when you say things like that, I just feel—"

"Darinrain," I said warningly.

"Yes, Your Majesty," Darinrain bowed his head, hiding a smile in the process.

"What an intriguing dynamic, *Creovis.*" The Oracle tilted her head to the side as if she were studying me, if she had eyes to do so. "You are not at all what I expected."

"What do you mean?" I chose not to hide the sharpness in my tone. Despite her breathtaking beauty, I still felt a drop of uneasiness fall into my stomach.

"Your very core was forged from absolute hatred and bloodthirsty vengeance," the Oracle said, gliding closer to me, "yet your fight has always been to protect the ones you learned to *love*. Such contradictions are not accidents, *Creovis*. Even the blackest forge leaves room for light to bleed through the cracks. The one born of ruin becomes the keeper of its undoing."

"You can call me the *Creovis* as much as you want, Oracle, but that is not *who* I am."

"You proved that much when you defeated Sinivir, *Xiaye*." The Oracle spread her long fingers wide. "Which brings me to the reason I brought you both here. If the Creators have made contact with you, that means the time for the *Creovis* to return to the Realm of the Creators has come. You now seek the Brothers, do you not?"

"You think you can help us?"

"My dear, I did not become an Oracle simply because I acquired certain gifts!" Her smile became unhinged once again. "I know *things*."

"Any *things* you would like to impart upon us, then?" Darinrain asked as he folded his arms over his chest. I flashed a look at him out of the corner of my eye.

"Indeed, Story Teller. You already know from your own teachings that a Creator's control and Essence can only truly be removed from Creation if they are either defeated within their own realm, the Realm of Creo, or defeated in the Realm of Creation if they are foolish enough to not leave their Essence apart from their form. Sinivir, of course, was arrogant enough to fight you, Xiaye, with his Essence fully intact within the form he took in the Realm of Creation. The other Brothers will leave theirs within their realms if they choose to enter Creation."

"You're saying our only option of liberating Creation from the control of the Brothers is to fight them within the Realm of Creo?" I clarified.

"Indeed," the Oracle breathed, as if her mind had already wandered far from where we stood.

"Oh, the others are going to love this!" Darinrain boomed with a crazed grin. "Such a challenge! Sparring in the Queen's Guard can be exhilarating enough with the right partner, but fighting a Creator head-on would be—"

"Deadly." The Oracle's head snapped towards Darinrain, and his smile dropped. "Sinivir was the weakest of the five Brothers, and he chose to fight with the full might of his power in Creation. That is nothing compared to the extent of each Brother's power within the Realm of Creo. You will be fighting them in *their* home, where mortals are not meant to exist."

"Could a mortal harm a Creator in Creo?" I asked, assuming the Oracle wouldn't bother talking to us about the Realm if there wasn't a way for us to defeat the Brothers.

"Of course," the Oracle murmured, turning towards me and advancing slowly, "The Creators are arrogant. Such a time, with more power than any other being in existence, has convinced them they are untouchable. Your defeat of Sinivir may have frightened them enough to try their own hands at controlling Creation and destroying you, but it did nothing to knock them off their pedestals. Mortals are not meant to be able to enter Creo, so the Brothers have never created any kind of true defense against their attacks. Their powers are strong, but their bodies will be as weak as your own. You just have to get close enough."

"It is that easy?" Darinrain huffed.

"Becoming close enough with a person to kill them does not always mean you have to touch their skin with your blade, Story Teller," the Oracle hissed. "There are other ways."

"Those are?" I asked sharply.

"Ah, that I cannot tell you." The Oracle turned and began gliding away. "I am not interested in Summum's wrath should my tongue go too far."

"Summum?"

"A story for another time, *Creovis*." The Oracle paused. "I can, however, tell you the way into the Realm of Creo. I have no loyalty to the Brothers."

"You could not have led with that information?" Darinrain grunted. At my piercing gaze, he raised an eyebrow. "I *know* I am not as impatient as you, Xiaye. If I am annoyed enough to be blunt, *you* must be seething."

I didn't dignify him with an answer, but of course, he was right. I was just much better at hiding my rising frustration.

"I had to test you, *Creovis*," the Oracle said in a breathy, sing-song voice, "I needed to read how badly you wanted it. If you were an appropriate vessel."

"If I—what?"

Suddenly, her fingers had wrapped like coils around my arms, and her face was a mere few inches away from mine. Up close, she smelled... like a dream. Like a fresh, ethereal dream. Behind her, Darinrain had moved to grab his staff and, realizing it was gone, froze, his eyes focused intently on every move the Oracle made.

"Understand, *Creovis,* that the only way for you to enter the Realm of Creo is to use the power of one who has been there before. You must invite the Essence of Sinivir to exist within your own power."

"In my . . .! But he tried to—"

"It is not *him* you are inviting back into Creation, simply his Essence. *You* will have control over Sinivir's power, and he will not be able to do a thing if you do not allow it."

"There is no way in *hell* I will allow *anything* of that bastard to exist near me," I growled.

"Then there is no way in all of Creation that you will be able to defeat the Brothers before they have the chance to destroy everything you have ever known, *Xiaye.*"

My chest rose and fell with each anxiety-filled breath as I stared at the eyeless face of the Oracle. Her scent became too overwhelming, nearly causing me to faint as it fogged my brain. Invite part of the Fifth Creator *back?* When he had already killed so many before? How could I do something like this, and return to my people as if there was nothing wrong, much less ask them to put their trust in me as their Queen?

"Xiaye," Darinrain spoke, his voice calm. My sight refocused as I flicked my eyes behind the Oracle. His own navy gaze held so much emotion, so many words he could speak, but dared not to. "You are the only one who can."

The only one who can. One day, you'll understand, Creovis. I turned back to the Oracle's pulsating skin. "There is no other way?"

"If you want to be able to bring your warriors with you to battle, this is the only way you can do it. Sinivir's power, combined with your own, can transport you and whoever you choose into the Realm of Creo. It is the only way you will ever be strong enough for the Brothers to see you as anything more than a little nuisance."

I gritted my teeth. "Tell me how."

The Oracle smiled. "It will be the most painful thing you have ever experienced."

"What?" I whimpered, and then it hit me. Every single bone in my body, radiating from where the Oracle had wrapped her fingers around my arms, shattered. It was the lucid, articulate agony of being methodically dismantled and rebuilt with the memory of suffering threaded into every ligament, every gap between marrow and muscle. My skin held the violence for a moment, stretched and translucently red, but then it ripped open as shards of bone burst through. I tried to scream, but the sound was never able to leave my burning throat.

But the pain was only the surface, a warning.

Within the void of my body, something was being summoned and spliced into the blueprint of my being. It felt as if my blood was evaporating and being replaced with something *alien,* a memory of someone else.

"*Never* forget who you are, *Creovis.* It will be apocalyptic if you do," the Oracle whispered, and I knew no more.

CHAPTER 7

"Xai? Xiaye!" Avenlae's frantic calls jolted me back awake. The scent of heated leaves and the dry foliage of the underbrush shoved itself into my nostrils, and the suns stung my eyes. Avenlae's fearful silver gaze swam into my field of vision, his pupils contracted into thin black lines. Gradually, the canopy of the forest took shape behind him, emerald leaves appearing too energetic for the sluggish shadow that weighed heavily in my mind.

"She was okay just a moment ago!" Darinrain's panicked voice sharpened my hearing. "I did not see what happened! She was—she was just fine, I swear!"

"For once in your life, *shut up,* Darinrain!" I heard Notien hiss before the underbrush crashed as she tore through it.

"I-I'm okay," I said quickly, although my mouth felt as if it was stuffed full of cotton. I coughed again as I pushed myself up, hardly feeling the scratch of branches against my arms as my head began to spin.

"I will eviscerate him," Avenlae hissed as he caught me, holding my back and baring his canines in the direction of a second body crashing through the leaves and branches around us. Notien appeared first, emerald leaves slapping against her golden cheeks. Her round navy eyes flashed at the sight of Avenlae crouched next to me, and she immediately turned, catching Darinrain in the chest as he burst out of the foliage.

Two things happened at once—Avenlae jerked as if he were about to charge Darinrain. Without thinking, I raised my left arm as if to block Avenlae from his chosen target, although a more alert mind would have known there was not a damn thing I could've done to stop him from killing Darinrain.

What actually happened when I raised my left hand was that a vivid red and gold shield seemed to spring from my skin and harden the very air between Avenlae and Darinrain. Everyone, including myself, froze and stared at the nearly translucent waves of ruby and gold that moved across the shield, much like waves move across water. I had made plenty of shields during my time honing the *genepotentia* of the Creonex, but that color... that was *Sinivir's* color.

"The transference is complete," came the Oracle's voice. Who appeared next to Darinrain, however, was the *Matri Me'liev.* "You control the Essence of Sinivir now, *Creovis.*"

Avenlae's eyes slid over to mine, and I felt the pressure of his palm along my spine lessen. His ears stayed pinned against the braids along his scalp as he hissed, "*What did you do?*"

Against my better judgment, I ignored his rigid stance and turned my attention to the *Matri Me'liev* as Notien released her grip on Darinrain. Waves of hot anger pulsed through the *lyceliah,* enough to frighten me. *Not here.* "What... what do I do now?"

It was such a simple, yet idiotic question. The *Matri Me'liev* smiled, an expression that appeared so warm on her lined face, but that had seemed so predatory upon the face of the Oracle. "Victorum, Bellum, Fames, then Mors.

That is the order you must go in. Each Brother suspects that He is stronger than the one that came before Him, so attacking from the fourth Brother to the first will not cause as much panic. Trust in Sinivir's Essence to lead you to the realm of each Creator, but *not* anything more." The old woman bent close, her expression becoming serious. "I will watch over the Delfungaye. I imagine Kaigar already knows his place. If you are to do this, *Creovis*, you must leave now. Begin your journey before Mors has the chance to strike first. He will not touch us here on Silvacastra if he thinks you are more of a threat."

"So I have to *make* myself more of a threat," I whispered.

She nodded. "Remember, the Brothers *can* be defeated. If you can get close enough, you can discover the thing that gives true strength to their power. All you have to do is exploit it."

And then she was gone. As suddenly as the *Matri Me'liev* had first appeared, she melted back into the underbrush. The four of us left on the ground watched the swaying of the branches in stunned silence for a moment longer.

Turning slowly, as if she were breathing deeply to remain calm, Notien said, "*Explain*."

I glared at Darinrain to keep him quiet before I began. "I have a way into the Realm of Creo, where the Creators exist. That involves the control over Sinivir's Essence, hence the absorption of his power into mine."

Avenlae's eyes widened. "His power *exists* within you? *That* is what I feel?"

I turned a quizzical look on him. "Y-you feel it?"

Avenlae pulled his wings in close to his spine protectively. "I feel *hatred.* It is so faint I have to focus to name it, but it is there." He shook his head, his face softening. "Xiaye, what have you done?"

"What I *had* to do," I said, looking away from him, and searching for assurance instead in the navy gaze of Notien. "Sinivir's power is the only key we

76

have to entering Creo. Likewise, combining it with my own will provide us with the best chance we have of defeating the Brothers. I, I did this for Creation." I lowered my head, familiar guilt beginning to eat away at my resolve. "I had to. I have to do whatever I can. The stakes are too high."

"A sacrifice for the lives of many," Notien murmured. My eyes stayed on the ground.

"You would not have done it if there was another option presented to you," Notien sighed. "The idea and repercussions of this choice to immediately take offensive action scare me. But I trust you, Xiaye. Your people trust you. Kaigar has already begun to reorganize his units to prepare for your absence—he did not even fight Saetyl on it."

Your decision is foolish, and I refuse to say that I support it, came Vindicta's voice echoing in our minds, *but... I understand. We'll talk after my hive has been reorganized.*

I sighed, lowering my head into my hands. "I had to. I know it's terrifying for all of you, but I **had** to."

"She did not want to," Darinrain piped up, keeping his eyes on the ground and his voice soft. "The Oracle claimed that absorbing the power of Sinivir's Essence was the only way we would be able to enter the Realm of Creo and have a chance at defeating the Brothers."

"The Oracle? Realm of Creo?" Avenlae growled, turning murderous eyes back on Darinrain. "If I wanted more of your stories, *Je'quiet,* I would have ordered you to speak."

"Avenlae!" I snapped, pushing myself to my feet and raising the feathers along my wings. "That's enough. Your aggression isn't helping anything."

Avenlae's glare snapped to me, molten and wounded all at once. He hated when I used that tone — the one that reminded him I could command him, that we were not equals in the eyes of anyone but ourselves. His jaw flexed, a muscle twitching as if to bite back words that would have burned us both. Then, with a flash of his canines, he stepped back and dropped his gaze.

"Besides," I continued, choosing again to look at Notien while I spoke, "he's telling the truth. Our *Matri Me'liev* is the mortal form of the Oracle of Delf. The only reason Darinrain and I know anything of the Brothers now is because of her. She was able to transfer control of Sinivir's Essence to me and stated that his power would be the only weapon we would have against the Creators. This is the *only* way."

Notien studied my eyes for a few tense moments. "Do you realize how hard it will be to convince the others to believe you?"

"We have Vindicta. She can help me transfer the memories to all of you so you will know whatever I do." Another wave of anger hit me through the *lyceliah,* and I sucked in a breath through my teeth, trying to control my own emotions.

"The Oracle has given us our only chance at survival," Darinrain said, finally lifting his eyes. "What choice do we have but to take it?"

Notien let her gaze drift over to him, worry creasing her forehead between her eyebrows. "It is more than we had last time. That is what I keep telling myself."

"*This* is bigger than what we were up against last time!" Avenlae roared, his anger finally exploding as he faced me. "You want to *enter* the Realm of Creo, the very place the *Brothers* call home? With the rest of us, the mere mortals? Based on a tip from Darinrain and the words of a crazy old woman?"

"*I* have the power to—"

"Yes, yes, *you* have the power! *You,* the immortal, *might* have the power to threaten the Creators. What the hell are the rest of us supposed to do? Go to watch you kill yourself?"

"Avenlae!"

"My King, you are just feeling—" Darinrain began.

"I will *end* you if you say one more word!" Avenlae unsheathed his rapier, holding the blade steady across Darinrain's throat.

"Stop!" Notien shrieked. All eyes turned towards her, and, finally, silence fell. Notien held her hands up, palms turned out, and her ears were flat against her platinum hair as her eyes darted between all three of us. "It is terrifying right now for *all* of us. What we are about to do is unprecedented. There are no *Je'quiet* stories to advise us what to expect, and no orders from the General or past Queens to tell us what to do. But there is Xiaye, Queen of the Delfungaye and *Creovis*. She is the reason Creation was freed from the control of Sinivir, and, as far as I am concerned, she is the only one I would follow into battle against the rest of the Creators. If we lose that trust and continue to fight amongst ourselves because of whatever path she believes we must take, we all might as well slit our own throats now to save ourselves the torture of the deaths the Creators will give us."

Tears stung my eyes, tightening my throat and blurring my vision. I looked away from Notien, afraid to show her weakness when she had just put all of her faith in me. I glanced over at Avenlae, whose blade still rested against Darinrain's throat, right over his jugular vein. Gradually, Avenlae lowered his rapier, the muscles in his arm quivering as if they were fighting to slice the blade across Darinrain's neck instead of surrender.

"Av," I started, but froze when his eyes met mine with a hiss. Without bothering to step back, Avenlae leapt into the air, a claw on the joint of his wing ripping across Darinrain's temple. Darinrain staggered back, his hand flying to the gash that began to bleed freely down his cheek and neck. I gasped, but it was Notien who got to him first, moving his hand away so she could assess the severity of the wound.

"You should head straight for the Healer's Nest," Notien said, wincing as she let Darinrain apply pressure to the gash again, "It is a deep wound, but not one that will leave a scar if the Healers get to it soon."

"His damn temper," I snapped, tilting my head to get a better view of Darinrain's injury as he took a few deep breaths. "It's alright, Darinrain, I'll speak to the King —"

"No," Darinrain hissed as he looked over at me. "It was just discipline. I deserved it."

"What?"

"You may have been harmed with me. I did not protect you adequately, so the King was right to discipline me."

I glanced over at Notien, trying to understand Darinrain's logic. She gave me a tiny shrug, confirming that this was what they believed. I just shook my head, sighing before saying, "Will you be okay to make it to the Healers by yourself?"

Darinrain tried to give me an incredulous look, although the swelling along his eyebrow made him look more inquisitive. "My Queen, I survived Creation's War, but you ask if I am capable of flying over to the Healer's Nest?"

Both Notien and I raised an eyebrow at him.

He rolled his eyes. "Yes, of course I can get over there. It is just a scratch—my brain was not rattled around all that much."

"It may not have been rattled this time, but I do not believe it has never been rattled before," Notien said under her breath as Darinrain jumped into the air. I smiled softly as I watched the form of Darinrain flicker between branches and leaves above us. And then, as quickly as the moment of rest came, it was consumed by anxiety. A new energy, one powerful and terrifying, was buzzing through my veins. It felt as if the energy was positioning itself strategically, spreading through my body to await the first signal to strike.

"Xiaye?" Notien asked, pulling my eyes back down to her. "Shall we leave, too? You will have to meet with Kaigar before too long."

I nodded, trying to refocus my thoughts. My mind had been scattered, filtering through emotions and thoughts that were alien, things that didn't belong to me. Every fiber of my being wanted to rebel against the thing I had **chosen** to take in, and I had to control it, the power, and myself. *This is the only way,* I thought almost desperately, de*spite what they say, you know this is the only way to destroy them all.*

Notien and I took to the air, gliding back to the Queen's Nest in silence. Once again, the Delfungaye bowed and raised drinks to me as we moved through the central hub of the tribe. *They don't even know. They don't even know what I've done...*

Before me hung the first set of armor ever made for me by the *Glae'atii.* I stood alone in my chambers after a meeting with Kaigar. He outlined to me the plan to protect the tribe while its rulers and most dangerous warriors were gone, as well as advising me not to address the Delfungaye as a whole yet.

"Our people have known fear for far too long," he had said wearily, "give them a little more time to know peace. Should you fear our planet will become involved in this new battle, we will address them then."

I ran a finger along the matte black surface of the shoulder plates, avoiding the reflection of my silver and red eyes in the helmet of my armor. *This new battle.* Crimson inscriptions in the swirled lettering of the Delfungaye universal language ran along the organic curvature of the torso, added in after the Creation's War. Cracks, scratches, and nicks had been repaired, and I had no need of the armor since. Dried blood had been washed away, and the suit itself had been reinforced to handle the strength of my power.

But can it handle mine? Came the harsh whisper of Sinivir from the deepest shadows of my mind, causing the hair along the back of my neck to stand on end.

"Xai."

I gasped, flicking my eyes up to see the mottled reflection of Avenlae behind me in my helmet. I slowed my breathing before turning to face him as he held up a plate of fish and the fresh vegetables of the season. Eyeing him, I reached for the plate, studying his face and posture for signs of what kind of mood he was in. I could sense a stirring uneasiness in Avenlae through the *lyceliah,* but nothing more. That anger that had frightened me before was gone.

Wordlessly, he led me to a small table in our room positioned next to a window, where we could watch the sun set over the horizon. He began to eat, but still, I watched him. The silence was so heavy that it pressed in on my chest, making it difficult to breathe.

"Can you hear him, then?" Avenlae asked suddenly. "Sinivir."

"No, not really," I responded, the white lie rolling off my tongue effortlessly, "It's more like a distant memory of him that stirs here and there."

"Is that safe? Having him within your mind?"

I narrowed my eyes. "Sinivir is not in my mind, merely his powers. With his powers come wisps of his Essence, nothing more. Besides, I imagine my will to control him and remain myself is far stronger than his ability to attempt to separate himself from me."

"I hope so," Avenlae mumbled into his plate.

I ground my teeth and sighed, setting down my utensils as calmly as I could. "Speak honestly, Avenlae. You may not get another chance to."

"You think I am not aware of that?" Avenlae snapped, his silver eyes burning as they met mine. "I can *feel* him, Xiaye. I can feel Sinivir through you. *He* is the reason I go *insane* almost every night, watching you die in front of me over and over. I see the death of my family, the death of my mate, and I feel the pain so vividly it nearly tears open my chest every time. And now, he is *right there*. As if he could reach through you and touch me." A sheen of sweat glimmered across Avenlae's skin. "*That* is terrifying."

"I didn't... I hadn't thought of it like that," I said quietly, knowing I should've said something better, something more.

"No, you did not, nor did you bother to even *talk* with me about something like this before doing it."

"Well, it's not like I really had the chance to think it through—"

"*Do not* make excuses."

"*Do not* act like you have control over *my* actions," I snapped, the words heavier than I meant them to be. Regret lingered in the air between us, but I couldn't take them back. "I did what I had to. You can feel everything I can through the *lyceliah,* so you know I'm right."

The whisper of his warmth caressed my skin as Avenlae moved around the table to crouch before me. Tentatively, he curled his fingers around mine, the tenderness of his touch forcing me to look around into his moonlight eyes.

"You are all I have, Xai," he murmured, "*let* me fight to protect you. Let me keep you grounded, protected from *his* hatred."

"You think I can't control Sinivir's power on my own?"

"I know you. You have your own vengeance, but it is similar enough for him to use it against you. I can *feel* it, Xiaye."

"And I can feel your repulsion," I seethed, standing and moving swiftly for the door. "I have more details to confirm before we leave tomorrow. I'll return momentarily."

Nothing waited for me outside of the Queen's Nest. Truly, there was nothing more for me to prepare before the morning. But I couldn't be in that room with Avenlae. I couldn't be around him, feeling his fear, and knowing it was directed at *me.* His disgust, disappointment—it was too much.

Why do you run from him? Vindicta's voice floated into my mind, calm, strong, and reassuring. She came up to rest behind me where I sat at the top of the Queen's Nest, the Suns' set giving her pale scales a golden glow. Her prismatic eyes were curious as she lowered her head next to me.

"I… It's not him I'm running from exactly," I whispered, reaching a hand out and scratching her scales absentmindedly.

No, it is not. You are running from the truth Avenlae tells you.

"Sometimes I hate that you have access to my mind."

No, you don't.

I smiled softly, looking out over the darkening forest. "I don't want him to be right. I-I want to feel confident in the steps I'm willing to take. To feel confident that I'm not a monster, and won't become one. I… I want to know I'm doing the right thing, that my and my friends' sacrifices will mean something… in the end."

Vindicta laid her head on the bark next to me, blinking all six eyes up at me. *He can indeed feel the darkness that surrounds Sinivir's Essence within you. I can feel it, too.*

My heart sank, and a lump rose in my throat.

That doesn't mean you were wrong to absorb his Essence into your power, Xiaye. There would be very little chance that you'd even have a chance at defeating the other Creators if you hadn't.

"I know. But I don't think anyone else fully understands that."

They don't want to. Avenlae least of all. He loves you too deeply, and the instinct to protect is overwhelming.

"What am I supposed to do about that, Vin? The action has already been made. I can't just, just spit out Sinivir's Essence and be done with it."

Let Avenlae protect you.

I blinked, then looked down at her. "Let him?"

You need him as much as he needs you, especially now. For once, allow him to protect you. It will keep Sinivir's hatred at bay.

I gazed back out to where the suns had set below the canopy. Warm fires were lit within the dewdrop nests of my people, and soft tribal drums beat in the distance as the Delfungaye nightlife began. None of them knew. Nobody knew what kind of danger they were in.

"I should let him protect me the way I want to protect my people," I whispered.

Indeed. Vindicta sighed, her nostrils flaring for a mere second. I laid my head down upon hers.

"And you'll protect my friends if I can't, won't you?"

Always.

"And… the King?"

If the day should come.

"Thank you, Vindicta."

Thank you, *Creovis.*

CHAPTER 8

Night had fallen completely by the time I returned to the Queen's Nest. Guilt still settled sickeningly in my chest and stomach—that was really what kept me away. But there was the start to a mission looming on the horizon, and there was no more I could do to prepare for it besides rest.

Avenlae looked up from sharpening his knives as I entered the room. I paused in the doorway, shifting back and forth on my feet, trying to find something to say. Even with our bond, I couldn't tell if he wanted me there or if he wanted to continue the argument. Avenlae set the knife he was working on to the side, stood, and moved towards me, his ears pressed submissively against his hair. His wings moved forward, brushing their feathers hesitantly against me as he paused about a foot away.

"I... I did not mean to speak so aggressively towards you," he murmured, lowering his eyes.

"You had every right to," I whispered, wrapping my arms around myself. This was what Avenlae and I struggled with—vulnerable intimacy. Years together still hadn't helped.

His throat fluttered as he swallowed. "I just…"

"Let me explain," I raised my head, the Creonex warming around my hand. "Let me show you why I did it."

Avenlae lifted his eyes, their irises shining in the low light of the room. I closed the distance between us and pressed my left hand against his temple.

I never told Avenlae what I went through when Sinivir imprisoned me. The topic never came up, and it was a part of my trauma I tried desperately to shove as deep into the shadows as it would go. I thought perhaps I could outlast the memory by denying it oxygen. But some wounds don't starve, they throb, fester, fermenting in the dark and growing deeper roots.

That night, the last night we spent on a peaceful Silvacastra, I showed Avenlae the memory that almost killed me to relive. I transferred to him the feeling of my heart cracking at the thought of his death. I showed him the torture, the burning cage bars, the way Sinivir made me believe that my love was a weakness meant to be purged, the way his voice filled my head until I couldn't tell which screams were mine. The reason I feared Sinivir as much as he did. And when I opened my eyes, Avenlae's tears mingled with mine.

"*That* is what I need to save Creation from. Sinivir is **nothing** compared to his Brothers, and I **have** to do anything I can to gain an advantage in the fight I'm about to start. I-I have to protect **you**, Av. I… I'll break if they… if they kill you."

Avenlae cupped my face in his hands, lifting my head to kiss me softly. Then he pressed his lips against my forehead and wrapped his arms and wings around me in an embrace flooded with warmth. "Let me be your strength, Xai," his voice rumbled against my cheek as he pulled me against his chest, "You are not going up against the Creators alone, nor do you have to face the darkness of Sinivir's power alone."

Avenlae ran a hand through my hair, resting his palm against the nape of my neck. "Let me help you remember that, *Le'eseia.*"

The golden light of the rising suns illuminated the emerald leaves of the *Laizuteek* forest the next morning. Those living in and visiting the forest slept on, the light not yet bright enough within the dewdrop nests for them to stir. The air swirled lazily with the sweet songs of small creatures, the beginning of what would become a welcome melody of calls as the morning wore on.

I would not hear those calls. Neither would Avenlae, Darinrain, Notien, Saetyl, or Vindicta. It was almost insulting that we stood in our full armor on such a peaceful morning—even more so that we wouldn't even stay long enough to enjoy it.

Kaigar stood before us, dressed only in what was required of him for leading the training of the Queen's Guard later that day. One eyebrow was furrowed, the other twisted and pulling at the scar that blinded his right eye. "This is your final chance to turn your back on this, My Queen," he said to me, his gravely voice low. "You do not have to take on this battle."

"But who else will?" I asked, sliding a knife into a well-hidden sheath along my thigh.

The General gave me a long look, one that I felt I couldn't look away from.

"You can't tell me you would forgive me if I turned my back on this threat, and it became the end of the Delfungaye and Creation," I said softly, stepping closer. "We fought for what we have, now. I have to ensure we can keep it."

Still, for a few more tense moments, Kaigar didn't drop his gaze. Finally, with a sigh and a step back, he whispered, "Yes, *Creovis.*"

A thrill of energy shot through my body, a power I was unfamiliar with. I sucked in a breath as I watched Kaigar disappear into the trees before us, heading back to the training grounds of the Guard. The power wouldn't settle, no matter how hard I fought to force it down. It wasn't my power, after all.

It was the excitement of Sinivir's Essence—I was taking it home.

Notien rested her head on Saetyl's shoulder as I prepared myself to create a portal to the Realm of Creo. Saetyl's hand stroked through Notien's platinum bob mindlessly, as if unaware of the comforting motion. Vindicta paced back and forth behind us, her matte black armor clinking softly as she moved.

"What a lively group," Darinrain scoffed as he spun his staff, testing its balance.

"Are we not *entertaining* enough for you?" Avenlae growled behind me.

"My King, we are about to embark upon a battle for the freedom of all Creation! We are about to face our mortality, are we not?" The smile on Darinrain's face was almost maniacal. "Do you not feel the adrenaline? The anticipation?"

"I would prefer to feel the satisfaction of your *silence,* Darinrain," Saetyl said through gritted teeth.

Notien's navy eyes reflected a sense of resolve as she sighed, raising her head off of Saetyl's shoulder. "It is now or never, Xiaye."

I looked over at her as she pulled her scimitar from its scabbard strapped to her waist and fastened her helmet over her head. "Lead us on, My Queen."

Yes, do lead on, little Creovis, hissed Sinivir in the back of my mind, his smile evident in the inflection of his voice. My head twitched, involuntarily moving to respond to the sound of Sinivir's voice. Instead, I shook my hand, rolling my head around to disguise the twitch as a movement to calm my anxiety. Then, following suit with the rest of my team, I set my helmet over my head.

Vindicta stopped pacing and moved to stand in the middle of the group, allowing Saetyl, Notien, and Darinrain to climb up her armor onto her back. Avenlae was to fly ahead with me (since there was no way I would ever convince him to stay behind with the others), and Vindicta was charged with protecting the rest of my team. None of us knew what we were entering into, and I was the least fragile target of our team if I were to be spotted in the air as I scoped out the place. Avenlae's presence, however, would prevent me from "doing anything stupid", as Saetyl had pointed out.

I raised my left hand, the Creonex burning against my skin as I pulled from the restless power in my chest. For the first time, I spoke directly to Sinivir, reaching for the shadows in my mind that encircled his Essence: *Take me to your first Brother.*

Ah, won't Victorum just be delighted! Sinivir cackled as his Essence turned the filigree of the Creonex to deep crimson. The heat of the metal spread through my veins, igniting red-hot flames along my feathers and burning through my eyes. A beam of energy burst from my palm and cracked open the very image of reality before us, opening a buzzing portal into a world of red, gold, and black. As soon as the portal was open, I snapped shut the connection between Sinivir's Essence and my power, letting my arm fall to my side.

"And so it begins," I whispered under my breath before, with a last vestige of hesitation, I stepped through the portal.

Careful, Creovis, came the whisper of Sinivir, *protect the mortals. They cannot transition into this world in the same way that you and I can.*

I paused, only the front half of my body through the portal, my wings out and one arm thrust towards the sky, the sign for the warriors behind me to stop. Looking back at my team, their helmets on, wavering on the threshold, I felt rising conflict in my head.

"How—"

Allow me.

"I can't trust you."

He is not wrong, Xiaye. Vindicta clicked at me, stepping forward. *I would not trust him either, but he speaks the truth.*

"Why do you hesitate, Xiaye?" Darinrain called to me.

"It is not safe yet," Avenlae answered, keeping his eyes on me as he moved close enough to touch my hand.

Use him, Sinivir hissed.

"What?"

GRAB HIM. Sinivir's voice filled my head, taking hold of my muscles and wrapping the fingers of my left hand around Avenlae's arm before I had the chance to stop myself. I gasped, eyes widening, but unable to let go or close off the flow of Sinivir's power. Spreading from the metal of the Creonex that touched Avenlae's armor was a web of pure gold. It wrapped around his body in mere seconds, then shot across the ground to spread up Vindicta's tentacles, legs, and tail. From her scales, it jumped to the armor covering Darinrain, Notien, and Saetyl, until our entire group glowed brighter than the suns that rose above Silvacastra.

Then, just like that, the glow was gone, absorbed into the bodies of each of my team members. I let go of Avenlae's arm, my breathing loud in the silence that swelled in my ears.

They are safe now, Sinivir whispered, and then he was gone, quiet and dormant deep in the back of my subconscious. It had all happened so quickly, in the span of only a few seconds, and I appeared to be the only one who had seen the web of gold. Avenlae's head tilted, his voice crackling through the comms in my helmet. "Is everything okay? Xai?"

"I, yes, yes," I said, composing myself. "We can enter."

Carefully, Avenlae followed me through the portal, his head darting around as he took in the surroundings. I stayed still, watching as the rest of the team entered the portal, and even as the portal snapped shut with an ear-shattering *crack.*

Why? Why had Sinivir done it? Why did he stop me to protect my mate, my friends? The Essence of Sinvir was no longer accessible for me to interrogate, so, ultimately, I turned away from the dark shadow that used to be the portal and looked out over the Realm of Creo.

Before us stood the crooked silhouette of Castle Victorum, its reputation lingering vividly enough in Sinivir's memory for me to know the name. A legion of fir trees stood solemnly around us, their pines woven into an inky tapestry. The castle itself was as red as the blood coursing through our own veins, and the sky, shadowed by maroon clouds, was backlit by a golden glow of no true origin.

In that suspended world of silence, each breath felt amplified. Instead of a soft breeze or the earthy smell of underbrush, there was only a void—a barren lack of true life. Its stillness reminded me uncomfortably of holding your breath, waiting for something to happen; this hush too taut to sustain peace for long.

"We should not be here," Avenlae said, just loud enough for me to hear.

"No mortal should," I responded, looking over the sharp peaks of the castle turrets. It looked for all the world like an artfully twisted pile of broken, blood-soaked bones whose flesh still stubbornly remained. I shuddered, then rolled my shoulders back, stretching out my wings and pulling my rapiers from where they rested across my back.

I'll track you on the ground. Signal what you see, Vindicta said, shaking her head and slithering into the shadow of the trees.

"I find myself disappointed in the lack of excitement," I heard Darinrain scoff as they moved away.

"Speak louder, then. I am sure the enemy simply has not heard you yet," Notien snapped, and I felt as if I could hear her eyes roll.

Avenlae spun his swords once, moving next to me. "I will follow your lead, then, My Queen."

"Follow close, Av," I said, taking a long look at the sky before leaping into the air, "I've no idea what I'm leading you into."

No wind buffeted our feathers, yet it was effortless to stay in the air. Beyond the castle was a vast expanse of dry, cracked ground as grey as death. **What kind of world is this to exist in?** I thought to myself as Avenlae and I swooped down to weave through the towers of Castle Victorum, looking for an entrance. No calls from guards were answered by our appearance, no movement was observed along the ramparts surrounding the castle, and no shots of enemy fire were fired. The structure lay still and dead beneath us as we surveyed its shadows.

"I do not like this, Xiaye," Avenlae called through the comms in our helmets, "why has nothing tried to stop us yet?"

A Creator needs no protection, Sinivir chuckled in the back of my mind.

I gritted my teeth. "You said it yourself earlier—mortals aren't meant to be here."

"We will mount a surprise attack, then? How invigorating!" Darinrain's voice was much too delighted, even through the crackling of the comms.

No need. Victorum will know we are here. He will sense the Essence of Sinivir. He simply doesn't see us as a threat, Vindicta hissed within our thoughts.

"There is the entrance, Xiaye," Avenlae said, gesturing to a break in the bloody exterior of the castle, "open and unguarded."

"Do we enter?" I asked him, circling back around and hovering far above the shadowed archway that led into the vast expanses of the castle.

"Do we, My Queen?" He responded, his helmet tilted in such a way that I knew his ears were drawn forward, and his eyes were bright as he watched me through the darkened visor.

Do we? Kaigar was wrong. **Then** was my final chance to turn my back

93

on the Creators, enjoy what time I had left with Creation. That moment, I could either return to Silvacastra to spare myself and my friends the pain of more battles, or… suffer through the fight to liberate Creation from the control of the Brothers. It was the point of no return.

And so I dove, Avenlae's order for the rest of the team to meet us ringing in my ears. It was freedom or death. Perhaps it was death or death, and we just didn't know it yet. But I had to take the chance for freedom. I had to face everything that stood beyond that shadowed archway of Castle Victorum.

Vindicta clicked the blades of her tails together as Darinrain, Notien, and Saetyl craned their heads to look into the archway that rose formidably before us. The rustle of our wings was the only sound in the entire world. Set deep within the stone were two doors of wood darker than the night. And everything was so ***still.*** Any one of us could reach a hand forward to touch those doors, and yet there was no alarm sounded, no movement within the castle to suggest that we had been seen.

"Should we knock?" Darinrain asked, stepping to the forefront of our group. Soft hisses from the rest of the team met that statement. He shrugged. "I just did not know if you were waiting for an invitation."

"Prove yourself helpful, Darinrain, or I may find a dungeon to stash you in," I grumbled, igniting my wings with golden flames so there would be enough light to guide us into the castle.

"Now, Xiaye, is that really something you should be saying in front of our King?" Darinrain said, his smirk infuriatingly in place as he and Avenlae pushed open the doors.

Avenlae growled, smacking the pommel of his sword across Darinrain's helmet with a crack that seemed to echo infinitely. The fire of my wings deepened to a maroon. "I swear, I will ***eviscerate*** both of you if you can't find a way to ***grow up—***"

"Oh, tut tut!" An arrogant male voice swelled from the impenetrable shadows within the doorway, colored with an accent that sounded as if its owner had too many teeth. Darinrain's, Avenlae's, Notien's, and Saetyl's heads twitched as their ears searched for the direction of the voice. Vindicta hissed, crouching low to the ground and narrowing her six eyes. My flames reverted to gold as I looked around, hoping to see anything but solid black. Reaching over my head, I withdrew my rapiers, stepping over the threshold. There were only desolate stone walls on either side of me, bare and, somehow, spotless. The floor I walked on was as black as the doors, and my steps echoed as if the ceiling soared far above us.

"Now, what kind of little band is this? I dare say I'm *intrigued,*" the voice came again, its inflection that of a hunter finding prey he's been forced to chase for far too long. Suddenly, the shadows were swirling, swallowing the doorway behind us. The light of my wings no longer penetrated the darkness as we gathered together, our weapons drawn as Vindicta rose onto her back legs. A growl rumbled deep in her chest as she extended her head over top of us, preparing a paralyzing scream.

Within the swirling shadows, flames erupted, spinning with blinding brilliance until they were caught along white marble walls. There were no torches on the walls; instead, fire itself snaked and coiled across veins of gold in the marble, glowing in pulsing rhythms, as if alive. The light revealed floors polished to a mirror-black sheen, reflecting twisted silhouettes of all present, warped grotesquely by perspective. Shadows slunk away from the twisting fire of the walls, their darkness clinging to the ceiling, thickening the corners, and draping across pillars as if they were artfully placed decorations. And there, at the apex of it all, sat a man on a throne carved from white filigree so intricate it seemed impossible for mortal hands to have shaped it. No, not a man. A creature?

A Creator.

His skin was the color of snow, marred only by jagged black scars—battle scars. His eyes had no pupils, no whites; they were smooth golden orbs glowing in the firelight. They were angled in an almost feline face, accentuated by the black high collar that extended up from his chestplate. Golden horns wrapped and branched around his head, and he was dressed in scant white armor that appeared as if it had started its life as the thickened, horned hide of some animal. The Creator's torso remained bare, hardened by muscles that he didn't even need. He lounged across the throne lazily, his legs kicking over the arm of the throne as he slouched against its back. Pressing one elegantly clawed hand to his cheek, he smiled stonily, his black fangs seeming to ooze over his lips.

"Well, hello, little mortals. What brings you into the presence of Victorum, Creator of the First Universe?"

CHAPTER 9

There is no way out, Vindicta said, clicking softly behind us. I glanced back—the doorway we had entered through had indeed disappeared.

"Ah, Vindicta, my dear Brother Bellum's prized Creation!" Victorum roared, pushing himself forward on the throne. "What a treat! I remember when Sinivir stole you and your kind. Pathetic, really. A child's tantrum."

An anger that was not my own clenched in my chest. I took a deep breath. *Do not forget, you're the one in control...*

"And these winged beings... I must look closer." In a single second, Victorum had crossed the vast throne room and held the bottom of Avenlae's helmet between two claws. In the same instant, arrows of pure gold had shot from his skin and hovered inches away from each of our hearts. With a lazy flick, Avenlae's helmet was clanging across the stone floor behind us, his braids flopping down over his shoulders.

Victorum smiled, his teeth a black void. "Why do you look upon a Creator with no fear, mortal?"

Avenlae bared his fangs, and his ears lay flat against his braids. Victorum cocked his head to the side, and I felt my pulse quicken as he growled, "A worthy adversary to conquer."

Instinct took over. The First Creator was fast, but not as quick as my impulse to protect. A crackling whip of violet wrapped around Victorum's wrist stopped the golden arrow mere centimeters from Avenlae's temple. Slowly, his head turned towards me, black fangs bared.

"*Creovis*," he hissed, his voice as harsh as the shriek of metal. The golden arrow in his palm was reabsorbed into his skin as the First Brother flicked my whip from his wrist. I curled my fingers as the whip disappeared into the Creonex and Sinivir's disgust threatened to cloud my mind. Victorum crept towards me, firelight dancing off his crown of horns, his feet as silent as the paws of a cat. His breath hissed through his fangs as he stepped around me, the golden orbs of his eyes moving up and down. Complete silence filled the throne room, as golden arrows still held each of my team members hostage.

Finally, Victorum stepped back, drawing himself up to his full height with a sickening smile. He spread his clawed fingers, the golden arrows turning to sand and flowing back into his skin as he said, "Perhaps we have started off poorly. It is only that it has been so long since new mortals have entered Castle Victorum."

Bodies materialized from the walls surrounding us. Vindicta hissed, lowering herself over us as her tongue flicked around at the beings that began to take shape.

"Oh, none of that now," Victorum said, "they are my people, my *vaevictis*. They are a part of my castle, my home. They are the mortals that have been liberated from the suffering of their worlds."

The *vaevictis* were all dressed in identical robes of gold and white, their eyes all round, black orbs. Their skin was as white as Victorum's, with delicate golden lines racing across their faces, as if their skin had been pieced together like mosaic glass. Each smiled at us as they moved closer, their hands folded into the long sleeves of their robes.

"You see, they are identical, so that no individual has more than their peer," Victorum said, sinking back onto his throne. "There is no greed, no guilt, no fear, no pain, here. There is only me, their Just Creator, and, now, you, mortals."

"We're not here to stay," I called to him, keeping an eye on the advancing robed *vaevictis*.

"Ah, not even for one meal?" Victorum tilted his head, placing one hand close to his neck, in a mockery of offended feelings.

"We have demands that must be met." I tightened my grip on the hilts of my rapiers.

"Those demands can just as easily be voiced over food, little **Creovis,**" Victorum said, sitting forward. "My people have done nothing to threaten you. Yet, you would choose to lead with violence?"

A few gasps flitted around the circle of robed people. They halted, their eyes now wide as they glanced around at each other. I stared for a long time at Victorum, at the unreadable gold of his eyes, the way his body was frozen in its position, the picture of *perfect* control. The warrior in me fought against the visceral anger writhing within Sinivir's Essence. Manipulation was dripping from Victorum's words, but what was he trying to manipulate? What was his goal? Why hadn't *he* led with violence, as his Brothers had?

As much as I wanted to spring forward and drive my blades into Victorum's chest, I knew it wasn't the right time. There was too much we didn't know—an attack was too risky until we could figure out what kind of threat his *vaevictis* posed. I lowered my wings, extinguishing their fire, and slipped my rapiers into their scabbards across my back. Haltingly, the rest of my team did the same, but Vindicta stayed as she was, her eyes locking onto each one of the robed individuals around us. She was trying to read them, to understand precisely what they were.

"That's better, isn't it?" Victorum leaned back and smiled, but there was no kindness in his face. "Allow my people to lead you to a room in which you can rest while food is prepared. I have no need of it, but I do enjoy partaking in the tastes of mortals every millenia or so."

A soft laugh followed us out of the throne room as the white and gold *vaevictis* closed in around us, herding us into a hallway leading off to the left. Vindicta hissed again, curling her lips at the surrounding *vaevictis* and sliding the blades of her tails together.

"Are you sure about this?" Notien whispered, sheathing her scimitar at her hip, but keeping her hand on its hilt.

"We need more information," Avenlae responded, reflections of the *vaevictis* moving across the front of his helmet as he scanned the hallway.

Saetyl and Darinrain moved to either side of Notien, staying silent but poised for attack. The glow of the fire within the walls slithered alongside us, illuminating no more than a foot ahead of the led *vaevictis.* The golden people seemed to glide along the floor, and their movements made no noise. They weren't meant to be seen or heard. They were the background, the decorations, the subtle additions to the castle to give it barely a drop of life.

Vindicta clicked softly, twitching her frill. *I cannot get a read on them. They have no thoughts.*

What? I thought back.

They have no thoughts, Xiaye. Those creatures have no minds.

"We have arrived, Visitors," said a soft, feminine voice. I turned away from Vindicta, unsettled but forced to hide it. A doorway of black shadows rose above us, immune to the light of the glowing walls.

"More shadows," Darinrain scoffed. "Such an unoriginal design. Lazy, if you ask me."

"Nobody did ask," Saetyl grumbled.

"Our Great Creator has prepared a room for Our Visitors to stay in," said a *vaevictis,* ignoring the whispers of my team.

"And how did your 'Great Creator' know to have a room ready?" Notien asked.

"Victorum knows all, and so is prepared for all," answered a different *vaevictis.* Their voices were all the same, soft, feminine, robotic. As one, they stepped to the side, turning to face the shadowed doorway. Drops of fire oozed away from the wall, splitting into spirals of filigree that coated the blackened surface of the door. With a groan, it swung open, allowing the flow of the fire to spread across the walls within. Without a word, the *vaevictis* moved forward, brushing past us to enter the room. At Vindicta's insistence, we entered before the final *vaevictis* could come close enough to touch her.

Five shimmering curtains of gold lined the circular walls on either side of us, and an archway foretold the opening of a cave at the far end of the room. The walls were still marbled white and gold, with fire burning along their crevices. There was nothing on the shined onyx floor beyond the reflections of Vindicta, my team, and the circle of *vaevictis* that lined the wall. The air within the room was completely still—not too hot, not too cold, and barely even there.

"You will find more comfortable clothing has been placed within each of your lodgings." A *vaevictis'* voice echoed, and each extended one robed arm to gesture to the curtained-off doorway next to them. "Our Great Creator requests that you change into something more befitting of your time here within His Castle."

"And if we refuse to?" Avenlae snapped.

Every arm dropped, and each black eye focused on him. "Victorum insists," echoed every ***vaevictis.***

"So we'll comply," I responded, tilting my head forward in a subtle bow. "Are we allowed our privacy?"

"Yes," they bowed in unison, then began to file out of the room. One ***vaevictis,*** the last one left, stepped up to me. "You are to be given time to rest before your meal. We will collect you when it is time to meet with Our Great Creator."

"Do we have to stay within this room?" I asked.

Something flickered within the depths of the ***vaevictis'*** colorless eyes, and its face twitched, pulling at its golden lines. Then, it smiled, showing perfect, golden teeth. "It is… recommended." The creature vanished, and the air it left behind felt too still, too watched.

Avenlae's hand brushed instinctively against the blade at his side.

"Recommended," he muttered, almost to himself. The word curled through my thoughts like smoke, carrying the weight of a command disguised as kindness.

My stomach turned. We weren't guests here. Not really.

For a moment, we stayed in the silent stillness of the room, our heads bobbing around as we studied the space. Something had to be hidden in the shadows that still clung to the ceiling over us, or behind the curtains that shimmered although there was nothing in the room to make them move. But there was no sound, no other movement. There wasn't even a smell.

"Strategically, I understand your hesitation, My Queen," Saetyl said, finally breaking the silence, "however misplaced I think it is."

"We are dealing with powers we hardly understand within a realm we knew even less about," Avenlae said, turning to face the rest of the team. "We have to tread carefully. What do we know about the ***vaevictis?***"

"Vindicta reported they have no minds," I said, tilting my head up at the

Voxmor Queen. Her eyes stood out as kaleidoscopic jewels against the monotonous white, gold, and black of Castle Victorum and its inhabitants. Curling her tails in close, she lowered herself onto all fours, saying, *They have no thoughts, no consciousness to store them in. It is as if they do not actually exist.*

"A shared delusion, then?" Darinrain said, spreading his arms wide to the rest of us. "Ah, we have all reached a new height in our relationship!"

"They're probably some kind of reflection Victorum created," I said quickly, preventing anyone else from responding to Darinrain. "Little copies of something he can use for entertainment."

"Does that mean they are harmless, though?" Saetyl asked.

"How dangerous could they be if they cannot think for themselves?" Darinrain shrugged.

"*You* are still dangerous, are you not?" Avenlae said.

"Why, thank you for noticing, my friend!" Darinrain exclaimed. "I strive to be the deadliest warrior, so that My King will—"

"We can leave *him* here for Victorum's entertainment," Avenlae grumbled.

"I second that," Saetyl interrupted the rest of Darinrain's proclamation.

"Enough," I growled as Vindicta moved away from us, sniffing along the walls and curtains, her tongue flicking to taste the air.

"I agree with Xiaye's approach," Notien chipped in. "The *vaevictis* may not be physically harmful, but something tells me Victorum knows whatever they know. He may listen and watch through them, so we must be vigilant and watch our backs."

I could not sense the First Creator within the vaevictis. Vindicta clicked behind us, *but that doesn't mean he cannot access them. Change into whatever clothing they have brought for you, and buy me more time to see if there is a mind for me to infiltrate.*

I nodded. "Keep whatever weapons on you that you can. We will meet

103

back in this common space."

"If this Creator 'knows all', do you suspect he predicted what room we are each going to choose?" Darinrain asked, and we turned towards the outer wall of the room.

"Should you pick a room and find a dress within it, I am sure one of us can help you with the bodice and skirts," Notien said with a smirk as she stepped towards the golden curtain in front of her.

"I find myself offended you would assume I would not already know how to don something so fashionable," Darinrain quipped back, ducking through the curtain of the room next to hers.

I rolled my eyes as Avenlae and I headed towards the curtained-off doorways next to the cave meant for Vindicta. Avenlae moved in front of me, sniffing the air with his ears up and forward, assessing the movement of the golden curtain.

"Unfortunately for you, Notien, there is a quite dapper suit in here, which I do not require *any* assistance in styling!" Darinrain's voice echoed behind us, followed by a grumbled, "If I could be so lucky," from Saetyl.

"If there was anyone poised to strike behind this curtain," Avenlae growled, turning back to me, "they likely would have already chosen Victorum's wrath over listening to the ramblings of that idiot."

"Let Darinrain find what little joys he can," I said, pressing a small kiss to Avenlae's cheek as I swept past him. "Who knows how much more time he'll have."

Without waiting for a response, I reached out and pushed the curtain aside, shocked at the cold, weightless touch of the cloth. It was like pushing aside a gust of polar wind. Beyond the shimmering gold was a tiny, simple room. The walls extended back just far enough for me to step into the space, and a modern yet straightforward mirror created the back wall. Before the mirror was an outfit suspended in the air. The bodice was a jagged entanglement of gold, white, and black cloth, featuring a geometric pattern with no discernible beginning or end. Gold pants, skin tight, dropped from the waist of the bodice, and behind them was a train of pure white. On the ground next to the outfit was a pair of simple, black, ankle-high boots: no heel, no bulk, no ties.

What the hell is this? Carefully, I pulled on the dress, its material feather-light enough that it felt like I wasn't wearing anything at all. The silk cape fluttered to the floor behind me as I slipped into the boots, then checked my reflection. That dress had been tailored to me. I'd never worn something that fit so naturally in my life. Instead of spinning in the mirror, admiring the shape the bodice gave my body, or how the sheen of the pants made their material appear as if it were just my skin, I reached for my rapiers, tightening their scabbards across my chest. I didn't care that they were visible — something about the perfect fit of the dress set my nerves on edge.

You think my Brother was able to conquer the First Universe without knowing anything?

I gasped, falling back against the side wall of the little room as Sinivir's voice slithered through my mind.

You are right to keep your weapons, Creovis. Keep them all.

"What do you mean, 'conquer'?" I hissed, my eyes darting around the room as if Sinivir was going to materialize from one of the shadows.

Go looking, Creovis. You want to know who Victorum is? The answer lies in the very place where he calls himself the Great Creator.

Closing my eyes, I listened to the sound of my breathing, felt the now frantic thrashing of my heart. *It's not real;* you *control* him.

But what if he was right?

Outside of my little room, the rest of the team was gathering. Vindicta still prowled the walls of the common room, her tongue flicking out along the walls as she investigated every space she could find. Notien and Saetyl were dressed similarly to me, each with their weapons still strapped to their hips. Notien was elegant and willowy, moving with the same grace as the fabric she wore. Saetyl, however, just looked petulant.

"My Queen, we really should have a dress like that designed for you!" Darinrain said with a wide grin as he strode forward, insultingly resplendent in a golden suit with black undershirt and waistcoat. Avenlae joined me then, adjusting the cuffs of his identical suit jacket. I'd never seen him in something so… human.

Unfortunately, I found that I liked it much more than I wanted to admit.

He, on the other hand, made no effort to hide how his silver eyes slid over my body. "As long as you can fight in that…" His gaze lingered just a moment too long. "You make it hard to look anywhere else."

"What is the point of forcing us into these things?" Saetyl snapped, rolling her shoulders and glaring around at the rest of us as if we had all been in on the secret.

Manipulation, Vindicta clicked, ambling back over to us. *It is a reminder that this is* his *realm. You're meant to be unnerved. It makes it easier to control.*

"What do we do now?" Notien asked, her eyes darting between Avenlae and me. "Wait for the *vaevictus* to return?"

"Not all of us," I said quickly, cutting Avenlae off before he could respond. "I'm going to head back into the throne room. Something tells me there's more to this palace than meets the eye, and I'm going to find it."

"By yourself?" Avenlae asked, his voice sharp.

Vindicta growled as Notien narrowed her eyes at me. "You want to leave us here alone, waiting for the ***vaevictus,*** while you go off and explore?"

"Wrong choice," Saetyl grumbled.

"I have my powers, you will have Vindicta," I shrugged. "She can contact me as soon as something happens."

It's as if you didn't just hear me say that Victorum aims to remind you that we are within the Realm of Creo. We have no ***control over anything here,*** Vindicta hissed.

I sighed, exasperated. "The ***vaevictus*** practically threatened us at the mere idea of leaving this room. I have powers to protect myself, but I have no idea if I can protect all of you if the ***vaevictus*** come after all of us."

"Oh, because ***of course*** they would not care if just ***one*** of us left the room," Dainrain quipped with one eyebrow raised.

Avenlae's jaw tightened. The shift in his posture was small, but it changed the air around us — colder, heavier.

"You think I can stay here while you are in danger?" he said, voice low and rough at the edges. "I would feel it, Xiaye. Every second. Do not ask that of me."

"I'm trying to protect all of you!" I raised my voice. "I have no idea what I'm going to find out there —"

"And yet that is the exact risk we all took in agreeing to even enter the Realm of Creo with you in the first place," Saetyl interrupted. "We either go together, or not at all. You may be our Queen, but here, we are all the same in the eyes of the Creators. We will be targeted with or without you, Xiaye. So, you might as well lead with backup."

I met each of their gazes, their determination set. ***What fiesty little things,*** Sinivir hissed through my thoughts, the hint of a smile in his words. I shook my head, turning away from them all. "Fine," I said, heading towards the giant doors at the front of the room, "It's all of you against me, anyway."

"Do not think for one second that you would act any differently were the circumstances different," Notien said with a smirk as she fell into step next to me.

"Careful, Xai," Avenlae whispered, quiet enough for only me to hear, "I can feel when he speaks to you. Do not allow him to manipulate you away from us."

Your mate has learned well! Sinivir cackled. I took a breath, staring forward at the door as we approached it. *Ignore him, ignore the fear, ignore the worry.* The second we left the room, we were either going to walk straight into a punishment, or I was going to learn that Sinivir was capable of helping me. I needed to know which.

The same hallway with twisted, flaming marble awaited us on the other side of the door, its shadows seeming to creep curiously forward. No sound echoed from the end of the empty hallway — just a silent glow through an archway. Our boots didn't even make the slightest squeak on the polished black floor as we moved forward, Avenlae, Notien, and I at the front, and Vindicta following behind. There were no other doors along the marbled walls we passed, and no **vaevictus** materialized from the flow of white, black, and gold. But the castle was watching. A feeling enveloped us as we entered the throne room. Castle Victorum knew. Its shadows coiled around pillars and slithered from corner to corner, evading the glow of the fire within the walls. I stood in the middle of the room for a moment, watching the movement of the fire and shadows as the other members of my team spread out. **Something** was wrong. It was just a feeling, as if I were being sent a message from the Castle itself, but a message without words I could understand. It was the way the shadows shifted, the glow of the flames within the walls around Victorum's throne, the way the throne's filigree looked so... so organic...

"Xiaye."

My head whipped around as Notien said my name. She stood on the other side of the room, watching me from next to an ornate golden table. I walked over to her, the shined surface of the table alight with the stars of the night sky. But there were spaces within these stars, void of color or light. It was an alien sky, one I'd never seen before, and with these black holes swallowing everything around them.

"That is not our universe," Notien whispered, her navy eyes wide.

I frowned. "Is—is this the First Universe?"

She nodded slowly. "It must be."

"But… where are all the planets?" I asked, looking back down at the depiction on the table. "Why haven't the people of the First Universe said anything about those—"

"I remember recommending that you stay within the room prepared for you," said a smooth, melodic voice. A *vaevictus* appeared before Notien and me, the hood of its robes pulled down to reveal how its golden veins pieced together its skull. Black eyes followed the movement of Saetyl, Darinrain, and Avenlae as they moved to stand with Notien and me. But the *vaevictus* made no acknowledgement of Vindicta slithering into position behind it, her serrated tails poised over her head.

"Your 'Great Creator' knows all," I responded flatly. "Surely he knew we wouldn't stay cooped up for long."

"Perhaps," the *vaevictus* tilted its head. "That is why I was placed here. There are things within Castle Victorum that must be protected."

"Oh?" Avenlae asked, his ears pinned against his hair. "What things are those?"

"Secrets," it whispered.

I glanced up at Vindicta, who shook her head imperceptibly. *Victorum isn't here.*

"What are you?" I asked, stepping towards the creature.

109

Its head twitched as its lifeless eyes snapped over to me. "I am the *vaevictus.*"

"*Who* are you?"

This time, one of its eyes twitched. "I am the *vaevictus.*"

Darinrain reached over his head, grabbing his staff in a slow, controlled movement. "That was not the right answer. *Who* are *you?*"

The twitch extended to include the entire *vaevictus'* body, like a glitch in a machine. "A secret of Castle Victorum," it said, its voice now different, distant, wavering.

I took another step towards the *vaevictus* as Vindicta began to raise herself onto her two back legs. "Did Victorum create you?"

"Our Great Creator made all," the *vaevictus* replied, a slight tremor in its arms covered by robes. "And now, we should return to the room made for *you.*"

One more step, and I was close enough to the *vaevictus* to see the texture of its skin, and the way it stretched between each vein of gold. I stared into those black, lifeless eyes long enough that my own began to burn. But I *needed* to see it. I needed to know that there was *nothing* within that creature.

But there was.

One blink, and I could see the eyes behind the blackness, the mind trapped within a prison of white skin bound by gold. The *vaevictus* wasn't a creature—it was a shell.

Fighting to stay calm, I asked, "Who *were* you?"

A ripple passed through its face, its eyes flickering from black to something almost familiar. "We were… many. Once." Its eyes darkened, and its smile turned brittle. "All things serve still," it whispered, almost to itself. "Even what remains."

Then shiver ran across the *vaevictus* shell, and both eyes twitched before it lowered its head. "It has been so long since mortals have come to Castle Victorum."

"I do not think we are going to get any more information out of it," Saetyl said gruffly behind me.

Hold your position, Vindicta growled. Behind me came the whisper of blades being drawn from their sheaths, but I kept my eyes on the *vaevictus.* "Why haven't mortals come to the Castle?"

It raised its eyes to mine, with a secret pleading. "Because there are no mortals."

My breath caught in my throat as I took a step away from the shell, glancing over at the table that depicted the First Universe. The gaping holes of complete nothingness were still there, more stark than the universe's brightest star. *No mortals...* "But w-we have treaties with civilizations in the First Universe—"

"And our Great Creator knows *all,*" the *vaevictus* intoned, its eyes narrowing. "Tell me, Visitor, have you seen the throne of Castle Victorum?"

My eyes slid to the white throne at the front of the room. I felt frozen, repulsed. Forcing myself to move, I made my way across the room. The shifting shadows told me Darinrain, Saetyl, Notien, and Avenlae followed me. I wanted to tell them to stay back, to save them from whatever was on that throne. But I couldn't take my eyes off of it. I couldn't stop staring at the intricate filigree, the matte white of the material, the organic movement...

A strangled cry left Notien's throat. A scuff told of Darinrain's sudden halt.

And I stopped breathing.

The throne was made of *bone.*

CHAPTER 10

The filigree was a labyrinth of bones woven together. They twisted and intertwined with each other, carved meticulously, forming a grotesque spectacle. Whispers of secrets seemed to lift from the bones themselves, tales of warriors, of lovers, of **children,** now reduced to mere fragments in Victorum's horrifying tapestry. The air suddenly felt charged with tension and thick with the smell of decay, a reminder of what had built that throne.

Haltingly, I turned back towards the ***vaevictus.*** It lifted one arm, letting the loose sleeves of its golden robes fall back. Its entire arm was metal.

"Oh God," I whimpered, the realization hitting me in wave after wave. ***You want to know who Victorum is? The answer lies in the very place where he calls himself the Great Creator.*** Sinivir's voice echoed in my mind as I turned to my team. Their eyes were wide and terrified.

"Where… where did those bones come from?" Saetyl asked, her voice hoarse, as if she didn't want to know the answer.

I swallowed. "The mortals."

Notien covered her mouth, her eyes welling with tears.

"We need to leave," Avenlae said, looking over my shoulder at Vindicta. "Can you sense where—"

"Leaving before an offered meal is quite rude, I've heard."

I ripped my rapiers out of their sheaths, whirling around to the entrance of the throne room as Victorm stalked forward. His golden eyes shone with the glow of the fires along the walls, his crown of horns casting jagged shadows. The black scars against his snow-white skin stretched as he moved, and he curled his lips back from his pointed, blackened teeth.

Behind me, Vindicta hissed, moving to crouch behind us as Avenlae, Notien, Saetyl, and Darinrain stepped back, fanning out beside me. "Oh," Victorum purred, "what has the little mortals so distressed?"

I swallowed. "What did you do to the people of the First Universe?"

Victorum blinked slowly, then cocked his head to the other side, still prowling ever closer. "Whatever do you mean, little Creovis?"

The Creonex warmed around my hand as I adjusted my grip on my rapier. "Exactly what I asked. What did you do to all of those people? All those civilizations, those innocent lives?"

The golden orbs of Victorum's eyes slid across each of our faces, a slight twitch to his ears. A snarl pulled his lips away from his teeth as he turned back to me, angling his horns down far enough that their twisted crown cast shadows over his face. "I *saved* them. I *liberated* them."

More rustling came from beside me as each member of my team settled themselves into an attacking stance, the joints of their wings pointed towards Victorum. "Wrong answer," I hissed.

"I protected them from a life of pain and suffering!" Victorum's voice rose, the heaving of his chest warping the tracks of the onyx scars. "Do you know how much the mortals of Creation lost during Creation's War? But now, my Creations, my little mortals, will not have to feel that kind of pain again. I've gathered their little souls and taken them away from the suffering of their mortal lives. There is no judgment here, no pain, no loss, no greed. They simply are, as they were *always* meant to be."

"Yet their bones built the very throne you sit upon," Saetyl snapped. "What kind of message is that? 'Step out of line once, and your limb will end up here?"

"Once arriving at Castle Victorum, they had no need of their mortal bodies," the First Brother growled, "and I am free to do with them whatever I please. Besides, I'm their Beloved Creator—why wouldn't they want to become a part of my throne, the very symbol of my power?"

"You killed *all* of them?" Darinrain said incredulously. "You destroyed the entirety of—"

"They asked for this!" Victorum roared, lunging toward us as spittle flew from between his teeth. "Hidden away in their little rooms, their little worship chambers, *praying* to their Gods to be released from the pain of their existence. That is *all* you mortals do now, is *beg* to be liberated from suffering!"

"They ask for *guidance,"* Notien said, raising her scimitar, "not death."

Victorum growled as he began to pace before us, his restless energy palpable. "I don't care. I don't *care* what you mortals say. *I* am their Great Creator! The First Universe has always been mine to conquer, and now it is mine to rebuild. I am everything those mortals ever need, everything they ever wanted, and I have given them the liberation they asked for. And *you,* Creovis, you bring these fragile beings to my castle to disrupt a system that has been in place long before you ever *existed!"*

"We are here to *end* your reign," I replied, spinning my rapiers as I angled my wings down, their blades facing the Creator. "Creation will be free, either through your death or ours.

Victorum grinned, a smile of malice and hatred. "There has only ever been *one* Creovis before you. I wonder if you will be as easy to destroy as *he.*"

Calm yourselves. As soon as he is distracted by Xiaye, we'll be able to make our move, came Vindicta's voice in my mind. There was no sound of acknowledgement from my team, but neither did Victorum back away from me.

He can't hear her! Sinivir cackled, and red flames erupted along my feathers.

"Ah, dear Brother," Victorum said, clicking his claws together as he eyed the flames, "you think this time will be different? You think you can stop me?"

"*Enough,*" I snarled, as jagged bolts of crackling gold energy surged down the blades of my rapiers, "Are you going to fight me, or just keep running your mouth about it?"

"Oh, Creovis," the First Creator taunted, molten gold dripping like venom from his eyes, tracing down his pallid, sickly cheeks. "Did nobody ever warn you to be careful what you wish for?"

Spread out! Came Vindicta's order not a moment too soon, for a barrage of golden arrows launched themselves with lethal precision toward each of my team members. Simultaneously, Victorum dove towards me, black teeth bared and claws extended. I barely parried his attack, but the sheer force behind the blow sent my arm snapping violently back, leaving me vulnerable and struggling to regain my stance. Notien sprang from the wall to my left, intercepting another strike from the First Creator as electricity buzzed out of my feathers, scattering dust around us. Crossing my rapiers in front of me, I caught Victorum's claws in a desperate clash of steel and fury. Golden arrows flew from his skin, shrieking through the air to relentlessly pursue my team.

Keep moving! Vindicta called out to us, the echoes of her screech throwing off the aim of the arrows. Stray crimson sparks from the energy burning

115

my wings incinerated each arrow on contact.

I spun, breaking the deadlock between the First Brother and me, just as Darinrain lunged forward. His staff's blade sliced clean through the joint of Victorum's left shoulder, severing flesh and leaving the arm dangling grotesquely by a mere strip. Victorum's scream was a cacophony of agony as golden blood gushed down his limp, swinging arm. Molten streaks of gold had carved into his cheeks, glowing with fierce intensity as the First Creator glared around him. We were all poised to strike as soon as Vindicta gave the order. They had figured out Victorum couldn't hear her, but she could hear *everyone*—it only made sense to defer to her leadership, despite my power in the fight.

Saetyl spun her ax to my right as the rest of the team moved restlessly around the room, ears twitching, waiting for the First Creator to make another move or for orders to echo in our minds. Tendons and sinews writhed violently, twisting and knotting themselves together as they attempted to reattach Victorum's severed arm to his shoulder. *If we could just cut him up faster than he can heal...*

"You lead your team well, *Creovis*." Victorum's claws lengthened, and the streaks down his cheeks began to gouge viciously into his neck, carving a path of raw, searing flash as they burrow into his chest. He ground his black fangs together, drops of coal smearing down his chin. "But they are simply annoying little flies!"

BRACE! Vindicta's voice burst into our minds, and Darinrain shot across the room to Avenlae as Victorum's skin began to glow gold. Vindicta loomed over me, frill fully extended, and let loose a scream that cracked the very stone walls that enclosed the battle. The gold of Victorum's power flickered from the intensity of the Voxmor Queen's shriek, and we all fell to the ground, our hands over our ears as we tried to protect ourselves from the violence of the

116

sounds. The First Creator's arm stopped healing, and his blood flowed anew, pooling below him and splattering onto his feet.

LET ME FIGHT HIM! Sinivir shrieked in the back of my mind. I shook my head, holding tight to my control, and snapped out the buzzing lavender whip from the Creonex around my left hand. Another snap, and the whip was wrapped around Victorum's hanging arm, ripping it the rest of the way off before he had the chance to stop me. With a roar, faster than a blink, he had swung his other arm around, his claws tearing deep gashes into the side of Vindicta's face, cutting her scream short. Her tails shot over her head as she stumbled to the side, still ready to defend herself if Victorum continued his attack. Saetyl sliced her wings forward, their blades cutting into the First Brother's torso as she swung her ax around. Even after losing an arm, Victorum was still faster than we could track as he caught the handle of Saetyl's ax in his claws, stopping it inches away from his other shoulder.

"Silly little girl," he cackled, "you flew much too close."

Arrows burst from his horns, diving straight for Saetyl's throat as he hoisted her from the ground. Notien let out a primal scream and flung her wing wide to shield Saety's head. Five golden arrows pierced mercilessly into Notien's feathers, each one hitting with a sickening thud.

"NO!" Saetyl cried, hearing the pain in Notien's next scream. I ripped the whip across Victorum's face, trying to distract him as quickly as I could. At the same time, Vindicta lashed out with her tails, targeting Victorum's head. With a howl of rage, a golden arm exploded out from the socket on his right shoulder, clawed hand snatching Vindicta's tails in mid-air, halting them before they could even graze his crown of horns.

"Insolent little ***mortals!***" he screeched. "Let me ***destroy*** you!"

"You haven't learned yet," I said, raising myself up and sending golden

117

power across my armor and wings. "Creation belongs to *no* Creator."

"Oh, is that so?" Victorum hurled Saetyl across the room, sending her crashing into a stone wall above where Notien huddled to protect her bleeding wing. Notien darted to Saetyl as she crumpled to the floor, a vein of vibrant blood beginning to drip down the back and side of her neck. Victorum whipped around, driving the blades of Vindicta's tails straight into the stone wall behind him, effectively trapping her as she shrieked with pain. "You have no idea what you're up against."

He flicked his claws, and golden arrows went sailing over my head. For a second, one single second, I thought he had somehow made a mistake and misjudged. *He missed!*

But the cry of pain behind me tore through my chest like a jagged blade. Avenlae's wings had been brutally pinned against the stone, bright blood staining his sparkling silver feathers where the arrows sank into the rock. Darinrain hurled himself to the ground, desperately trying to support Avenlae to lessen the pain of his weight pulling against the arrows.

Let. Me. Destroy. Him. Sinivir hissed, and my wings once again burned with the crimson fire of the Fifth Creator's power. When I turned back to Victorum, I could see the reflection of my glowing red eyes in his two golden orbs. His black fangs appeared as he smiled.

"Yes, Brother," he cackled, "face me! Conquer *me* for everything I took from you!"

I slammed by rapiers into their sheaths and walked forward, Sinivir's hatred a wildfire scorching through my veins. Surrendering control to him hurt every fiber of my being, yet my fury blazed hotter than the searing torment. Electricity burst from my hands, crashing into the stone with a vengeance, carving blackened scars all around me.

118

"Oh dear, Big Brother," Sinivir's voice came from my mouth, "you hurt her mate. Remember the last time you meddled in love?"

Something moved in the depths of Victorum's golden eyes. Was it… fear?

"Yes, I remember," Victorum raised his claws, "I remember how *good* it felt to make you *beg!*"

I swung my arm across the room, burning black streaks into Victorum's face, arms, torso, legs, everything. Saetyl spun and protected Notien with her body, forks of lightning barely missing them in the corner.

No! Don't hurt them! I tried to cry, but Sinivir had seized control and overpowered me effortlessly. Victorum slashed out with his claws, but I was able to twist out of the way of his attack as easily as if he had simply warned me of what he was going to do. With a sharp flick of my other hand, I marred the First Brother's once-pristine white skin, branding it with more blackened scorch marks of my power. He spun, claws extending into talons, slicing through the air with such blistering speed that his movements were nothing but a violent blur.

But Sinivir knew them. He *knew* this fight.

Not one claw touched me. Not even close. I had never felt this kind of power in my body, this *untouchable* power. The air around me rippled—alive, electric—and I realized it was me. My power. My pulse.

It was exhilarating. Terrifying. Every nerve in my body sang with something that wasn't supposed to exist, a force too large for my hands, too violent for my heart.

Victorum's golden eyes widened as his skin began to blacken, his horns burning to smoking stumps. I could feel his fear—and I didn't stop. My hands, glowing red with Sinivir's power, locked around his wrists. The heat of it devoured everything, even the part of me that wanted to be afraid.

"You remember this, don't you?" It was still Sinivir's voice passing over

119

my lips. "You must remember what I told you, Brother."

Victorum bared his fangs. "I remember your weak, *pathetic—*"

A pulse of energy roared through my body. That was all it took—just that one pulse. Crimson electricity burst through Victorum's skin, a fierce glow emanating from every inch of his being, burning him from the inside out. He continued to grin—a defiant, maniacal grin—as his body turned as black as night and started to disintegrate into nothingness. That unsettling grin was the final piece to succumb to the ash, and only when it vanished completely did Sinivir finally release his control over me.

There was a thump behind me, and I turned, trembling, to see that the arrows holding Avenlae's wings against the wall had disappeared, releasing him to the ground. Notien whimpered in the far corner as Saetyl shifted to maintain pressure on the wounds along Notien's wing, ignoring the still steady drip of blood from a gash along the back of her head.

"A-Av, are you—are we... is everyone okay?" I asked, trying to keep my voice steady.

All injuries are relatively minor, Vindicta clicked as she moved towards Saetyl and Notien, her tongue flicking out as she assessed Notien's wing.

"Can you stand, My King?" Darinrain asked.

Avenlae's jaw tightened. "I do not need your hand," he said, using his wings to steady himself even as they trembled. He pushed Darinrain back—too forcefully, too defensive—and looked away, as if the motion alone erased the moment of weakness.

"Av, are you s—" I started to say, but a sudden shift in the stone beneath our feet cut me off. A deep, ominous rumble reverberated through the walls encircling us. All ears stood straight up, and Vindicta's hiss sliced through the air as dust cascaded from the ceiling.

We need to get out, she commanded, curling her tentacles around Saetyl and Notien to move them out of the corner. Suddenly, another deafening rumble shook the air, and we were all thrown to the ground as the entire room convulsed and shifted, threatening to tear itself apart.

"Xiaye, you want to go ahead and crack open reality?" Darinrain called to me as he and Avenlae crawled over to us, wings twitching as they prepared to fly. "This would be a perfect opportunity to do so."

"Yes, I'm aware!" I snapped as I felt the Creonex warm around my left hand. The problem wasn't my ability to create a void—the problem was that I didn't know where to warp us *to.* Sinivir was being stubbornly silent, and I had expected a moment longer for us to decide our next plan of action. Violet power was crackling along the filigree of the Creonex, but, at the moment, that power wouldn't take us anywhere.

"I cannot believe I have to agree with that man," Avenlae hissed as a crack shot through the middle of the room and the floor began to tilt, "but get us the hell out of here, Xiaye!"

"I-I'm trying!" I cried, reaching again for Sinivir's power, but I got no response. I couldn't just take us back to the tribe: with Victorum gone, the other three Brothers were sure to come searching for us.

With a horrendous crunch, the floor began to tilt straight down, sparks flying where the jagged edge scraped along the wall. Our wings gouged deep scratches into the stone as we scrabbled to find any purchase.

Oh, how perfect! Sinivir cried as a pit of pitch-black nonbeing opened beneath us, and my fingers slid off the edge of the stone.

What wonderful timing! Sinivir roared as my ears filled with the screams of my teammates. A beam of red energy burst from my hand and opened into a swirling void that felt like a rush of cold water when we passed through

121

it. The calm was only temporary, for after the rush came the solid smack of our faces onto dry, hard dirt. Dirt that was as black as the pit we had nearly fallen into. Dirt that had no smell.

Gasping, coughing, I raised my head, my eyesight fading in and out of focus. Images of beings stood in a crowd before us, but I couldn't find the strength to do anything about it. They were silent and still, waiting for something...

In the next second, my vision focused. The beings were the last memories of the people of the First Universe, watching as we writhed in the blackened sand, trying to catch our breath and assess the pain of injuries. Their bodies shimmered, pushed by a wind none of us could feel. Then, in unison, they bowed their heads forward, the bow of millions of people, as the sand began to swirl away the memories of their bodies. I stayed frozen, staring, trying to understand how we were seeing them, who they were, and what they meant.

I knew he would find you next, Sinivir cackled as something pierced my neck, and Avenlae screamed.

I didn't even have time to react. I spun dizzily around, saw shadows force Avenlae into the sand, and then my vision went black.

CHAPTER 11

My consciousness returned in the shock of cold and the bitter smell of coppery blood. I coughed, shaking my head and flailing my limbs as I tried to stand. The world was still dark. Was I blind? Weight pulled against my wrists and legs as something metal clanged rancorously around me. Was I chained?

Tentatively, I lifted my wings, trying to feel how close the walls—no, the **bars** were. I couldn't fully extend my wings in any direction. Pressure clenched my chest, and I began to pant, panic closing my throat.

Calm now, Creovis, Sinivir whispered in the back of my mind. ***You're right where you're meant to be.***

"W-where—?"

"Xiaye? Xiaye, is that you?" Darinrain's voice echoed off of walls I couldn't see.

Relief almost made me cry. "Darinrain! Where are you? Where are we? W-what's happened?" I choked out.

"I-I do not know, exactly. They have taken Notien, Saetyl, and Avenlae, and I think they have Vindicta—"

Shut up, both of you! Vindicta's voice snapped in our minds. ***Show them*** no ***fear if you want the chance to live.***

"Who the hell are 'they'?" I hissed.

The ground beneath me trembled as massive doors suddenly swung open before me. I raised my hands and ducked away from the light that stung my eyes, but the vibration of the floor didn't stop. I tumbled to the floor as the cage lurched, and the smell of blood became almost suffocating. Coughing again, I blinked my eyes rapidly, trying to adjust to the light of the world I was being pulled into. As my cage moved forward, primal dread froze my body.

Behind me, a tiny cage was towed that held Darinrain, followed by a third that held Vindicta. Our clothes were torn and stained, hanging from our limbs in pitiful rags, and Vindicta had been stripped of her armor. We entered into a procession of beings whose armor dripped with fresh blood of black, crimson, green, and purple. No matter the color, all blood smelled the same.

Rising around us was a monumental colosseum, its stone the mottled appearance of viscera. In the stands sat the most aggressively disgusting creatures I had ever seen. They blinked their glowing, beady little eyes as they screamed, jeered, clicked, roared, and applauded multiple limbs. Some flapped wings, others snapped pinchers, and more rubbed the blades of their limbs together to create a cacophonous screech. These were the creatures of the Second Universe, the very same monsters the Voxmor had evolved to coexist with. Suddenly, Vindicta didn't seem so menacing.

Violently shredded bodies were still being cleared from the stained floor of the colosseum as our cages moved along the outer walls, pulled along by spindly humanoid beings in chains. Darinrain's ears pressed tightly against his skull as his head darted around, pupils contracted. He kept his wings folded

124

tightly ac\urls of acrid grey smoke spiraled into the air, while a tangled mane of coarse grey hair trailed from the crown of its head down its neck and splayed across its broad, muscular chest. The beast's sinewy frame and massive hands suggested it was bipedal, and it kicked out a hooved leg lazily as it lounged back against the bodies.

However, it wasn't the thing itself that made me sick.

Chained next to it was Avenlae. A dirty loincloth barely clung to his body, and his hands were shackled with such ferocity that I could see drips of blood falling over his fingers. A brutal metal muzzle was clamped over the lower half of his face and was anchored painfully to the top of his skull. His wings, too, were ensnared in chains that ripped feathers from flesh, dripping vibrant blood with every slight movement. Avenlae's eyes were wide with torment as they darted frantically across the crowd, his ribs straining with each ragged breath and his muscles quivering uncontrollably.

"Avenlae!" I shrieked, my voice desperate and cracking.

His eyes met mine, widening as his pupils constricted. He darted forward, fast enough to almost wrench his arms out of their sockets as his chains tightened, carving even deeper into his flesh. A blackened creature made entirely out of smoke appeared behind him, wip raised.

I screamed as the whip cracked across Avenlae's bare back, throwing myself against the bars of my cage. *"No! Don't touch him! STOP!"*

Avenlae collapsed, blood curving along the indentations of his muscles as it flowed from gashes across his spine. Crimson flames erupted along my wings, and a red-hot energy exploded from my skin. A pulse of energy burst from my hands and disintegrated the bars of my cage. The screech of pure rage from my throat echoed throughout the colosseum as I flew towards Avenlae, a sword of ruby materializing in my palm.

An iron grip coiled around my wings, yanking me to a brutal stop mid-air. Agony shot through my spine as the weight of my body dangled helplessly from the base of my wings.

Do not move, Xiaye, Vindicta said from below, her voice tremulous with fear.

"That is a power I have not witnessed in a long time," came a low, warbled voice—the slithery voice of a thousand violent men.

Be smart about this, Creovis, Sinivir whispered. *Bellum always did play with his food before deciding whether or not to eat it.*

I gritted my teeth, biting back my cry of pain and trying not to answer the Fifth Creator as the creature who held my wings spun me to meet his beady little eyes. "Have we caught my brother's *Creovis*?" Bellum growled. A disgusting smile parted his snout. "You like my little Mercenary, do you?"

My eyes darted treacherously towards Avenlae, who stayed curled up on the ground. Bellum grabbed Avenlae's chains and dragged him across the mountain of bodies, forcing him to stand. Avenlae's terrified silver eyes met mine, pleading, crying.

"The last of the *Y'araye!* Perhaps my favorite prize in all of Creation, little *Creovis.* I always wanted one, but Mors never let me keep them. A pity," Bellum pouted. "I always did enjoy watching them kill."

He leaned in close enough that I could smell coppery blood on his breath. "Do you know the best way to get a *Y'araye* to fight, *Creovis*? The best way to make them kill everything they see?"

I clenched my jaw shut. *Don't speak. Don't show fear. Don't move.* I didn't even know if the voice in my head was my own, Vindicta's, or Sinivir's. Pure terror gripped my body as a deadly laugh rose from Bellum's throat.

"Find their mate," he hissed, his claws tightening around my wings, "and make them feel *pain.*"

Crackles of red energy forked over Bellum's fingers, and, with a pause just long enough for a breath, it began to surge into my body. My spine snapped backward as an agonizing shriek tore through my lungs like wildfire. Blinding whiteness consumed my vision, and every muscle convulsed violently. The torment was beyond endurance, tearing my very being to shreds. In that moment, I was obliterated—I knew nothing, felt nothing, became nothing, but endless anguish.

I didn't know how long the torture lasted. As abruptly as it had begun, the pain ceased, and my body trembled violently as my spine relaxed. The pain of my weight hanging from my wings no longer registered, and I panted in quick, shuddering gasps. Below me, Avenlae thrashed, his wrists and wings pouring rivers of blood as he fought against the merciless constraints. Another scream echoed across the colosseum, a sound so raw it seemed to shatter the very atmosphere. Vindicta's cage rocked as she threw herself against the unyielding bars, tails cracking and sparking against the metal.

"Yes, little Warrior!" Bellum roared over the cheers of the crowd below us. Avenlae's cries were loud enough to be heard through his muzzle.

"Stop," I whimpered. But I wasn't speaking to Bellum—every time Avenlae writhed, his chains ripped deeper into his flesh. I couldn't watch him destroy himself in a desperate attempt to get to me. I had to save him, to help him. *I* had to protect *him.*

"Ah, my Voxmor Queen fights to get to you, too, *Creovis*." Bellum raised me to his snout once more. "Power truly does transfix all, doesn't it?"

Sinivir's anger flared deep in my chest. "You would know, wouldn't you?" I heard myself speak, but it was a warbled version of my voice. "You have no idea what it is you hold, Bellum. You have no idea the weapon you have enraged."

"This is what you've been reduced to, Brother?" Bellum cackled. "A mere Essence residing within another's form? It is a mortal form, isn't it?"

The fiery rage that pulsed through my veins begged me to move, **to fight,** but my body wouldn't respond. Bellum snorted. "Fine. We'll test the power of your **Creovis**, Little Brother. I hope this one is better than the last."

Bellum conjured a black cage from the stack of bodies next to him and tossed me into it. New aches formed in my limbs as I was sent tumbling back to the dirt floor, where Darinrian and Vindicta stayed paused in their cages. "To the holding cells!" Bellum barked as the enslaved creatures began moving us again. "Tomorrow, we will see how deadly **Xiaye** can be."

"No, NO!" Came another screech, this time from across the colosseum. Two more cages had been dragged onto the floor, these two holding Saetyl and Notien. One of Notien's wings hung limply down, a liquid of mixed blood-tinged fluid and green pus oozing from where Victorum's arrows had gone into her feathers. Behind her, Saetyl clung to the bars of her cage, her copper skin appearing more golden-toned as the cage rocked over the uneven ground. Thick plaques of congealed blood caked her hair and neck, and her golden eyes were only half-open.

"Vindicta?" I gasped, trying to pull myself closer to the bars of my cage.

She's alive, Vindicta said, clicking loudly behind me, **but that head wound needs to be treated.**

"Xiaye!" Notien screeched, reaching for me even though we were on opposite ends of the colosseum. More shrieks of applause roared through the stands above us, the creatures hissing and screaming for the new arrivals.

"What timing!" Bellum roared, clapping his colossal hands. "We have all of our Players, don't we?"

"Darinrain," I called, facing him as my eyes widened. "What is happening?"

"You ask me as if I've been here before!" He hissed back.

It's a game to him, Vindicta growled, curling her tails over her head. **Bellum enjoys a performance. And we are the entertainment.**

The movement of our cages halted as more chained, spindly creatures dragged Notien and Saetyl's cages closer. "Xiaye, what do we do?" Notien called frantically.

"Be calm," I responded, stumbling to the other side of the cage so Notien could see me better. "Try to be still."

"'Be calm'?" she seethed. "There are still the intestines of dead creatures *all over* this colosseum, and you want me to 'be calm'?"

The more fear you show, the more likely it is that Bellum will choose you for a performance, Vindicta said, lowering her growl to a purr to mollify Notien.

"Shall we choose the first Players, Creator?" hissed one of the creatures of shadow, its green eyes gleaming.

"Indeed," Bellum rumbled, "I have already chosen the Creovis, but who do we want to enter the colosseum with her?"

"With me?" I gasped, fear coiling itself tightly over my chest.

The crowd cheered viciously as the shadow creature moved toward Notien, whose eyes had grown round with tiny, pinhole pupils as she pressed herself as tightly as possible against the back bars of her cage. But they all *shrieked* as the creature moved past Notien... and approached Saetyl. The jeers of the beasts in the stands rose in a wall of sound as Bellum nodded, another stream of smoke curling away from his nostrils.

"N-no, you c-can't!" Notien cried, flinging herself into the other side of her cage as the creatures of shadow began to unhook Saetyl's cage from hers. A creature whirled around and struck out with a wicked whip, and gashes bubbling with blood opened a long Notien's arms and shoulders. Falling away from the bars, she turned to me, the floor of her cage quickly becoming slick with her own blood. "Do something! Please, Xiaye, *do something!"* she begged desperately, her voice cracking as it rose again to a shriek.

129

"You cannot," Darinrain said beside me, his own navy eyes wide as he watched. "They will kill her for the simple joy of it."

"H-how do you know?" I asked, but was unable to tear my eyes away from the sight of Notien sobbing and screaming while the shadow creatures began to pull Saetyl's cage towards a gasping hole in the wall of the colosseum.

"It is entertainment," Darinrain swallowed. "That is what Vindicta said, is it not?"

"How **could** you?" Notien wailed back at me. "How could you just stand there?"

Don't you cry, Vindicta said forcefully as tears burned my eyes. *Don't you dare show them how this affects you. Bellum will make it worse.*

"How could it be any worse?" I whispered, trying not to flinch at Notien's keening cries as she slumped to the floor of her cage, defeated.

"I do not know," Darinrain responded, his voice hollow. "I do not want to know."

Our cages lurched again, and I began to take a step forward, towards where Notien still slumped in her cage.

DON'T MOVE. Sinivir's voice cracked through my mind, paralyzing me where I stood. I couldn't speak or move: I could barely even breathe. The cage tilted, and I was looking into a sky of turbulent clouds, ripping and tearing at each other in a mockery of the colosseum below. And then the darkness of shadow consumed me as massive doors were hauled shut, and Sinivir released my body. Stumbling forward, I caught myself on the cage bars, sucking in lungfuls of air.

"W-why are you all still here?" I asked, lowering myself to the cold floor of the cage. "Why did they take Saetyl, but keep me with you?"

Because we are the other Players, Vindicta growled. *I don't know when we're expected to enter the colosseum, but we are expected to entertain.*

"My Queen," Darinran said softly, "I hate to admit it, but I am beginning to regret agreeing to join you on this mission."

I aimed a glare at him in the dim light of the tunnel we were being pulled through.

He held up his hands. "I thought I owed you honesty."

Not helpful, Darinrain, Vindicta growled, beginning to pace around her cage. Moments later, the cages halted, and the rumble of a door lifting from the ground echoed through the tunnel. Clanks cried sharply as the spindly creatures worked to unhook Vindicta's cage from Darinrain's.

"Wait!" I called, rushing towards the other end of my cage.

Leave them be! Vindicta snapped, whipping one of her tails against the bars so the shine of sparks momentarily lit up the tunnel. *You can't give these creatures any reason to use any of us to torture you.*

"B-but I can't let—"

You must! Vindicta let out a small shriek as the creatures began to pull her into a new room, one that was pitch-black, tiny, and damp. *Remember who you are, Xiaye, and protect your emotions.*

A door of thick, chizzled rock slammed down from the top of the tunnel, closing off Vindicta's new prison and shielding her from my mind. Her silence was a new kind of terrifying—she was a lifeline in that brutal, unforgiving realm.

"It is just us now, Your Majesty," Darinrian said, his voice weak.

I took a breath, my chest tightening with unrelenting fear. "It's just us."

CHAPTER 12

I crouched in the corner of a dim cell. The floor felt cold and slick beneath me, but I couldn't discern what coated it. I enveloped myself in the fragile protection of my wings. My body felt drained of strength, leaving only numb indifference. I didn't know where Notien was, I didn't know where Saetyl was, and I couldn't protect Avenlae.

"It is not hopeless, My Queen," Darinrain said softly from the cell next to me. Only dirty bars separated us, and he had stayed close to them while I hid in my darkened corner. "It… it is just a game. We just have to play the game."

"Explain yourself," I snapped.

Darinrain's ears swiveled: he was listening for anyone else in the cells around us. "He is going to make you fight, Xiaye. You just have to give him a good show. That is how we survive."

"What makes you think I can fight right now?" I pushed myself up, frustration masking some of my pain.

"I know you can. If it comes down to it, I know you will."

"Darinrain, we are stuck in a cell with no weapons, no idea where the rest of our team is, with the threat of a Creator looming over us, and all you can tell me is 'you have to fight'?"

"We are in a colosseum. The game, the 'entertainment', must be whatever fights Bellum designs."

"How'd you figure that one out?" I grumbled.

Darinrain shrugged. "When I became the last *Je'quiet*, I decided to study the most iconic periods of the history of each civilization. Gladitorial games in the Colosseum are from the humans, no?"

A heavy door groaned open above us, its edge slamming into the stone wall with a sharp crack. Harsh, blinding light flooded Darinrain's cramped cell, casting stark shadows on the damp floor. Darinrain recoiled from the sudden brightness, a low hiss escaping his lips as he turned his head away. I pressed myself deeper into my corner, the cool touch of the Creonex gradually warming as power rose in my chest. *Careful, Creovis*, Sinivir whispered, he's right. *You must plan each move.*

I gritted my teeth and watched shadows move across the stone entrance to the cave that held our cells. There was some scraping, a clink of chains, a call from some unseen creature. Then a lifeless body was hurled into the cell, landing with a dull thud. It tumbled over the stone a few times before coming to a halt in front of Darinrain. The figure lay motionless for a moment, its ragged breaths barely audible in the oppressive silence. Meanwhile, the flickering shadows at the cell's entrance began to recede, making way for the Creatures of Shadow. These eerie figures, with their gaunt, skeletal forms, stepped into the cell, their dried, leathery hands gripping whips tightly.

Suddenly, the body moved. It shot upright, legs skidding wildly against the floor with a desperate, muffled scream. I jerked forward as the horrifying realization hit me—it was Avenlae, frantically struggling to escape the advancing creatures. Darinrain shoved himself off the back wall of the cell, placing himself between Avenlae and the razored whips of the Creatures of Shadow.

"Wait, please!" he begged, his hands held out before him. His onyx wings spread behind him, shielding Avenlae. "H-he has had enough, has he not?"

One of the creatures made a long, drawn-out hiss that eventually dissolved into words. "It disobeyed the Master."

"Yes, well, that is what happens when you get between a **Y'araye** and his mate," Darinrain responded, a hint of anger in his voice.

One of the creatures raised its whip. Darinrain ducked down, hands out and ears pressed against his temples. "Okay, okay, just—your Master wants a show, right?"

The creatures exchanged looks with each other.

"We will play the game. All of us. You will get cooperation if you just leave him here for a moment."

Hisses echoed through the shadows. "Who are you to promise that? Master has already chosen his two Players. They do not have a choice."

"I am the only one in our group who has not been tortured. That should tell you something, should it not?"

One of the whips cracked against the bars closest to me. My eyes watered as I caught a whiff of metal.

"I swear on my life," Darinrain said, keeping his head low. Avenlae moved to stand, but was pushed back down by Darinrain's wing. "Leave him here until tomorrow. They will all play your games. If not, your Master can kill me however he chooses."

"Darinrain," I hissed.

Say nothing! Sinivir snapped.

134

Glowing green eyes glanced in my direction. The creatures of shadow remained silent for a moment, appearing to contemplate Darinrain's proposal. Avenlae's wheezing breaths became the only sound in the cave.

"Fine," a creature hissed. "The Master no longer needs the *Y'araye*, anyway."

I stayed still for just as long as it took for the creatures to leave the cave, plunging us back into semi-darkness. Darinrain turned as soon as they were gone, folding his wings with a gentle rustle and crouching down to Avenlae. I crept hesitantly across my cell, my heart pounding with fear of what kind of state I would find Avenlae in. Darinrain moved with deliberate care towards Avenlae, his eyes respectfully averted and his neck exposed in a gesture of cautious vulnerability. When Avenlae didn't hiss or jerk away, Darinrain brushed a hand across the metal muzzle clamped across Avenlae's jaw. Avenlae trembled, the softest whimper escaping his lips.

"Oh, My King," Darinrain spoke quietly, "what have they done to you?"

"Av?" I said, my voice breaking. His anguished silver eyes met mine, and another muffled cry came from the muzzle as he pushed himself across the floor. Tears ran tracks through the dirt and dried blood on his cheeks as Avenlae pressed his forehead against the bars of the cell, wrapping his raw hands around one of the bars. My throat clenched as I reached through, my fingers trembling as they brushed against the small part of his cheek exposed above the muzzle. With my left hand, I gently rested my fingers on his temple, prepared to soothe him with every peaceful memory I had, yet his agony was insurmountable. His mind was utterly shattered by the torture he endured and the searing ache of the chains over his wrists and wings.

I sucked in a breath, trying to quiet my cries. *No, you have to be strong for him! He can't know you feel his pain right now,* I thought, watching the trembling of his muscles.

135

"Xiaye," Darinrain said. I looked past Avenlae's bloodied shoulder to meet Dainrain's worried navy eyes. "It is bad, Your Majesty."

"I know," I hissed. "So, when were you planning on telling me how to make it better?"

Darinrain frowned.

"The game, Darinrain. What the hell is the game?"

He swallowed. "It is my best guess at how to get us out of here."

"Do you know where the rest of our team is, then?"

"No, only Vindicta. However, if we play along, I think we can reach them. This colosseum is a stage, Xiaye. This is just entertainment for him and those he has deemed worthy from each civilization in his universe. You see how he chose Saetyl? The individual in our group who garnered the most visceral response from Notien. They loved it."

"I'm not asking to avoid a fight," I said, shifting to support Avenlae as he slumped against the bars. My hands didn't tremble, but my voice did. "I need a way out. Tell me how, who to deceive, what to say. I'll perform, I'll lie, I'll bargain, but I won't shed innocent blood."

Darinrain's head tilted. "You fight. You kill. You win. That is how the humans did it, no? That must be how we do it."

I stared at Darinrain, my eyes widening. A growl rumbled deep in Avenlae's throat, but he didn't move from where he lay against my arm. "Who... what am I supposed to fight?"

"I do not know."

"Do I have to win more than one fight?"

"I do not know."

"What the hell am I supposed to do, Dairnain?" I shouted, my voice shrill in the small space. "You're telling me I have to fight my way out of this place, but not who or what or how many? What about Saetyl? There's no way she can fight with me in her state."

"That is all the information I have, and it may not even be accurate—"

"That's not good enough!"

Darinrain whipped his head to the side as if struck, exposing his neck and breaking eye contact with me. A soft touch on my wrist immediately calmed my anger as I glanced down. Avenlae's silver eyes met mine, tired and pained. He couldn't speak, but the plea in his gaze was clear without words. I slowed my breathing, closing my eyes momentarily as I fought to control my emotions.

"I know your fear, My Queen," Darinrain murmured, eyes still on the dirt floor, "we are all afraid. I just bargained my life away in hopes that you and the rest of the team would willingly play along with Bellum's game if it meant we would be free of this place and its torture."

"And what if the game is torture?"

Darinrain raised his head slowly, then looked at me out of the corners of his eyes, as if terrified I would kill him where he stood. "They want to be entertained, Your Majesty. Entertain them. That is how you save all of us."

Your Historian speaks the truth, Sinivir hissed. *My Brother loves to see blood spilled. Kill everything you see in as violent a manner as possible, and maybe he'll be willing to barter a deal with you.*

"It's disgusting," I spat, but I didn't even know if I was responding to Darinrain or Sinivir.

"It is the only choice." Darinrain's eyes wavered. "Please, Xiaye."

I followed the path of a lone tear as it slid down Darinrain's golden cheek. He had never cried before, not that I had ever seen. He was supposed to be the only one of us who was untouched by the horrors we'd seen. Darinrain was the only one of us who could still smile in a fight, who could joke as Avenlae glared daggers at him, who could find humor in every situation.

But not this one.

Not when he had just bet his life on me.

The sight of him undone made my lungs forget how to work. My fingers clenched white on the bars; my stomach turned. If Darinrain could break like that, then nothing felt safe anymore. I leaned my forehead against the cold metal, wishing it were Avenlae's warmth instead. I mentally reached out, searching for Vindicta, but there was no response. The rest of my friends could all be dead, for all we knew. *And I have to slaughter whatever Bellum puts in front of me to save Darinrain and Avenlae.*

You killed plenty of Voxmor during Creation's War. You even tried to kill me. This shouldn't be that difficult, Sinivir grunted in my head.

"I killed creatures I thought had taken everything from me," I whispered. "I killed you because you took everything from me. But to kill something or someone I don't know?"

"Whatever Bellum puts you against will be trying to kill you with just as much determination," Darinrain said, deciding not to question who it was I spoke to.

He'll like you even more if you torture your opponent. I could almost hear the smile in Sinivir's voice.

I swallowed down bile. "Sinivir says I have to torture them."

Avenlae's hands wrapped around my wrist, his eyes darkening.

Darinrian lowered his head. "It is a show. You have to… perform adequately to survive."

I closed my eyes, feeling the tightness shift from my throat to my chest, a sensation that was both familiar and unsettling. The act of killing wasn't the problem—Sinivir was right in that regard. I'd killed in battle before without a second thought. Yet the creatures I was preparing to fight against… I knew

138

nothing of their stories, their histories. Were they innocents, prisoners like me, forced to fight for survival?

Is that not what war is, little Creovis? Sinivir whispered. *Just a bunch of creatures fighting to see who will survive.*

"What have I gotten us into?" I murmured, resting my head against the cage bars, almost against Avenlae's forehead. He whimpered again, shifting his weight around as if trying to find a position in which the pain of his injuries would be slightly less.

"I am sorry, but you must be still, My King," Darinrain said softly. "When you move, you begin to bleed again."

Avenlae lifted his head, just barely, and turned so that Darinrain could see the profile of his face. A drop of blood, shining crimson, welled from the bottom of the muzzle that pressed into his throat, and dripped down his neck.

Darinrain's jaw tightened, and he looked up at me. "Just play your part, My Queen. I will play mine."

I swallowed. "Entertain Bellum?"

"As best as you can. Keep him distracted. I will do whatever I can to unite the rest of the team and find a way out of here."

"You're so confident."

"I have no choice but to be," Darinrain sighed, watching as Avenlae relaxed back up against the bars, blood oozing from the gashes torn into his back, arms, and shoulders. "There is hardly enough time to get us out of this place."

"There isn't enough time."

"Have some faith in my capabilities, Your Majesty."

Avenlae growled, effectively (and finally) shutting Darinrain up for the evening.

Somehow, I managed to sleep propped up against the bars of my cage with Avenlae slumped across from me. Darinrain respectfully kept his distance, cocooning himself in his wings in the opposite corner of the cage he shared with Avenlae. Whether we slept for hours or minutes was unclear, with no sign of time passing beyond a door slamming open and streaming blinding light into our cells. Avenlae and Darinrain hissed as they shrank back into the stone wall of their cell. Power fired to life in my chest, warming the Creonex as I blinked, fighting away the cloud of sleep in my head. Creatures of shadow moved down the sloping entrance to the cave, their hisses making my ears twitch as they neared. A few green eyes met mine, followed by hoarse cackles, but the group stopped before Darinrain and Avenlae's cell. Avenlae whimpered as his feet kicked out from under him, slipping in the dirt as he fought to get away from the advancing guards. This prompted another round of cackles, and one of the creatures in the back of the group cracked a whip.

The Creonex glowed around my hand as I pushed myself off the ground, moving towards the front of my cell.

Then, I wasn't moving anywhere. I was immobilized, frozen with burning energy, fighting to be free of my skin.

If you dare attack Bellum's victae, you will lose everything you have fought so hard to protect, Sinivir hissed.

No matter how fiercely my anger burned behind my eyes, I couldn't move, couldn't fight against Sinivir's hold. ***I will kill you for this!***

You already have, Sinivir sneered.

Avenlae let out a muffled cry as the ***victae*** entered the cell, fanning out across the entrance to bar the path of any who tried to escape. One of them cracked a whip again, and, by the way Avenlae moved his head, I could tell he was baring his canines under the muzzle.

You're going to force me to sit here and watch them torture him? I shouted in my head.

You want him to live, don't you? Sinivir responded, sounding annoyed.

The *victae* advanced, hissing and clicking together their shadowed claws. Avenlae's eyes widened, his pupils contracted so thin they were but a line of black. He scrambled, pressing himself as tightly as he could to the back wall, but the blood on his limbs slackened his grip across the stone. The whip cracked a third time, a sound as sharp and clean as a guillotine. This time it landed, the tip wrapping around Avenlae's upper arm and tearing away a strip of flesh. He shrieked, a thin, keening wail that forced his metal muzzle deep into the skin of his cheeks and jaw.

"Wait!" Darinrain called, darting out from the back wall. "Just wait. I will get him for you."

"The Master wants the *Y'araye* now, Glider," a *victae* hissed.

"And your Master will have him if you let me give him to you," Darinrain said, drawing himself up to his full height, wings flared. "He wants a cooperative prisoner, does he not? How would he reward you if you brought him a dead *Y'araye*? Your Master would never get another one, you know."

Yellowed fangs flickered around the shapeless faces of the *victae*, yet they remained at a distance. Interpreting this as a response, Darinrain faced Avenlae, his black wings spread to block the view of the *victae*. I wanted to scream, wanted to throw a knife into Darirain's skull for thinking he could just give my mate to the ones who tortured him. But I did nothing. I stayed held in place, my body beginning to ache from how hard I was fighting against Sinivir's influence.

Darinarin knelt where Avenlae had slid down the wall, fresh blood dripping anew from some of the worst lacerations between his wings. The rise and fall of his chest was frantic, and his muffled whimpers echoed throughout the cell.

"Please, My King," Darinrain said, his voice soft enough for only us to hear. He kept his eyes on Avenlae, for once not dropping his gaze. Darinrain lifted one golden hand, resting his fingers across the side of the metal muzzle chained to Avenlae's head. "It is just a game. You just have to play along. I will get us out of here, but I need you to give me the time to figure out how to escape. Can you perform long enough for that?"

Avenlae's eyes searched Darinrain's face, but he didn't jerk away from the other man's touch. He stayed there, staring at Darinrain with terror in his silver eyes as his body shook and bled.

"Please, Avenlae. Trust me." Darinrain's voice cracked with the desperation in his plea. After a few deep breaths, Avenlae nodded once. Darinrain moved his hand down to the manacle around Avenlae's wrist and pulled, helping the Mercenary to his feet before shoving him at the victae. Finally, Sinivir released his hold over me, and I stumbled forward, wrapping my hands around the bars of my cell as if they would just melt at my touch.

"Avenlae!" I cried out, pushing a hand through the bars as the victae pulled him up through the entrance to the cave.

One silver eye met mine—one moonlit silver eye filled with tears.

"*Fae'yeerium*," Darinrain whispered beside me, "do not let him die."

"'Do not let him die'?" I said through gritted teeth as my power made the bars burn bright red. Darinrain pushed himself away from the metal as I rounded on him. "What the **hell** does that mean, Darinrain?"

"H-he just has to cooperate," Darinrain said, shaking his head and pinning his ears back against his skull.

142

"*Damnit*, Darinrain! What the hell do you mean? You keep talking bout this 'game' and that we all 'have to perform' but what if you don't know *shit!*" I screeched, a flare of red-hot electricity bursting from my skin and cracking across the cave. Darinrain threw himself to the ground, covering his head as pieces of the stone ceiling smacked into the dirt.

"I-I know, My Queen, b-but it will make sense—"

Suddenly, the dirt beneath me shifted. I rocked backwards, stumbling as the floor began to move.

"What's happening?" I asked frantically. Sinivir cackled in my head as Darinrain raised his eyes, watching as the floor began to shift up. Dust rained down upon my back as the ceiling yawned open, unleashing the deafening roar of a bloodthirsty crowd. Panic surged through me like a live wire. *Wait, wait, I'm not ready!* I thought desperately as I clawed my way to the edge of the floor. By the time my fingers reached it, only a narrow gap remained between the filth of my cell and the blood-soaked battlefield of the colosseum. Darinrain's eyes pierced through the thin slice of shadow, and his parting words thundered in my ears like a death knell:

"Entertain them, Xiaye."

CHAPTER 13

I shoved myself to my feet as the ground shuddered into place beneath me. Crackling tendrils of golden energy raced along my skin and through my feathers as my power ignited. Spinning slowly, I took in the enormity of the colosseum—towering levels of stained stone seats loomed above, teeming with vile creatures that screeched and jeered at my appearance. The pit floor was a mire of congealed blood and blackened dirt, the stench of rotting flesh filling my nostrils and making my stomach churn. A *victae* threw my rapiers across the pit and I dove for them, strapping the scabbards across my back as quickly as my trembling fingers would allow.

At the front of this macabre arena sat Bellum, his throne carved from the bodies of his victims, Avenlae chained to his side like a broken doll. Bellum's beady black eyes narrowed as he snorted out a plume of grey smoke from his squashed snout. "It is time, *Xiaye*," the Second Creator growled, baring his blackened fangs. "Did my little Brother make you as powerful as his last?"

If I live to see the end of this, Sinivir, you owe me some answers, I thought as I ignited my wings into golden flames.

I owe you nothing, Sinivir hissed, pushing the heat of his power out through the Creonex, causing crimson flames to dance among the gold of my wings.

Bellum leaned forward, grinning. "Yes, *this* will be fun. Give us a show, little *Creovis.*"

"Only if you agree to my terms!" I shouted up to him.

The crowd became as silent as if they weren't even there. Avenlae's nostrils flared as he stared down at me, but he didn't move. I could feel his heightening fear through the *lyceliah,* but I fought to push it back and remain focused on Bellum.

The Second Brother cocked his head to the side, his little ears pushing forward. "Oh? I'm listening."

"If my fight *entertains* you, you let my team go *alive.*"

You're a complete idiot, Sinivir seethed in my head.

"That is not playing the game, Xiaye," came Darirain's voice from somewhere beside me. I chanced a glance—his cage had been moved up to the far side of the pit.

Bellum chuckled, sending puffs of smoke across the colosseum. "Ah, but to be entertained is subjective, don't you think? You want to bargain your life on whether or not Bellum the Creator is entertained by how well you survive?"

"No," I replied, clicking together each of my fingers of my left hand, allowing the anger of Sinivir's power to flood my veins so my power became the color of blood. "I'm bargaining on whether or not you're entertained by how well I *fight.* I don't *have* to survive."

Avenlae's scream tore through the silence of the colosseum just before the crowd roared their approval. He nearly twisted his elbow out of its socket as he fought to be free of his metal chains, his skin completely stained by his own blood. Bellum laughed maniacally as he wrenched the chains, snapping Avenlae's head back as he fell to his knees, bearing the whip of a *victae*.

Don't react, Sinivir whispered as bile rose in my throat.

Blood began to flow in rivulets down Avenlae's ribs as the whip tore through his back and wings.

Do not react! Sinivir said again, but I couldn't stop the shaking of my limbs, and my eyes watered as I tried to swallow down my nausea.

It's just a game, it's just a game.

"I have never seen what becomes of a *Y'araye* when his mate dies," Bellum jeered, waving off the *victae* after its last lash of the whip across Avenlae's back. "Fine, little *Creovis*. Should I be entertained by your *performance,* I will let your team go in the exact state they're in."

No. Before I had the chance to protest, an uncontrollable rage consumed me. Red fury burned through my body, and I craved to annihilate anything that dared cross my path. *Give me a damn victim,* I thought, scanning around the pit of the colosseum. Something was pushed out of an opening in the wall before Bellum, but it was clouded in shadow. A *victae. Perfect.*

A primal growl erupted from the creature's chest, vibrating violently through the pit as it prowled towards me. I reached up and unsheathed my rapiers, raw power crackling against the stone walls, tearing down the matte black blades with a menacing hiss. The *victae* reached for its weapon, and I surged forward, rapiers raised, ready to strike.

The creature lunged with a speed that belied its massive size. I twisted out of the way as its claws slashed where my head had been moments before, retaliating with a brutal swipe of my blade. The rapier collided with metal; it was parried.

"Come on!" I shouted, anger boiling over that the *victae* had enough skill to evade *me.* Sinivir's power poured a deep, hellish crimson into the flames along my wings, bathing the colosseum in an eerie red glow. The *victae* turned

146

and made a guttural growl with an echo of a voice behind the sound. Someone else was screaming, begging, but I couldn't hear who. I didn't *care* who cried—that creature was going to die.

I charged again, feinting to the side to avoid a wide, savage swing of the *victae's* claws and slashed my blade against its side. The thing screamed, its green eyes ablaze with fury as it twisted out of the way of my next assault. Each swipe of its claws and bladed weapon sang with lethal intent, narrowly missing my throat as it advanced, movements becoming cold and calculated. I deflected blow after blow, power surging from my rapiers and body as wrath writhed under my skin.

"Why won't you *die* already!" I screeched, the air thrumming with raw energy and the thunderous stomps of the creatures in the stands rising around us. Bellum reveled in sadistic laughter as the *victae* darted forward again, causing me to duck and roll out of the way of the vicious swing of its blade.

"Dance, little *Creovis*! Dance for me!" he roared, rattling the chains that held Avenlae.

Avenlae.

With a cry of anger, I unleashed a torrent of magenta power that tore mercilessly into the *victae*. The creature let out a blood-curdling scream as it was hurled to the dirt floor with a sickening thud.

But it still breathed.

I closed in, sheathing my rapiers with an ominous finality as I loomed over the body of the *victae*. "You want a show?" I called to Bellum. He grinned, flashing his blackened tusks.

I reached down, seizing its arms in a death grip.

"Here's your fucking show!"

My power detonated with a ferocity I'd never felt before, coursing through my veins like liquid fire. The world vanished, eclipsed by the agonized

147

wails of the *victae* as I wrenched its arms back, my foot grinding into its spine.

With a grotesque snap, its arms were entirely torn off its shoulders, a fountain of blood painting the dirt floor of the colosseum.

The air was thick with the metallic tang of viscera, and the red of the colosseum bled into a chaotic blur as the chants of the crowd hammered against my skull. Strength seeped from my body like a dying flame as I surveyed the colosseum, its walls reverting to their stained, desolate grey. A scream pierced me like a blade, and I whipped to my right, taking in shuddering gasps as my power disappeared.

Notien was there, plastered against the bars of a cage, her face contorted with sheer terror. She screamed, her cries raw and desperate, vomit splattered on the ground where she clawed through the bars in a futile attempt to escape the nightmare.

"N-Notien?"

Dairnain stood completely still in the cage next to her, his eyes wide and face the color of sand as his wings hung limp.

What have you done? Came the sound of Vindicta's wavering voice.

I clenched my hands, shocked at the sound of her voice. And I felt feathers. *Feathers.*

My heartbeat became the only sound I heard as the world spun in slow motion, surreal and serene. I *felt* the blood drain from my face as I looked down.

It wasn't a *victae* I had fought. It was Saetyl.

And her wings, her black, *whole,* beautiful wings, were in my hands.

My legs buckled beneath me as horror consumed every fiber of my being. My scream dissolved into a retch as everything in my stomach poured onto the dirt, mingling with the growing pool of blood gurgling from the stumps on Saeytl's back.

Burn her! Sinivir ordered, but I couldn't move. I was stone—frozen in a haze of terror, every muscle convulsing, my vision swaying in sickening waves.

"I didn't know," I sobbed, my voice rasping as bile and tears coated my tongue. "Shit, I didn't know, I didn't know!"

Do as he tells you NOW, Xiaye, Vindicta commanded, pacing the length of her cage to my left. *Saetyl is going to die if you don't stop the bleeding.*

"I didn't know, I didn't know," I kept repeating, sitting in my vomit and feeling the touch of warm blood as it flowed close to my leg. Blood... so much blood... it soaked the battlefield... *I felt it through my armor as I hugged her, hugged Saetyl... mercy, mercy, MERCY!*

GET UP! Sinivir snarled, his power lancing through my bones. My knees forced straight, every joint screaming as he forced me to my feet.

"I didn't know, I didn't know, I DIDN'T KNOW!" I screeched as I stumbled closer to Saetyl's body, as if screaming would stop me from having to see her, to *feel* the mutilated muscle and sinew along her back. Notien shrieked ever louder, cutting through the uproar of the creatures in the stands as they called for me to finish off my opponent.

"No, no, no, no," I sobbed as I rocked over Saetyl, my fingers trembling and slick with her blood.

Burn her, Sinivir hissed, his power vibrating through my body.

"I can't, I can't—no, no, no!" The plea cracked apart as my chest cinched tight, my heartbeat hammering against Sinivir's will. I could still move—just barely—but every command I gave my body met his strength pressing back, grinding me into obedience. My hands shook inches from Saetyl's back. For a breath, I thought I'd stopped him—then heat surged up my arms, violent, red, alive. My fingers touched her skin before I could scream again, and the world filled with the smell of burning flesh. Her spine spasmed as she opened her mouth in a silent scream.

"NO!" Notien's and my shrieks merged into a single keening wail as her body convulsed one last time before going limp.

Drag her over to me, Vindicta ordered, her tone ice-cold. *She's still alive. I'll protect her.*

"W-what?" I choked, tears blurring my vision into a storm of grief and guilt.

You cauterized her wound. If you want her to live, you will do exactly *as I say,* Sinivir growled.

Numb, my limbs heavy as stone, I grasped Saetyl's arms in shaking hands and hauled her limp form to the front of Vindicta's cage. Every step was like wading through quicksand.

"I didn't know," I told her, repeating the only other words I could speak. *Please believe me! Damnit,* please *believe me!*

It was Bellum, Sinivir said. *That is his power, to turn friend against friend. He can force anything to fight. You have to kill him now, Xiaye, while you're free of his influence.*

I lifted my gaze to the summit of the colosseum, where Bellum sat upon his throne of bodies, crowned in shadow, a grin of triumph carving across his face as he watched the visceral sorrow below him.

Use that anger you know so well, Creovis, Sinivir hissed gleefully.

I didn't know what to do. Every emotion, disgust, pain, horror, rage, terror, ripped through my mind. It battled against the confines of my skin, and I began to hyperventilate as I stumbled to the middle of the pit. The crowd shrieked its approval, and the very walls of the colosseum rattled with their celebration.

Entertain them, Xiaye.

I sank to my knees, my eyes meeting Avenlae's. The anguish in those eyes, the exhaustion…

150

I bowed my head, clutching myself tightly as I relinquished every shred of control. A scream tore through my throat, raw and unrestrained, while lights exploded behind my closed eyelids. I screamed, and screamed, and **screamed,** letting loose every drop of power in my body in a cascade of tormented grief. The onslaught only stopped when all the air had left my lungs. I stayed huddled on that unforgiving, blood-soaked, dirt floor, shivering, hoping that if I just kept my eyes closed, it would all end. We would be done. *I* would be done.

"Get up, Xiaye. Now!" A hand wrapped around my arm and yanked me to my feet as Darinrain hissed in my ear. I blinked, scanning my surroundings and trying to focus on him. The colosseum had gone mercifully silent, and the acrid smell of smoke permeated the air. My power had shattered the bars of the cages that held Notien, Darirain, and Vindicta, but Avenlae remained untouched. Notien immediately ran for Saetyl, her breath coming out in wheezing sobs as she ducked under Vindicta's tentacles.

"My, my, little **Creovis**," Bellum grunted, "that was quite the performance."

"L-let us go," I managed to say, leaning back against Dainrain for support.

"Now, hold on." Bellum ran a finger across the bottom of his snout, then used a claw to toy with the tip of one of his tusks. "I haven't decided if I am entertained."

"She has done enough for you, has she not?" Dainrain barked back, his muscles stiffening.

"She **killed** all of my **victae**," the Second Brother growled, raising himself out of the throne of corpses. He leapt down into the pit, his wiry mane streaming behind him. Avenlae was dragged behind him, crying out as the chains tightened around his body. Bellum dangled Avenlae in front of us, and my whole body ached as I felt his pain. "She owes me a debt now."

Attack now! Sinivir's voice thundered, nearly sending me back to my

151

knees. The air was electric with anticipation—*everyone* wanted the Second Creator dead. The blood, the screams, the horror: it all ignited an inferno within me. Shock and grief became distant memories, but anger? It *consumed* me.

You fight him with my *power, Xiaye,* Sinivir roared as Bellum drew forth a broadsword, flinging Avenlae to the dirt.

Notien, stay with Saetyl, Vindicta said with a hiss, her two serrated tails clicking together.

"I owe you *nothing!*" I seethed, combing my power with the growing pulse of Sinivir's. Several volleys of raw energy exploded from my left palm as I advanced towards the Second Brother, the Creonex burning hotter than the Silvacastra sun.

Bellum deflected each shot with a lazy flick of his fingers, his lips curling into a smirk as grey smoke poured from his nostrils. He spun his broadsword, the blade still dripping with fresh blood. Golden lightning burst from my palms as I drew my rapiers, charging headlong towards the Creator. His colossal form towered over me, a titan looking down upon a peasant.

But I wasn't the only one filled with fury.

Darirain darted around behind Bellum as his beady black eyes stayed trained on me. Vindicta bounded up behind me, using her snout to launch me into the air. For the briefest moment, the Realm of Creo was silent as I was suspended in the air, my rapiers raised over Bellum's head.

"Vengeance created the very weapon that will destroy you," I said through clenched teeth just before the air came rushing up to meet me. I dove towards his head, power building in my chest. At the same time, Vindicta leapt onto Bellum's side, clawing her way through his flesh and sinking her tails into every vulnerable spot she could find. The Second Creator swung his sword around to block my attack while snapping his tusks just a hair's breadth from Vindicta's throat. Flaring my wings, I twisted sharply to land on his back, sinking my rapiers into his shoulders. Bellum's enraged bellow ricocheted off the stone walls of the pit as he clamped his hands around Vindicta's throat. Yet her scream made the entire colosseum tremble. *Nothing* could escape the paralyzing scream of a Voxmor. All the air left my lungs as I fought against the agonized pressure threatening to shatter my ears and skull. *Hold on,* I reminded myself, tightening my grip on my rapiers, *just hold on.*

Haltingly, Bellum raised his broadsword as Vindicta continued to stab with her tails. *No, no!* The wicked blade pointed straight at her head. I had to do something, but that *scream*. It was taking everything in me to remember to hold onto my blades buried deep in the Creator's shoulders, and Sinivir just laughed in my head. Bellum sung the sword down, the blade piercing into Vindicta's scales.

"NO!" I wailed, driving my power into the metal of my rapiers. Then, it wasn't Vindicta who was shrieking, but Bellum as his body burned with the might of pure *genepotentia* tearing through his flesh. My skin began to blister all down my arms as I pushed my body to its max, forcing every drop of power I had to the thing that tortured my mate. Something grabbed onto my wings, ripping with so much force that I felt the bone snap. I shrieked as I was thrown over Bellum's head, my power weakening as the ground approached. The pain from impact nearly made me black out, and nausea came in waves as my entire back pulsed, my wings limp on either side of me. Shaking, I pushed myself onto my arms as Bellum threw Vindicta against the stone wall. She stayed where she was, crumpled and silent. I reached out to her mind, but there was no response. *No, no, no...*

"Well, this may have been the *greatest* performance I have yet witnessed," Bellum spat, his whole body smoking as he turned towards me. "But it's over now. What a sad finale for the little *Creovis.*"

Sinivir continued to laugh in my head as his Brother raised his sword, bearing down on me. *Just make it quick,* I thought, unable to feel anything past the pain of my wings and spine as I closed my eyes.

There was the singing of his blade as it sliced through the air, and then there was nothing. No pain of my body being cleaved in half, no sting of my head being separated from my shoulders. But there was something warm dripping onto my head. I frowned, opening my eyes to see a growing pool of black blood. Something gurgled above me. I snapped my head back.

Darinrain had sent his staff *through* Bellum's neck with the point of its blade protruding from the back of his skull. "You do not get to decide who lives or dies," Darirain hissed, yanking the staff from Bellum's skull with a pump of his wings. More black blood pooled down Bellum's chest and shoulders, soaking his wiry mane as he stumbled backwards, dropping his broadsword.

"How—?" I whispered as Darirain dropped to the dirt, spreading his wings wide to protect me from any further attacks. But the giant Creator collapsed, his blood the very last to soak into the dirt of Bellum's Colosseum.

My Brother's greatest weakness, Sinivir sneered. *He could be killed by anyone he could not provoke into war.*

"Why couldn't he influence Darinrain?" I asked out loud, my voice weak, and Darnrain's ears twitched as he spun his staff, reaching back to strap it across his back.

Darirain was quiet for a long time before responding, "Because I will *never* fight those I have chosen to love."

CHAPTER 14

W*need to get moving.*

I gasped as Vindicta's voice cut into my mind. Waves of pain rippled through my body, making each movement a struggle as I pulled myself onto my knees. My eyes darted to where Vindicta had been thrown. She shook her head, dark blood oozing from beneath her scales, but the flow was slow. *It isn't safe enough for us to tend to injuries here.*

"I don't know if I can send us anywhere," I said in a weak voice, trying desperately to stay conscious with the ache of my broken wings.

Did you not learn anything from our war, Creovis? Sinivir growled. *This is mortal pain. You are far beyond that kind of limitation.*

"I'm also far from being able to use my power like that," I grumbled.

Vindicta growled as she neared, baring her fangs. *If you can just open a portal, I can carry you and Saetyl through. We should return to Silvacastra—Saetyl will need the Healers. There's no sense in taking her further into the Realm of Creo.*

Darinrain nodded, able to hear Vindicta's voice in his head. "I will get Avenlae."

Mortals, Sinvivir scoffed, and he took hold of me. My entire body went still, and I choked in a breath. Off to my left, I heard Avenlae's whimper and rattle of chains—he could feel what was happening through the *lyceliah*. Pressure began to build in my wings, the pain so intense I saw white. I wanted to scream, to vomit, to shake, *anything* to distract from the pain, but I was held prisoner as Sinivir painstakingly *wove* each of my bones back together, fiber by stabbing, aching fiber.

I sucked in a lungful of air as he finally released me, collapsing face-first into the gritty dirt, my chest heaving with each strained breath. Chains rattled, a muffled whimper sounded. Coughing, I summoned every ounce of strength I had left to push myself upright again. My hands shook uncontrollably as I reached out for Avenlae, seeing how dull his silver eyes had become. Darinrain helped him over, his hands slipping on the fresh blood that still flowed from where the whip had torn open Avenlae's flesh.

"Help him," I begged Sinivir, my voice barely a whisper through the tightening of my throat, "Please help him."

Get everyone out of this realm, first, Sinivir sighed.

Reluctantly, I dragged my hands away from Avenlae, closing my eyes to concentrate on the surge of power within me. Every second was precious, both for Avenlae and Saetyl's sake. But I refused to look over to where she lay, to see the horrific damage *I* had done. The pain was gone from my wings and back, but a deep-seated guilt twisted and coiled around my heart. I raised my hands, allowing Sinivir's power to take over as he conjured a shimmering void of gold before us. Crackles in the Realm of Creo unfurled to reveal the fringes of the *Laizuteek* forest, just skirting its southernmost border. It was as close as anyone, apart from the Delfungaye, could venture to the tribes central hub, where the Healer's Nest was. Throwing my arms back, I pulled to void over us, snapping it shut in the sky.

Grass and moist undergrowth crackled softly beneath my legs, releasing a rich, earthy aroma that was nearly impossible to resist. I wanted to collapse, to fill my lungs with the scent of the plants, the breeze, the essence of Silvacastra. As I lowered my head, my gaze met Avenlae's. His eyes had become dark, their shine gone, their glow faltering. He could barely keep himself upright, his muscles trembling with the effort to still breathe. I set my fingers against his metal muzzle, letting my tears flow freely. "Help him," I begged.

Avenlae shook his head, leaning back on Darinrain for support.

Xiaye. Vindicta's voice was soft but firm. I grit my teeth through the ache that bloomed in my chest as I dragged my gaze over to where Notien clutched Saetyl's limp form to her chest, her tears leaving trails in the mud across Saetyl's face. Vindicta stood behind them, her tails clicking together as she scanned the trees for threats. *Help Saetyl first.*

Hesitantly, I stood, moving towards Notien with my hands locked at my side. *I didn't know, I swear I didn't know...*

"Stay away from me!" Notien shrieked, fumbling to pull Saetyl even closer to her.

I stopped about a foot away from them, frozen in place as if Notien's fear held me there. "I-I just want to help," I whispered, unable to push more strength into my voice.

"I watched what you did to her!" Every one of Notien's words felt like a stab to the heart. "I watched you *rip* her wings from her back like they were *nothing!*"

If you don't let her help, then there is nothing more we can do for Saetyl, Vindicta growled. It may have seemed harsh, but I understood the need for directness. The pain Notien was going through—the pain *I caused*—was almost unfathomable.

"I will *kill* you if you touch her again," Notien hissed, canines bared and her ears flat against her hair.

My eyes widened as tears blurred my vision. I couldn't speak, couldn't move. I wouldn't have even tried to stop her if she had darted forward to slice my neck. I deserved it, her wrath, her hatred.

Suddenly, Vindicta's tentacles wrapped around Notien, dragging her up from the ground before she had the chance to react. With the touch of one tentacle to her temple, Notien went limp, her eyes glazed and unfocused.

Do it now, Vindicta clicked, closing all six of her prismatic eyes. *I cannot keep her in this state for long.*

I dropped to the ground, reaching for Saetyl with hands that felt weaker than the grass that flattened beneath me. My heart ached with the need to help her, yet I couldn't bring myself to look at her face, at anything beyond my fingers. I reached inward for Sinivir's power, the power of the Creator.

It is not my power that you need, he sneered. *It is* yours, *Creovis.*

C-can you give her wings?

You can create something new, but you cannot replace what has been lost, Sinivir said. *There are rules in Creation, too, Creovis.*

"What do I do?" I whimpered, tears splashing onto Saetyl's blood-stained skin. "H-how do I help her?"

There was no answer from Sinivir. I couldn't even sense the shadow of his Essence swirling around the Creonex. The longer I stared down at Saetyl, the more ragged and desperate her breaths became, each one a struggle against the inevitable. Above me, Notien stirred in Vindicta's tentacles.

Damnit, do something, *Xiaye!* A voice screamed in my head, and

I screwed my eyes shut, reaching deep within the *genepotentia* that vibrated through my veins. ***Do something, do something, DO SOMETHING!***

Energy crackled along my skin, but it was wrong. It was too much, too hot, too aggressive.

Protect her, protect her.

The energy cooled, a soothing presence that wrapped around my arms as if it alone held my hands over Saetyl's torn body. The touch of calming blue spread through me, a serene wave that stilled my mind, blanketing my anxiety and shielding my thoughts from Sinivir.

Help her. You can because you have to.

Gritting my teeth and tightening every muscle in my body, I released the blue, the wave of calm, the protection. I concentrated its flow through my hands, fighting to control its strength. ***Help her, help her, help her.*** The longer I held my hands over Saetyl's body, the weaker my own became. It was as if I were transferring my own lifeforce to her.

That's enough, now, Sinivir's voice echoed in my head, as if from far away.

"I-is she alive?" I heard myself ask weakly.

Yes. Alive and stable. Cut the connection, Creovis.

I inhaled deeply, dropping my hands and severing the flow of energy through the Creonex. As I opened my eyes, the world seemed to tilt and sway, a dizzying dance of colors and shadow. There was a small flash of gold—Saetyl was stirring.

"Good," I whispered, trying to push through the darkness growing along the edges of my vision. Vindicta clicked somewhere beside me, and I heard the sound of a body dropping. The image of Saetyl before me faded, and my limbs suddenly felt full of lead.

"But... Avenlae," I tried to say, but all I heard was a slurred murmur from my lips. There was a shriek, and suddenly I was on my back, my eyes flying open to stare up into the enraged face of Notien as she bared her canines and held her dagger to my throat.

"What did you do to her?" she hissed, pressing the blade along the quivering of my jugular vein.

"I-I helped, Notien," I stuttered, terrified to move lest the dagger slip. "I h-healed her—"

"I will bleed you *dry* for what you have done, you—"

A silver wing slammed into the side of Notien's face, whipping her head around and sending her flying off of me. The dagger made a shallow nick just under my jawline as it tumbled from her grasp, the sting keeping my adrenaline high. I rolled away, brushing a finger across my neck and feeling the slow drip of blood as I pushed myself to my knees. Avenlae stood over Notien, his wings angled to point their claws at her as she kicked away from him. Notien knew never to challenge him, even as weakened as he was. Shaking her head, she moved to grab her dagger, but stilled at the low growl that rumbled up from Avenlae's chest.

"Notien." Darinrain's voice cut through the tension as he stepped forward, ears up and wings flared.

Once again, like some sick loop, I dragged myself off the ground, but stayed in a crouch. Exhaustion was again weighing down my limbs, and I knew I'd be no help if I tried to step in. Notien flicked her eyes up to Darinrain, curling her lip for a second before backing away from both men, back to where Vindicta was helping Saetyl to sit up. Avenlae watched her retreat, then stumbled back, his wings twitching out to keep him upright. Darinrain swooped an arm under Avenlae's wings, keeping his navy eyes lowered as he tried to steady his king.

Darkness began to creep into the corners of my vision as I jerked to catch Avenlae before he fell to the ground, but my legs didn't respond. My arms flopped back to my sides as Darinrain helped to guide Avenlae over to me, and Avenlae's acceptance of Darinrain's assistance spoke to how severe his injuries were. His eyes were half-closed as they met mine, and his breathing evolved into shallow pants.

"Saetyl, your ax," Darinrain called over his shoulder. Moments later, Vindicta let Saetyl's ax fall from her tentacle. Darinrain picked it up, swung it several times, and broke the manacles around Avenlae's hands. Avenlae sighed, letting his arms rest limply against his wings, their blood staining the silver feathers crimson.

I bit down on my lip, forcing myself to stay present. *One more time,* I pleaded as I reached for the warmth of the Creonex, *let me heal one more time!*

Darnrain moved the blade of the ax to the chains that held the muzzle over Avenlae's jaw, preparing to cut them away.

NO! Vindicta's order came as a shriek that made everyone cower away. Avenlae's eyes widened as he realized Darinrain was clutching the chain of his muzzle, and he began to shake his head, frantically trying to wrench himself away from Darinrain. Shocked, Darinrain immediately dropped the chains and ax, throwing his hands into the air and bowing his head low to expose his neck to Avenlae. I looked to Vindicta, who sniffed the air as if to check that Avenlae's muzzle hadn't been disturbed.

You cannot remove the muzzle, she said, stepping away from Notien, who supported a bleary-eyed Saetyl.

"What?"

Avenlae whimpered weakly, pressing trembling hands to the bottom of the muzzle, where the metal pressed into his neck. Darinrain glanced between

161

Vindicta and me, his ears swiveling as if Vindicta's voice could be heard outside our minds. He stayed where he was, though, afraid that any sudden movement would startle Avenlae.

If you remove that muzzle, his throat will come out with it.

The full force of nausea blurred my vision and made my mouth water as I tried to control a retch. "H-his throat?" I stuttered. Darinrain's face turned the color of pure sand.

Avenlae turned stricken silver eyes on me, a tear cutting a track through the congealed blood and grime on his cheek. The strength in his core failed, and he sank into the underbrush, ribs heaving as his slight shock of adrenaline faded.

How typical of my Brother, Sinivir sneered in my head. *He always had to have the final say.*

My stomach twisted. I turned away before anyone could see my face, pressing a hand to my mouth as if I might be sick. The truth sat behind my teeth, burning. "How do we save him?" I forced out, hoping they wouldn't hear the echo of Sinivir still in my head.

You don't. You can't heal him fast enough to save his life if you remove that muzzle.

"I can't just leave him to die!" I hissed. "Tell me there's something we can do."

There is something I can do.

"Tell me, teach me, send your power through the Creonex, anything—"

No, Xiaye, you can do nothing. You aren't strong enough. But I am. Only I have the strength to wield genepotentia fast enough to heal his throat before it rips.

I stared at the ground, breathing through waves of nausea and dizziness. "I won't release you."

You don't have to. Just give me complete control for a moment.

"No. Not anymore, never again."

Don't, Xiaye, Vindicta warned, her clicks coming closer, *it's not worth the damage.*

Just a moment, Creovis. That is all the time I will need, Sinivir hissed hungrily. His power thrashed within me, craving release.

"No!" I said through gritted teeth, feeling the touch of a breeze along a sheen of sweat coating my face.

You can hide your voice from the others, Sinivir, but not from me, Vindicta growled. *Stay as you are.*

"Xiaye?" Saetyl's hoarse voice floated over to me.

"I won't let. You. Hurt. Him." I had to fight to speak each word as all my energy went into suppressing Sinivir's power.

I promise I won't, little Creovis. We need him alive, Sinivir said, coiling his power around my body. *You're about to no longer have a choice.*

The sound of shuffling in the grass grew louder along with the clink of chains.

"GET AWAY!" I shrieked, throwing myself away from where Avenlae shifted to reach for me. He flattened his ears against his matted hair, pressing his wings against his raw spine.

"Xiaye, what is—" Darinrain started, but was cut off by my scream as Sinivir's power ripped into my muscles. Avenlae's pupils contracted as he tried to pull from whatever strength he had left, flapping his wings to try and lift himself from the ground. His blood splattered across the grass as Vindicta dove forward and wrapped her tentacles around his arms and torso. She pulled him close to her scaled chest, easily immobilizing him as she arched her tails over her head, their deadly blades pointed down at me.

163

CREOVIS

My vision went completely white with agony as Sinivir's power burned through my veins, devouring everything I was. I couldn't hold on anymore. My body was no longer mine. With a snap of my neck, I let go of my own existence.

Protect them. Protect them all.

CHAPTER 15

AVENLAE'S POV

Xiaye's body jerked around the grass, dust, and dead leaves flying. The *lyceliah* snapped, and that feeling Avenlae had gotten so used to left with a stab of ice. He fell back to the ground, wheezing and clutching at the crippling pain spreading through his chest as Vindicta loosened her hold around him. *No, no, no.* His thoughts spun in frantic circles as he tried to hold himself up with one shaking arm, watching Xiaye twitch. Darinrain stood frozen behind Avenlae, his navy eyes wide as he stared at the scene before him. Notien moved in front of Saetyl, spreading her wings wide to protect her mate. Finally, Xiaye's body stilled, vacant blue and silver eyes staring unblinkingly at Avenlae. His nails pierced his skin as he scratched at his neck, gasping for breath through the pressure that constricted his throat. *Move, Xiaye, please move...*

Her veins suddenly glowed red, spider-webbing across her alabaster skin as her lips drew back into a sneer. The color flowed into her eyes until they were as crimson as the blood that dripped from every place Avenlae's skin had been ripped open.

"Well, Avenlae, it has been a while, hasn't it?" She spoke, but her voice was Sinivir's as she rolled onto her knees, smiling at the stretch of her wings.

Within an instant, Avenlae's pain was gone. He was able to breathe, yet he felt completely numb. His eyes flicked around the clearing—everyone else was frozen. Not with fear. No, they were quite literally *frozen,* suspended in time. Avenlae pressed his ears against his hair, lifting his wings into a defensive position as he moved his feet under him. He had no weapons, but a *Y'araye* didn't need weapons to be dangerous.

"Careful, Warrior," Xiaye said, cocking her head to the side, "You try to hurt me, and you hurt her."

Is she—

"Yes, she's alive." Xiaye rolled her eyes, Sinivir's voice exasperated. "Mortal bonds are so pathetic."

Avenlae narrowed his eyes, standing slowly, his muscles primed and ready. *What do you want?*

"Nothing impractical," Xiaye smirked as she, too, rose to her feet. She let her wings drag behind her as she began a sedate pace around Avenlae. "I just require you *alive*."

I would rather—

"You'd rather die than make a deal with me, you'd rather die than do anything to hurt your mate—save me the melodrama," Xiaye growled, whipping around to face Avenlae and sliding a finger along his neck where the muzzle came perilously close to the flutter of his vein. "Would you rather *die* than protect her?"

Avenlae swallowed.

"You know Xiaye is determined to kill my brothers. She will keep going back into the Realm of Creo, no matter what it costs her. She won't rest until every Creator is destroyed." Xiaye raised her bloody eyes to Avenlae. She was so close he could breathe in her scent... but it wasn't **her**. The eyes, the voice—it wasn't his mate. "You would rather die now than protect her as she faces my last two Brothers? I don't need to tell you how vicious they are."

Avenlae continued to stare, trying to hold his breath to keep his mind clear.

"As I said, I just need you **alive,**" Xiaye hissed, clicking the metal of the Creonex against Avenlae's muzzle. "I'm the only one with the power to keep you alive, and you're the only one with the influence to keep Xiaye going towards her goal. Easy enough, isn't it?"

Do not touch—

Before he could react, Xiaye wrapped her fingers around the muzzle and ripped it from Avenlae's face. His mouth gaped in a silent scream as he felt the searing pop of his throat being pulled from his neck, but then Xiaye's left hand was holding his flesh together, and his skin warmed as a golden glow emanated from the Creonex. Her eyes glowed red as blood as she pulled his head down by his neck, whispering, "Now **you** owe **me.**"

My consciousness returned as quickly as if I'd just been woken up from a fitful sleep. I gasped, my eyes wide as I became aware of myself and my hand wrapped around Avenlae's neck. Blood dripped down the front of his grimy chest, and I immediately felt bile rise in my throat.

"Av, I—you—what—?" I stuttered, terrified that if I moved my hand, I would see his throat hanging by threads of sinew. Trembling, I slowly lifted my head, my eyes locking with his. The muzzle was gone, leaving only faint impressions etched into his sunken cheeks. His breath came in rapid, shallow bursts, and I felt the panicked flutter of his pulse against my fingers.

"A-are you…?" I whispered.

Slowly, he wrapped his fingers around my wrist, carefully prying my hand away from his neck. There, a scar stretched across his throat, vivid and raw. It remained a haunting reminder of Bellum, but no blood seeped from its bubbling surface. His heart continued its steady thrum, evident in the flutter of veins on either side of his neck, returning the shine to his irises. A flood of tears brimmed in my eyes, a turbulent mix of fear, anger, and profound relief washing over me. I didn't even know what to say or how to react.

"Is he okay?" I heard Darinrain ask behind me, but I couldn't answer him. I couldn't move, couldn't breathe, couldn't speak.

Avenlae's fingers brushed against my cheek as he whispered, "Xai."

The sound of his voice nearly broke me. I choked back a sob as I wrapped my arms around him, breathing in his scent to prove to myself that he was *alive.* His chest shuddered against my cheek as his body seemed to melt around me, and his wings pressed against my back.

After a moment, I felt his head lift, prompting me to step back and glance up at him. Avenlae was fixated on something behind me, his ears up and forward. A spike of anxiety quickened my pulse as I turned around, anticipating a new threat. But it was only Darinrain behind me, his ears up as well as he surveyed Avenlae and me. Behind him, Saetyl was sitting up, leaning her raw back against Notien. Sinivir had gone conspicuously silent, his Essence retreating far enough into the shadows of my mind that I couldn't reach him.

The King survives. Vindicta's soft voice echoed through all of our minds as her six eyes darted between us, moving out from behind Avenlae. She sniffed along his arms and back, the gashes left from the whips of the *vitae* already half-healed. Darinrain looked back at Saetyl and Notien, then returned his gaze to us, a smile forming on his lips.

"We all do," he said breathlessly. "We all survived."

"Notien, go alert the Healers," Avenlae said beside me, watching anxiously as Saetyl winced and closed her eyes.

Notien's eyes narrowed as she glanced at me. "I will *not* leave Saetyl her with—"

"That was an *order*, Notien," Avenlae growled, flashing his canines.

She immediately lowered her gaze, hissing as she turned her head towards Saetyl.

"Do not disrespect him," Saetyl whispered weakly.

I will protect her, Vindicta said as she ambled over, resting her tentacles across Saetyl's back as a low purr rumbled in her chest. Notien fixed her gaze on her mate for a moment, narrowing her eyes as she clenched her jaw. Then, without another word, she rose to her feet. In one fluid motion, she leaped into the air, her departure as swift and silent as a whisper. I felt Avenlae's weight as he leaned against me, exhaustion pulsing through our *lyceliah.*

"My King, let me help you," Darinrain said, lowering his eyes and holding out his arm as he moved to support Avenlae.

"It's alright, Darinrain, I've got him," I said, shifting to hold Avenlae's weight.

No, Xiaye, Vindicta said, wrapping more of her tentacles around Saetyl, who groaned. *We need to start moving towards the tribe. Saetyl needs the Healers as soon as Notien alerts them.*

"I am fine, Xai," Avenlae murmured, pulling himself away from me, only swaying slightly. My eyes met Darinrain's, and he positioned himself beside Avenlae, just close enough to catch the King were he to fall. Vindicta helped Saetyl to stand, then began walking, keeping the tentacles of one foreleg around Saetyl's waist to support her as she moved. My power rippled through my chest, ready to be used at a moment's notice as we began to make our way through the undergrowth. I watched Saetyl's winces as she walked, the twitch of her arms as she tried to find her balance without the weight of her wings on her back, and the paling of her face. My throat tightened and I looked forward, blinking away tears.

You didn't know, Sinivir whispered, then fell mercifully silent once again.

My mind writhed, tangled in fractured thoughts as I tried to search for the right words, something that could somehow mend the damage I had done to Saetyl. But how could I possibly *apologize* for tearing off her wings, stripping her of her very freedom and autonomy?

The light of the sun pierced through the canopy in jagged lines, echoing my shattered thoughts. A soft rustle of my wings along the undergrowth disrupted our silence, like whispers of guilt lingering in the air. Darinrain's hand flicked as Avenlae stumbled ahead of me, but he didn't touch the King as he righted himself and continued onward, his new scars stark in the daylight.

What the hell have I put them all through?

Calls came from the trees ahead of us, and flickers of suns' light reflecting off of feathers paused our trek. It took mere moments for the Healers to reach us and load Saetyl onto the stretcher. Notien didn't look at me once—it was as if I were invisible. Then, Avenlae was denying their assistance, Notien was demanding they return to the tribe at once, and Avenlae was ordering Darirain to follow them and speak with Kaigar.

And I remained silent.

I felt like I was drifting outside my own body, a hollow figure amidst the chaos surrounding me. My thoughts wavered on whether or not I should even return to the tribe. A small part of me was screaming for me to go back, to make amends, but doubt gnawed at my resolve. Once they discovered what I'd done, where my team and I had been, would the tribe remain loyal to me? They couldn't. *I wouldn't...*

"Xai."

I blinked, my thoughts silenced. Birdsong echoed through the trees, their leaves rustling in the calm breeze that swayed through the undergrowth. Avenlae stood before me, his wings curled tightly against his back. His silver eyes moved over me, over the ripped and grimy undershirt I'd been in since Bellum's Colosseum, the frayed braids that somehow survived a battle with two Creators, over the blood that had long since dried on my skin. But there were no bruises, lacerations, or scars on my body. I was a *Creovis*—I couldn't be permanently hurt like the rest of my team. But damn, I wanted to be. I *wanted* to feel the pain, to be unable to escape it. I deserved to bear *their* pain, to suffer under the pressure of it.

But in that moment, I could still feel absolutely nothing.

"We should return to the tribe. There is nothing more we can do out here."

I nodded to him. It took a second for his words to actually reach me, and Vindicta pressed her tentacles gently across my back to encourage me to move.

Your people need you.

"Why?" I asked before I could stop myself.

"You are their Queen," Avenlae said. "They will need reassurance now that we have returned."

"They won't trust me. They shouldn't."

Avenlae sighed, wrapping his wings around me and pulling me against his chest. "They do not know what happened."

"And you think Notien won't tell everyone she sees?"

"Saetyl will keep her calm."

"Saetyl has no reason to keep Notien quiet. She should hate me even more." I clenched my jaw, trying to hold back the tears that threatened to fall against Avenlae's skin. I took a breath, breathing in the scent of his sweat, blood, and feathers.

She holds no hatred for you, Xiaye, Vindicta said, clicking as she moved around us. *She was just as blinded to the fight as you were. She alone knows what truly happened.*

"You're not supposed to enter anyone's mind without their permission," I snapped, then immediately regretted my tone.

This time, I believe it was warranted, Vindicta growled, and the sounds of her ambling through the forest quieted as she moved away from Avenlae and me. Avenlae pressed his lips to my forehead, whispering, "You cannot hold on to your regret, Xai."

I pressed against his chest, trying to push him away from me. "How can you say that to me? You're not the one who-who *ripped* Saetyl's wings from her back. You're not the one who just took everything from her—"

"But she still lives, does she not?"

I nodded, feeling heat in my cheeks as anger filled my thoughts.

"She is a warrior. She will adapt."

"She is *Delfungaye!* She has spent her life in the *sky* and in the trees, Avenlae! I *took* that from her!" My voice broke as I stepped away from him, unable to stop the tears from blurring my vision. "I t-took *everything...*" I took in gulps of air, unable to control my breathing as I grabbed at my chest. Suddenly, the air was stifling, the suns were too bright, and the chirps of Silvacastra's animals were *too loud.* "I didn't know, I didn't know, *I swear* I didn't want to!"

"Breathe, Xai," Avenlae murmured, staying calm as he cupped my face in his hands. His wings rubbed rhythmically against mine, grounding me in the moment. "Saetyl still has her life. You have not taken everything from her. She is a Delfungaye warrior, and will adapt to this new way of life."

"But she shouldn't *have* to," I whimpered, taking a few gasping breaths.

"Yes, and you should not have *had* to be forced to take the Delfungaye

172

throne, or put your life on the line to sacrifice for the survival of Creation over and over. But neither reality nor the Creators care what we believe we do or do not deserve. Our only choice is to adapt."

He brushed away the tears that continued to trail down my cheeks. "Notien's hatred will pass: it will just take time. And you must remain strong for her and for Saetyl. It may be hard for you to see, but they need you now more than ever, My Queen."

"You can't be strong for them instead?" I asked with a watery laugh.

"No Xai," Avenlae whispered as he pressed a kiss to my cheek. "I have to be strong for you."

Even as he said it, I felt a tremor in his hand, the confession of weak muscles. I bit my cheek, trying to tear my eyes away from the fresh scar across his throat. I didn't deserve this from him. I didn't deserve his support or his love. But I *needed* it. ***Harden your resolve—you've hurt enough people for a lifetime in one day.***

I swallowed down my emotions, packed them up, and shoved them into the darkest shadows on the edges of my thoughts. I shrouded myself in the numbness, in the inability to feel.

"Let's return, then," I said, my gaze locked on his silver eyes, deliberately avoiding all of his scars. He searched my face, a heavy silence expanding between us. Then he reached his hand out, interlacing his fingers with mine, a gesture I'd taught him while introducing him to human ways. The guilt surged through me, nearly bringing me to my knees again, but I forced it down, again biting the inside of my cheek until I tasted the metallic tang of blood. Physical pain was a refuge, clearer and simpler to handle.

We walked the entire way to the tribe. We could've easily flown—Avenlae was gradually regaining his strength, and I knew how much he hated to walk. But he stayed on the ground for me, allowing me to endure the very confinement I'd imposed on Saetyl. His hand never left mine, his grip steady and unwavering, built for climbing and combat. Mine was deceitful, lacking the resilience to trust myself. Sinivir was still silent, but I could feel his presence threading through my thoughts. He, alone, knew all. He knew everything, every fear and confession I couldn't voice to those I should've trusted most. And that was disgusting.

Vindicta was waiting for us at the base of the trees, clicking up into the canopy at other Voxmor slithering by. As we approached her, she dropped onto all fours, lowering her front end to the grass. *We should get you to the Healers, My King,* she said with a soft click.

"I do not need them, now," Avenlae said, a spike of fear surging through our *lyceliah.*

I'm afraid I must insist. Sinivir appears to have healed you well, but I do not trust him. Let your Healers confirm that you have no lasting injuries. I will take you to them.

"I can fly," Avenlae growled.

If Vinidicta had eyebrows, she would've raised one. *Your growls and hisses don't work on me, Avenlae. Ride willingly, or I will carry you to the Healers and make sure the whole tribe can watch you dangle from my tentacles.*

Avenlae looked over at me, his eyes sharp. I shrugged. I didn't have the strength to make any decisions. Avenlae lowered his ears, a flash of hurt in his eyes before he released my hand and climbed atop Vindicta's back.

Return to the Queen's Nest, Xiaye. I will gather all who need to speak with you once we know the King is okay.

I nodded as she slithered up the tree. A part of me felt immediately agitated: probably Avenlae's emotions. Spreading my wings, I leapt into the air, but I didn't feel the wind in my feathers. It didn't awaken me, or calm my whirling thoughts, or ease my pain.

Delfungaye nodded and bowed as I passed. I didn't even look at them. I didn't stop to speak, to wave, to acknowledge my people. I couldn't take their stares, not now.

I landed roughly on the balcony of the Queen's Nest and stumbled into my quarters, my breathing becoming uneven as my muscles clenched across my chest. Echoes of Notien's screams rang in my ears, and the weight of Saetyl's... her wings, the pop of them separating from her spine... the blood... *so much blood.*

I swallowed heavily, trying not to vomit as my body began to tremble uncontrollably. I tried to find that numbness again and blanket it over my mind, but I was too lost. I was too lost, too terrified, too guilty, too angry, too broken, too deadly—

A loud knock came at the door. I gasped, the echoes of the battle with Bellum fading. I stayed frozen for a moment, waiting for the sound to come again. And it did, along with a careful, "Your Majesty?"

I moved to the door, reached out for the door handle, saw my hand shaking. Taking a deep breath, I rubbed my hands down the rough texture of my pants, trying to push my emotions back into their dark corners. I opened the door, looking up into the worried navy eyes of Darinrain. His staff was gone, likely stored in his nest, and he had changed into the traditional wrap and harem pants of the *Fyr'aeset.* The jagged tattoos up his skull were vibrant in the warm light of my quarters.

"Y-yes?" I stuttered, cursing myself for still sounding so weak.

Darinrain furrowed his brows. "I have spoken with Kaigar to brief him on our progress in the mission."

I felt my blood turn cold. "You told him?"

"Yes."

"Everything?"

175

"…Yes."

My eyes widened as I stepped back. Darinrain moved into the room, his ears up and wings close to his spine. "W-why?" I asked, breathless. "Why did you tell him?"

Darinrian sighed, his eyes softening. "Saetyl is one of his warriors. As General, he deserves to know what happened to her."

I shook my head, unable to speak from the fear that clenched my throat.

"Xiaye." Darinrain lowered his voice. "You cannot blame yourself for what happened."

"I can't—Darinrain, *I* and I alone held her wings and… and—"

"You did not know it was her you fought. Saetyl does not blame you."

"How can you *say* that? Why is everyone *saying* that?"

"Because I have actually spoken to her." Darinrain crossed his arms over his chest. "What has happened has happened. You cannot change it, and imprisoning yourself in one moment will only serve to hurt you more."

I looked away from him, breathing deeply to calm the fury that writhed within me. I couldn't even tell if it was my anger or echoes of Avenlae's emotions through the *lyceliah.* "Is there anything else you need to report to me?"

Darinrain remained quiet for a moment. "You still have a team behind you, Xiaye."

"I'm sure Notien wouldn't agree with you."

"Notien will move on. Give her time to process what has happened, and she will come back to you."

"She shouldn't," I mumbled, looking around the room to avoid Darinrain's gaze.

"Your Majesty, I must request your eye contact."

I ground my teeth, clenching my fists to stop the trembling of my hands. Hesitantly, I looked up at Darinrain. "You are my queen, but you are also my friend. It is painful to see you blame yourself so harshly. You are not alone in your pain right now. I told you to play the game, to perform. How do you think I feel now, after watching…" His voice trailed off as his navy eyes seemed to shine with emotion.

"How could you have known?" I asked him, frowning. "You didn't tell me to hurt her. You were doing what you could to keep us all alive, Darinrain. You're the reason we survived at all."

"Exactly." He tilted his head, his ears forward. "How could *you* have known? Bellum's power let you see whatever he allowed you to see. He fed your anger, your vengeance. And now you imprison yourself within it."

"Don't tell me how *I* feel, Darinrain," I said, raising my feathers slightly.

"Someone has to." He shrugged as he turned to leave the room. "You are not listening to yourself or your mate. Maybe you will listen to a friend."

I stared at the empty doorway long after Darinrain left, as if I were still fighting with some remnant of him mocking me from just outside my quarters. Every part of me was begging to accept the suggested forgiveness in Darinrain's words, but it wasn't his forgiveness I needed. ***Don't act like you deserve it,*** I thought, digging my nails into my palms, craving the pain. When that didn't hurt enough, I moved my nails to my wrist.

Now, Xiaye, Sinivir's voice cut through the silence, startling me. ***As entertaining as it has been to watch you try to tear yourself apart, we still have a mission to complete.***

"You think I give a damn about your 'mission' right now?" I hissed, turning away from the doorway.

It is as much my mission as it is yours. You forget, I have access to the entirety of your mind—I know vengeance still burns into each of your thoughts.

177

"What your Brothers did to you is not my concern."

But what they've done to you, and what they will do to Creation, is, Sinivir retorted. *You'd be lying if you claimed you no longer crave revenge for what Bellum did to you and your little friends.*

"Stay out of my thoughts, Sinivir," I growled.

You trapped me here. That was your choice.

"I did that solely to gain access to your power. Your opinions don't matter to me."

Well, now, who is most cruel, then? You or me?

I opened my mouth to answer, but no words came out. The obvious answer was Sinivir, since only one of us had nearly caused the destruction of all of Creation. But who was I to place blame? I wasn't innocent. I'd taken autonomy away from Saetyl, someone who had become one of my friends, someone who was loved by my closest friend—

Oh, save me the HYSTERICS! Sinivir's voice cracked through my skull like a whip, and my knees buckled as I gasped and held my head. My eyes screwed shut as my temples throbbed and the echoes of his roar gradually dissipated. *Your guilt is so mortal, so self-centered. You picked a fight with the Creators—the fact that your entire team has their lives is a miracle. If you can't handle the consequences of a war with those who made you, then sit here and let them kill you.*

"You had the choice not to go," came another voice, one that rasped after years of yelling orders.

I released my breath in a drawn-out hiss, searching *deeply* for the patience to speak to another person. *I should have closed that damn door,* I thought, spinning to face the front of the room.

"I stood with you, telling you you had the choice to *stay here,*" Kaigar said, his silver and damaged white eyes narrowed.

"You know I didn't have that choice," I replied. "I *never* had that choice."

"Do I know?" Kaigar moved forward, raising his wings. "Do I really? Did your team know? Do they know everything?"

"What the hell are you talking about—"

"The *risks,* Xiaye!" Kaigar roared. "Did they know *exactly* what you were taking them into?"

"They *chose* to—"

"My best warrior has returned with her wings torn *completely* off! Our King appears as if he were nearly ripped into pieces, and the *Je'qeuit's* eyes are hollow. And I do not even want to know if the rumors I have already been hearing are true!"

"Remember your place!" I seethed, raising my wigs in turn.

"Oh, I know my place," Kaigar rumbled. "I serve my people, *all* of the Delfungaye. Do you?"

"How *dare* you ask that question, after seeing *everything* we just sacrificed—"

"What did *you* sacrifice? You have no scars!"

"I want them!" My voice rose to a shriek. "The Second Creator shattered every bone in my wings, and I *want* to feel that excruciating pain. When we returned here, Notien held a knife to my throat, and I *wanted* that blade to slash my neck, to feel my own blood pouring out of me. Cut me now, drive your sword through my chest, hack off one of my wings, tear the skin from my face, I don't care! *Anything* is better than being okay enough to watch *them* suffer."

Tears streamed from my eyes, soaking my cheeks and neck. Kaigar stared, silent and still. Wisps of white hair poked out from the braids that ran the length of his skull, obscuring the scars that tore their way across his left temple.

"You could have stayed," he said finally, his voice cruelly soft.

"Yes. And then I would have been okay enough to watch *all* of you die."

The General dropped his gaze, sighing, his massive, scarred shoulders dropping. "And you'll have to go back?"

"Y-yes," I responded numbly.

He shook his head. "You have to address our people."

"And tell them what? What do I say that they will believe?"

Kaigar lifted his gaze, his eyes piercing. "The truth, Xiaye. You must tell them the truth."

CHAPTER 16

A soft breeze rustled through my hair. Upon it came the scent of fresh leaves, night sky, and a hint of the food and drink in the *Laizuteek* and *Hopyroque* bars that came alive in the tribe as the suns set. Their blaze had just disappeared over the horizon, blanketing the sky in a deep violet and darkening the shadows of the forest. I sat within those shadows, within the leaves of a tree that overlooked the middle of the tribe, just close enough to see my people. They bobbed to the beat of tribal drums, their drinks warming their veins and brightening their lazy smiles. Children darted through the nests, reenacting scenes of Creation's War from the stories they had been told. Mothers watched on, fixing the clothes their children had torn while they gossiped about the recent news they'd heard. But it wasn't about the Creators. It wasn't about how one of their most decorated and infamous warriors had had her wings completely torn off. They didn't know about it. Nobody else knew.

It was absolutely *cruel*.

It was your choice to lie to them all.

"Shut up, Sinivir," I whispered, and his shadow slithered away into the recesses of my mind. Off to my right, Avenlae stood on the highest balcony of the Healer's Nest, talking with Kaigar in hushed tones as their silver eyes darted across the tribe. I folded my wings even tighter against my spine, even though I knew there was no way they could see me. Pinpricks caused the hair on my neck to stand on end; it was the feeling of Vindicta searching for me through her connection to my mind. I forced out a small dusting of Sinivir's shadow to block her out.

I thought you wanted me gone? He sneered.

"I want to *control* you," I said through clenched teeth.

You want to control yourself.

I balled my left hand into a fist, trying to calm myself before I snapped back at him. He could sort through my thoughts to know my response anyway.

You really think you stand a chance against the rest of my Brothers by yourself, Creovis?

"I'm not talking to you about this right now," I grumbled as movement around the Healer's Nest caught my eye. *Just a Healer entering for their shift. Damnit.*

You spent too much time among the humans before they fell, Sinivir hissed. *This self-pitying is becoming quite annoying.*

"I'm so sorry I have emotions, Sinivir," I shot back as I continued to study the entrance to the Healer's Nest. At the same time, I could feel Vindicta's presence getting stronger. A sense of restlessness came over me, and I shifted on the branch, my wings twitching.

You're weak and whiny. I could practically hear his eyes roll in my head.

"And just like that, I suddenly feel so much better," I mumbled, my eyes narrowing as there was movement at the entrance to the Healer's Nest again. This time, a woman with golden skin and sleek, black wings was leaving, her arms wrapped tightly around her torso as she flew, her eyes cast down. Notien had finally left.

I leapt from the branch, gliding along the canopy of the trees to stay out of Notien's line of sight and keeping my scent high above her. Upon reaching the Healer's Nest, I climbed through the branches, taking myself in among the leaves and avoiding the windows of wards as I made my way around the massive structure.

"Where is she, Sinivir?" I whispered, reaching for the power that buzzed in my chest.

The entrance is right below you, he quipped.

"Yeah, and I'll bet Notien has stationed someone to guard Saetyl's room, so waltzing in through the door isn't an option. Where is she?"

His sigh sent shivers of unease down my spine, and I bit the inside of my lip to stop myself from cringing. Suddenly, my eyesight went red, and the panels of the Healer's Nest disappeared. The internal structure of the Nest was outlined in red before me, and the figures of Healers and invalids moved around before me. Up to my left, across the nest, a prone figure glowed, the only one without wings.

She does have a window, O Stealthy One, Sinivir growled.

Using the branch above me for a boost, I pulled myself into the air, a few flaps of my wings carrying me over the top of the Healer's Nest and to the other side. It was darker there, away from the central hub of the tribe, so I didn't have to cover myself with the thickest leaves of the tree. I climbed towards Saetyl's window with the help of the claws at the joints of my wings, switching between my grayscale eyesight and the red of Sinivir's sight to ensure I was climbing to the right place. In one swift movement, I swung myself into the open window of Saetyl's room, blinked a few times in the brightness of the artificial light, then had to arch backwards to avoid a knife as it flew within centimeters of my nose, close enough that it cut through the very end of my hair as I fell back.

Knowing I couldn't stabilize myself into a good defensive position fast enough, I let myself drop to the floor so I could roll into a crouch, grabbing one of my own knives from my boots as I did so. Saetyl was sitting straight up in her hospital bed, another knife already in her right hand as her fiery eyes bore into mine. Her forest-green hair had been braided into two simple Dutch braids, and her torso was wrapped tightly with blood-stained bandages, but… she looked so much smaller without her wings.

"I thought we had agreed you would throw a knife at me only *once.*"

"I am sorry, I did not realize who it was diving through my window at first," Saetyl rasped, flipping her knife around to sheath it with the hint of a smirk curling her lips under her tusks. I took a breath and replaced my own knife as I stood, a weight in my stomach as I glanced around the room.

"It is a hospital room, Xiaye, not a prison in the Realm of Creo," Saetyl said as she reached to take a sip from a crystal cup of water next to her. "Nothing is hiding in the corners here."

"Old habit," I whispered, trying to find the courage to look her in the eye. Wires dangled from the ceiling above her, draping over the headboard of her bed like shimmering strands of a web. They coiled around her neck and spine in a sleek, serpentine embrace. A faint, ethereal light pulsed rhythmically through the wires as she moved, as if they were attuned to the electrical impulses racing through her spinal cord.

"This is how they prepare me for placement of artificial wings," Saetyl explained as she watched my eyes move over her wires. "The wires help to sync the artificial joints, muscles, and nerves with my brain and spine. The base of the wings is already attached, but they must be trained to recognize and respond to the orders sent from my brain. At least, that is how the Healers explained it to me." She shrugged. "They used much larger words that I did not even know existed in our language."

I felt a slight smile tug at the corners of my mouth, a breath of relief that she wouldn't be confined to a life on the ground, but I fought to suppress it. I had no right to smile or laugh when she was hooked up to wires like a puppet. Not when I had put her there.

"Is it painful?" I asked, my voice lacking any real strength.

"Not anymore." Saetyl shook her head. "Honestly, Xiaye, if you had not nearly killed yourself to heal me, they would not have been able to give me artificial wings. It is thanks to you that I will be able to fly at all."

Tears stung the corners of my eyes. "It won't be the same."

She pursed her lips. "No, but the world stopped being the same when we entered the Realm of Creo. We must adapt."

"But, Notien—"

"Pah," Saetyl curled her lip, "let Notien be angry. Let her work through her pain on her own. She is still ruled by her fear, as many of us have been for so long."

I shook my head. "But… but I *ripped* your wings from your back!"

"And I killed what part of you was mortal in front of *all* of Creation!" Saetyl threw her hands up. "You are still here. I am still here. I will still be able to fly because you tried to heal me so quickly. I say we are even."

I stared at her, my eyes widening and jaw dropping. My mind felt like a jumbled mess of puzzle pieces, and I didn't even know how they were all supposed to fit together. Words stayed on the tip of my tongue, becoming tangled as I tried to figure out what I was supposed to say.

I approve of this one, Sinivir said, quite unhelpfully.

"I don't—how can you—why don't you hate me?" I stuttered, taking a step closer to her.

"Did you really come here for me to yell at you? Berate you and carry on about how unfair life is and what you have done to me?" Saetyl raised an eyebrow. "We both knew life was unfair long before this. I agreed to go into the

185

Realm of Creo and follow you wherever this journey led us. None of us knew what was going to happen, yet we followed you anyway. None of Creation knew what was going to happen in the Final Battle, and yet they followed you anyway. My wings… they are just another casualty of war."

I looked away from her, hiding my face as a tear slid down my cheek. "But they didn't *have* to be—"

"Becoming a Delfungaye Warrior means accepting that your life is no longer in your hands," Saetyl snapped, forcing me to look back at her. "It means we put our lives at the mercy of whatever we must do to protect our people and accept the consequences, no matter what they are."

My breathing became uneven, and parts of the room blurred as a knot rose in my throat.

"I still *have* my life, Xiaye. I may not have my wings, but I can survive without them. I can still serve you as my Queen, and the Delfungaye as my people. I am *not* broken. Neither are you."

But I *was* broken. Long before I ever met Saetyl, I had been broken. Wasn't she?

I remembered her once, shaking with rage, begging to be hated so she could feel something clean. I'd told her she wasn't a monster; that mercy was still in her, no matter what she'd done. I hadn't realized then that mercy cuts both ways. Now she offered it back to me, and I wanted to reject it — to make her hate me so I wouldn't have to forgive myself.

I didn't turn my head away when another tear dripped down my cheek, and my throat tightened so much that I could no longer speak. Was it relief that she somehow forgave me? Was it anger that she didn't hate me when I wanted her to *so badly,* so that my guilt could be fed? I didn't even know. I just began to cry. Ugly, loud, raw sobs, my cheeks soaked with tears that would dry my skin enough to make it crack. And Saetyl watched. She said nothing more, but she sat with me as I tried to understand the emotions coursing through my mind. I wanted her forgiveness, but more than that, I wanted her fury. I wanted her hatred so that it would validate my own. To know that I had stolen her wings *and* that she just forgave me so readily was more painful than to just wrap myself in the anger of those who had to bear witness to what I had done.

Gradually, the tears dried, and an intense throb replaced the grief in my head. I had made it to the side of Saetyl's hospital bed, leaning on the warm, fluffy white comforter that covered her legs.

"You always have been too hard on yourself," Saetyl said, brushing a hand up my arm.

I scoffed, rubbing the back of my hand across my eyes. "That's how I've survived. Nothing teaches you faster than negative reinforcement."

"That may be so, but you have not been alone for the past six years. Do not forget that."

When I didn't respond, Saetyl's fingers pressed lightly against my forehead, raising my eyes to hers. "You have my permission to forgive yourself, Xiaye. Let us say nothing more about it. There are things in this realm and others that are much more important than what kind of wings I have."

I gave her a soft smile as her golden eyes glowed, and the wires diving in and out of her skin continued to pulse. Perhaps she would move on. Maybe she would adapt well to her new wings and fly with them almost as well as her old ones. Notien would love her, support her—Avenlae would teach her to fight with these new wings. She would move on.

But I wouldn't. I was going to force myself to hold this tight, to keep it hanging within my mind, a reminder of what the Creators could make me do, what we had to lose, and that I would *never* allow myself to become that monster again.

CHAPTER 17

The middle of the night on Silvacastra held a peace I had never found before, even on Earth. A scent of fresh leaves, the calm river, and a hint of wind from the crest of the mountains far off to my right moved over me, and I filled my lungs with it. My skin reflected the light of Silvacastra's small blue moon, and the stars flickered along the swirls of the Creonex that cooled over my hand. There, on the topmost branch of the Queen's Nest, I could look out in any direction and see for miles above the forest. I could hear the calls of nocturnal creatures, their voices disguised to sound like the very wind that carried their scents, the rustle of the trees swaying, or the flow of the river.

There are few planets such as this. Vindicta's voice startled me, and I nearly fell right off my perch. She pulled herself up to join me, her tentacles and claws holding her steady so far off the ground.

She is right, Sinivir spoke, his voice oddly calm. There was something behind his voice, something I hadn't heard before. Vindicta flinched: she could hear him, too. *My Brothers didn't believe in diversity as much in their little experiment.*

"And you did?"

There was a reason I gave all of Creation the ability to choose, Creovis.

Vindicta snorted. *Most of the other planets within the universes that can sustain life have a theme, so to speak. Mine is filled with the most vicious creatures in all of Creation. Some have the most beautiful and elegant beings you'll ever lay eyes on. And still others are covered in water, and their inhabitants have never even seen land.*

"What about the other Allied Worlds? I've only been to a few. Surely they're not all so... monotonous?"

The Creators made their planets specifically to host their intelligent life forms, Sinivir sighed. *Earth was the first planet I made that was different.*

I about choked on the very air I breathed. *"You* made Earth?"

I did. Sinivir's voice *sounded* like a shrug. *It was meant to be a joke, and then Fames began to use it as a dumping ground for any species he created that he didn't like. When the planet suddenly took on a life of its own, he used it for target practice.*

"With what?"

An asteroid.

"Are you serious?"

Then he turned his back on it for just a moment, and the humans appeared. And they just... never died. When I breathed consciousness into Creation, Fames could no longer touch Earth.

Or any of the other planets, Vindicta clicked. *Bellum even left my planet alone for generations before Sinivir arrived.*

I had to wait for the right time, Sinivir sneered.

"And you've overstayed your welcome," I muttered, sending a pulse of power from the Creonex into my mind to force Sinivir to back off. When my thoughts quieted, Vindicta nudged me with her snout, clicking. *Avenlae will be discharged from the Healer's Nest shortly. You should wait for him in your chambers.*

I sighed, lowering my eyes from the moon and scanning the tops of the trees. No part of me wanted to return to the reality of being the Queen of the Delfungaye. I didn't want to look in the eyes of my people or my King, for how could they trust me? My people knew nothing of what I had done, and Avenlae did. Surely he was as disgusted by my actions as I was?

The only other member of our little party who is still upset over this is Notien, Vindicta said, nudging me again so that I lay against her scales.

"Vindicta, I *tore off* her mate's wings."

No, Bellum did. Neither of you was aware of what was going on. She was trying to kill you just as viciously as you were her. You just have more power.

I shook my head, digging my nails deep into my palms. "I don't understand how you're all able to let this go so easily."

Because we know *who you are, Xiaye. Bellum pulled from the most profound anger you and Saetyl had, and forced you to use it against each other.*

"So that part does exist within me?"

It exists within everyone and everything. How do you think the Voxmor once nearly took over all of Creation? Vindicta lifted my chin with one of her tentacles as she lowered her head. *You cannot hate something that is so integrally a part of you. You must control it. Train it so that you may use it only when you call to it, not when someone else does.*

I nodded. "And Notien?"

She will come around slowly. Give her the space to sort through her own feelings. Besides, she is not the only one who has ever cared deeply about you. Vindicta cocked her head to the side. *Avenlae is approaching your quarters. Go to him, My Queen. He will need you now more than ever.*

Almost as silently as she had approached, Vindicta slithered down the branches of the Queen's Nest and disappeared into the shadows of the night. A fragile peace enveloped me, one that I knew could be shattered with a mere breath of anxiety. I wanted to stay there, to be lost to the night, to the distant nocturnal calls and fresh breeze. But I knew Vindicta was right. I could feel Avenlae's pain, his fear, his longing through the *lyceliah.* He needed comfort, solace, even if he would never ask for it.

I dove around to the balcony jutting out from our quarters, hoping to stay in the darkness for just a second longer. No light shone through the windows of the French doors—apparently, Avenlae felt the same. I folded my wings tight to my spine, savoring their pressure and weight, and tried to enter the room as quietly as I could. The fear I felt from Avenlae was volatile, and it wouldn't take much to set off his instincts.

Two moonlight eyes pierced mine the second the balcony doors closed behind me. Their intensity was enough to silence the coiling whispers of Sinivir on the edges of my thoughts. Avenlae sat on the bed, his wings wrapped around his body. This was an incredibly protective stance, one used in times of tremendous distress. Breathing deeply, I crossed the room to the bed, trying to figure out what to say to him. What was I supposed to tell him? I'm sorry? But for what? Was I supposed to say that it was okay, it was going to get better? No, we both knew that was a lie. Nothing was going to get better, not while there were still Creators left in existence. Should I have asked him what he needed from me? Was he okay? Of course not—

"You are alive."

I paused, half of my body leaning onto the bed. Avenlae's voice was… different. There was a harshness to his tone, the sound of something lost. My eyes grazed over the fresh, bubbling scar across his neck.

"Tell me you are alive," he demanded, his eyes glowing ever brighter.

"I'm alive," I said, my eyebrows knitting together as I sat in front of him, glancing around the rest of his body for more new scars, more places where those beautiful tattoos had been disrupted.

Gradually, his wings lifted away from his body, revealing a light black *Fyr'aeset* wrap around his torso, breathable in the humid air of the forest. He lifted his hands, almost timidly, to hold mine. I stayed silent, letting him lead me and show me what he needed and what he wanted. His calluses scraped against my skin as he pulled my palms against his chest, just over his heart. It beat, steady, strong, just under my fingertips. I could feel him breathe, feel his lungs expand, and his ribs press into my hands. ***I'm alive.***

His fingers brushed across my cheeks, my jaw, my neck. The silver of his eyes shone in the welling of tears that threatened to fall down his cheeks. "You are alive," he said again, his voice barely a whisper, "even though I could not protect you."

"Av, there was nothing you could have—"

"No." I flinched at the sound of his voice. His wings stretched toward me, wrapping around us both, and his hands cupped my jaw, holding me as if he alone were keeping me tethered to our world. "They could have killed me, Xai. So many times, they could have taken my life from me, and there was nothing I could have done to stop them. But they did not. They ***toyed*** with my pain, my blood. It was so easy for them, so effortless to enjoy the sound of my screams."

His breath came in quick pants as he moved closer. "I am ***nothing*** in the Realm of Creo. I have no power and no strength. I have no way to keep you safe. I. Am. ***Nothing.***"

"You are ***everything*** to me, Av," I said, trying to calm my own voice, "You… you keep me stable, grounded in who I am."

For a moment, we were silent and still, just staring into each other's eyes, taking in the new scars, the new guilt, fear, and sadness that crept behind our gaze. Then, Avenlae moved forward, brushing his cheek across mine in a nuzzle as he inhaled my scent, caressing my skin with his lips until he reached my mouth. "Remind me you are alive," he murmured, pressing his lips against mine. When he pulled away, his eyes were the very moonlight that poured into the room. "And that you are *mine.*"

My fingers dug into the sharp line of Avenlae's jaw, my nails scraping stubble as I pulled his mouth back over mine, arching into his body as his arms wrapped around my back. As his tongue ventured into my mouth, reminding me of how sweet he tasted, my hands made quick work of the light wrap he still wore. His wings caressed my feathers, sending electric shivers rippling my spine and into my stomach. As soon as his wrap was on the floor, he was tugging impatiently at my top, moving his mouth across my neck and collarbone, nibbling and licking at the sensitive skin while I sank into the feel of his warm skin against my fingers, his muscles taught. His teeth grazed my collarbone, and I hissed, my nails raking down his back as I pressed myself closer.

The cool night air raced across my skin and tightened my nipples with anticipation as Avenlae threw my top to the side, running his hands up my torso, his calloused palms rough against my shuddering skin. Pressing my palms to his chest, I pushed him back against the bed, the air leaving his lungs in a ragged gasp as he hit the blankets.

His eyes—those damn moonlight eyes—burned into mine as I straddled his hips, my thighs framing his body. Leaning down, I dragged my tongue along his chest, tasting the salt of his sweat, the heat of his skin. He groaned, his hands gripping my hips, his fingers digging into my flesh as I moved over his neck, teasing him with slow, torturous strokes. I covered his mouth with mine, parting his lips with my tongue as we wrestled with the rest of our clothing, removing

193

it with a fervor that spoke of the need coursing through our bodies. This wasn't a moment of pure lust, of not being able to keep our hands off of each other because we just *looked* good enough. This was the reminder that our hearts still beat. This was a reminder that his skin was still warm, that I could still feel him, that we could still love each other. This was just *different.*

I rubbed against him, and Avenlae groaned as he bucked his hips into me, throbbing need pulsing between my thighs. I couldn't keep in my own moan as we pressed our hips together again, my thighs slick, his body shaking and ready.

"Le'eseia," he purred, hands guiding me, pulling me onto him, and him into me. I sighed, feeling his pulse mingle with my own.

"You," I whispered into his ear, "are *mine."*

I began to rock back and forth, the sound of his groans, gasps, and calls fueling me on. Avenlae responded to every move I made, his muscles clenching, vibrating, his breath hitching, his mouth as fervent as mine, and his tongue just as heated. He was mine, I was his. That was our constant. Each other.

We were alive, we were alive, we were *alive.*

"NO! G-GET AWAY!"

The scream shredded the darkness, yanking me from deep sleep. I flailed, disoriented, heart hammering, trying to figure out if I was dreaming or awake. The room was swallowed in pitch blackness until that tortured wail cut through again, hoarse and fractured by damaged cords. *Avenlae.*

I vaulted up, turning to comfort him with the Creonex already warming around my left hand. But before I got to him, his wing whipped out, striking me across the face. Pain blossomed in my cheek and down my neck, hot and raw. I tumbled backward off the bed, hip and knees grazing the floor as Avenlae screamed again, limbs caught in the sheets as he thrashed.

"Do not touch me, *do not touch me!*"

Stumbling to my feet, I pressed a hand to my jaw—my cheek throbbed in time with my pulse. Avenlae was a storm of panic, bucking and twisting against something only he could see. His breath came in harsh wheezes, his voice cracking in and out from the strength of his shrieks and the damage to his throat. I lunged forward, fingers closing around his wrists. He unleashed a shriek so fierce it felt like broken glass in my ears. His eyes were wide and wild with fear.

"Avenlae, it's me!" I called to him, trying to make my voice louder than his cries. "I-it's okay, nobody's trying to hurt—"

His wings slammed into my ribs in brutal, bone-crunching thuds. Hot pain erupted beneath my skin, but I anchored the claws of my wings into the headboard. Avenlae writhed like a wounded animal, every sinew straining.

"Avenlae, *please!*" I begged, but my voice was lost in the sound of his shriek as he cried to be freed.

The door to our chambers burst open, cracking against the walls. Between my feathers and the frantic beating of Avenlae's wings, I saw Darinrain in the doorway, his eyes wide and his staff in his hands.

"My Queen, what is—"

"*Help me!*" I cried, just as one violent heave from Avenlae lifted me off the bed like I weighed nothing.

Dropping his staff, Darinrain darted to the head of the bed, pressing his arms across Avenlae's chest and using his wings to pin Avenlae's against the headboard. Avenlae roared in panic, body arched, tears carving paths down his face.

"NO! Stop, stop, please! Don't—get *away from me!*"

Darinrain's arms shook with the monumental effort to hold Avenlae down. "What is happening?" he panted.

195

"It's just a nightmare," I called to him over another intense cry. "I can't get him out of it!"

"What about the Creonex?"

"Does it *look* like I can reach his temple right now?" I snapped, another violent thrash nearly sending us both crashing into each other.

"Can you hold him?"

"What?"

"I have an idea. Can you control him for just a moment?"

"I—"

Before I could answer, Darinrain sprang off the bed. Avenlae seized the chance, sending me skidding to the footboard. I scrambled back up, trying to reach for his arms again as he rammed his fists and wrists into the headboard hard enough to make his knuckles bleed.

Darinrain paused in the doorway. "On a separate note, My Queen, did Avenale get you that wrap?"

"Darinrain!" I shrieked as I was tossed into the air again, and Avenlae let out a gut-wrenching cry.

"I am going!" he called as he darted out the door.

"Avenlae, stop!" I cried, pressing the full weight of my body against him, trying to still the storm of muscle and feathers. "It's Xiaye! You're here, you're home. Listen to—"

"Do not touch me!" he shrieked. "L-leave me alone!"

He twisted forcefully, trying to wrench himself free, and I hated having to hold him there, hold him still while he was trapped in whatever hell his mind had created. It was the worst I'd ever seen him—he wasn't protective or aggressive. He was absolutely terrified.

At that moment, Darinrain burst back into the room, a crystal glass in his hand. He darted around to my right, seizing Avenlae's jaw and forcing the glassy liquid—bitter, acrid—into Avenlae's mouth. It was enough to strangle Avenlae's cry into a shuddering gag.

"Darinrain, what—!" I gasped, immediately releasing Avenlae's arms as he pitched forward, coughing violently.

"It is just a tonic," Darinrain said, stepping back and setting the glass on the table next to the bed, "but the stuff tastes truly awful."

We stayed there, motionless, watching as Avenlae gasped, ready to jump into action the second he began to scream again. His wings drooped, trembling, and sweat slicked his brow and feathers. Finally, his silver eyes lifted, his pupils gradually beginning to dilate as he looked at me. He drew in a shaky breath and wrapped his wings around himself, pressing his feathers tightly to his bare torso.

"Xiaye," he whimpered, his voice so fragile.

I shook my head. "It wasn't real. You're safe—we're on Silvacastra."

He blinked, stared at my blood-speckled cheek, and reached out with trembling hands to confirm I was real. Then his gaze dropped, grief flickering across his face as he traced a fingertip along the scar on his throat, then down his jaw. "They... they hurt me," he croaked. "It burned—"

"I know," I murmured, reaching out and lowering his hands. "But it's done, it's over. We'll never be back in Bellum's Realm."

Avenlae nodded again, still distant, then flinched as Darinrain shifted. Dainranin lowered his eyes, exposed his neck, and took another few steps back.

I sighed. "Let me get you some water, Av."

I moved to get off the bed, and Avenlae's hand wrapped around my arm in a vice grip. His eyes widened again, his fear visceral in their silver depths.

"It's okay, Av," I whispered, running my other hand down the side of his face, "you're safe here. It's just us."

197

He held me there for a moment longer before releasing me. I moved to the other side of the room, my bare feet almost silent against the wood floor. Darinrain followed me out the door into the dim, warm light of the Queen's Nest.

"You do not have to go far," he said quietly, gesturing to a small table outside of my chambers, "I brought a bottle of water with me."

"How did you know that would work?" I asked, grabbing the bottle.

"I did not," he shrugged, "but who can stay dreaming of anything at all with the taste of that tonic on their mouth?"

"Why have you had it?"

"My older brother used to use it on me anytime I misquoted our histories," Darinrain replied, a sad smile on his face.

"A good way to learn, I guess," I said, sharing in a soft chuckle before turning to head back into the room.

"My Queen," Darinrain voiced, stopping me before I crossed the threshold. "If Avenlae likes that wrap, I know a merchant from the *Fyr'aeset* who sews more that may be just your taste."

I glanced down at the simple, light onyx bed wrap I was wearing, shaking my head in disbelief. "How can you even think about that right now? After everything?"

He tilted his head, giving me a knowing look. "So much has changed, yes. So much has happened. But you are still my friend, which means I can still advise you on the ways of Delfungaye fashion."

I raised an eyebrow.

Darinrain set a hand to his chest in mock offense. "You question *my* interpretation of your style?"

"Good night, Darinrain."

"Good night, My Queen. I will have my merchant friend send over some of her pieces, and you can tell me all about how much Avenlae adores you in them."

CHAPTER 18

Morning dawned as it always had, warm and bright. Glints of dust danced through the rays of suns' light that streamed into our room, like little fairies I had read about as a child.

But my world wasn't the same.

Memories of the Realm of Creo flooded back, chasing away the daze of sleep in mere fitful moments. I filled my lungs with morning air, stretching carefully so as not to disturb Avenlae. He still slept next to me, the rise and fall of his chest slow and steady. It had taken hours to get him to fall back asleep after the night terror, hours of painstakingly transferring every memory I could think of through the Creonex. Some memories we talked about, others we watched silently together, wrapped in each other's arms. He needed this sleep, this time to heal. I didn't. I wouldn't allow myself.

After donning a **_Laizuteek_** tunic and loose pants, I glided into the tribe, taking the familiar route through the trees to find the merchant who sold coffee. A steaming cup, made exactly how I like it, was already set on the counter, its scent almost like the loving embrace of a long-lost friend. The merchant smiled at me, said she was happy to see me again, asked where I had been off to.

I lied to her.

It was so easy to make up a story, to hide the truth behind a smile, a small laugh, and something about the Allied Worlds and new missions. Kaigar had done well to keep most of the tribe from becoming suspicious that something was happening.

You have to tell them the truth, Xiaye. His words chanted through my thoughts as I flew back towards the Queen's Nest. **Why** did I have to tell them? Why did they have to fear the new threats of the Creators? We had already destroyed two of the Brothers, and the tribe was blissfully unaware. Why couldn't I just let them continue to live their lives free of the pain of war, especially one that hadn't, and likely wouldn't, affect them until it was over?

"Your Majesty."

I blinked, suppressing a cough as a small sip of my coffee tickled the back of my throat. The *Matri Me'liev* hovered before me, ripples of multicolored cloth streaming from her wings. Her soft, navy eyes crinkled as she smiled at me, deepening the wrinkles of her aged, golden face. "There is nothing to hide from me. You know my secret, and I can sense all of yours."

I glanced quickly around us, ensuring that the tribe still remained calm. "What brings you out here so early?"

She tilted her head to the side. "Oh, Xiaye, do not try so hard to protect yourself. I am here to check on you."

"Is that so?"

"Come, now. We will head to the Queen's Nest together."

Knowing that to dissuade her would be an insult, I gave the old woman a tight smile and began to glide next to her.

"I can feel the shift in the powers," the *Matri Me'liev* said.

I looked over at her out of the corner of my eye.

"I am speaking to you as the Oracle, *Creovis.*"

"Ah," I muttered. "Well, two of the Brothers are gone."

"Very good. And your entire team is still alive."

"Yes," I responded sharply.

"Should you not be proud of that? Grateful for their lives?"

I stopped gliding and hovered behind her. "They're alive, but at what cost?"

The Oracle turned, a gleam of starlight flashing in her eyes. "A cost they were all willing to pay."

"How would you know that?"

"I am an Oracle. I know *things.*"

I scoffed, rolling my eyes and looking away from her.

"Now, Xiaye," the Oracle continued, taking on the tone of a mother reprimanding a child. "You cannot continue to punish yourself for everything that occurs outside of your control."

"*I* am the one who took them all into the Realm of Creo!" I hissed, fighting to stay quiet enough not to wake anyone in the nests closest to us. "On *your* advice! If I had left them here, everyone would still be in one piece, mentally and physically."

"Perhaps. And you would be dead."

I frowned at her, taken aback.

"Or, as good as," she shrugged, "seeing as you are not mortal."

"What are you talking about?"

"You *need* them, Xiaye. You need Avenlac, Sactyl, Notien, Darinrain, and Vindicta with you when you enter the Realm of Creo, if only to remind you of who you are. There, you are in the world of the Creators, of the very beings in All That Is Known who wield the power that you embody. You are not mortal and so cannot be harmed or killed by mortal things. But you *can* be harmed by the Creators. They can control you, manipulate you into whatever they choose, if you let them."

"So… so you told me to remember who I was so I could protect myself from the Brothers?"

The Oracle nodded. "Protect yourself from *all* of them, Xiaye." She looked me up and down once more. "One more thing. A Queen does not wallow."

I blinked at her. "I… what?"

"Pick yourself up and brush yourself off. This energy you are spending on blaming yourself is becoming pathetic."

My eyes widened as I watched her glide forward, my mouth open.

"You have to move on one day, My Queen," the Oracle called over her shoulder. "It does not matter how many times you try to repeat to yourself that you are at fault for any of this. It will not change what has happened, nor what will happen."

The rest of the day became a blur, an act in front of my people. It was filled with fake smiles, forced laughs, and more lies. Avenlae was with me, face stone serious, responses curt.

Hours bled together as I moved through the familiar rituals of leadership, acting as if it were just another day on Silvacastra, and nothing at all had happened while I had been gone. I met with my officers and Kaigar soon after speaking with the *Matri Me'liev* to review the status of border controls—no one questioned the heightened security. The officers assumed that tensions had heightened between the Delfungaye and another of the Allied Worlds, and that was the reason not only for the King's and my absence, but also for the reorganization of the Guard and Voxmor. I just let them continue to assume, despite Kaigar's exasperated glances.

Avenlae, however, couldn't hide his vigilance. He was never further than an arm's length away from me, his intense chrome eyes scanning our surroundings at all times. Outside of the Queen's Nest, he kept looking to the horizon, as if watching for a sign of one of the last two Brothers to appear. The *Matri Me'liev* assured me she couldn't feel any change in the Realm of Creation, and Vindicta never reported being able to sense the presence of the Creator. But Avenlae couldn't shake the fear.

I was finally able to escape the protective shadow of Avenlae mid-afternoon when Kaigar requested that the King preside over the Ceremony of Ranks and Weapons for the most recent trainees. Unable to sit still for too long and not willing to sit with my thoughts, I found myself walking through the halls of the Healer's Nest, tilting my head forward periodically as Healers and patients bowed to me.

Not sneaking around this time, Creovis? Sinivir sneered.

My smile felt strained as I bowed in return to a passing Healer, but I ignored the voice in my head. A few steps away was Saetyl's room. I hesitated, taking in the stark contrast of the pure white walls against the matte black door. There was no guard stationed outside, no indication of anyone inside. Yet, an invisible force seemed to keep me at bay. It was as if an unwritten rule barred my entry, pulling me in two directions at once.

"I have stared, too, but I cannot find a single speck of dirt in this place."

I jumped, whirling around with a hand to my hip where a knife would have previously been. Behind me was Saetyl, one forest green eyebrow arched as her fiery eyes danced across my face. In her hands was a glass of *anteel* and a plate of food that was still steaming. Her pulsing wires hung above her, plugged into a sleek box near the ceiling. She followed my gaze, looking up at the cables.

"It does look odd, but it gives me some freedom," she shrugged.

"Oh, uh, that's good," I said, trying to offer her a smile.

She shook her head. "Come on, Xiaye—Notien is not here."

"No? I would have thought she'd never leave your side," I said quietly as Saetyl stepped in front of me, unlocking her door.

"I love her with my entire heart," Saetyl chuckled, "but even *I* can get tired of her chattering."

"She really does know how to carry on a conversation," I agreed, checking around the room as I followed Saetyl to her bed. She reached up and swung the wires, sending the box across the ceiling, where it settled into the wall and reattached to its power source.

"That's incredible," I breathed, watching as lines of blue lights glowed along the top of the ceiling.

"You are starting to look too much like our King," Saetyl said, flopping onto her bed and moving a small table out from the headboard.

"What?" I grunted, leaning carefully on the covers.

Saetyl cocked her head to the side, looking me up and down. "You are checking all corners of the room and the ceiling. Do not think I could not see you do that as soon as we entered."

"I was well trained," I replied with a soft smile.

"So you say." Saetyl took a sip of her **anteel**, then began on her plate of food. "And how are the others?"

"They're…good."

"I do not know why you think you have to lie to me."

I sighed. "You've got more than enough to deal with right now without me adding more to it."

"Are you still stuck on blaming yourself for all of this?"

"I'm not blaming myself," I said, though my voice faltered. "I'm just not sure the person I had to become to win deserves peace yet."

"It is war, Xiaye. War between you and the Creators. Nobody agreed to join you in the Realm of Creo expecting to return the same as we were when we left."

"You're not the first to remind me," I mumbled.

"Then maybe you should start listening." She glanced up at me as she chewed a bite of food. "Take some. I grabbed too much, anyway."

"Don't offer too loudly. Notien might hear you," I said as I reached forward to take a piece of vegetable off of her plate.

Saetyl scoffed. "She knows I do not blame you for anything. She knows you did not do this intentionally, and, honestly, I think she misses you too much to continue to blame you."

"Really? It's hardly been a whole day since we got back."

"Yes, well, as soon as we arrived at the Healer's Nest, they determined I would be the perfect candidate for artificial wings. I am no longer in pain, I will be able to fly again, and, most importantly, I am not dead. So, Notien doesn't really have anything else to blame you for."

It was my turn to raise my eyebrow. "This is Notien we're talking about, right?"

Saetyl laughed. "She just has a lot of emotions to work through. Do not let her make you feel worse. Now, this time, be honest—how are the others?"

I took a deep breath before answering. "I haven't seen Vindicta this morning, but she was fine last night after I visited you. Darinrain is... Darinrain. And Avenlae..." I let my voice trail off.

Saetyl nodded, taking another sip of *anteel.* "Darinrain spoke to me about it briefly early this morning."

I watched her chew another bite of food, then reached forward for a slice of fish to nibble on. "I... I haven't seen him that bad before. Usually he's just protective, or he becomes aggressive, but..."

"Darinrain said he was screaming."

I winced. "Never say anything about it around Avenlae."

"Of course." Saetyl set her plate aside. "Will he let you help him?"

"He barely talks to me about what goes on in those night terrors. All he allows me to do is transfer calming memories through the Creonex to calm his mind before sleep."

Saetyl watched me for a moment, her golden eyes searching. "Notien would know better than I what you are supposed to do."

I huffed, looking down at the comforter. "I know. But I doubt she'll talk to me."

"Let me talk with her," Saetyl said, stretching, "I may be able to get her to move on and calm down. In the meantime, Avenlae likely just needs comfort."

"I already give him memories—"

"That is not what I mean. Do you remember the first time you entered my mind? You remember what you saw?"

I nodded slowly.

"You were the first person to ever tell me I was not a monster. That was one of the most monumental moments of my life. Perhaps Avenlae just needs to know he is not alone."

***

The entire day had felt like it lasted over a week. I kept checking the suns, trying to see if they had gotten any lower in the sky. When the shadows

206

finally lengthened, and the glow of the suns became a burning gold, I flew straight to the Queen's Nest, deciding that I had shown myself amongst the tribe for long enough. The feeling of a soft, silk wrap that allowed for better airflow was enticing, and I planned on lighting a small fire before sinking into one of the plush chairs with a cup of *anteel*. I wanted silence and solitude.

As I entered the room, I built up my defenses against Sinivir, ensuring that I could block him out for the evening. Upon Avenlae's and my bed was a stack of *Fyr'aeset* cloth wraps. Each wrap was a masterpiece, adorned with elaborate and intricate designs that seemed to dance with complexity. The cloth was soft as satin, inviting to the touch, and shimmered gently in the light, as if woven with threads of moonlight and stars. I smiled to myself as I picked up one of the wraps at the top, its fabric a deep sapphire blue, adorned with swirls of black that were darker than the night. Darinrain had been right—that merchant he knew created designs that were *exactly* to my taste.

Just as I had tied the wrap around my wings and covered my breasts, Avenlae entered the room, a soft wheeze in his breath. His eyes roved over my body, their irises beginning to shine a prismatic silver.

"Where did you get that?" he asked, his voice still raspy.

"Darinrain."

Avenlae's eyes immediately darkened.

I gave him a look. "He knows a *Fyr'aeset* merchant who he thought made wraps I would like."

"And how would *he* know what you like?" he grumbled, moving to the bed to glance over the assortment of clothes.

"He's just being kind," I said, hugging myself and lowering my eyes. There was a rustle as Avenlae sorted through the wraps, and then a sigh.

"I know. I… I did not mean to upset you."

I looked up at him, at how his ears pressed into his hair. It was braided simply that day, with most of the long, black swaths hanging to the middle of his back. Suns' light glinted off the gold of the ring pierced through his septum, jewelry that was more becoming of a king. Reaching up, I set my fingers along his jaw, gently pulling his face closer to mine.

"You're just overwhelmed. I understand."

"Are you not?"

"I'm in here and it's not even dark yet."

Avenlae smiled softly, his canines pressing into his bottom lip as he set his forehead against mine. "You are my safety, *Le'eseia.*"

"And you are mine." I kissed him softly, then stepped back. "Change. There's no way you're still comfortable in that."

Avenlae smirked, stretching his wings as he reached around for the hooks on the sides of his black vest of the Queen's Guard. "Would you assist me, My Queen?"

I raised my eyebrows, crossing my arms over my chest.

Avenlae's wings drooped slightly. "Would it help if I said I was still in pain from my injuries?"

"Perhaps, except I know you're healed," I said, smiling as I stepped forward to pull the vest off of him. It was hard to believe that just a day before, I was begging Sinivir to save Avenlae's life, and now, I was trailing my fingers down his chest, across the cracked tattoos separated by jagged scars. I could feel the warmth of life radiating across his skin, the movement of his muscles as he breathed.

That moment was easy to hide in. To tell myself that nothing had actually happened. It was just another one of Avenlae's nightmares that I had to calm.

A knock came at our door, shattering the peace. Avenlae's ears pressed against his hair as he glared behind me. "What?"

"It is Darinrain, Your Majesty."

Avenlae rolled his eyes, a growl rumbling in his chest. "Send him away."

I shook my head, stepping back and moving towards the door, hiding my smile from Avenlae as I turned the handle. "Good evening, Darinrain. Do you have something to report?"

Darinrain bowed, his grin showing the full length of his canines. "Not this time, My Queen. But you look absolutely resplendent in that wrap. Is that one of the ones I sent you?"

"What do you need, Darinrain?" Avenlae snapped behind me. I gestured for Darinrain to follow me into the room and swung the door wide. Darinrain made no effort to hide how he looked over Avenlae's bare chest and abs as he walked to a small table on the other side of the room, setting a small bag on one of the chairs.

"I would say I need the King to remain clothed, but..."

"Get on with it," Avenlae hissed, and I rubbed my temple, turning towards Darinrain to flash him a grin.

Darinrain lowered his eyes, angling his ears backwards as he began pulling an assortment of small jars out of his bag and placing them on the table. "It is actually you I am here for, My King. Do not worry, Xiaye can stay to chaperone."

Avenlae flashed his canines, stepping towards Darinrain with his winggs raised, when the *Je'quiet* picked up a ruby jar, plucking off the lid. Avenlae froze, sniffing the air, and his ears tilted forward as his eyes widened. "Is that...?"

"Sit, please, My King," Darinrain said, his voice smooth and respectful, as he stepped back and gestured toward the plush chair next to him. My eyebrows knitted together as Avenlae moved around Darinrain, watching intently as he began to organize the small jars. Leaning forward slightly, I inhaled cautiously, straining to detect even a hint of aroma, but my nose isn't anywhere near as sensitive as theirs.

As Avenlae sank into the chair, Darinrain straightened, standing for a moment at attention before Avenlae. "Please do not take offense at my accent: I did not have as much time as I would have liked to prepare."

And then, something remarkable happened. Darinrain began to speak *Y'araye.* Avenlae sat up, his ears perked, silver eyes gleaming with a newfound brightness as he heard the familiar cadence of his native tongue. Darinrain's hands moved gracefully, performing a ritualistic dance that mirrored the rhythm of an alien song. Occasionally, he would reach for a small, ornate jar, delicately retrieving a pinch of vibrant, colored dust. With reverence, he pressed the dust into Avenlae's chest, gently touched his temples, and let it cascade over his head. Avenlae remained utterly captivated, his entire being absorbed in the melodic words and the ritual. As the ritual concluded, Darinrain gracefully knelt on the ground, offering a deep bow that conveyed utmost respect and trust. Avenlae observed him intently, a profound expression reflected in his silver eyes, a mixture of awe and understanding.

When Darinrain stood, he glanced over at me, gave me a quick bow, then turned to head out the still open door.

"Darinrain," Avenlae said, leaning forward in the chair.

The other man stopped in the doorway, turning his head so that we could only see his profile, and the way his *Je'quiet* tattoos curled up his skull.

"Thank you."

Darinrian tilted forward again, another bow, then made his way out of our chambers. I turned back to Avenlae, watching as he examined the jars, his eyebrows furrowed as he touched a hand to the spot where a dusting of emerald powder was still on his cheek.

"What was that?" I asked, keeping my voice gentle as I stepped over to him.

He took a breath, then looked up at me, his eyes shining. "It was *Sa'noqho*, a Dream Cleanse. The oldest of the ***Y'araye*** rituals."

"Oh, Av," I sighed, sinking into the chair next to him with a soft smile.

"I have not heard those words in over twenty years," he murmured, his gaze unfocused. And suddenly, what Saetyl had told me made sense.

CHAPTER 19

"Y ou cannot hide forever," Kaigar grumbled as he escorted me out of the Queen's Nest, "if there was a way, I would be the first to tell you."

I rolled my eyes, stretching my wings as I prepared to take off from the back balcony. "Yes, but a feast? Right now?"

"The hunters brought back a *Zrafejik*. *Laizuteek* are preparing the *hi'pret*, and you know every *Fyr'aeset* mother will already be on the way to prepare sides. The tribes will have a feast whether or not you want them to."

"Do you have the numbers for a heavy Night Guard tonight?"

"I do."

"Fine," I said, stepping onto the railing.

"Xiaye."

I turned back to the General, the scar misshaping his mouth and eye pulling tight in his scowl. "The tribe has been quiet, peaceful. Going after the Creators—is it worth it?"

I studied Kaigar's lined face, and the places along his hairline where the years had caused his hair to become more silver than black. We hadn't spoken about the Realm of Creo since I had arrived back at the tribe nearly a month before. Kaigar had kept me at almost an arm's length, but the longer we were on Silvacastra, the more apparent his apprehension became. Finally, I replied, "If I don't, there will be no tribe to speak of."

Kaigar studied me with his one blind white eye and regular silver. I imagined he probably looked at my mother that way, years ago, perhaps every time she was faced with a decision. Did he have two silver eyes back then?

Did he study Novissime in that manner as well? When she decided to bring me back here, to train me, to ask me to be her heir?

"The Queens live so strongly within you," he said softly, "but do not forget yourself, Xiaye. Your determination is beyond what I have seen."

I nodded once, knowing that such moments with the General were too rare to dissuade. "You followed them, though, Kaigar."

"Indeed. And I follow you, My Queen. *They* will follow you when they know the truth," Kaigar said, nodding towards the central hub of the tribe. With that, he turned and was gone amongst the bustling of the Queen's Nest in midmorning.

I dove from the balcony, my mind tangled in his words so much that I barely noticed the wind rushing through my feathers. *Was* the battle I led against the Creators truly worth it? It *had* to be. Mors' silence had meaning. He was waiting for the right moment, waiting to see how far I would go. Right? There was a threat in the existence of the Brothers and their power.

The threat is how easily they can take control, Sinivir said within my mind, his voice lacking its usual sharpness. *My Brothers have been toying with you this far, but I can only hope that by the time Mors discovers how much of a threat* you *are, it will be too late for him.*

"And what about you? When this is all over, what will you do?"

That is for us to discover, isn't it, Creovis?

I clenched my jaw. "Don't make me regret bonding with your Essence, Sinivir. I destroyed you once—I will do it again."

Yes, yes, I am well aware, Sinivir growled, pulling his shadows back and silencing himself. I buried myself in the feeling of the wind moving over the parts of my skin that were exposed by the marbled white and grey uniform I wore, trying to send my anxiety away with the slipstream of my wings. *This is the right thing. I'm protecting my people—that's the right thing to do. Ensure their survival, no matter what.*

Behind the Queen's Nest, across the river, there still sat a clearing in the trees. It had been where Avenlae had trained me years ago when I was first brought to Silvacastra. Odd… suddenly, that time seemed so simple compared to where I was as I descended over the trees. Back then, I was learning how to fight. I didn't even know my place in Creation's War, and had never even met a Creator before.

Now, I was trying to kill every single one of his Brothers.

The sound of training swords cracking against each other echoed up to me as I swooped over the clearing, gauging a place to land. Darinrain looked up, noticed me, and moved to the side of the treeline, waving and grinning as I landed on the grass, tucking my wings in quickly to try and avoid being a distraction for too long.

"Dropping in to see the progress, are you, My Queen?" he asked, nodding his head behind me as if in signal to someone. I turned as I backed up to stand next to him, watching as Saetyl moved back into position to continue sparing. Notien stood across from her, rolling her shoulders with her eyes narrowed. It had been nearly a month since Saetyl had left the Healer's Nest with her new wings, and still Notien had not once met my eye.

Avenlae paced around Notien and Saetyl as they began their rounds, calling out corrections and moving Saetyl's arms and legs to help her form as she acclimated to the feeling of fighting with wings that responded half a second slower than hers had. The wings themselves were truly magnificent in their design and grace. They moved with an almost ethereal silence. Each feather was crafted from a light, iridescent material, shimmering with the brilliance of the suns, lifting and falling as if each individual feather could be controlled with Saetyl's mind. The wings were anchored to a sleek, silver metal spine, a marvel of engineering that seamlessly disappeared into her hairline at the nape of her neck.

"The Healers really outdid themselves," I said, my eyebrows rising as I watched Saetyl fight. Notien was going too easy on her, but perhaps that was what was needed.

"They really did." Darinrain nodded, crossing his arms over his chest. There was a sheen of sweat across his forehead, and his staff was leaning up against a tree.

"Were you just sparing with her, too?" I asked, gesturing over to his staff.

"Indeed." He winced as Notien landed a hit on Saetyl's ribs. "She is adamant that she trains day in and day out. She remains determined to strengthen herself enough to continue the mission with the rest of us."

I shook my head, turning back to face Darinrain. "I don't care what she tells me. I'm not taking her back to Creo."

"Good luck trying to tell **her** that."

"I'm not going to give her a choice."

And yet, what she does with her life is not your choice, Xiaye. Vindicta's voice bloomed in my mind as she moved out of the shadows of the trees along the treeline behind Darinrian and me. *There is no point in demanding that she stay here with the tribe. Neither she nor Notien will listen to you.*

"But it's safe here. The Creators haven't touched the tribe yet, so... so nobody dies here." Kaigar's words began ranting through my thoughts. *Did they*

215

know the risk? Is it worth it? Is it worth it? IS IT WORTH IT?

"Xiaye," Darinrain said, his eyes unnaturally serious as he met my gaze, "you cannot take this away from her. There are only two Creators left, so we are halfway there. It would be dishonorable for us to stop now, even if you were to order us to."

I studied the deep navy of Darinrian's eyes for a while, rubbing together the uneven surface of the Creonex along my fingers. There was still a part of me that didn't want to take any of them back to Creo, this little voice that refused to be silenced no matter what anyone told me. The peace was supposed to last many more years. My team hadn't asked for this new war, and they didn't deserve any of it, any of the pain or the fear. Especially when we had to do it alone, with only a few in our small team to lean on. And yet...

You need them, came Sinivir's voice, soft in the back of my mind.

I hate to say this, but Sinivir is right. Vindicta clicked, growling quietly, *You will not be able to finish this alone.*

Darinrain's eyes widened as he turned to Vindicta. "You can hear him? In *her* mind?" His eyes flicked back to me. "And he just speaks to you? Whenever he wants to?

"Unfortunately."

Darinrain wrinkled his nose and curled his lip, revealing a long canine. "How revolting."

"Thank you, Darinrain," I sighed, looking back to where Avenlae had called a halt to Notien and Saetyl's sparing session. The shadows had begun to lengthen as the suns began to sink closer to the tops of the trees, and the faint echo of chattering at the tribe had grown steadily louder as I'd spoken with Darinrain and Vindicta. Saetyl and Notien set aside their weapons as Avenlae went over a few final instructions. Darinain retrieved his staff, spinning it over his head and securing it across his back as he stretched his black wings.

"Shall we join them, My Queen?" he asked, tilting his head in a slight bow and gesturing towards Avenlae, Saetyl, and Notien.

I will see you in the morning, Xiaye, Vindicta said before she slithered back into the trees, back toward her hive. I nodded to her as she left, then turned to follow Dairnrain across the clearing.

"Her Royal Highness approaches!" he called, with a completely unnecessary flourish. Which was, of course, why he did it.

Avenlae took a deep breath, closing his eyes for a moment before he turned a burning glare on Darinrain. Saetyl grinned, her tusks pressing into her top lip as we approached, and Notien stepped behind her, keeping her navy eyes on the grass.

"My strength is returning," Saetyl said, bowing her head before rolling her shoulders. "I will be able to return to duty soon."

I swallowed hard, trying to control my expression. *I can't take you back out there.* "I can see that. You've always been a strong warrior. You don't think you could serve well here with the Guard?"

Saetyl raised an eyebrow at me, and I could hear a soft *tch* of disapproval from Notien behind her. I glanced over at Avenlae, who fluttered his wings and turned his eyes on Saetyl. *It's ultimately her decision... not mine.*

"Perhaps. But I serve my King and Queen first," Saetyl responded, tilting her head in such a way that it could almost be considered a challenge.

I bit the inside of my lIp, trying not to glance at Avenlae again. He would defer to her decision, only because he knew what it meant to have honor as a warrior. "Of course," I said, giving Saetyl a soft smile, "if you're still willing."

"What kind of question is that for you to ask?" Notien asked, stepping to the side of Saetyl and glaring at me.

"Notien," Saetyl growled, her voice a warning. Notien's wings twitched, but she didn't lower her gaze from mine. *That* was a challenge.

Avenlae moved forward, a low growl in his chest. The feathers along his wings rose, and he clicked the claws at the wing joints together. He didn't need to flash his canines for Notien to back down, though. She turned her head towards Saetyl, a muscle in her jaw twitching.

"We will take our leave now," Saetyl said, more so to Notien than the rest of us, "and prepare for the feast. Are we still welcome in the room at the Queen's Nest?"

"Always," I responded, taking a breath as Avenlae's feathers lay flat. Saetyl and Notien said nothing more as they turned to take off, Notien helping Saetyl get up into the air.

"Give Notien just a little more time, My Queen," Darinrian said quietly, watching as they disappeared over the tops of the trees.

"She has had enough time to decide where her loyalties lie," Avenlae grumbled, his ears pressing against his hair.

"She's been through as much as the rest of us," I said, my voice a little harsher than I meant for it to be. "I can't expect her to get over what's happened so quickly."

"You are too patient."

"Could the argument be made that you are too forceful, My King?" Darinrain asked, keeping his eyes very carefully just off to the side of Avenlae's face.

"An argument could be made that you interfere too much," Avenlae snapped.

"Ah, but only when it comes to you, Your Highness," Darinrain said with a mockingly sweet smile.

I rolled my eyes. "We should all head back to the Nest. The tribe will expect everyone to make an appearance, especially since we've been so absent recently."

"Now, Avenlae, what are you planning to wear? Should we coordinate?" Darinrain jogged to catch up with Avenlae as he made his way to the middle of the clearing to take off.

"If you do not move, you will be wearing my feathers somewhere on your face," Avenlae hissed.

"They would compliment my new *Je'quiet* robes very nicely," Darinrain said with a shrug, but he did back off as Avenlae spread his wings and leapt into the air.

"I don't know why you keep trying with him," I called as I stepped forward, stretching my own wings.

"He needs a friend, I think," Darinrain said, moving to the side so we both had room to take off.

"I don't think he wants one," I responded as we began to glide towards the Queen's Nest.

"Of course he does!" Darirain called, swooping around me with his sleek, giant wings, and that same unassuming smile across his lips. "You can make lovely company, My Queen, but, really, that man needs something a little less serious in his life!"

***

The light streaming into the windows of our chambers was a warm, golden hue, casting a gentle glow across the room as I meticulously braided Avenlae's hair. Each strand was silky smooth against my fingers, gliding effortlessly as I wove them together. A tranquil quiet had settled over us, and his wings tenderly draped across my legs, their weight comforting. His breathing was a steady, soothing rhythm, and I found myself slipping into the methodical pattern of braiding, mind blank and hands moving of their own accord. It was a moment we hardly had together, a moment of just existing within each other's presence.

Talk to him.

I blinked, pausing halfway through a braid. Was that Sinivir's voice?

Yes. Talk to him.

"Xiaye?" Avenlae asked, his voice harsh, laced with a whisper where his vocal cords had been damaged by the muzzle. A flicker of anxiety passed through the *lyceliah.*

I cleared my throat. "I'm sorry, I was just... thinking."

There lapsed another moment of silence.

"About?"

I tied off the end of the braid and started on the final, tilting his head to the side so I could work around his temple and ear. "What's happened. To all of us."

"Mors has left the tribe alone."

"What if... what if it was a lie? What if he never meant to hurt us, and just wanted his Brothers dead?" *Is it worth it?* I couldn't get those words out of my head. I couldn't stop returning to the question over and over, especially as my team recovered.

I wouldn't put it past Mors to manipulate mortals like that. However, Creovis, we both know Creation will never be safe for as long as the Creators remain in control, Sinivir hissed. I had become so accustomed to the sound of his voice in my head that I had to stop myself from answering him aloud.

"From what we have seen, I think we can agree that the Creators care very little for the civilizations within their universes. Sinivir was the only thing standing between us and the rest of the Brothers before, and now that he is gone, they may be starting to feel more confident. They may decide they no longer care about our ability to feel fear and pain."

They never did care for the pain of mortals, Sinivir growled.

Yeah, and neither did you. "There are only two Creators left, but the last two changed us so much. There are so many new scars, Av. So much new pain."

Avenlae reached up and gently placed his hand over mine, the warmth of his touch slowing my anxiety in my mind. I sighed, letting my fingers slip away from the end of his braids as he turned carefully to face me, his eyes searching mine with a quiet intensity. "Xiaye, *we* hold that pain and those scars, *not* the rest of our people. They had to hold the pain of Creation's War because there was no one until you who could stand up to a Creator. Our purpose in attacking the Brothers is to prevent our people from having to experience more trauma and fear."

"But I don't know if it's worth any of *our* lives," I said softly, feeling the sting of tears in the corners of my eyes, "and I'm terrified of being the reason I lose you or anyone else."

"Their death will be their choice, not yours, should it come to that. They, too, are choosing to hold the pain of this mission to spare the rest of our people. There is no higher honor for a warrior."

I set my hand against his cheek as I stared into his silver eyes, his face still split by an old scar that stretched from his temple to his jaw. "Sometimes I wish I could hold the pain for all of you."

"No, Xai, you cannot."

"What do you mean?"

Something rushed through the *lyceliah*. Something warm, comforting, golden, and powerful. *Love.* "You are not alone, *Le'eseia*."

I am not alone...

CHAPTER 20

The lights within the Queen's Nest had been dimmed, and the structure was filled with an unusual quiet. Most of the tribe was gathered out in the forest, and flickers of warm firelight filtered in through the windows, making the shadows dance. I glided down several levels of the Nest, heading towards the one room with artificial light still glowing from the doorway. Swaths of a white, silky skirt brushed against my legs as I landed, and beadwork along my bodice tinkled quietly. I hadn't had to dress so formally for my first feast on Silvacastra, but being Queen of the Delfungaye came with some traditions I would never be able to escape or change. Before, I'd always had Notien to giggle with as we tied up each other's hair and placed beadwork in our wings. Saetyl, Notien, and Darinrain were held to nearly as high a standard as Avenlae and I, having been an integral part of my fight in Creation's War. Having Notien with me to guide me in these traditions and help me prepare was always a comfort I… took for granted. Getting ready in peaceful silence with Avenlae wasn't awful, but it wasn't the same. It didn't bring me the same comfort.

And so, with a bag full of beads flung over my shoulder, I took a deep breath and crossed the threshold of Saetyl and Notien's room, their laughter echoing out into the massive, empty floors of the Queen's Nest. Saetyl's fiery golden cat eyes met mine through the mirror she and Notien sat in front of. She raised an eyebrow, but didn't drop her smile. Her forest-green coils had been piled into a fauxhawk down her head, and she wore an outfit more suitable for a warrior. She was never one to don a dress, no matter what the traditions were. Her uniform, a black pantsuit, still had Notien's feminine touch, though, with its traditional **Hopyroque** green and violet beadwork along the shoulders and midsection where the cloth broke.

"We'll be expected at the front of the Queen's Nest before too long, you two," I said, smiling softly at them.

Notien's head whipped around, her smile dropping as if I'd just slapped it off her face. "We will join you momentarily, then," she snapped.

"Ah, well, actually," Saetyl said, standing and rolling her eyes only for me to see, "that reminds me. I had something to, uh, pick up from the Healers."

"No, you do not," Notien responded with a frown, "I have all of your medications. They went over all of your discharge instructions with me— "

"Yes, well, they forgot something." Saetyl walked hurriedly to the door, brushing past me with a whispered, "Fix this before I go crazy!"

I dropped my eyes to the dark wood floor, tracing the intricate grain patterns with my gaze as I absentmindedly fiddled with the strap of my canvas bag. My mind raced, trying to find the right words to say to Notien. In Saetyl's absence, an oppressive silence filled the room, the air seeming to press into my chest.

"Do you need something?" Notien asked, her voice sharp.

I sighed, finding the courage to raise my eyes to hers. "Yes, actually. I was wondering if you could assist me with the beads on my wings? Avenlae can braid, but... well, that's about all he can do to help me with these things."

Notien stared at me for a long time. At least, it felt like a long time. It was as if her gaze alone was a line I couldn't cross, a wall that kept me at arm's length, and I couldn't take a step forward no matter how badly I wanted to.

Finally, I broke. "Look, Notien, I think you have every right to hate me. In fact, no matter what anyone else says, I *wanted* you to hate me. I wanted *everyone* to punish me."

Notien's eyebrows drew together in a thoughtful arch. Her eyes, initially sharp and focused, softened ever so slightly as I spoke.

"When we returned to Silvacastra, I spent the entire trek back to the tribe trying to figure out how to hurt myself, how to run away, and how I could even *dare* to have the audacity to look any one of you in the eye. That... that thing I did, that *disgusting* thing, is unforgivable. And everyone is so kind to me, even though I *wish* they would hate me as much as you do. Because then the guilt would be justified. Then I could be disgusted with myself and my existence, and know that I *am* too dangerous."

Notien stood abruptly, her feathers rustling as her ebony gown cascaded over her feet. Intricate ruby red beadwork clinked softly, trailing paths down her arms and around her waist as she moved forward, shifting with each deliberate step. I swallowed, my words caught in my throat, and felt a jolt of tension ripple through my muscles. She halted just inches from me, her gaze piercing as she looked down her nose. Although Notien was already several inches taller, the air of authority and presence she exuded made her seem to loom even larger.

"I will not help you hate yourself."

I blinked in surprise and had no clue how to respond. Her breath escaped in a soft, exasperated puff through her nose, and she lowered her eyes from mine. It was the first time in months that she backed away from eye contact, which indicated a challenge. "It is much easier to place the anger and pain onto someone else than to just accept what has happened. I watched you *rip* off her wigs, and, even though I knew, I could *see,* the horror in your eyes, that you did not even know what you had done… it was so much easier to hate you for it."

My chest tightened, and I gritted my teeth, attempting to suppress the overwhelming wave of guilt that took over my thoughts. I forced myself back to flashes of images from that moment: *the blood, the feel of her limp wings in my hands…*

Notien raised her head, her eyes glistening with tears. "I still have so much anger to work through and let go of. But, as much as I do not want to admit it now, I do not hate you. I did not want you to know, because I wanted someone else to feel the pain I was going through. Everyone around us seemed so ready to just accept and move on, but I could not. Not so soon."

"Because you love so deeply, Notien," I said quietly.

She smirked. "Not *that* deeply. Any other queen would have punished me severely for the amount of disrespect I have shown you."

"Well," I shrugged, "I thought it was warranted."

Silence stretched as we both glanced around the room, unsure exactly how to move forward.

"You know," Notien ventured, "I am only saying this because the King is not present. But those are not Queen's braids."

"I know. It would be such an embarrassment to present myself with warrior's braids to a *feast.* Whatever would the tribe *think* of me?"

Notien gave me a look.

I held out my bag.

"Oh, sit down," she said, snatching the bag from my hand and trying to hide her smile as she moved back to the vanity at the other end of the room. I grinned and followed her, laying out the skirt of my dress as I sat on the ground. Her fingers worked nimbly to take out my braids and rework them, taking strings of aquamarine beads and wrapping them around the updo. Just like that, normalcy began to return.

Almost.

The fire blazed as food was passed around the gathering. High above us, a tribal beat pounded through the forest, and Delfungaye swayed as they ate their fill. Voxmor, who had Riders, were coiled along the branches, taking bites from the plates of their chosen people. Vindicta rested behind me on the massive front-facing balcony of the Queen's Nest, a hunk of meat nearly finished in front of her. To my right sat Notien and Saetyl, talking animatedly with a few higher-ranking members of the Queen's Guard as Kaigar stood silent and still behind them. To my left was Avenlae and Darinrain, Avenlae uncomfortable in his traditional uniform, and Darinrain *much* too pleased in his *Je'quiet* robes as he attempted to converse with his King.

"The hunters have done well with this kill, have they not, Your Highness?" Darinrain boomed with a grin as he raised a glass of *a'ta'ya* towards Avenlae.

"Indeed," Avenlae growled, filling his mouth with another bite and chewing slowly, not to savor it, but to give himself an excuse to stay quiet.

"I guess this is a much-needed breath of fresh air for us, don't you think, Darinrain?" I said, humoring his attempts.

"It is, My Queen," he responded, bowing his head. "And you look quite resplendent in that gown, I might add. A powerful warrior, you may be, but you really do settle into your softer, feminine side quite well, Your Majesty."

I tried to smile as I attempted to figure out whether or not I was going to take his words as a compliment.

"Careful, Darinrain," Avenlae hissed with a flash of his canines.

"My friend, someone has to compliment our Queen!" Darinrain took a swig of his drink, adding in an undertone, "And I do not hear *you* saying anything to her."

"I do not feel the need to be so annoyingly conspicuous," Avenlae grumbled.

Darinrain's eyes brightened as his grin became even wider. "Nor, apparently, do you feel the need to correct me, My King! Did you hear that, Xiaye? I have just been *allowed* to call him my friend!"

Avenlae lowered his plate, his ears pressed tightly against his braids as he turned pleading silver eyes on me. "*Help* me."

I smiled, leaning forward and planting a kiss on his sharp cheek, just below his scar. "No."

He frowned, but a hint of a smile curled his lips. "Why do you so enjoy my suffering, *Le'eseia?*"

We all *do,* Vindicta chuffed behind us, finishing off the last bite of her meal. *You need the light of this night more than any of us, Avenlae.*

Avenlae aimed a look at Vindicta, who chuffed at him again, moving her snout forward so he could set a hand across her scales.

"Xiaye!" Notien called to me, her eyes shining. "Do you hear the change in the music?"

I tilted my head, confused, as my ears twitched. A knowing smirk spread across Saetyl's face. "She has not heard it, but *Avenlae* definitely has."

I turned back around, watching as Avenlae flashed his canines at her, the feathers of each Delfungay tribe swaying in his braids as he moved further back into his chair, as if trying to sink into the shadows. Indeed, the beat of the drums above us had changed, and with it came a soft melody of strings and wind instruments floating down through the leaves.

"A royal dance!" Darinrain gasped, setting his drink down and rising to the railing of the balcony in a flourish of deep navy robes. "Is that what our people want? A dance for the King and Queen?" His voice boomed out across the trees, and a call of cheers and whistles rose out from the branches.

"I will slit your throat," Avenlae growled up at Darinrain.

"Ah, but you will have to catch me first," Darinrain answered, leaping from the balcony to hover before us, his arms outstretched.

This is going to be wonderful to watch, Vindicta clicked, moving forward and touching her snout to my shoulder.

"You're not supposed to be egging them on," I said to her, rising out of my chair and smoothing my skirt.

I enjoy it, sometimes, she said, flicking a tentacle against the back of Avenlae's head to make him stand as well.

I shook my head, extending a reassuring hand out towards Avenlae as he begrudgingly trailed behind me to the railing that overlooked the crowd below. Our people erupted into a joyous cheer as we ascended into the air, navigating to the center of the gathering. As we did, the *hi'pret* sheet was lowered to keep the flickering flames at bay. I moved to face Avenlae, our wings beating in rhythmic unison so we could hover close to one another. He swallowed hard, nervously fidgeting with the collar of his uniform, tugging it upward as if seeking comfort. I wrapped my fingers around his hand, feeling the warmth of the Creonex as it emanated a soothing blue glow, silently transferring a wave of calmness to him.

"No one can see the scar from here, Av. No questions will be asked."

His moonlight eyes shone as our people quieted around us, waiting, the anticipation palpable. "I think, perhaps, you will owe me for this, Xai," he whispered.

"And I imagine you won't let me forget that I do," I said, glancing around as the music changed again, a slow, sweet melody. "Do you know this dance?"

"Unfortunately," he breathed, wrapping an arm around my waist as he cupped the nape of my neck with his hand. "I will lead you."

That was a little-known fact about Avenlae. For as fierce and deadly a warrior as he was, he was a beautiful dancer. It was a skill that no one would expect from him, because it was a skill he did not show off to anyone save for me. And it wasn't beautiful in the way humans were, with their ballroom dances, sways, and elegant arms. It was not beautiful in a way that was learned with perfect postures in sparse dance studios. The dance of a Delfungaye was so much *more.* It was the dance of the birds, of the wind, and the sky. It was the rhythm of beating wings and falling feathers. It was aerial acrobatics done with the same grace as clouds drifting away and splintering against a blue sky. And Avenlae knew every beat, every note, every crescendo of every dance, even the most traditional ones, even the ones that I had never been taught.

His body moved with the same control as it did when he fought, every muscle synchronized with each movement, so in tune with the music that when it changed, he did not have to think about what the next step was. We moved from the center of the *hi'pret*, and the calls of our tribe rose up through the branches as I spun away from Avenlae. He followed, catching me and picking me up by the waist, before dropping through the air, releasing, and catching me again. My beads clicked in rhythm with the beat, and the coat of his uniform billowed behind him, mimicking the canopy of leaves above us. We rose, fell, and spiraled through the melody of the song, my eyes never leaving his. And for a moment, just one, at the very end of the dance, the music stopped. The Delfungaye were quiet. And it was just us.

Just Avenlae and I suspended in time, arms around each other, gazes locked.

Just him. Always.

And then the sky broke.

229

CHAPTER 21

It began with a soft rustling through the leaves, quiet enough to be mistaken for the sound of a breeze. Then the cheers of our people gave way to shouts of fear as the trees began to sway, for the whole *world* was trembling. Avenlae dropped my hand as his head whipped around, eyes wild, hands reaching for well-hidden knives. I could feel the thrum of panic like a pulse, quickening as the ground rippled violently beneath the forest's underbrush. Vindicta shrieked from the Queen's Nest, launching Saetyl into the air and calling to her hive members, who began to secure themselves more firmly to their branches as their Riders joined them. Then came the very roar of Silvacastra, the sound of the planet in pain. It was as if the fabric of the world itself had been cast into a tempest—a violent, unrelenting madness.

Prepare yourself, Sinivir warned as our power began to rage through my veins, a violet blade materializing from the Creonex as the rest of my team flew up to join Avenlae and me. More Delfungaye took to the air, unable to stabilize themselves on trees that swayed so far we thought they'd just snap in half at any second.

With a massive **crack**, the night sky above us **shattered.** It broke into a million little pieces, like a broken mirror, violet, glowing cracks zigzagging farther out than we could see.

"Sinivir," I called, spinning around in the defensive circle we had made, "what's happening?"

Billows of shadow rained down from the cracks in the sky, blacking out the stars and showering the forest in an inky, melting greyscale.

Mors, Sinivir growled as the shadows began to take shape before us. The very moment his grey eyes snapped into existence, the torture of Silvacastra stopped. The entire planet became silent and still, the Delfungaye suspended, frozen in the air, and only Vindicta left to slither along the tree branches. Avenlae, Darinrain, Notien, Saetyl, and I hovered before Mors, all of our weapons drawn, despite how useless they were. I narrowed my eyes as soft gasps left the lips of my team—to them, it was **Fae'yeerium** appearing in the flesh.

"Tick tock, little **Creovis,**" Mors hissed, the sound of his voice making my skin crawl. "You have a decision to make."

"And what is that?"

Mors began to circle us, but his eyes stayed on me. "You seem intent upon making my Brothers disappear, and they have been too weak and ignorant to stop you. But you see how easily I can **break** your little planet. How easy it is for me to **suck** the very life of your people out of their bodies. **I** am not like my Brothers. I will not give you the chance to fight back."

"You've allowed me to so far. I'm still alive, aren't I?"

"What do I care whether my Brothers are here to control Creation, or banished to the Realm of Summum? With them gone, the fate of Creation is left to **me.**"

Choose your words carefully, Creovis, Sinivir whispered, his shadows coiling in my mind.

231

"Why don't you do something about it, then?" I snapped. "If it's so *easy* for you, just kill us! Just finish everything!"

I could hear the shifting of my team around me, their hands tightening on their weapons as Sinivir sighed in my mind. *That was most decidedly* not *careful.*

Mors narrowed his eyes, sliding his silver claws together as the shadow of his body began to swell. "I may no longer have my Creonex, but *do not* doubt my power, *Creovis!*" His voice rose like a thousand screams. "I wanted to give you *one* final chance to make a choice, to *survive.*"

Without warning, torrents of smoke exploded out from his body, coiling around Avenlae, Darinrain, Notien, and Saetyl, rendering them utterly helpless before they could even blink. Their weapons clattered pitifully against the branches, swallowed by the shadows beneath us. I whirled around, my blade flashing as I aimed to sever the dark tendrils binding Avenlae next to me. But in an instant, something wrapped around my hand, tightening so fiercely that I shrieked, convinced that my wrist would splinter into pieces. Icy blades dug into my neck and jaw, wrenching my head back to face Mors as he loomed closer. A jolt of power left my body, a message from Sinivir to tell Vindicta to *stay away.*

"You ask me to end things, little *Creovis?*" Mors hissed, flashing silver fangs as his claws slid along my skin. "I know you can sense that I can destroy you, right now. In front of those you hold most dear. How *sweet* it will be to witness their suffering, to *feel* their—"

He froze, his entire form taut. His claws trembled ever so slightly. Then he yanked my face toward him with a force that sent a searing pain through my neck as one of his claws sliced into my flesh. The scent of death suffocated the air as he leaned in closer and whispered, *"Sinivir."*

Power burned under my skin, an inferno of rage that wasn't mine.

Mors released me, retreating, his fangs bared in a grin stretched unnaturally wide. Then he began to laugh, to cackle, a cacophony of clashing metal and the screech of grinding chains. "Your vengeance isn't even *yours, Creovis!*" he shrieked, his voice a jagged knife. "You have embodied *his* hatred! This is even better than I imagined."

My veins crackled with barely contained magenta power, and I was blinded by a sea of *red.* I was engulfed by the ferocity of Sinivir's emotions, helpless to rein them in. It was as if I were watching myself from afar, watching as someone else used my body as a puppet dancing to *their* violent tune.

"Come to me then, Brother," Mors taunted, "do what you want with Fames. But end it with me. This time, you can *feel* what it's like for me to take *everything* from you again."

I *exploded.* Fiery tendrils of red-laced *genepotentia* surged out from me, consuming Mors' shadows in a maelstrom of searing crimson flames. The sight etched into my memory was the silver glint in his eyes and the menacing gleam of his fangs just before Silvacastra was plunged back into the abyss. "Come to me, Brother, and finish this."

The world vibrated with raw energy, an almost deafening hum resonating through the air—like the charged static just before a storm breaks open. Heat danced across my skin, sizzling as a cool Silvacastra breeze swept the forest, a return to night, to movement, to life. Whistles and chirps met my ears as Delfungaye swooped around, checking on their friends and family, looking for the wounded. Vindicta clicked and vibrated her frill, summoning her hive members to assess them and their Riders.

Now, they knew. They all knew. There was no secret anymore.

And my team stared at me with wide silver, navy, and golden eyes.

"What do we do, now, Xiaye?" Notien asked, her voice an echo of emptiness.

I looked around at each of them, at their scars, their empty hands. My heart thrashed against my chest as my lungs drank in the fresh, potent scent of the forest. The Creator had left Silvacastra untouched. He could've ripped the sky away, cracked the planet in half, snapped us out of existence. But he left Silvacastra as it was.

Because of Sinivir.

I swallowed. "We go to Mors, and we end it."

CHAPTER 22

"We *end* it?" Avenlae growled as he followed me back to our chambers. "That is your answer?"

"It's all we *can* do," I said, my mind racing as I began taking stock of where my new armor and weapons were.

"All the Delfungaye tribes know, Xiaye. They all *know* what we are up against now. They are terrified, and your answer is 'We go to Mors, and we end it'? We just do as he says?"

"Avenlae, what the hell else are we supposed to do?" I snapped, whirling around to face him. "The only way to ensure the safety of our people is to destroy the Creators, you said so yourself. And you saw what Mors can do. You think he'll back off if we just hide here for long enough?"

"No, but I think what you are ordering us to do is suicide."

"I'm *ordering* you to do what it takes to save Creation. You stood by me when we did it before, and not even a few hours ago, you were telling me why we *needed* to go back to Creo. Why is now any different?"

"Because I actually listened to what Mors said. Did you?"

"'Come to me, Brother, and finish this.'"

Avenlae's eyes darkened. "'Your vengeance isn't even yours.'"

A thrill of anger writhed in my chest, and I took a breath, trying to calm it.

"Even now, I can feel his fury within you, Xai," Avenlae pleaded, taking a step closer. "What if Mors is right? What if all of this hatred is not yours? What if you are only going after the Creators because Sinivir has manipulated you to believe—"

"Shut *up,* Avenlae!" I shouted. His eyes widened as his ears pressed back against his braids. "You weren't saying *any* of this when we first began this mission. You didn't even agree with me when I brought it up earlier *today.* You can't back out on me just because you're *afraid.*"

A sting of pain passed through the *lyceliah,* strong enough that it almost made me gasp. "Afraid?" Avenlae said quietly, moving away from me as his wings lowered. "I do not have to be afraid of your death, Xiaye. You cannot die. I do not even have to be afraid of my own death, for it will be one that will happen in battle. But I can *feel* you changing. I can feel the darkness grow stronger within you. That is more painful, for it is as if you are dying slowly from the inside."

"*I* control myself, Avenlae. *I* have control over Sinivir. Maybe it's *you* who's changing. Maybe you're finally realizing you're not invincible. That I don't *need* you to protect me. Maybe you're finally realizing that *I'm* the one with the power."

His head snapped toward me, eyes burning with gold light. "*Power?*" The word cut through the air like a blade. "You think this is about who has more of it?" He took a step closer, and his wings flared wide enough to brush the walls. "You think I fear for myself?"

For a heartbeat, I saw it—his mask crack, the raw panic behind his fury. Then he looked away, feathers trembling as he forced them to lower. "I have fought Creators and beasts without flinching," he said, voice low, rough with restraint. "But watching you become something I cannot protect you from—" His jaw locked. "That terrifies me."

He turned sharply, half his face hidden behind a wing, the warrior's mask snapping back into place. "I will help protect the tribe," he said, his voice cold again. "But I will *not* help you kill yourself."

"Ahem."

I whirled around at the sound of someone clearing their throat behind me, the Creonex flashing gold around my hand. The *Matri Me'leiv* stood, hands clasped before her, a soft smile on her golden-lined face. "Am I interrupting?"

I opened my mouth to dismiss her, but Avenlae spoke over me. "No. The Queen and I are done."

Before I could respond, he had turned and leapt from the branch, gliding down to the entrance of the Queen's Nest. I watched him, trying to breathe evenly through the frustration that was making my muscles tense.

"His fear is warranted, My Queen," the *Matri Me'leiv* said, stepping forward to stand next to me, "Even without his own body, Sinivir is a very powerful Creator. He feels more deeply than his Brothers, and so you can feel him more strongly than yourself at times."

"How would you know that?" I asked tersely.

"You forget I have been alive millenia longer than you," she murmured, watching the movement of the Delfungaye below us as officials gathered to speak over preparations to place the Delfungaye tribes back into readiness for war.

I sighed. "And you don't look a day over 100 years."

"Being immortal has its perks."

I tried to smile. "Can the immortal part of you tell me if I'm doing the right thing? Is there some prophecy at play here with another decision I need to make?"

"Yes. And no." The elderly woman tilted her head at me, the beadwork in her hair tinkling. "Not all of my prophecies come to fruition in the way I expect them to. The currents are shifting in the universes and realms, My Queen. Something is building, changing over the last month. There is unrest, but I do not know from where."

"And what am I supposed to do with that information?" I asked, turning an exasperated look on her.

"Xiaye, I cannot tell you where to go from here," the *Matri Me'leiv* said, her eyes darting between mine, "The next several decisions must be your own. All I can tell you is that Creation will never be safe while the Creators still have a hand in the game. They care not for the feelings and survival of mortals. We are nothing more than entertainment for them, and, for now, they are *entertained.*"

She turned and moved down the branch, her wings dragging lightly behind her as she joined a *Laizuteek* and *Fyr'aeset* woman waiting far behind her, both dressed in traditional robes and beadwork. My eyes trailed after her as she left, and I really wanted nothing more than to fire off a little burst of energy at her. She spoke in riddles and expected me to decipher their ambiguity with complete accuracy. How was *I* supposed to extract a decision from her words? *Creation will never be safe...* Was I supposed to act now? Was I just supposed to prepare my people for their inevitable extinction?

Another stab of fury tore through my mind. I moved into my chambers, slamming the door and pacing as I tried to calm my emotions. And *was* it even mine? Was this really Sinivir and his hatred towards *me?* Towards the situation?

"Of all the times to be silent," I seethed, "you choose *now?*"

Sinivir made no response.

"Damn coward," I spat, my pacing growing more frantic. I craved release—I wanted to hit something, throw something else, and scream. I wanted to tear something apart, or maybe fight someone. Anything that would expel that racing, burning energy within me. I breathed deeper, my nostrils flaring, wings twitching. Someone needed to tell me what the hell to do. Someone needed to make sense of what was wrong with Avenlae, how much time we had to protect the Delfungaye tribes, how to destroy Mors, and how to separate myself from Sinivir. I wanted my own mind back. I wanted to be able to control my ***own*** emotions.

These are ***your emotions, Creovis,*** Sinivir whispered, his voice echoing in the room.

"No, they're yours," I snapped. "Control yourself."

You and I are almost synonymous now, he said, ***and you have taught yourself how to feel more vividly than any other creature.***

"No, this is ***your*** anger!" I shouted, pulling at the beads of my dress so fiercely that the thread broke, spraying aquamarine beads across the wooden floor. "You keep giving me your hatred and rage!"

Spiteful little thing, aren't we? Sinivir said mockingly.

"***You*** are!" I shrieked, ripping again at my dress. I couldn't control it anymore—the ***fury,*** the pure indignation burning through my thoughts. "It's all ***you!*** You and your—your arrogance, your pitiful jealousy, your endless, meaningless fight for a vengeance that's not even mine!"

LOOK, CREOVIS! Sinivir roared, using his power to whip my head around to face the mirror across the room.

My reflection… wasn't mine.

There stood a creature draped in tattered white rags that dripped shattered aquamarine beads. Its skin, a ghastly, pallid grey, starkly contrasted with the glowing crimson red of its eyes, which burned with a deep-seated malice. Down its shoulders and back was hair as red as freshly spilled blood, falling against wings that blazed with magenta flames.

WE are vengeance.

A primal scream tore from my throat as I hurled myself to the floor, scrambling away from the mirror. I buried my face in my hands, icy terror coursing through my veins. My muscles began to tremble as I pressed my palms into my cheeks, gulping air in ragged, panicked breaths, the horrifying reflection burned into my eyelids. *It's just a trick,* I tried to tell myself, *it's just one of his tricks. It's not real.*

Gradually, with several more deep breaths, I moved a finger. The mirror still stood before me, reflecting nothing more than the simple Queen's chambers. My hands shook as I set them on the floor, pulling myself forward, crawling, terrified to stand, for what would I see? My gasps became quiet sobs as I neared the mirror, and cool tears fell from my cheeks. *What will I see, what will I see, what will I see...*

And then she was there. One silver eye, one red. Dark hair fell in messy, wavy tendrils where the braids had fallen out. Feathered wings that fell in a black-to-white gradient folded tightly behind her. And tears blotched her fair cheeks red.

I pressed a hand to my reflection, watching my face contort as I cried harder. Big, ugly, painful sobs ripped themselves from my chest as I curled up against that mirror, hugging myself, rocking back and forth on the hard floor, wondering what I had **become.**

I gasped, startled awake by something. It wasn't a sound, a touch, a light. I was just awake. Then I was in pain. I had somehow fallen asleep, still curled against the mirror, and my body ached from being crumpled against the wooden floor. I hissed out through my teeth as I pushed myself upright, moving my limbs to work out the stiffness in my joints as my head throbbed from behind my eyelids and through my ears. Was that what had woken me, then? Just pain? ***Nothing new.***

I sighed, pushing myself off the floor. A few tattered pieces of my dress fell from my chest and hips as I shuffled over to the bed. Seeing the empty, still-made covers set forth a dull ache in my chest that I tried to ignore as I pulled my torn dress off my body and found a light ***Fyr'aeset*** wrap to put on. It wasn't bright, just a soft, simple grey. I frowned as I began to pull it on, a dull ache racing down my right arm. Odd, but I figured I had slept in an awkward position. ***That's what you get for throwing a tantrum,*** I scolded myself, moving back towards the bed as I spun my arms in wide circles, trying to loosen up my muscles.

Pain shot down my leg. I stumbled, barely catching myself on the bed. Breathing through the pain, I looked down, trying to find what I had mistakenly run into in the dark of the room. But there was nothing there. The skirt of the ***Fyr'aeset*** wrap fell only partway down my thighs, and there was no cut or bruise on my skin to blame for the pain. I stared at my leg as the pain ebbed away, suddenly *very* awake.

Then Sinivir spoke one word, a word that sent a shiver of fear down my spine. ***Avenlae.***

I didn't even bother changing. I ripped my rapiers down from where their scabbards hung, strapping them over my nearly see-through wrap as I burst out the French doors of my chambers. The night was clear and bright with the small blue moon and stars shining down onto the forest, as if nothing had happened mere hours before.

I stepped onto the balcony, closing my eyes as I breathed in the scent of the night. Turning my power inward, I searched out the ***lyceliah*** in my mind. At the forefront was the golden cord that kept Avenlae and me connected, and through it, I could feel his pain and exertion. He was fighting; he must have been. ***Come to me, Brother, and end this.***

241

"No, no, no," I whimpered, focusing my power on that cord. The other Creators **knew** Avenlae was my weakness. They **knew** they could use him to get to me, and now...

A golden trail shot out of my chest, diving into the trees in the direction of the training clearing behind the Queen's Nest. I leapt into the air, beating my wings and directing my power into the Creonex, preparing for a fight. Leaves and small branches cut into my cheeks as I dove through the canopy, too frantic to slow my descent. Another pulse of pain exploded across my ribs, and I whimpered again, pushing my wings until they burned. **Just get to him, just get to him.**

I finally landed a few feet from the clearing, unsheathing my rapiers and moving towards the treeline. Whatever Avenlae was up against, I would need any advantage I could get. I moved to a small break in the underbrush, folding my wings tighter against my spine so as not to give away my position. Small twigs and rocks sliced into my bare feet, but I ignored the pain. I didn't have time to feel it. Pushing up the branch of a juvenile tree, I peered into the clearing, my muscles tense. Avenlae was there, whirling around, wings spread and rapiers out. But it wasn't a Creator he was fighting.

It was Darinrain.

And they weren't **fighting**—they were sparring, both bare-chested and with sweat glistening on their skin. But how was Darinrain landing any hits on Avenlae? He was notorious in the Guard for being the one warrior nobody sparred with because they couldn't land a hit. No one could win against him, least of all Darinrain, who enjoyed the fight too much.

Within a minute of me watching them, I got my answer. Avenlae had landed on the ground after fending off a complicated attack pattern from Darinrain's staff, and had just moved in for his own attack when something appeared to choke him. He dropped one of his swords, hacking, his face twisted in pain as he grabbed for his throat. The coughs made him double over, strong enough that I could see his muscles convulse over his ribs and stomach.

Darinrain lowered his staff and moved closer to Avenlae, holding a hand out, but careful not to touch him. "My King?"

Avenlae took in a few ragged breaths as the coughing calmed and spat a glob of blood onto the ground. He stayed bent over for a moment longer, just breathing as another drop of blood fell from his lips.

Darinrain backed away and picked up a crystal bottle of water, handing it out to Avenlae. "We should leave it here, My King. You need rest."

"That is the longest I have lasted," Avenlae said, his voice hoarse, "but it is not good enough. I have to keep working."

"Your Highness, you have done enough for tonight. Your body still cannot keep up—"

"Well, it **has** to!" Avenlae snapped, clicking the claws of his wings together over his head. Darinrain dropped his head down, exposing his neck and lowering his wings so that their feathers parted the grass at his feet.

I was about to step forward to diffuse the situation when I felt something wrap around my wrist. I gasped and ducked down, turning with a rapier raised across my face. Vindicta stood behind me, half of her face concealed in shadow.

Leave them be, she said calmly, dropping her tentacle from around my arm. I frowned at her, but stayed quiet and turned back towards the clearing. Avenlae was standing and had taken a drink out of the bottle, but his chest still rose and fell in shuddering breaths. Darinrain stayed still, his eyes on the ground and his wings as low as he could hold them. Avenlae moved the bottle around in his hand, sinking the blade of one of his rapiers into the dirt. "I… I have to protect her," he said softly.

"We all do," Darinrain said, daring to raise his head slightly, as if trying

243

to check Avenlae's stance. "You, too, have to be reminded that you are not fighting this fight alone."

They remained quiet for a moment. "You... you fight without fear, Dairnrain."

"I am a Delfungaye warrior, and I serve my Queen and King. There is no room for fear."

"But in Creo..." Avenlae faltered, looking around as if he were searching for words. "In Bellum's Colosseum, you knew what we had to do to fight back. You knew how to beat him in his own game. How... how do you fight without fear?"

Darinrain lifted his head. His eyes met Avenlae's. And Avenlae **let him.** He allowed Darinrain to hold his gaze. "My King, how would you fight in the Realm of Creo **without** fear?"

"Do you not?"

Darirain tilted his head, a soft smile on his lips. "In the Queen's Guard, I watched all of my friends die during Creation's War. So I stopped taking anything, including my own life, seriously, or becoming friends with anyone. What did it matter? Everyone was going to die in the end."

"But you did not."

"No. And neither did you, Xiaye, Notien, or Saetyl." Darinrain averted his gaze, his voice heavy. "I have known the four of you longer than anyone else in my life. I was **terrified** when we entered the Realm of Creo. Terrified that the pain of losing any of you would be more than I would be able to cope with after all this time. But that meant I had to do whatever it took to ensure we would all survive." He bent down and retrieved the rapier Avenlae had dropped, handing the hilt out to him. **"Use** your fear, My King. You, who have lived through so much, have everything to draw from. If you want to protect our Queen, use your fear."

244

Avenlae took the hilt, holding eye contact with Dainrain for a moment longer before the other man averted his gaze. Avenlae would never look away first, but the fact that he even **allowed** Darinrain to look him in the eye at all was almost more shocking than realizing before that it was Avenlae's pain I was feeling. I ducked back behind the underbrush and turned back to Vindicta, a question in my mind that I didn't even need to voice.

They have been training here whenever they've had a chance since we arrived back from Creo, she said, staying in the shadows, *usually at night. Avenlae made sure Darinrain and I wouldn't tell you, for he worried that, if you knew how hard it had become for him to fight, you wouldn't allow him back into Creo if you went to continue the mission.*

"But I felt his pain. How have I not felt it before?" I whispered.

She held up a few tentacles.

"*You?* You've kept me asleep?"

I can block the lyceliah for some time. It takes a lot of energy to do so, but disobeying Avenlae also wasn't an option.

I shook my head at her. "I can't even be angry with you because I know you're right."

She tilted her head as if she were shrugging.

I glanced back over to where Avenlae had forced Darinrain into another round of sparring. "I can't let him back into Creo. You knew that when he asked you to keep this a secret from me."

I did, Vindicta said, her voice sounding tired in my mind, *and yet, I couldn't dishonor him to tell him there was no point in training. There is permanent damage done from that muzzle Bellum put on him. Sinivir kept him alive, but there are some things you just can't heal when a mortal's throat is ripped out.*

245

"How long is he able to last before another attack?" I asked.

Much longer now than before. I believe he's gotten to about five minutes now. But this is just sparring—we don't know what a real fight would be like. And he needs much more time than we have to rehabilitate himself back to being close to where he was before.

I watched Darinrain and Avenlae spar for a little longer, knowing that Darinrain was holding back as they fought. He could see as well as I could how tired Avenlae's body was.

"You know what I must ask of you," I said to Vindicta.

She clicked softly, moving her snout forward to nuzzle under my hand so I could lean on her as a tear rolled down my cheek. *I have known since the first night I had to block the lyceliah. He is mine to protect, My Queen.*

CHAPTER 23

I t was truly a miracle that the coffee bean survived Creation's War.

How an ancient plant and drink had lasted so long was a complete mystery to everyone, but as the suns rose over the horizon, I held my cup of coffee tighter to my chest, relishing in the peace the taste brought me. I was alone on one of the very top branches of the Queen's nest, still dressed in my *Fyr'aeset* wrap, my hair a tangled, wavy mess falling over my shoulders and down my back. And I chose, for once, not to care. I needed a moment to myself to sit and not care about the world around me. I needed peace and clarity.

So, I needed coffee.

Avenlae had come back to bed later in the night, just a few hours before the suns began to rise. I feigned sleep, remembering the promise I made to Vindicta that I wouldn't let on that I knew about his secret. That meant, however, that I crept out of bed as soon as the suns brightened to room enough for the night-vision grayscale to fade from my eyesight. I didn't know what to say to him. There was this tension between us, the strained memory of what I had said the night before, and the fact that I knew how much our last venture into the Realm of Creo had weakened him. I wanted to find a way to **make** him stay on Silvacastra, but I knew there was nothing I could do to change his mind. Nothing I said was going to be significant enough for him to abandon his mate when he knew where I was going. Which was why I was alone, watching the suns rising, plotting ways to distance myself from Avenlae so I wouldn't have to figure out how **not** to tell him to never set foot near a Creator for the rest of our lives.

The leaves rustled behind me, and I turned, lowering a hand to the hilt of a knife hidden at my hip. In seconds, Notien pulled herself onto the branch next to me, also dressed in a *Fyr'aeset* wrap.

"I told you you would grow to love these," she said, pinching the material of my skirt.

"That you did, and then Darinrain brought me more," I said, taking another sip of my coffee. "Where is Saetyl at this early hour?"

"Oiling her wings," Notien sighed as she moved to sit next to me. "Never thought I would say that to you. 'My mate is off oiling her wings.'"

I chuckled with her, lowering my cup to rest on my lap. We stared off into the suns' rise for a moment, allowing the morning breeze to move through our feathers, and the warmth of the suns to soak into our cheeks.

"Everything has changed," Notien said quietly.

"I know," I responded, my chest tightening. "And it won't... it won't go back."

Notien nodded, her blonde hair seeming to glow in the early morning light. "I want it to. However, sometimes I find myself wanting everything to move forward faster, to push us past this time. So we can look back when we are on the other side, in awe of how we got there."

"We did that before, didn't we? At the end of Creation's War?"

"We did. When I hugged you, crying for all those we had lost along the way, crying that you were still alive, and you were going to spare Saetyl. It is so… wrong that we are back here, again. Back in the middle of it, wondering what the world will be like in the end."

I lowered my eyes, staring into the steam that rose from my cup as my thumb traced its edge. Memories of those days returned. The memory of meeting Notien and Darinrain, fighting Saetyl, all of the training, all of the fear. And back even further was the loneliness of Earth, of having no one. "I think," I breathed, "I just wanted… a family that survived. I wanted to know people who *lived.*"

"You built a family, did you not, Xiaye?" Notien replied, turning her round, navy eyes on me. "Our little team. And any one of us would be dead without you."

I raised an eyebrow.

"I speak the truth! It is only because of you that any of Creation survived Sinivir's attack. Even if *I* do not want to admit it."

"I deserve that," I said, rolling my eyes.

"As long as you agree," Notien chuckled. "But still we survive. Much different than before, but we are all alive. You know people who lived because *you* made it so, Xiaye."

"Then what…" I started, pausing for a moment as I felt my throat tighten. "What happens when I make the wrong choice? If everyone has survived because of me, what happens when—"

"Stop," Notien snapped, but her eyes were still soft and kind. "Do not speak like that. I, I have been unfair to you, after Saetyl lost her wings. I put my anger on you. But, beneath the pain, I never stopped trusting you, Xiaye. And you cannot lose trust in yourself."

"Everything I've done… has been for you. For all of you."

Notien tilted her head slightly, a soft smile on her rosebud lips. "I know, Xiaye. It is why I cannot stay angry with you. *You* love so deeply."

I leaned over, resting my head on her shoulder. "You should stay angry with me. Even so, I'm so grateful to have you back."

Soft pressure spread over the top of my head as Notien leaned her head onto mine. "I know."

We should have stayed there. We should have stayed on that branch to watch as the suns rose to their full height, as the colors of the forest grew more vibrant and the air warmed. *We should have stayed.*

But the branch shuddered beneath us as Vindicta hauled herself through the leaves, clicking frantically as her frill vibrated, opening and closing over and over.

"What is it?" I asked, wings twitching as I moved my feet under me.

They're here.

"Who? Who's here?"

Sloviyankae.

"What? Why?" Notien looked around as if she would be able to see *Sloviyankae* crawling up the branches beneath us.

Inquiri's hive is bringing the survivors. They just crossed the northern border.

"Survivors?" I gasped. "Vindicta, *what* has happened?"

Come quickly, she hissed, her head darting around, intercepting transmissions from both her hive and the other Queen, Inquiri, of the hive near the *Fae'oteek* mountains. Then she dove back into the tree, slithering down its branches and into the undergrowth.

"Get Saetyl and Kaigar," I said to Notien, flinging away my cup. *I'll get a new one, anyway.* "I'll wake Avenlae and meet you in front of the Queen's Nest."

250

Notien gave a single, decisive nod before leaping into the air, her massive onyx wings helping her to glide far into the trees. Dropping through the canopy, I glided down to the balcony jutting out from Avenlae and I's chambers, wind rushing through my tousled hair as I landed on the wood planks. I flung the French doors open, my eyes landing immediately on where my new armor hung, having been delivered from the *Glae'atii* just that morning.

"Get up," I called to Avenlae as he stirred groggily in our bed, "we've got company."

He sat up, blinking a few times before realizing I was taking down my armor. "What is happening?"

"Vindicta said the *Sloviyankae* are here, just past the northern border. Except she called them survivors." I turned to him after pulling on the top half of the matte black, form-fitting armor, its crimson details burning in the golden suns' light. My armorer had added more accolades along the chest and shoulders of the armor, detailing the story of Creation's war. "She won't tell me more. She's too distressed."

Avenlae bolted out of bed, moving to the rack next to me where his armor hung, all silver and gold shining, with insignias of the *Y'araye* and Delfungaye royalty intertwined along the chest and back. "Do you think it is a sign?"

"I think it's a message," I said, starting to place sleek knives in the sheaths up and down my legs. Avenlae had his armor in place in just a few smooth, practiced minutes and had twisted my hair into a simple braid a moment later. His hair fell loose and straight around his shoulders and down his spine, a testament to how deadly and powerful a warrior he was, as he needed no extra adornment. With our rapiers strapped across our backs, we made our way out the front of the Queen's Nest. The morning air had become crisp with anxiety as we approached where the rest of our team waited, watching as a concerned General hovered before them.

"There is only one reason the *Sloviyankae* would come here unannounced," Kaigar said as we hovered around him. "Something has happened to their queen."

"Vindicta reported that Inquiri was bringing us survivors," I said, looking off into the trees in front of us, watching for the tell-tale swaying of branches that would signal the approach of the Voxmor hive.

"I alerted the Healers," Notien said, her hand on the hilt of her scimitar at her hip, "they are ready to take in the injured if there are any."

"Vindicta's hive is preparing to either fully or partially absorb Inquiri's," Saetyl said, her gleaming metal wings silent as they sliced through the air, "depending on how many there are."

"What?" My head whipped around to Saetyl, even as the trees began to sway before us. "What do you mean? We know the count of the Inquiri Hive."

"Not anymore," Darinrain murmured, watching as the first Voxmor appeared in the branches, several *Sloviyankae* hanging from its back.

Within moments, the trees at the heart of the tribe came alive as Voxmor, accompanied by *Sloviyankae* Riders, ascended from the undergrowth, causing the trunks to swirl with the pale-scaled bodies slithering up. Many Voxmor split off from the mass to offload their injured at the Healer's Nest, clicking and shrieking to communicate as their ranks reformed.

"There are so many," I said, my voice empty. The *Sloviyankae* being taken into the Healer's Nest had entire limbs and sections of their bodies that were... **mummified.** They were just dry, grey husks of tissue, as if all the color and life had been sucked out of them.

"I will go," Notien said, placing a gentle hand on my arm before she dove down to assist the Healers and take count of how many *Sloviyankae* were to be kept within the Nest. Clicking drew my attention back to the crowd before me. Vindicta was perched upon a branch that jutted out in the middle of the hive members, and from her back slid Havyeque, his slender ears twitching at all the sounds around him. Darinrain and I descended to meet him on the branch, and the movement of the tribe and hive stilled.

"What's happened? Where's Queen Klaecyia?" I asked.

Havyeque looked between Darinrain and me, almost panting, as if he couldn't figure out what to say or do. "Sh-she… she is dead."

My eyes widened, and I felt as if I'd been punched in the stomach. "H-how?"

Havyeque lowered his head, staring off into the underbrush. "Death."

I glanced over at Darinrain, who shook his head and said softly, "We should get you to the Healers."

"Y-you do not understand!" Havyeque cried suddenly, darting forward and wrapping long fingers around Darinrain's arm. "It was her! Death. *Fae'yeerium.*" His eyes moved over to me, and he spoke as if pleading for me to believe him. "She came to us in the flesh. H-her claws, they opened… the smoke came. It swallowed ***everything.*** Left behind ***nothing.*** The Queen ordered that I-I flee. That there should be someone who survives who can take c-care of our-our people." Again, Havyeque's eyes unfocused, as if he was watching his memory play out in front of him. "We took the ***gueirags*** as far as we could, those of us who escaped the smoke. The smoke had already flushed out the Inquiri Hive, and there were barely enough to take us the rest of the way here."

Less than half of Inquiri's hive remains, Vindicta said, bowing her head. ***They will be absorbed into my hive.***

"And Inquiri? Did she survive?" I asked.

She does for now.

"For now?" I turned to Darinrain, but he looked just as confused as I did.

253

Two queens cannot inhabit the same hive. Once her hive is fully absorbed by mine, Inquiri will die.

I shook my head. "Y-you can't just kill her—"

You do not understand, Vindicta clicked, *it is the way of our species. It is her choice to do this. When she knows her hive is safe, her connection to them will be severed, and she will pass peacefully.*

I stared at Vindicta, wondering how many times she had to do something like this in the past.

"My Queen," Kaigar said behind me. I took a breath before facing him. "What are we to do with the *Sloviyankae* survivors?"

"H-Havyeque," I said, trying to steady my voice, "who leads your people now?"

He raised his head, white tendrils of hair coming loose from his braids. "Me. I am the only one who survives in the Queen's inner circle."

I gazed at Havyeque for a while, struck with the urge to hug him. He looked so frightened and lost, his coal eyes wide with a mix of fear and confusion. The magnitude of this tragedy was unlike anything the *Sloviyankae* had ever experienced. They had been spared the full extent of the horrors of Creation's War that had ravaged the rest of the Delfungaye. But now this war, the fight between the Creators and me, had taken almost everything from them within a few hours. The devastation hung in the air, suffocating, as if the very atmosphere was heavy with despair.

"They will be given sanctuary for as long as they need," Avenlae said, his hoarse voice still commanding. "I trust you and Saetyl will be able to oversee the integration of the refugees."

"Yes, My King," I heard Kaigar say. A gust of air blew past me, the rustle of wings and whine of mechanical parts. "We should have told them."

"I *know,* Kaigar," I growled. "I don't need you to scold me—"

"I said *'we',* Xiaye." Kaigar sighed. "We should have warned everyone before this. I am not innocent—I knew, and I said nothing."

Glancing back as Kaigar left, I caught Saetyl's golden eyes before she followed the General. They held fear, but also a fiery resolve. She knew. I knew. *Everyone* knew.

This had been a warning.

The Voxmor were absent from the tribe for the day and into the evening while they performed the ritual to absorb the Inquiri Hive, and observe the passing of their Queen. The surviving *Sloviyankae* and multitudes of *Laizuteek* began to set up walkways throughout the tribe to ensure the refugees could travel as needed. Avenlae called in the outer *Fyr'aeset* and *Hopyroque* tribes that had separated off into their territories at the end of Creation's War. As far as either of us was concerned, the entirety of the Delfungaye was now at risk.

The Queen's and Night Guards convened with Saetyl and Kaigar in the evening as the other tribes arrived, reorganizing units with the added numbers of warriors. This was, fortunately, a simple task, for the warriors from each tribe had already fought and trained together almost six years previously. Yet their excitement over being reunited was short-lived—they all knew the reforming of the Delfungaye Guard meant the species was once again under attack.

Darinrain led Havyeque to the Queen's Nest and spent most of the day setting him up in a room and just sitting with him, talking over what had happened and calming the other man down as best he could. I didn't blame Havyeque for his fear. I'd been shoved into the role of Queen of the Delfungaye just as suddenly, and the fear during that time had been staggering. And after having just watched so many of his people have the very life sucked out of their bodies... I couldn't fathom his horror.

Notien came to me at the Queen's Nest as the suns were beginning their descent, and the forest started to fill with a soft golden glow. "The wounded are being treated to the best of our ability," she said, rubbing her palms up and down her bare arms. She had changed into the harem pants and cream wrap of the *Fyr'aeset* soon after assisting the Healers, as her armor was no longer needed. "Many of them are going to lose their limbs."

I shook my head, watching several **Sloviyanke** climb nimbly across branches and walkways. "Can they be replaced with prosthetics?"

Notien shrugged. "I do not know yet. The Healers will have to create prosthetics specific to the **Sloviyankae,** as they are just different enough as a species that we cannot use the ones they make for our tribes."

"They'll have to work quickly to make those prosthetics," I replied with a sigh. "The **Sloviyankae** rely on their limbs so much more than we do. If it were just wings, it'd be different. But their wings are used to climb just as much as their arms and legs. They depend on them—"

"Xiaye." Notien stepped forward, putting her hands on my shoulders. "We will help them. The fact that they are alive and have somewhere to stay is enough for now."

"But **none** of them would be in this situation if I'd never gone to Creo," I whispered.

"No, they would not. Because, instead, they, and we, would all be dead," came Darinrain's voice behind us. The brush of his wings across the wooden floor of the balcony moved closer until he stood on my other side.

"He is right, you know," Notien said, rubbing her hand across my upper back. "After seeing Mors, how he spoke to you, how he treated us… We had to do something to scare him and stop the other Creators." She turned my head so I had to look her in the eye. "In many ways, I have no right to say this, for I spent so much time trying to doubt you and blame you for all that has happened. But you have done what has needed to be done. You have done what no queen before you would have the courage to do. And you will see the end of this. I will do whatever I can to see the end of it, too."

She gave me a soft smile before moving away to leap from the balcony, soaring to where Saetyl had just appeared from the meeting place of the Guard. Darinrain stayed next to me, quietly watching the two of them glide towards a tree that housed a small *anteel* tea shop within its branches.

No more waiting, Creovis, Sinivir hissed in the back of my mind, his Essence coiling around my thoughts after he'd stayed quiet for so long. *The next time Mors enters this universe, it will be to destroy it.*

"Why?" I asked out loud, forgetting that Darinrain was still next to me.

Why? I would think you could remember what he told you the first time—

"No, why didn't he destroy us already? Why isn't he here now?"

Remember his words, little Creovis. "I may no longer have my Creonex." Without it, travel into the universes is restricted, and using his power while leaving his Essence in the Realm of Creo takes much more energy and strength.

"What has Sinivir told you?" Darinrain asked, touching a finger to my wrist as a calm reminder that he was there.

I shot a glance at him, my eyes flicking away almost immediately as I tried to shove the presence of Sinivir into the recesses of my mind. But I couldn't deny his words. Not when I knew their truth the very second Havyeque had told us *who* had attacked the *Sloviyankae.* "We have to go back, now."

257

"Go back?"

"To the Realm of Creo." I turned to face him, clenching my jaw to fight back tears. "But I can't take all of you with me."

Darinrain gave me an exasperated look. "My Queen, everyone has already told you they are aware of the risk—"

"Yeah, and so am I!" The words came out too sharp, too fast. "Everyone keeps saying they understand what they're walking into, but none of you listen when I say I'm the one leading you there. Saetyl still needs more time to adjust to her new wings, and Avenlae—" I bit back the tremor in my voice. "Avenlae isn't fighting like he used to."

Darinrain closed his eyes. "I told him Vindicta would not keep a secret from you for long."

"She only told me *after* I had already seen you two sparring together."

His navy eyes popped open as he looked down at me. "Well. You know, there was one night when I forgot to tell her we were training, so, assuming that is the night you witnessed, you cannot be *that* upset with me because, technically, *I* am the one who made sure you would find out."

I shot him a look that should have singed the feathers off his wings.

Darinrain gave a low laugh that didn't quite reach his eyes. "My King is stronger than you think, Your Majesty. His body remembers pain, yes—but his pride heals faster than his wounds. He has made progress since we returned to Silvacastra."

I folded my arms, trying to look composed, though the truth was simpler: I didn't know how to stop being afraid of losing control.

"If it makes you feel better, My Queen," Darinrain added quietly, "I'll take responsibility for his life when we return to Creo."

"No," I said quickly, "that is not your job."

"Whose is it?"

"Avenlae's. He would never allow you to protect him."

"He does not *have* to know."

I raised an eyebrow.

Darinrain grinned down at me. "He has raised the same eyebrow at me before! Does that mean, then, perhaps we are friends?"

"Avenlae doesn't have friends."

"Ah, well. He has me whether or not he likes it." Darinrian shrugged. When I didn't answer, he touched a hand to my arm. "So do you, Xiaye."

"I know. You *are* my friend, Darinrain." I looked back out over the tribe, the firelight from the nests growing brighter as the sky above us darkened. "Damnit. It's not really my choice, is it? Whether or not any of you return to Creo with me?"

"No, My Queen. It never really was."

"You'll help protect Saetyl then, won't you?"

"If that is what you ask of me."

"Yes. I'll take care of Avenlae if you and Notien help Saetyl. No matter what happens." My voice cracked, and I raised a hand to my throat as my eyes welled with tears, as if my fingers alone could steady my voice. "We have to protect them."

I felt gentle, strong arms wrap around me, and then Darinrain's chin on my head. "We will, Xiaye. No matter what happens."

More tears slid down my cheeks as Darinrain hugged me. It wasn't a tender embrace, but rather one of support and strength. It felt as if he were attempting to bear my burden if only for one moment.

Then came a sting of pain through the *lyceliah.* I turned my head just in time to see a flash of silver feathers as they moved out of the doorway back into the Queen's Nest behind us. Avenlae had seen. And he had walked away.

259

CHAPTER 24

Apprehension gripped me as I stood outside my own bedroom door, unsure whether to push it open. Avenlae was in there — I could hear the sound of him sharpening the blades of his rapiers. But there was something else, a strange emotion swelling within me. It was something I was feeling through the *lyceliah*, as if it was generating a force field, compelling me to stay away.

It had been decided moments before that my team and I would travel to the Realm of Creo once more in the morning. We all knew we had to complete the mission, whether we wanted to or not. Yet, as I stood there, staring at the silver vines that snaked their way up the door, the prospect of entering my own chambers felt as daunting as entering the Realm of Creo without any idea what awaited us.

You are stalling over something so trivial, Sinivir scoffed. *Mortal woes have always seemed so ridiculous.*

"I'm not mortal," I hissed, balling my hands into fists. "You wouldn't understand. You don't feel."

Silence met my retort. In fact, the shadows of Sinivir's Essence

seemed to retreat, as if hiding themselves further back into my mind, where *I* couldn't reach *him.*

I didn't know if I enjoyed or hated the solitude when I hadn't been the one to choose it.

One last silent second, and then I pushed open the door. Soft firelight flickered across the room from the fireplace, bathing our chambers in the ambience of reverie. Avenlae didn't bother to look up from where he worked on his rapier, his second laying to the side, already gleaming. His armor hung close to the door, and he was dressed in a black tunic of almost sheer material. The scar up his sternum and across his face stood stark against the deepening shadows of the tattoos that raced across his skin, their designs broken periodically by new scars from Bellum's Colosseum.

Wordlessly, I removed my armor, my eyes darting across the walls and furniture as I searched for the right way to approach him. My skin tingled as it was exposed to the open air, and I lowered my wings around myself as I moved to the wardrobe to find a small satin romper. Something easy to get into and out of. *What do I say? Nothing? Is he angry? Hurt?*

"Your silence is nearly deafening, Xiaye."

I let out a puff of breath, adjusting the straps of the romper over my shoulders. I turned, and his glowing moonlight eyes were on me. Avenlae had set his rapier aside next to the second, both of their blades shining and deadly. His muscles were tense as he stayed where he was, the air thickening around him.

"So is yours," I said softly.

"What is the meaning of it?"

"I could ask you the same."

His eyes narrowed. "I could die tomorrow. But you will not. So why do you choose not to speak to me?"

"Perhaps because you have murder in your eyes."

He did nothing but continue to stare.

I sighed. "Or maybe because I *know* you have multiple reasons to be angry with me. And since we're returning to Creo tomorrow, I don't want to spend tonight arguing."

Avenlae tilted his head to the side. "Then perhaps you should leave."

I frowned, taking a step back, trying to hide the pain that was growing in my chest.

"You made it very clear before that you do not need me. I saw you tonight. With him. You do not want me either now, do you?"

"Av, that was nothing —"

"*Do not* lie to me, Xiaye," Avenlae growled, standing. "You owe me more than that."

"I'm not lying," I snapped, moving towards him as the heat of anger raced through my mind. "Darinrain is my *friend.* You know that. Be angry with me for things I've said, not lies you've told yourself."

His eyes darted between mine as his chest rose and fell. I could see the primal anger in him, in the way he breathed, the way his muscles nearly trembled. *This is instinct,* I told myself, trying to hold my ground. The Creonex warmed around my hand, prepared for defense.

A few more tense moments, and then Avenlae looked away, his wings folding close to his spine as his ears pressed against his hair. "I know," he whispered.

"What?"

"I *know,* Xai." The exasperation in his voice cracked. "As much as I want to fight the man, I… I know Darinrain is no threat."

I threw my hands up. "Then what is going on with you? Why are you acting like this?"

262

"Because *I* should have been there for you," Avenlae said, turning pained silver eyes back on me. "You should have felt safe enough to come to me. Instead, you scolded me for being *afraid.* You are not looking for strength in me — you are seeking an outlet for your anger while finding comfort in others. When did I become that to you?"

My throat tightened the longer I stared at him, unsure if I wanted to hug or hit him. I didn't even know if I wanted to kiss away the hurt and fear in his eyes, or if I wanted him to *feel* it as viscerally as I did. "N-no, Av," I stuttered, moving close enough that I could almost feel the beat of his heart through the thin fabric of his tunic. "Y-you're so much more than that to me. You know that."

"Xai."

His gaze felt like it could paralyze me. **Speak, damnit. For once, just talk.** "I... I took you to Creo. You only went because of me. You a-and everyone else. And now you've changed. You look different, you sound different. Your nightmares have changed. You wake up screaming in absolute terror, not anger." The longer I talked, the quieter my voice became as tears dripped down my cheeks, flowing down my neck and across my chest. "Saetyl's lost her wings, and I nearly lost Notien. And I know you've noticed Darinrain trying to hold everyone together, horrified that he'll lose all of us. I **took** you there. I took **all** of you there! But you all **refuse** to stay here; here it's safe. None of you will let me protect you. And you're the only one capable of understanding how all of this feels!"

Avenlae said nothing at first. He only watched me — watched the way my shoulders trembled, the way my tears hit the floor like ash. The silence stretched, heavy but not cold, until he moved closer.

When he reached for me, his hands shook faintly, though his touch was careful — reverent. His callused fingers brushed away the tears as if afraid to hurt me. "These wars have changed all of us," he said quietly. His voice had softened, the growl gone. "Whether we fought for you, for the Delfungaye, or for Novissime, none of us were going to be the same as we were before Sinivir."

He hesitated, and then pressed his lips to my forehead, a slow, uncertain kiss that lingered like a promise. "You need to stop carrying what isn't yours to carry, Xiaye," he whispered against my skin. "You keep trying to hold us all together, but we chose this. We chose you. You don't owe us the weight of our own pain."

My breath hitched. "I just... I just want to protect everyone."

"I know," he murmured. His arms came around me then, pulling me gently into his chest. The steady rhythm of his heartbeat was a quiet anchor, his wings folding around me like a shield. "But you can't save everyone, Xai. Not in war. All you can do is keep fighting, and let the ones who love you fight beside you."

For a moment, I let myself melt against him. The smell of metal and smoke on his skin, the rough warmth of his hands in my hair, the quiet certainty in his words — they pulled me back from the edge of breaking.

When I finally spoke again, it was barely a whisper. "We still have to go to Creo in the morning."

Avenlae exhaled slowly, brushing a final tear from my jaw with his thumb. "Then we will go," he said softly. "Together."

***

The golden light of suns' rise was so treacherously bright. For the first time in my life, I wanted night to fall again. I wanted the entire world to be sunk into darkness, because that would mean the morning would never come, and the time to return to Creo would always stay just out of reach. I had kept so close to Avenlae that night, but I couldn't even bring myself to hug him before we were dressing in our armor and sheathing our rapiers across our backs. To have then embraced him would've felt as if I were trying to say goodbye, and I couldn't face it. I *wasn't* going to say goodbye to any of them. Not Avenlae, Saetyl, Notien, Darinrain, or Vindicta. I was *going* to bring them home, just as I had before.

And we weren't returning to Silvacastra until the Creators were destroyed. We were finishing it.

But first, I was going to tell our people the truth. I was going to find it within myself to tell them *everything.*

Kaigar had been quick to spread the word that the Queen would be addressing her people the very second I told him. He didn't even ask me what I was going to say to them. He expected me to tell them every damn painful detail. And now I stood before them all, armor in place, rapiers crossed behind my back. A queen dressed as a warrior for the first time in almost six years. Yet, the forest was completely silent. Not even a breeze dared to rustle the leaves. Silvacastra was waiting. Would I speak, or would I lie?

Eyes darted to Avenlae next to me, and craned to see Saetyl, Notien, Darinrain, and Vindicta flanked behind us. Time to see if all the rumors were true, if reality was better or worse than what the gossipers had made up in their minds.

I'd stood before the Delfungaye like this once before, once when Creation's War felt bleak, and Death seemed inevitable. Once when I had been forced to take over rule of a civilization I barely knew, after the death of the only person who could teach me. I had spoken to them then. But why did it feel so much harder to open my mouth now? Why was it, when I looked out among the golden, navy, silver, and black eyes that stared up at me, at the copper, golden, and white hands wringing, holding weapons, brushing absentmindedly against throats and cheeks—*why* couldn't I talk?

The air felt heavy in my chest as I took another breath, stepping

265

forward, away from my team. *Tell them.* Guilt dried my tongue the second I opened my mouth. "It's no secret, now, what we all saw a few nights ago, and what happened to the *Sloviyankae.*"

"It never should have *been* a secret!" Someone yelled, earning a growl from Avenlae. Several people shifted, their feathers lifting slightly. They wouldn't say anything in agreement, not with their King watching, but their body langauge told me enough.

I swallowed, trying to regain some composure. "No, it shouldn't have. I should have come to you all in the beginning. I should have warned of the dangers we now face as soon as I became aware of them. But a fight such as what we're in now... How could I have told you? Barely half a decade after Creation's War, how was I supposed to tell any of you that the threat became *four* Creators?"

Another silence fell over the forest, but this one wasn't complete. Soft whispers slithered through the crowd as they shifted again, the tension becoming increasingly unstable. But it wasn't fear: it was anger.

"The Fifth Creator's Brothers seek to finish the job he began. Two have already been destroyed, and my team and I must leave again to face the final two."

Whispers became murmurs, which grew still to jeers. My fingers trembled as I tried to keep them clasped in front of me, searching for the right thing to say. "I can promise all of you, we will not rest until we have—"

"You have already fought them before?" Came the yell of a warrior.

"I-yes, we had to. But, you must understand—"

"What about *our* warriors? What about those who have trained for this?" Another shouted.

"I-it's not as easy as you think to enter the Realm of Creo—"

266

"But you know how! And you told no one!"

As their voices rose, I glanced over at Avenlae, whose ears pressed tightly against his braids. He seemed to flinch at their words, as if their voices pierced him as deeply as they did me. I swallowed, digging my nails into the back of my hands as I fought to keep my head up and find my voice. "We wanted to assess the threat before bringing the information to our people. This kind of panic was what we were trying to avoid —"

"What good did that do?" Yelled a *Sloviyankae* warrior, his black eyes narrowed as more agreed with him. "We have no home to go back to! Our brothers and sisters are dead, all because you kept your little *secret!*"

"N-no, that's not—we thought we were protecting—" But it didn't matter what else I had to say. The branches swayed as the cries and shouts of the Delfungaye echoed beneath the canopy. They looked straight at me, the claws of their wings angled down, their canines flashing.

And my voice was gone, lost in the wave of anger and fear pulsating from the crowd. The world disappeared, the sky gone, the trees dissolved, and it was just me, alone, facing this monster *I* created. I froze and just watched. I couldn't even hear their words, just their roar.

"How *dare* you!" Saetyl bellowed, her voice slashing through the jeers of the crowd. Her call, the call of a warrior, was one they listened to and heard. Again, the forest fell silent, paralyzed with anticipation. Her forest-green curls caught the rays of suns' light that was able to break through the canopy as she stared around at the crowd, daring them to continue to hold her gaze. "How *dare* you insult your queen! You know nothing of what she has been through to ensure your lives!"

"We know nothing because she tells us nothing!" shouted another *Sloviyankae* woman.

"And would *you?*" Saetyl growled, rounding on the woman. "If you had seen the horrors she has, had fought the battles she has, would *you* be able to find it within yourself to spread the fear?"

Gold, navy, silver, and black eyes shifted between each other. A soft rustle moved through the crowd, a whisper. Saetyl drew her shoulders back. "I was there. I have seen what our Queen has done, listened to your whines and your cries, but now, you hear *me*. You are all terrified by the mere appearance of Mors. But we have been to Creo, and we have seen the Creators for what they truly are. We fought them on *their turf!* But you want to berate your Queen for leading us there? For taking on the burden of battle so *you* would not have to?"

"What is the reason for keeping the warriors out of battle?" sneered a fellow *Hopyroque* man.

"What do you think happened to my wings?" Saetyl cried, flaring her metallic feathers. *"This* is what happens when you face a Creator. The loss of my wings was just a *taste* of their fury. *We* chose to take the pain of this battle to spare our people. And your Queen, instead of hiding within the Queen's Nest, barricaded by soldiers and the lives of her people, has chosen to stand with us on the frontlines."

As the echoes of Saetyl's voice faded, the forest seemed to grow darker. The branches of the trees bent forward, pulling the tribespeople closer together. A breeze moved through the leaves and fluttered along the wings of the Delfungaye before it made its way up to me, and there it was — the smell of fear. My hands had finally stopped shaking, and I forced myself to look out among the crowd once more. Their eyes lowered, their heads ducked, and their wings tucked closer to their spines. I felt I should have said more, or found some way to inject a drop of confidence back into them. But what was the point? I couldn't deny the fear of my own team, knowing what we were planning on going back into. We would all be continuing the lie if any of us tried to say something to make the tribe feel safer.

"So, I say again, how dare *any* of you insult your Queen. Be grateful our scars are only *ours* to bear." Saetyl glared out at the crowd for a moment longer before turning to face me, determination set in the hard lines of her jaw and the crease between her eyebrows. Again, words failed me. I had no idea how even to begin to express what I felt. What could I say that was worth her defending me?

As if able to hear my thoughts, Saetyl said softly, "There is nothing more to say, My Queen. Leave the people in the protection of the General and Vindicta's hive: we have a battle to fight."

She bowed deeply before stepping past me to stand back in formation between Darinrain and Notien. Avenlae gazed over at me, silent as the crowd and just as unreadable. Then, he clicked a few times at the team and brushed past me back into the Queen's Nest, leading them to where we were supposed to have met that morning. Vindicta watched Saetyl, Avenlae, Notien, and Darinrain file past her, but she stayed where she was behind me, unmoving until I ordered her to. Taking a breath, I hesitantly looked back out over my people. There was no cheering, no bows, not even a whisper moving through the trees.

Then, one *Laizuteek* warrior moved.

He lowered his gaze to the underbrush, then lifted his silver wings straight up into the air, wingtips pointing towards the canopy above us. Gradually, the rest of the Queen's Guard behind him followed suit, and the movement spread as a ripple through the rest of the branches. The *Laizuteek* forest became mottled with sleek black and shining silver, blurred by the thrashing of my heart as it shook my vision.

This wasn't acceptance or respect. It was their goodbye.

CHAPTER 25

The team met solemnly in the training clearing, just moments after addressing the tribe. *Excitialium* blades lined Vindicta's tails and tentacles, and one arched over the middle of her head, gleaming as she slithered out of the treeline, clicking at all of us as our mental connection to her slid into place. No one spoke. We barely held each other's gaze.

Darinrain looked around at all of us, his staff strapped across his back. "One more time?"

Quiet nods met his statement. Saetyl's metallic wings shifted, the feathers almost sparkling. *Please survive.*

I turned away from them, breathing deeply as I reached for Sinivir's power. "Take us to Fames, then."

As you wish, Sinivir hissed, his power crackling through my veins before it broke open the very air before us. My breath caught in my throat.

The realm within the fracture appeared as the very embodiment of desolation and decay.

As if pulled against my will, I moved hesitantly forward, stepping into and through the void. I hesitated, each step forward feeling as though I was leaving my life behind, abandoning the comforting embrace of the Silvacastra suns. My eyes struggled to adjust to the oppressive darkness of this forsaken part of Creo. With a snap, the void shut behind as Vindicta stepped through, following us into the haunting silence. The realm was utterly devoid of motion. Nothing in the black sky or in the rivers of thick, luminous green liquid that stretched across the barren grey rock ahead of us like veins.

In the distance, jagged cliffs rose abruptly from the ground, their harsh outlines breaking the monotonous abyss of the sky. A dense fog clung to the landscape, casting a sickly haze that accentuated the sharp, menacing edges of this world. It was an eerie panorama, a place where the boundaries of reality seemed to distort and fade into a chilling oblivion.

"Quite the welcome," Darinrain said, his head on a swivel as he took a step forward. "My Queen, are you sure you have taken us to the Realm of Creo, or have we accidentally entered into the mind of our beloved King?"

Avenlae's deep growl was the only response Darinrain got.

"I may actually be the one to kill you, Darinrain," Saetyl rasped as she removed her ax from where it hung between her wings.

"Oh, do not steal that momentous moment away from Our King!" Darinrain said in mock offense. "Everyone knows his blade is the only one I wish to taste."

"Quiet, Darinrain," I snapped. Other than his irritating remarks, there was still no movement or sound in the realm. I couldn't even sense anything beyond myself and my team. "Do you feel anything, Vindicta?"

No. I sense no one. I do not like it, she hissed.

That is because Fames will wait for you to come to him, Sinivir said, his voice like ice. *He is not as aggressive as my other Brothers, but do not underestimate him. He is far more cunning.*

"Then let's move out," I ordered, stepping forward. The ground crackled under my feet, puffs of dry dust spraying into the air with each step. In that desolate realm, nothing stirred or thrived. It was a barren world, stripped of life and vitality, a place that had long since wasted away into obscurity. Not even the remnants of crumbling buildings or the brittle skeletons of dried plants marred the stark landscape. Only the jagged expanses of bare rock stretched out endlessly, accompanied by the eerie glow of the liquid that pulsed beneath the surface. The venous rivers carved their way through the stone, the only measure of the distance we had covered. Still, nothing came to us. The terrain remained unchanging, a monotonous expanse where no whirling smoke or drifting dust arose to conjure the form of a Creator.

"Are you sure you brought us to the right place?" I whispered.

Fames is here, Sinivir hissed. **He is watching you.**

I stopped, holding a hand up to my team. "Then how do we draw him out?"

"Is he close, Xiaye?" Notien asked, and I heard the sound of her unsheathing her scimitar.

You don't lure Fames out unless he finds you intriguing enough.

"And am I?"

Xiaye. Vindicta's voice cut through Sinivir and my conversation. I turned back to her, noticing her gaze fixed intently on the river beside us. The liquid, once still and luminous, has started to churn, its surface breaking into boiling, frothy bubbles. Tiny droplets flicked into the air, smoking and sizzling against the rock they landed upon.

No, Sinivir said, as we backed away from the oozing river, our weapons drawn. **But I am.**

The luminous green liquid continued to become more volatile, then, as one mass, it **moved.** A viscous glob rose out of the river, its corrosive touch scorching the stones as it slithered closer to us, growing taller and more menacing with each passing second. Wisps of smoke trailed upwards, and as the sickly grey hue of the stone seemed to deepen into the blob, it began to materialize into a form. Within moments, a creature of nightmares stood before us, the green liquid dissolving into two small glowing eyes. Its pallid skin was stretched tightly over the skeletal framework of its elongated fingers and face, yet in some places, the skin appeared to be grotesquely melting away from its gaunt, spindly frame. The creature's head tapered to a sharp point, eerily reminiscent of a plague doctor's mask, the likes of which I'd only ever seen once in an abandoned museum in the Precinct on Earth. Rags of robes hung loosely over the creature's violently hunched spine, where its vertebrae seemed on the verge of rupturing through its fragile skin. When it smiled, its lips peeled back to reveal teeth as black as obsidian, teetering on the brink of decay amidst its stark white gums.

"I wondered when you would be sent here, *Creovis,*" the creature said, its voice like a death rattle. "Your journey through the Realm of Creo has been... *fascinating.*"

"I don't need to hear what you think about me or the death of your Brothers," I responded, igniting my power to crackle down my rapiers and blaze across my feathers as Avenlae, Notien, Saetyl, Darinrain, and Vindicta began to spread out behind me. "Frankly, none of us care. Let's move on to the fight, and skip the speech, shall we?"

Fames showed his teeth again and made a hacking noise, a disgusting form of laugh. "You are audacious, *Creovis,* despite remaining unaware of the reason you fight."

I paused, studying the glow of his eyes.

Careful, Creovis, Sinivir whispered. *Listen intently to every word Fames says.*

Orders, Xiaye? Vindicta asked, hissing and clicking the blades of her two tails together. Avenlae and Darinrain stood on my left, their weapons drawn and wings lowered towards the Creator. To my right, Saetyl slid the feathers of her wings together, sparks flying, as Notien glanced over at me, trying to gauge the feel of the upcoming fight.

"Explain," I said, trying to steady the shaking of my hands.

"Oh, no," Fames shook his head, the bones of his body rattling. "It is not I who has the answers. It is my Brother who resides within you, who created you."

"My Queen?" Darinrain asked, his eyes flicking between me and Fames.

Stay calm, Sinivir cautioned.

"Has dear Sinivir told you *why* he wants us dead?"

"He… he wanted control over Creation."

Creovis… Sinivir warned.

Fames cocked his head to the side, sliding closer still. "Indeed, but *why?*"

I stared, counting each breath, mind racing.

"Tell her, dear Brother," Fames hissed. "Tell her *why* you wanted control. What *feeds* your vengeance?"

Ask him, Sinivir growled, his fury barely contained, *what they took from me.*

"*Scy'ak tho!*" Avenlae snapped, and Notien, Darinrain, and Saetyl moved into position to attack, their weapons raised and wings out, their blades angled towards Fames. Behind us, Vindicta raised herself onto her hind legs, baring her fangs as her frill shuddered.

ASK HIM! Sinivir screamed, nearly making me flinch.

"What did you take from Sinivir?"

Silence, complete silence, spread between the Creator and my team. No one moved and barely dared to breathe. Then, slowly, Fames lowered his head down to me until the very tip of his elongated face almost touched mine as he whispered, *"Everything."*

A red-hot rage ignited in my mind, burning my skin. It wasn't mine. I *knew* it didn't belong to me, but it took all of my mental strength to separate myself from Sinivir's hatred. I stumbled back, shaking my head and panting, trying to gain control over my own conscience. I heard Avenlae's order, felt the wind of wings and movement around me, but I couldn't even see straight. Something wrapped around me, cushioning my fall. Or was it holding me up? Had I even fallen? What was happening?

"Ah, little Brother, you were always so easy to hurt!" Fames cackled, his voice suddenly clear. The bleak world around me came back into focus as strength returned to my body. Vindicta had retracted her blades and had her tentacles wrapped around my torso to hold me up. Avenlae, Dainrain, Notien, and Saetyl stood before me in an attack formation, but Fames had moved away, stalking back and forth like a predator searching for a weak point.

"Is she okay?" Avenlae asked without taking his eyes off the Creator.

She stabilized, Vindicta answered, and a puff of her breath moved over me as she lowered her snout to my back, nudging me back onto my feet. I sheathed one of my rapiers, reaching my hand up to her nose.

"Something's wrong," I panted, "why didn't Fames attack?"

You weren't weakened for long enough, Sinivir snarled.

Perhaps you should stay out of this one, Vindicta seethed, her six eyes following Fames' every move.

"Like hell he will," I said, pushing myself off of her and grabbing the hilt of my rapier once more. "He's pissed."

"Now that I have your attention, *Creovis,*" Fames called, "I have... a *proposal.*"

275

Avenlae stepped back, turning silver eyes on me as he lowered his wings. We held eye contact for a moment. ***Anything to keep him out of this fight.***

"Speak," I ordered.

Fames bared his teeth, but said, "I know you were sent here. I know Mors told you to 'do what you want' with me. I have seen your battles with my older Brothers, and have watched how they died." He curled his fingers, then stretched them back out, each almost as long as Vindicta's tentacles. "Sinivir spoke truthfully. I am not as aggressive as the others. I am not as interested in bloodshed."

Only torture, Sinivir scoffed.

"But, my Brothers do like their games. They enjoy toying with the mortals they created. In that respect, I am not so different." Fames moved closer, his bones and rags swaying with each step. "So, I propose we play our own little game, ***Creovis.***" He reached into the rags that barely covered his ribs and withdrew a rusted metal object, which he held out for us to see. When he uncurled one finger, something dropped from a screaming chain that hung from his wrist.

A pair of scales.

"Should you win, ***Creovis,*** I will allow myself to be banished from the Realm of Creo without a fight. You will remain unharmed and will be allowed to continue your mission unhindered. I may even be convinced to reveal the secret to defeating Mors."

Darinrain's ears shot forward. Saetyl's eyes flicked over to us, and she adjusted her grip on her ax, leaning away from the Creator.

Fames drifted nearer, shaking the scales; the screech of the chain caused Avenlae, Darinrain, Saetyl, and Notien to flinch back. "Should you lose, however, you will be mine, ***Creovis.*** We shall attack Mors together, and then Creation will fall under ***my*** control."

All eyes fell on me. The world had gone quiet once more, and the fate of Creation rested upon one answer, one decision. ***Careful, Creovis.***

276

"What's the game?"

"A riddle." Fames' eyes appeared to glow an even brighter green as he spoke. "Give me that which you cannot lose.

That which can give as readily as it can take,

Which can love as easily as it can hate.

Give me that which can change everything it touches, but can choose to effect nothing;

Which can remain blind to its own virtue, but through which all of reality is perceived by its being.

Give me that which can create and destroy, can teach despair or joy, can spread and stop, can be remembered or forgot.

Give me that whose absence would be felt by all."

My pulse rose in my throat as I felt my mouth become dry. Avenlae's eyes widened next to me, and his hands tightened around the hilts of his rapiers. Darinrain's throat bobbed as he swallowed hard, his head turning haltingly to look over at each of us.

Notien began to shake her head, raising her scimitar higher. "No. I-it is a trick. There is nothing we can give you like that."

But there is, Vindicta said softly, her voice echoing in our minds.

"Do not say anything, Vindicta," Saetyl growled, rolling her shoulders and stepping closer to Notien.

They all know, Creovis, Sinivir hissed, *but do you?*

"Only one thing can love, hate, and whose absense is felt by all, whether or not it becomes forgotten," Darinrian murmured, turning back to face me as he lowered his staff slightly.

Ice raced down my spine as Fames leaned forward, holding out his scales. "Give me a life worthy of *mine.*"

Everything seemed to freeze, except for my beating heart. "A-a life?"

Fames rattled the screaming chain. "Tick-tock, *Creovis.*"

I met the terrified eyes of my team. No. No, I couldn't do it. I *wouldn't.*

You have to, Sinivir sighed.

"No," I began backing away from my friends. "No, I-I won't do it."

"Is there another choice?" Notien asked, her voice hoarse, and the screech of Fames' scales was her answer.

Avenlae tightened his grip on one of his rapiers. "Let me, Xai."

My eyes widened. "What?"

"I am King of the Delfungaye," he said softly, "In this war, my life is second only to yours, and you cannot die."

"Don't you *dare,* Avenlae!" I shouted, dropping my own rapier and manifesting the whip out of the Creonex. In seconds, it was wrapped around the wrist of his dominant hand. Darinrain moved forward and grabbed hold of Avenlae's other wrist, allowing him to hold his rapier, but not move his arm.

"It has to be one of us, Xiaye," Avenlae said, his voice steady. "One of us so everyone else can survive."

My vision blurred as tears welled in my eyes. "No. I'm not losing you. I said I would protect everyone, and I *will* protect everyone."

"Allow me, My King," Saetyl said, spinning her ax around, "I have already lost my wings. If Fames wants my pain, he can have it."

Before she could move, Fames' scales let out another shriek. "Exchanging broken parts for a Creator? How insulting, *Creovis.*"

"J-just wait," I stuttered, shaking my head again. "There has t-to be another way."

Darinrain looked back at Fames, who pulled his lips back to reveal his white gums and rotted teeth. With a sigh, Darinrain raised his navy eyes to mine.

"This is it," he said. "One of us for all of Creation."

A cold tear slid down my cheek as my chest tightened painfully. "I-I can't," I whispered.

Darinrain's eyes softened. "It is okay, Xiaye. You do not have to. Just promise me something."

"What?"

"Promise you will forgive me."

Before I could say anything, before I could even move, Darinrain pulled himself onto Avenlae's rapier, the blade going straight through his chest and out between his wings.

CHAPTER 26

E verything seemed to stop.

Time stood still.

I couldn't move.

But Darinrain's blood, so red and full of his life, cascaded down his armor and pooled at his feet. His body convulsed violently against the blade, his mouth frozen in a silent scream as blood trickled over his lip. Avenlae stood paralyzed, eyes wide with horror, his very soul shattered. His other arm dropped from the whip, and the sound of his first rapier hitting the stone seemed to reverberate endlessly in the absolute darkness of the Realm. There was a choking sob beside me as Notien crumpled to the ground, her hands clutching her chest in a futile attempt to hold together her heart.

But still, I couldn't move, trapped in my own helplessness.

Darinrain lifted a trembling hand to the hilt of the rapier lodged in his chest, blood streaming over Avenlae's fingers. With a heart-wrenching cry, Darinrain pushed himself off the blade, staggering weakly. Avenlae's blood-

drenched second rapier fell with a hollow clatter as he darted forward to catch Darirain before he collapsed.

"It is okay," he whispered gently, cradling Darinrain's head on his lap. "Stay still, it will not hurt as much."

Avenlae already knew there was nothing I could do about the life draining from Darinrain's eyes, yet he still looked up at me, tears already spilling down his cheeks.

"Oh, Darinrain," Saetyl whispered, her wings falling, "what have you done?"

"I-I... am the... only... weak link," Darinrain panted, each breath a rasping death rattle. His voice splintered, each word a struggle against the chaos erupting in his chest.

I shook my head, my entire body beginning to tremble as I crouched next to him. "No," I choked out.

"Do not speak," Avenlae said, cupping Darinrain's head in his hands, "save your strength."

"I am... sorry... My King," Darinrain whispered, blood blooming through his chest, "I have... none left."

Avenlae's shoulders jerked. "No, no, I am Avenlae," he said, his voice cracking, "Y-you call me Avenlae."

Darinrain managed a weak smile as he looked up at his king. "Finally." Then he cried out as his body convulsed, another hot rush of blood staining the ground.

"Xiaye, please—do something!" Avenlae's sobs wracked him, tears pooling around the scar across his face. "H-his pain, s-stop his pain!"

I should have been able to. I had the power to. But, hearing the cries from Avenlae, seeing the blood flow from the hole in Darinrain's chest... Terror pinned me as Darinrain's life seeped away. I couldn't fucking move.

Let me, came Sinivir's voice, soft in my thoughts. Something moved over me, and then my hand was reaching out. But it wasn't my power that flowed into the Creonex.

It was Sinivir's.

Tendrils of power as vibrant as Darinrain's blood flowed from my fingers into Darinrain's golden temples, and, immediately, his body relaxed. He took a few more shuddering breaths, then opened his navy eyes, staring up at Avenlae.

"I am... sorry I... never got to... call you my... my friend."

Avenlae's shoulders trembled uncontrollably as his tears fell onto the curves of the tattoos that arced across Darinrain's forehead. "You were not my friend, Darinrain."

As the final breath crossed Darinrain's lips, Avenlae whispered, "You were my brother."

Darinriain's eyes glazed over, staring at the black sky above us. His body stilled, and the flow of blood slowed to a pitiful trickle. Avenlae patted Darinrain's cheeks, his hands shaking as he realized there was no life left in Darinrain's body. "H-he heard me," Avenlae whimpered, taking in gasps of air so forcefully that his entire body rocked, "P-please tell me h-he heard me. T-tell me h-he knows."

I couldn't see him through my tears. My throat was so tight I couldn't speak, for I knew Darinrain's heart had stopped beating too soon. I stared at Darinrain's eyes, once so bright when he smiled. Now, they were dull and quiet. Now, his skin had lost its sheen of gold.

I would never hear him again. I would never see his grin. The world would never know a soul as bright as Darinrain's. And so the world would ever be the same.

282

Tell him Darinrain heard him, Sinivir coaxed, his voice so calm. *He needs to know.*

I just nodded my head. I couldn't bring myself to speak the lie to Avenlae.

He bent his head over Darinrain, his sobs raspy from the damage to his throat. But they still sliced through me, every single heartbreaking cry. Avenlae's tears swirled in the blood that pooled across his legs and across the stone beneath him. To our right came the choked sobs of Notien as she turned to rest her head on Saetyl's shoulder. A pressure against my back told me Vindicta had moved closer, protecting us as we tried to understand how Darinrain could be *gone*.

"Touching," Fames mocked, swaying the scales so that their chain squealed as he crept forward. "The sacrifice of a warrior who was too good for this world."

Fames cocked his head to the side, running a cracked tongue over his black teeth as he bent over Darinrain's body. Avenlae's head snapped up, and he bared his canines, thrusting his wings forward to protect Darinrain from the Third Creator.

"You protect him now, dear King!" Fames cackled. "Where was your protection when he was alive? Or did you simply not care until now?"

"How *dare* you!" Saetyl cried, tears shining against her cheeks as she held Notien. "You gave him no other choice!"

"I gave the *Creovis any* choice," the Creator hissed. "I said 'a life', but I did not dictate *whose.*"

I stayed where I was, frozen on the blood-spattered stone, staring at how still Darinrain's body was. Like a statue. As if he weren't even real. Fames' words and the cries of my team were just echoes in my ears, sounds I didn't quite understand. *Is it real? Is he really dead?* I felt like I couldn't move, couldn't react. My mind was lost, paralyzed by the idea of a reality in which one of my friends had died in front of me. In a place *I* had brought him to. *I led him to his death.*

Then, one phrase, spoken in the sickly whisper of Fames, cut through the numbness: "But, is he *worthy?*"

The screech of the scales' chain set fire to a fury like I had never known before. I didn't just see red, I *was* red, engulfed in violent crimson flames as my power thrashed within me like a wild animal.

"Is he worthy?" I growled, raising my head to stare into the glowing green eyes of the Creator I knew I was going to decimate. But it wasn't me who struck him down. Sinivir sent out a flare of my power, and one of Vindicta's tails shot out from behind me, embedding itself into Fames' abdomen, or what was left of it. He looked down at the tail sticking out of his body, as if confused about how it got there. Vindicta's second tail whipped around and stabbed all the way through his chest, in his left arm, and out the other, immobilizing him. Fames shrieked, dropping his scales as Vindicta's tails lifted him into the air while she stepped over where the rest of us still crouched. My flames disappeared as I watched her — for the first time in nearly six years, the look in her eyes frightened me. They were as bloody red as Sinivir's, and siliva dripped from her fangs as she hissed at Fames. Her tentacles wrapped around him, ensuring he had no escape as her head began to weave back and forth, her frill vibrating, a scream building in her throat.

He was worth more than you will EVER BE!

BRACE! Sinivir shouted, his shadows bursting through my veins. I gasped, then raised my hands to release his power just as Vindicta's jaw fell open. A warped crimson shield formed around us, but it didn't protect us entirely from the scream Vindicta released. It was the most visceral sound I had ever heard, one that seemed to shake the very fabric of reality itself.

Fames disintegrated in her tentacles, his skin peeling away from his bones and flopping into the green liquid of a river Vindicta held him over. He didn't struggle or scream; he couldn't, not against the sheer force of the shriek of a Voxmor Queen. The Third Creator, Third Brother, Fames, was reduced to ash in seconds, and there was not one thing he could do to stop it. A pile of ash floated to rest on one side of the scales he had dropped, but it didn't move. The ash weighed nothing.

And then the Realm of Creo was silent. The crimson shield faded, as did the crimson in Vindicta's eyes. Her frill lowered as she fell back onto four legs, flicking remnants of Fames from her tentacles. When she turned back to us, her eyes had returned to their prismatic brightness.

I only wish Fames could have suffered more, was all she said.

Notien moved away from Saetyl, tendrils of her platinum blond hair plastered against her cheeks where they stuck to her tears. She knelt on Darinrain's right, setting gentle fingers against his cheek as she stared down at him.

"I want him to smile," she sniffed. "I want him to… to say some idiotic thing to remind us we are all still alive."

"He did not have to die," Saetyl murmured, her voice shaking. "Of all of us, he deserved this death the least."

I watched them, feeling the touch of tears as they dripped down my cheeks. Pain constricted my chest and choked my throat, but I was torn between stepping back to comfort my friends and moving forward to destroy the last Creator, the last Brother who began that battle. I looked out towards the abyss of Fames' Realm, to the endless expanse of glowing green venous rivers and desolate, dry land. Mors was still out there. Even though Darinain was… even though he was gone, Mors was still there. He wouldn't wait for us to mourn. He didn't care.

"He deserves a ceremony," Avenlae choked out. "I will take him back. We-we will give him the memorial of a warrior."

"Not of a *Je'quiet?*" Saetyl asked softly.

"No, a warrior. That was what he chose."

Xiaye.

I tore my eyes away from the horizon and back to my little group, all huddled around the body of Darinrain. Vindicta had moved behind me, her snout next to my shoulder. *It is time to honor him.*

"Sh-should we?" I whispered to her, leaning against her scales without even noticing.

Yes, you should allow yourself to.

"I-I should have s-stopped him," I stuttered, lifting a hand to her nose, as if holding on for dear life, to protect myself from my own emotions.

"No, Xiaye," Saetyl said, standing and stepping towards me. "He made up his mind. I do not think he was ever going to allow any of us the chance to stop him."

It was his choice, Vindicta clicked, supporting me as I leaned more heavily against her.

Saetyl took a deep breath, trying to hold herself together better than any of the rest of us. "Vindicta, are you able to carry him back to—"

"No," Avenlae snapped, raising pink-tinged eyes, "I will take him."

"Av, are you—"

"I will take him." Avenlae moved around Darinrain's body, sliding his arms under his torso. As he lifted the body from the ground, sluggish blood began to drip down Avenlae's arms, staining the silver and gold of his armor. But he didn't seem to notice, or care.

And so it was Avenlae, carrying the dead body of our finest warrior, who led us out of Creo, leaving behind a world of silent death, and entering into a world that would never seem as bright or warm again.

CHAPTER 27

*D*arinrain isn't dead.

Don't look at the body — it'll be too real.

Any moment now, he's going to jump up and applaud
Vindicta on an excellent performance, and ask Avenlae if those really were
real tears.

Except he didn't.

The entire flight through the tribe, Darinrain remained motionless, his eyes stationary. Avenlae held his body, his own silver eyes focused in front of him. Vindicta slithered through the trees next to us, Saetyl and Notien followed behind us, their heads down and their hands crossed over their chests — a ceremonial stance of respect for a fallen warrior. Delfungaye from all tribes crept out of their nests to watch us pass, hands over their mouths and ears flat against their hair. Silence spread before us, but for the rustling of leaves from the *Sloviyankae* gathering among the branches. Members of the Queen's Guard bowed their heads, crossing their hands and fighting back tears. The grief of the tribe was tangible. It wasn't simply the death of a warrior.

Darinrain had been the final surviving *Je'quiet.* The whole history of the Delfungaye, the stories of their ancestors, had died with him.

I kept my head held high, but my eyes down on the underbrush below me. I couldn't find the courage to look anyone in the eye. Darinrain's death was on my hands, and no one was going to tell me otherwise. The promise I had made only the day before felt like such a slap in the face. *I will protect all of you.* Pitiful. Naive. He had warned me then. ***Damnit, you*** told ***me then...***

And my people knew we were no longer safe.

Darinrain was the first warrior to die since Creation's War. I could see it in their eyes — the trauma returning, the memories beginning to surface in their minds. I couldn't protect them anymore. Would they think me a liar? Would they hate me for trying to hide the danger of the Creators from them for so long? I wouldn't even defend myself if the Delfungaye decided to blame me for it all. I would deserve it.

When I finally did glance up, I saw Kaigar, who waited before the entrance to the Queen's Nest. His ears were forward as he stared at the body Avenlae held. With only one healthy eye, his sight wasn't as good as the rest of the tribe around him. As we neared, however, his lips parted as his ears flattened against his salt-and-pepper hair, and his eyes met mine. There was horror in those aged eyes. Darinrain was one of his warriors who had ***survived.*** It was as unfathomable to the General as it was to me and my team that his body was now limp and empty.

From the entrance to the Queen's Nest came the ***Matri Me'lieu,*** who flew to hover next to Kaigar, her hands crossed over her chest like the rest of the warriors. Kaigar didn't move — it was as if the realization that it was Darinrain Avenlae held kept the General frozen in place, trying to understand where it all went wrong. I lowered my eyes again: I didn't know if I could stand seeing more of their pain.

Our procession stopped once we reached Kaigar and the *Matri Me'liev.* Kaigar reached a hand out and, hesitantly, touched his fingers to Darinrain's cheek, as if to feel if there was any warmth left in his skin.

"How?" was all he said. But no one answered. None of us knew how to.

The *Matri Me'leiv* gestured off to her left, and, in moments, members of her nest had appeared, their hands out to take Darinrain's body off to be prepared for a Celebration of Passing. Avenlae stared at them, his eyes widening as he tightened his grip on Darinrain's body.

"Av, i-it's time to let go," I said quietly, placing a gentle hand on his arm. My words seemed to startle him, for he made a soft gasp, then looked down at Dainrain. A tear slid down his cheek, then splashed onto Darinrain's. Saetyl moved forward and touched Avenlae's shoulder. Slowly, he looked up at her as she set her hand on the back of Darinrain's head.

"There is nothing more you can do for him," she said softly, "let them take care of him, now."

"W-we have to burn him," Avenlae said, as if in a trance.

Saetyl nodded. "I know."

Finally, Avenlae loosened his hold and allowed the other *Fyr'aeset* to take Darinrain away. We all watched until he disappeared, and then we watched some more. He should've popped right out of that nest, arms spread wide as he bowed, expecting praise for how long he stayed still. But he didn't.

"Was it worth it?" asked the *Matri Me'leiv.*

I felt like the air had been sucked out of my lungs as I turned to look at her. Her navy eyes, lined with years of life, stared deep into me. If I looked long enough, I could almost see the vibrancy of the Oracle within them. "If you ask me that again," I said, "I will slit your throat."

She bowed her head once. "Do not forget, Xiaye, that the help of a

Creator is never free. And there is still one last Brother."

I said nothing, just held the old woman in my gaze. Cautiously, I reached for Sinivir in my mind, but he remained just out of reach. *The help of a Creator is never free.* Hadn't I already paid enough? Hadn't we all?

I sighed, tightening my hold on Avenlae's arm. "Alert us when Darinrain has been prepared for the Celebration of Passing. We will hold it at suns' rise tomorrow, out in the golden plains. That's where he should've been."

The *Matri Me'leiv* bowed once more, then glided off to her nest. Kaigar looked down at me, his eyes softening. "One more?"

I nodded.

"Are you sure?"

"I have to."

He gave me a long look, one filled with a fear I had never seen in the General. "Do not lose yourself, Xiaye."

I lowered my eyes. "I already have."

With a slight tug, I led Avenlae past the General and into the Queen's Nest. It was quiet, since all of its usual inhabitants had left to see if we really were bringing back the body of a warrior. Saetyl and Notien silently broke away from us to find sanctuary in their room on a lower level of the Nest. Avenlae said nothing as I took him up to our chambers, and then sat numbly on the edge of the bed as I shut the doors, locking them to ensure that we would remain alone. When I turned back to him, he stared at the wall ahead of him. Darinrain's blood still coated his armor and stained his skin. That was why Avenlae was so afraid to look around — he couldn't bear to catch a glimpse of the blood still caked on him. I swallowed down the lump in my throat, knowing that it was time for me to remain strong. I moved over to him and began to work on his armor, loosening the straps that held it in place around his wings and torso. He did nothing to stop me, but nothing to help me, either. It wasn't until his chest was bare and I had laid the top half of his armor in a shadowed corner of the room that he spoke.

"I-I did not want to."

I turned, and his silver eyes were anguished. "I d-did not want t-to, Xai. I did not w-want to."

"I know," I said, collecting a basin of water and a rag, and moving back over to him. With gentle persuasion, I pushed him onto the floor in front of me, soaking up the water in the rag.

"I-I could not stop h-him," he said, his voice pleading as if he thought I wouldn't believe him.

I bit my lip, fighting back my tears, before repeating what Saetyl had said: "No one could've, Avenlae. Darinrain made up his mind."

Avenlae watched as I began to scrub the blood from his hands and arms where it soaked through parts of the fabric of his armor. His hands trembled and his breathing became uneven. "H-he heard me. He heard m-me."

I nodded, but I couldn't speak.

Stop.

I flinched, hearing Sinivir's voice.

He needs you, Xiaye.

My eyes widened. It was the first time he hadn't called me *Creovis.* And his voice… it was so gentle.

Because you do not need to be the Creovis right now, he needs you to be Xiaye.

My eyes began to burn as my chest tightened. I glanced at Avenlae and saw his cheeks, once again glistening with fresh tears. The constant flow had left his skin dry and raw. I didn't even know how he still had tears to cry.

291

I let the rag slip from my grasp, my sigh heavy wth exhaustion and empathy. Gently, I raised my left hand, cooling the Creonex because I knew it would be soothing against Avenlae's raw skin. As he leaned his head into the palm of my hand, his shoulders began to tremble with renewed sobs, each one piercing through me. "Avenlae," I said, my voice wavering, "you didn't kill him."

I could see the pain in Avenlae's heart from how the force of his cries took his entire body hostage. I stopped fighting my tears as I spoke to him, even when they took my voice. "And he knew. Darinrain knew you were brothers without you having to tell him. He didn't need to hear you to know. And no one blames you. It wasn't your fault."

I cupped his jaw with my hands, my voice barely a whisper. "He loved you. And this w-won't make him hate you."

Avenlae's wings slackened and slid to rest against the floor. As he leaned forward, his tears dripped onto my arms while he collapsed into them, surrendering the weight of his pain. His cries tore into my heart, splitting it down the center, ripping apart every bit of my resolve.

My strength shattered like glass. When he clung to me, I broke. I broke with him. We stayed locked together, his body heaving from the aftershocks of his sobs, and my silent grief matching his. The forest outside grew dark as I held him, taking out his braids and running my hand through his hair over and over until he could breathe normally again. Gradually, he slumped further into me, exhausted, defeated. I breathed deeply, searching for inner strength to pick both of us back up.

"To bed, Av," I whispered, pushing softly against his chest. He picked his head up, his cheek close enough to mine that I could feel its warmth. His moonlight eyes still glowed as they met mine, swollen as they were. His head moved up to my neck as he brushed his mouth across mine and breathed in my scent.

"I love you, Xai," he murmured, "and I will protect you."

"I love you, too," I responded, pressing my lips to his cheek. I let him believe he was the one protecting me. That night, I let him hold me when we finally crawled into bed, letting him hold on so tightly that it was as if he thought I was going to disappear if he let go for even a moment.

I let him believe he was protecting me. It was easier than facing the silence that waited if I didn't.

It was still dark outside when Vindicta used her telepathic connection to wake us.

It is time, My King and Queen, she said, her voice soft. **We must honor Darinrain.**

I sucked in the breath, feeling the stiffness in my muscles from staying so still, curled tightly in Avenlae's arms all night. Avenale stirred, a slight tremble in his movements, as if coming to the realization that the events of the day before had been real. I sat up wordlessly, pressing my wings against my back as tightly as I could. *It's time to move,* I told myself, gathering strength. *Just this next hour. Get through this next hour, then you can prepare for what comes after. But, right now, you have to move.*

I got up from the bed, stepping across the room as if my body was on autopilot. Tucked way in the very back of our wardrobe was the ceremonial attire for a Celebration of Passing. My fingers shook as I reached for their hangers, careful not to disturb the delicate beadwork. *Just this hour. Just this hour.*

Avenlae lay still in the bed as I moved back over to him, flicking flames from the Creonex into the fireplace before the bed to bathe the room in a soft glow. His eyes remained fixed on the ceiling as I laid out the mask, beaded and braided top, and thin fabric bottoms of his mourning suit.

"We have to get ready, Avenlae," I said quietly, separating the parts of my outfit — the mask, the dress, the beadwork meant for my wings.

"I know," he murmured. "But I... should I even attend?"

I let my hands fall as I just stared at the beadwork of the two outfits. *Just this hour. Breathe.* "It wasn't your fault."

Avenlae swallowed hard, the scar across his throat stretching.

"Besides," I said, looking over at him, "you know Darinrain would never forgive you if you didn't attend *his* Celebration of Passing."

The smallest smile tugged at the corners of Avenlae's mouth. "Indeed, he would not. I expect he would curse me."

"I expect he would haunt you," I shrugged.

Avenlae sighed and pushed himself up, silver wings stretched on either side of him. "He would. He already does."

Reaching up, I touched his cheek, then ran a finger across the stubble that had begun to grow along his jaw. "Only for a bit longer. His spirit will be at rest as soon as the suns have risen."

"Yes, but my mind will not forget his eyes," Avenlae whispered as he took his beadwork top into his hand, spinning the beads between his fingers.

I wanted so badly to find a way to take the memories from his head. Avenlae's mind had tortured him for nearly his entire life, and the fight to destroy the Creators had only added more volatile fuel. But all I could do was help him dress, smooth the feathers of his wings, and braid the length of his straight, black hair. I had the power to heal a body that could be healed, but not to heal a mind that had been so thoroughly damaged.

The forest still hadn't begun to lighten when I left our chambers in my emerald dress, lines of beadwork clicking together behind me as I walked. A few levels below, a light shone softly through a closed door. I gestured for Avenlae to head out of the nest where I knew Kaigar and Vindicta were waiting, and he made no protest. I glided down to the door, knocked once, and folded my arms across my chest. *Your hour is almost done. Then you can take a moment to breathe and start all over again.*

The door opened, and for a moment I saw nothing but dim light inside. Then Saetyl stood at the threshold, her hair unbraided and falling in forest-green ringlets over her shoulders. Half of her face was veiled by a mask of green and violet beadwork, and her golden eyes were steady as she looked down at me.

"I-I'm sorry," I said, trying to keep the waver out of my voice, "but I need Notien. I didn't want to ask Avenlae to—"

Before I could finish my sentence, Saetyl reached out and pulled me into the room, wrapping her arms around me and setting her chin atop my head. I gasped, frozen, almost... afraid. But not of her—I was scared of the grief that ached in my heart the second she embraced me. With the gentle touch of her hand on the back of my head, she pressed my cheek onto her shoulder, her heart a soft beat against my skin. Her embrace was anchoring—deliberately, insistently so—like a force meant to hold me there, in that moment, no matter how hard I tried to drift away.

"It is okay for you to be weak right now, Xiaye," Saetyl whispered, tightening her arms around me and stroking her finger through my hair.

The words hit me with more force than I expected. Something inside me snapped, and the breath I'd been holding escaped in a shuddering, weak sob. My knees became weak, and I sagged against her, but still, Saetyl didn't let go.

Another set of arms, more gentle than Saetyl's, wrapped around me, tentative at first. I knew by the kindness of the touch that it was Notien, even before she laid her head on my shoulder and her blonde hair brushed over my eyes. "I know you have been strong for Avenlae. Let us take a moment to be strong for you," Notien said, her voice shaking.

295

For a moment longer, I tried to suppress the guilt and despair that had been coiling around my thoughts. But it was so strong. And it **hurt.** It felt as if my chest was collapsing in on itself, and suddenly, I had no idea how I had been able to stand for so long. How had I been able to hold Avenlae the night before when **this** was the depth of my own grief?

We stayed there, suspended in the hush of their dim-lit room, bent together as we held each other. And… we cried. Quietly, Notien, Saetyl, and I cried together. For that moment, they were my only gravity, the only things that held me in a wave of grief.

And yet, the moment was not forever. The Silvacastra suns were still going to rise, whether or not we had each gathered our strength. I took several deep breaths, wiping my tears and controlling my emotions long before I felt like I really could. Notien took my hand and led me over to the vanity in the corner of the room, setting me down as she grabbed a brush and began to run it through the length of my hair.

"I keep expecting Darinrain to come through that door, all dressed up with a few cups of **anteel** to share," Saetyl said, gazing at the entrance to the bedroom. "I do not know if my head has actually come to terms with him being gone."

"Everyone has been watching the doors," Notien said, beginning to braid my hair, "We have all been watching for him to come back. He was always the first to rise, to gather us all together."

"I kept waiting for him to get up," I whispered, one last tear rolling down my cheek, "as they were carrying him to the **Matri Me'leiv's** Nest. I-it's like I don't understand why he won't move. I don't understand his absence."

Notien's braiding slowed. "Oh, that was why he was worthy."

"What?" Saetyl asked, looking around at us.

I heard Notien sniff behind me. "He held us together. He did not know it, but it is his absence that is the loudest."

We fell into silence as Notien finished the braids in my hair, tying them together in a royal style I'd never been able to replicate on myself. I hated that she was right. Even with all of his sarcastic comments, his unrelenting optimism, even the way he flirted with Avenlae to get a rise out of his King, Darinrain was the member of our team none of us ever imagined dead. He just seemed too good for death, too joyous, too alive, too strong. And he was the one who always had something to say to every one of us. Something to make us forget the insanity of what we had set out to do. He *was* our strength.

Moments later, we found ourselves outside of the Queen's Nest, joined by Avenlae, Kaigar, Vindicta, the *Matri Me'leiv,* and… Darinrain. He was adorned with the intricate beadwork of his people, shimmering in ruby red and deep onyx against his golden skin. Delicate flowers matching the hues of the beadwork formed the bedding upon which he rested. Beside him lay his staff, carved with spiritual vows and prayers of the *Je'quiet.* His hands were crossed over his chest, fingers curled together in the traditional Delfungaye warrior gesture of respect —a symbol of the honor shown to him by the tribe upon our return. He was so… peaceful. Darinrain knew pain no more.

High above, the branches of the trees were lined with Delfungaye and Sloviyankae, each holding luminescent flowers that glowed softly in the dim light, creating a radiant path through the forest leading to the vast plains beyond. Riders and their Voxmor moved gracefully through the canopy, scattering vibrant flower petals that cascaded down like a colorful shower over Darinrain as he was moved. Vindicta rose to join the Riders as the procession began. Tribe members soared to join the tail of the procession as we passed, while the Sloviyankae adeptly kept pace in the surrounding branches, their presence a constant, agile movement.

Gradually, the sky above began to illuminate, ablaze with the vivid hues of the suns' rise, painting a breathtaking tapestry of color. Avenlae kept his head down, his breathing becoming more uneven as the density of the trees

297

began to lessen, forcing the Sloviyankae to join the Riders on their Voxmor as they came down from the canopy. As the first golden rays of suns' light cast the Silvacastra plains in a pure glow, we stopped. Before us, tall golden grasses swayed rhythmically in a gentle breeze, whispering secrets of the plains. The *Fyr'aeset* warriors moved ahead, forming a protective circle around an area where the grasses had been meticulously cut. In the center stood a marble pedestal, its edges raised high to prevent any stray flames from igniting the plains. Taking a deep, steadying breath, we all descended, forming a close-knit group among the plains, our attention focused on the *Matri Me'leiv* as she directed Darinrain's body to be placed gently upon the pedestal. Avenlae's hand sought mine, his fingers trembling slightly.

> *He isn't ready. None of us is prepared to say goodbye.*

I felt the cold touch of Sinivir pulling himself to the forefront of my mind as the *Matri Me'leiv* launched into her ceremonial call-and-response song.

> *You honor him well,* he said, his voice calm.

> *We shouldn't have to,* I thought, clenching my jaw as my throat tightened painfully, *not like this.*

Sinivir remained silent through the rest of the ceremony, but he didn't disappear into the back of my mind like he had done so many times in the past. He stayed where I could feel him, as if he wanted to bear witness to the Celebration of Passing for Darinrain. Avenlae stayed composed, but I could feel his pain through the *lyceliah,* and it took everything in me to remain standing, to keep my head held high and watch as emerald flames began to consume Darinrain's body. *He's gone.*

But something was wrong.

Dark smoke began to pool around the pedestal, smoke that never came from the flames. Gasps came from the crowd as the *Fyr'aeset* around the pedestal began to back away. Shouts rang out from the *Sloviyankae,* cries of fear, spearheaded by Hoviyeque's yell, "It is her! *Fae'yeerium!*"

The cloud of smoke grew, spinning, writhing as it began to take shape. "Get them out of here!" I called back to Kaigar. "I don't care where you go — the mountains, deeper into the forest, underground — anywhere *far* from here."

"Your Majesty—" he began.

"I said *go,*" I growled, ripping the mask from my face as I turned back to where the cloud of smoke had formed into the shadowed body of Mors, his claws sparking as they rubbed together, and his glowing eyes wild with malice.

"This is the part where *I* take his soul, isn't it?" Mors hissed. "Or am I too early?"

Voxmor shrieks filled the air as the Riders moved into formation in front of the flock of Delfungaye taking to the sky. Vindicta flared her frill, passing along orders to her hive as she slid the blades of her two tails together, raising herself onto two legs.

Mors cackled, his voice like the sound of thousands of crying souls. "You intend to stand your ground dressed like *that?*" he mocked. "Oh, *Creovis,* I had hoped you would put up a better fight."

"I thought *we* were supposed to come to *you,*" I responded, the Creonex glowing deep magenta around my hand.

"Yes, well, as my dear Brother knows, I get *impatient.*" Mors stalked closer, the shadows of his body gathering. "So, what will it be?"

I glanced around. Saetyl and Notien stood by me, even though their hands were empty. And pure hatred radiated from Avenlae as he stared up at Mors, his canines bared.

Leave the weapons to me, Sinivir growled, the heat of his power beginning to surge into my body.

I rolled my head as energy crackled along my skin, spreading onto my feathers. "Fine," I said as crimson flames leapt onto my wings, "let's finish this."

CHAPTER 28

I stepped forward, spreading my arms wide. Sinivir's powers surged through me, an overwhelming torrent of red-hot rage. The emerald dress of mourning I wore was incinerated instantly, replaced by magnificent crimson armor that clung to my form like a second skin. My hands felt the familiar weight of my matte black and crimson rapiers, shimmering into existence with an almost imperceptible hum. My wings, vibrant and fiery, flared brighter than ever, their flames dancing and leaping like living creatures. Their flames leapt onto the clothes of Avenlae, Notien, and Saetyl, the fire weaving itself into intricate patterns until each was adorned in armor of shimmering onyx. Vindicta was last, her scales covered in sleek ebony armor accented by blades along her head, tentacles, and flanks.

I nodded at Mors. "Your move."

His silver fangs gleamed in a maniacal smile. "I may enjoy this as much as I did the *last* time, *Creovis.*"

Vindicta's tentacles swept under me, launching me into the air. I dove towards Mors, rapiers spinning as his claws met me midair. As Vindicta launched the rest of our team into action, the clash of metal against claw echoed through the air with a sickening screech. Mors' strikes held power I'd never felt before, and each parry reverberated through my bones. His claws moved faster than any blade had in training sessions, and the only thing keeping me alive was Sinivir's focus on creating well-placed shields.

Just keep him distracted! Sinivir cried, his voice piercing through the chaos as I narrowly dodged a strike, then immediately thrust my rapiers up to parry another. The sheer force of Mors' claws sent me crashing to the ground. I rolled back, spreading my wings to stop the momentum of the fall, my chest heaving, pulse pounding in my ears. Before I could move, Avenlae dove in, slicing the blades of his wings across Mors' face. Mors shrieked, his claws flailing high to seek out Avenlae's chest, but the warrior had already twisted around for another attack. Notien surged in from behind, her scimitar cutting a menacing arc toward the back of Mors' head. As the Creator spun to confront her, Saetyl clunged forward, her ax cleaving through what should have been Mors' chest, and Vindicta screamed, her tails arched over her head as she charged into the melee.

Leaping into the air once more, I flicked my wrist, my left rapier lengthening into a crackling whip that snapped around Mors' raised hand as he focused on attacking Vindicta. I yanked the whip back, locking eyes with his wild, glowing gaze just as Vindicta tore into the shadows that composed his body. His fangs shone as he screamed, Vindicta's claws digging into his shadows and her tails diving straight into the top of his head as she sank her teeth into his shoulder, thrashing her head around. Saetyl spun and swung her ax, its blade cutting straight through the Creator's wrist, and his claws fell, limp, onto the golden grass below us.

With a roar of rage, Mors erupted in a plume of smoke, the force sending Vindicta skidding across the grass. Sinivir threw a shield up just before the shockwave hit me, but it pushed Saetyl, Avenlae, and Notien several feet back. No blood dripped from the arm where Mors had lost his claws, but his eyes blazed with an infernal glow as he glared down at us.

"So that's how it is, is it?" he hissed, the smoke of his body beginning to bubble. "You think a little help from my dear Brother will help you?"

Suddenly, the smoke began to solidify. Mors shuddered, then *grew*. His body crackled grotesquely, bones grinding together, smoke liquifying and coalescing to become skin, and he morphed into a *creature*. Black horns spiraled over his head, and his face tightened into the chilling visage of a skull, its bones sharp and menacing, its razor-like fangs bared. Another set of arms burst from his torso, and the stub of his wrist regenerated a hand whose skeletal fingers lengthened back into gleaming, metallic claws. From the vapor where Mors had once floated, powerful legs emerged, their massive talons digging deeply into the earth beneath. "How will Sinivir help you fight *death,* mortals!" Mors cackled, all four hands brandishing metallic claws the length of my wingspan.

Blood-red energy crackled down the blades of my rapiers, fueled by Sinivir's seething hatred. As a fierce wind tore away Darinrain's ashes, my team and I closed in on the last Brother, our crimson and onyx blades gleaming in the warmth of the rising Silvacastra suns. Vindicta hissed, curling her tentacles and shaking her frill. In that moment, without a word passing any of our lips, our minds were in tune. We were going to liberate Creation, or we were all going to die trying. There was no other way.

A crack of crimson lightning shot across the sky, blazing through my wings as I dove towards Mors. Sinivir's scream echoed in my ears as Mors' glowing white eyes met mine, and his fangs slid apart in a rabid shriek. His claws rose below me, and I twisted, using the blades along the top of my wings to block the attack. Barely regaining my balance, I slashed my right rapier downward to fend off another claw, then hurled myself backward, my left rapier arcing over my head to parry the deadly thrust of Mors' horns. Sinivir threw out a shield over my chest, and I was nearly flung out of the sky again as Mors' second arm slammed against the red shield. With two frantic bursts from my wings, I propelled myself back just far enough to have a second to recover as Avenlae swept in to engage.

Mors' third arm snaked, intercepting Avenlae, preventing him from reaching me. But Mors's white eyes never left mine. Instead, I watched in horror as another **head** erupted from his torso, horns, fangs, and all, to focus on Avenlae. Suddenly, something smashed into my head, sending my helmet spiraling into the plains below. My vision blurred, agony pounding in my temples. Pain exploded across my back and ribs as I hit the ground, rapiers falling from my grasp as my lungs spasmed to pull in more air. The world spun, and the fight with Mors seemed to be occurring far off in the distance.

Did you forget, Creovis, Sinivir growled, his power yanking at my limbs, *that you CANNOT DIE?*

My vision snapped back into focus as I staggered back to my feet, adrenaline pumping through my veins. Blood streamed down the side of my face, but the pain was gone. Before me towered Mors, a macabre colossus of flesh and bone, his form constantly mutating into new horrors. His other two arms had sprouted their own monstrous heads as they battled with Saetyl and Notien. The entire back half of the Creator had twisted into a nightmarish image of a Voxmor whose screams matched the intensity of Vindicta's.

Notien carved her way through the chaos with lethal precision, her scimitar a gleaming blue as it sliced whorls in the air. But I could see she was tiring, even though her eyes still burned with unyielding resolve. Her parries were gradually becoming slower, and each of Mors' attacks was forcing her closer to the ground.

New rapiers materialized in my hands as I sprinted towards her, wings aflame, taking me into the air. *Again. Dive in again and again!* A cry stung my throat as I thrust my blades forward, barely blocking a blow that would've severed one of Notien's wings if I had gotten there even a second later. Mors cackled, sliding one of his arms around to skewer me from behind. I flung my left rapier into the wrist of that arm, altering the trajectory of the claws with enough time for me to push myself off of them and flip over the wild buck of his horns. I swung my left hand around, firing a burst of magenta energy into Mors' primary head. He shrieked, his monstrous form recoiling, if only for the briefest moment. But that moment was all my team needed to seize back their advantage.

That one. Focus on that one, I thought desperately. My team just needed to hold on long enough for me to attack the main head on Mors' body. *That's it. That's it.*

I forced every ounce of strength into my wings, diving and twisting around Mors' claws, fixated on his opaque eyes. The air was suffused with the sharp, metallic tang of blood where Mors had cut through parts of armor on Saetyl, Avenlae, Notien, and Vindicta. Each slash was shallow, but they were enough to begin to sap their strength, inch by inch.

My heart thundered in my chest the closer I got to the skeletal face that hissed down at me. Forks of magenta power exploded against the charred skin of Mors' body as his claws spun, always *just* too close. Silver scratches crisscrossed my crimson armor, each one a glaring reminder of how narrowly I evaded him. The scorching heat of Mors' breath seared my cheeks as I moved ever closer, his furious hiss a warning I had to ignore. Across from me, Avenlae twisted in midair, his onyx form weaving through the Creator's relentless strikes with powerful grace. He crossed his rapiers in front of him, shoving away another brutal attack from Mors' claws. With the moment of reprieve this gave him,

Avenlae reached up and ripped his helmet off, spitting blood from his mouth before preparing for another strike.

I was running out of time. Avenlae wasn't going to last much longer.

With a guttural cry, I pushed myself off of one of Mors' arms, agony burning through me as his claws sliced my wings and raked across my back. But it didn't matter. The time was *now.* Sinivir channeled his power into the deep gashes in my body, and my skin began to glow as gold as the suns above us. I raised my rapiers above my head, arching my back and tightening every single muscle. There was a moment when the slightest flicker of fear entered Mors' ashen eyes as they watched my blades fall. And I felt a thrill of victory. I *scared* him, the final Creator, the last Brother. I *did* it.

With all the force I could muster, I sank my rapiers into the sockets of Mors' eyes, pushing wave after wave of pure golden *genepotenia* through the blades and into his body. His shriek rattled my skull, fighting against the power I was forcing out of my body. Forks of crimson lightning exploded down from the sky, searing Mors' already blackened skin as Sinivir's scream joined that of his Brother. And I was frozen, just a vessel for power. I was nothing but desperate that this would save my people, my team, my friends, and my mate.

Something crushed my wings. I shrieked as the pain nearly blinded me, and I was ripped off of Mors' face. My body was slammed into the ground as if I were a helpless ragdoll. Coughing, gagging, gasping, I dragged myself up, my entire body trembling violently as I tried to get up to respond to the panicked calls of my thoughts: *get up, get UP, PROTECT THEM!* Sinivir again pulsed his power out through my veins, fighting to heal the wounds of my body and block the pain. But he, too, was weakening. A dull ache still throbbed as I stumbled, trying to stand while still panting and coughing. My wings dragged helplessly behind me, their fire extinguished.

Saetyl was thrown to the ground next to me, her body flipping across the grass sickeningly limp. I wheezed, forcing myself to run to her, even as the world began to tilt. She shook her head, blinking her golden eyes as sparks flew from her metal wings. Her body jerked, the wires along her spine malfunctioning as her wings froze, bent at awkward angles.

"Behind you!" she cried, her hand up as if she could manifest her own shield.

I spun, crossing my arms and sending out a pulse of energy that blocked Mors' claws, but sent me back into the flattened grass. I rolled onto my hands and knees, still wheezing, unable to reach for the power that would release me from the mortal body I stayed in. Avenlae had temporarily distracted Mors as he dove in around his main head, the blades of his wings slicing across the Creator's eyes that leaked their pale ichor from where my rapiers had pierced the bulbs. Mors raised two of his arms, the slicing of his claws forcing Avenlae to twist and flip around in midair to avoid their blades. Another swipe of the final Brother's claws sent Avenlae diving to the ground, rolling across the dirt and stopping in a crouched position with his rapiers held to either side of him. He bared his canines, then flapped his wings as he pushed himself off the ground.

Then he faltered.

Avenlae's chest heaved as he fell to the ground again, violent coughs forcing him onto his knees as bright red blood dripped down his chin.

"No," I whimpered, struggling to get to my feet, but Mors had already seen. One of his lower arms darted forward, striking like a snake.

Seemingly out of nowhere, Vindicta appeared, leaping over my head. Her tentacles wrapped around Mors' claws, changing their direction just enough to miss where Avenlae crouched. But her shriek took on a heart-wrenching pitch as the Creator's claw *kept* moving, tearing Vindicta's front leg off her body. Her black blood sprayed across Avenlae as she landed in front of him, still screaming and trying to balance as she fell forward onto three legs.

"NO!" A yell tore from my throat, a sound of both my and Sinivir's panicked cries. I forced myself up, ignoring the pain of my wings dragging behind me as I tried to run to Vindicta.

TO ME! Sinivir ordered, his voice carrying from my mind to the Voxmor Queen. She whirled around, but wouldn't leave Avenlae, who gasped for breath behind her, his eyes wide with terror.

Red consumed my vision. Energy pooled into the Creonex, then shot from my hand in a burning magenta beam that collided with the torn flesh where Vindicta's leg had been. Her black blood spread like spiderwebs over her pale scales, but its flow slowed as my power cauterized the crater in her side. I stopped running as the power weakened, then died, taking nearly all of my energy with it. Swaying, I tried to remind myself to breathe and keep my eyes **open**. There was still something I had to do. I wasn't done. But I was so **tired.**

A scream forced me back to the battlefield. In a moment of clarity, I looked up. Mors' claws descended toward me, the suns' light reflecting off their edges. But, this time, what could I do? My wings were shattered, useless. I barely had the strength to keep my eyes on his claws as they came ever closer. I couldn't be killed, but I **could** be destroyed. And now, I would be.

But someone threw themselves in front of me.

A body slammed into me, thrown backwards from the force of Mors' claws ripping through its flesh. **That wasn't real,** I thought as I fell back. **Th-that wasn't real, that wasn't real!**

But the pain of the body landing on top of me was. The burn of my muscles fighting to pull me out from underneath the deadweight was real. The feeling of bright blood pouring over me, spraying onto my armor, its metallic stench, was undeniable. And that platinum blond hair… The world reeled and narrowed to a point of pain and blood.

"NOTIEN!" Saetyl screamed, her arms out, reaching for her mate as her body still jerked from her malfunctioning wings. An echoing cry wrenched forth from her throat as she collapsed, her pain filling the air, a single raw note that hung in the plains.

I couldn't move, not even to wipe the blood from my eyes. The impact had pinned me to the ground with Notien's body sprawled across my legs. I held Notien's head in my hands, cradled it in my lap. Her navy eyes were glazed, her rosebud mouth parted in a half-formed gasp, and a trickle of blood across her jaw. That was the shape her death took: unfinished, unfair, a sentence cut off mid-consonant. Her sleek wings lay on either side of us, the feathers shifting only with the wind that blew across the plains. I touched Notien's face, the fine silk of her hair, the blood-slicked curve of her cheek. My hands, weak and shaking, left bright streaks across her golden face. Mors' claws had gouged a hole into her torso, ripped her body into ribbons of bloody sinew. Her heart… her heart was gone. She had died almost immediately. No power within me could fix a wound so deliberate. Notien had thrown herself in front of me, had absorbed the entirety of that blow, and it ended her. But her skin was still warm. How could she be gone when her skin was still so warm? "N-Notien," I whimpered, tears dripping over my nose. "W-why? H-how could y-you?"

Saetyl's shrieks hit me, gripped my heart, pounded against my skull. My tears fell in hot, blinding sheets onto her face, and with each drop that struck, I felt the ghost of memory—the riverbank where she first smiled at me, sunlight flashing on the water; her laughter as she pressed the cup of *a'ta'ya* into my hands, its taste sharp and sweet; the warmth of her fingers combing through my hair before the **Weigt'ri**, the quiet strength in her voice as she told me I was ready; her arms around me just hours ago, steady and real.

They came all at once—*too fast, too bright*—crashing against the moment in my hands. I could almost feel her laughter in the tremor of my fingers, hear her voice in the shallow rattle of her breath. But my hands were shaking, slipping, and her warmth was already fading.

I raised my head, struggling to breathe through the pressure of tortured sobs. Vindicta kept her gaze on Mors as he cackled, and flared her remaining tentacles over Avenlae to keep him behind her. He watched me, his silver eyes round, his ears flat against his hair. There was nothing any of them could do. Our strength was spent. And as Mors drew back all four of his arms, his claws spread, I knew.

They were all going to die, and he was going to force me to watch.

Pain, like nothing I had felt before, took hold of me. It was the pain of despair, of terror, of grief, of anger, of helplessness. It wrapped around every fiber of my being, throbbing, tearing, tightening over everything I was. I was losing *everything,* including myself.

And I *screamed.* I threw my head back and screamed so hard my throat seared as if it had exploded from the force. My whole body felt as if it burst from the pain, energy pulsing outwards in throbbing waves. A flash brighter than the suns shone behind my closed eyes, and I sucked in a breath.

The world had become silent. It had become still. Was this death, then?

Taking in shuddering breaths, I lowered my head, cracking my eyes open. A grey amorphic blob was suspended before me in the middle of a world bathed in white. There was no heat, no cold, no color, no feeling. I glanced down—Notien's body was gone. Instead, there was just an extension of the amorphic form. I scrambled out from underneath it, but it didn't react. It just stayed there. To my right was the golden outline of Vindicta, and, under her,

Avenlae. To my left was the crouched form of Saetyl, with a pulsing red mark in the center of her form. Was that her pain? The breaking of the bond between her and Notien?

I choked out a sob, covering my mouth with my hand. To *see* the extent of Saetyl's pain drove home how *real* Notien's death had been. She had jumped in front of me, sacrificed her life without a second thought. And I had *promised* her we would… we would sit together after it was all over…

A voice called to me, its sound as soft as a whisper carried on the wind. I gasped, hastily wiping the tears from my cheeks as I spun around. Still, the nebulous grey form hovered before me, its edges slowly unfurling like wisps of smoke, reaching out towards the radiant golden silhouettes of my team. But I could hear something within it. I couldn't understand the words, but the voice… I had heard it before.

Go to it, Sinivir said, his presence calm in my mind.

"W-why?" I asked, my voice weak.

Trust me, Xiaye.

I stared at the cloud, my hands still hovering protectively over the lower half of my face. My body quivered, fear coiling tightly within my chest. I didn't want to. I didn't want to do it anymore. I wanted to be done. Nothing within that grey form was going to be worth more pain.

Trust me, Xiaye, Sinivir repeated, his voice slow and calm.

Shuddered breaths became quick pants as I took a step towards the grey form. Nothing happened. I took another step. Then another. I moved as if pulled by an unseen force, as if I'd given over control of my body. Clutching my hands protectively close to my chest, I approached the enigmatic form, close enough to reach out and touch it. It hung there, suspended in time, unwavering. There was no sound, no smell, no feeling. But when I narrowed my eyes, I realized the cloud was made up of millions of tiny, colorless spheres, like little particles. Each was frozen in its place, a minuscule fragment of a whole. Holding my breath, I reached out a tentative finger.

The very second my hand came close enough to touch the cloud, the tiny spheres burst apart, opening a pathway that beckoned me further into its depths. There, only a few feet in front of me, was a glowing golden orb, its surface as smooth as that of a calm lake. I held the orb in my gaze, feeling each beat of my heart as if it were the most precious movement in my body, in my world.

And the orb **called** to me, in those words I couldn't understand, but in that voice I knew. Because it had been the voice that had first spoken to me through the Creonex. And those were the words it would speak to me, alone, cold in a leaky bunker. Back before I knew anything.

I crept closer, still but for my feet as they moved across the opaque ground. Whispers darted around the grey cloud, faster, louder, more persistent. When I was right in front of the orb, close enough that its golden glow was all I could see, I heard it.

Name me.

And I knew. Without Sinivir's prompting, I **knew**.

"Creovis."

A ripple passed over the surface of the orb, its once smooth appearance now alive with movement. It began to spin slowly at first, then gained momentum. The surface fractured, releasing hundreds of streams of golden light that danced and intertwined. The strands wove themselves together from the ground up, forming the distinct shape of a man. His features were intricate, carved from the light itself, and he gazed down upon me.

"Who speaks of me?" he asked, his voice the very sound of velvet, with the heat of fire.

311

"Xiaye," I responded, my voice so quiet compared to his.

He tilted his head to the side. "You are the Second, then, aren't you?"

"I-I am."

"And I am Vita, the First." He tilted his head forward in a slight bow. I stayed as I was, tears drying on my cheeks as my eyes flitted around the golden light that created his body.

"It is done?" he asked after a moment of silence.

"W-what?"

"The Brothers—have you come to destroy the last?"

I nodded, feeling a tightness in my chest.

"At last," Vita sighed, the light within him beginning to flicker. "It is done."

He turned and began to walk through the grey cloud, its tiny spheres like black holes within his glow.

"What?" I called, taking a few steps forward and reaching out a hand towards him without thinking. "W-wait!"

Vita's eyes, still burning, met mine. "What do I-I do now?"

He tilted his head again, as if studying me. "The universe is yours, now, Xiaye, the Second. Take it. Protect it."

CHAPTER 29

A shockwave cracked through my body. My vision went white, as if the world disappeared for a moment, and then the pain returned. My body felt as if every bone had shattered, and a pressure returned on my legs. My scream echoed in my ears, and the white of my vision gradually began to darken as my eyes adjusted to the light of Silvacastra's suns, now almost dim compared to what had been the glow of Vita, the First Creovis. My chest heaved as I struggled to breathe through the throbbing and aching of every inch of my body. I lowered my head, my eyes resting on the still body of Notien, where she lay over my legs. There was no golden glow within her, no sign of light. Just the drying blood over her cheek, the gurgle in her throat, and the trickle from the ribbons of flesh that once was her torso.

A ragged gasping came from my left. Saetyl dragged herself closer, unable to keep her body still as sparks from her wings' wires sent jolts through her body. But her fiery eyes never left Notien. She dragged herself over to us, placing her bleeding fingers over Notien's cheek. Saetyl couldn't speak through her sobs, but the tenderness of her touch as her hand roamed over Notien's body said everything. She was trying to understand what she saw, trying to figure out how to accept it and say goodbye. *Because how can Notien be dead when her skin is still so warm...*

Vindicta limped over, moving slowly enough that she could keep Avenlae protected by her body. In the middle of the field, a mass of black smoke began to dissipate. Some of it coated the golden grasses like ash, some of it started to swirl in the wind that never stopped waving the grasses of the plains.

It's done, Vindicta said, her voice shaking as she neared, *Mors is gone. I do not know how, but he is gone.*

Avenlae collapsed in the grass next to me, his breathing sharp and his winces showing how painful each wheeze was for him. I looked into his silver eyes, seeing pain and fear. No celebration or relief. Just grief.

"We're done," I said to him, tears flowing anew down my cheeks. "We're finally done."

Vindicta lowered herself down behind us, sighing as she curled around our little group. She pressed a few of her tentacles against Saetyl, lifting one up to her temple to help calm the frantic signals from her brain. The jerks became less violent, until parts of Saetyl's body just twitched here and there as she pressed her forehead to Notien's. Her dark green ringlets, free from their braids, settled against the blood-caked strands of Notien's hair. A breeze brought with it the tang of blood, most of it drying in the flattened grass and over my hands. More of Saetyl's tears dripped into Notien's glazed navy eyes, appearing to make them wider, rounder, more... more innocent.

I stayed there, holding Notien's head, unwilling to let her go. I rocked us both, a slow motion born of grief. Like Saetyl, my hands still mapped the curve of Notien's cheeks, the point of her ears, the corners of her mouth that had always smiled so readily at me. All unnecessary details now, functions of a body that would never move again. How could this be all that was left of Notien? Of the first true friend I'd ever had. How could she end so abruptly, when she had marked the very beginning of what my life had become?

I slumped my head onto Avenlae's shoulder, trying to control my breathing so I could allow Saetyl the moment to grieve the loss of her mate. She was a ruin, still trying to bury her face deeper into Notien's neck as if she could somehow find the whisper of a pulse. Her wings, usually singing with their low electrical hum, now made only the occasional click: the dying memory of a signal. I would be able to grieve, in time. But not then. The others needed that time more than I did. They needed to keep their illusions, for just a while longer, that we were still whole.

Something floated down in front of me, landing softly on my right arm.

I glanced down, blinking back tears as my brain, still dazed by shock, sluggishly tried to recognize what the object was. At first, I thought it was snow—a single flake twisting in the suns' light, then two, then a calm flurry. But that was impossible, as we were too far away from Silvacastra's poles for snow to ever fall. I blinked again, and another flake spun down to land on my wrist. Carefully, I reached over and brushed the flake with a finger. It dissolved under my touch, leaving behind an oily sheen, a coating like that of an insect wing.

The next piece landed on Notien's cheek, a flat, rectangular scrap. There was color inside it: a gradient, a streak of blue fading to gold, a vanishing point of scarlet at the edge. It looked, impossibly, like... a scrap of *sky.*

I jerked my head up, suddenly aware of a great silence pressing down on the plain. The golden grasses were still moving, but the wind had stopped. The crackles of small fires had quieted, and their flames had died. Even the dark ash of what was left of Mors had drifted to lie still upon the soil. It was as if the entirety of Silvacastra was waiting for something, poised on the edge of a blade. Hardly daring to breathe, I raised my eyes to the sky.

Those scraps *were* pieces of the sky. The sky was *crumbling* right above us.

"W-what is h-happening?" Saetyl stuttered, seeing more pieces of the sky as they floated down to rest on Notien's body. But I couldn't answer her.

"Xai, what did you do?" Avenlae asked, his voice raw and hoarse, as his head darted around, seeing the black holes begin to widen in the sky above us. But I couldn't answer him either.

I was watching the world begin to disappear right before us.

Vindicta leaned closer to us, a small shriek of panic escaping her throat. I couldn't say anything to any of them. Because what terrified me more than the growing abyss in the sky was that *I* had done it. *I* had brought the destruction of this planet, of my people.

It is the failing of the universe, Sinivir said, his shadows moving purposefully through my mind. *Without the power of the Creators, there is nothing to hold together the fabric of the four universes.*

I watched in awe as the sky began to unravel, counting my breaths, *one, two, three...* as time stopped. Saetyl, Avenlae, and Vindicta were suspended in motion, their eyes wide and filled with the encroaching darkness that was slowly devouring their planet. But not mine. I was staring at Sinivir as he materialized before me. He appeared younger than when I first met him, his physical presence both haunting and mesmerizing. His crimson hair fell in a silky waterfall, a few braids pulling back the hair around his face. His eyes, a rich sanguine hue, were softer now, exuding a gentle warmth despite their harsh color set into the ethereal alabaster of his skin.

The help of a Creator is never free... The universe is yours, Xiaye. Take it. Protect it.

"This... this is what I was meant for, wasn't it?" I asked him. My limbs trembled, not with exhaustion but with the absolute clarity of final purpose. I looked to Sinivir, whose shadow bled red and malachite across the frozen field. "I was made to destroy your Brothers."

The words hung between us, unfinished, a question and an accusation at once. The Fifth Creator gazed at me. Not with the impersonal cruelty I remembered, but with some echo of longing, as if he mourned a future that could never come to pass.

"Yes. And no," Sinivir said. "You were the only thing I ever created that was strong enough to destroy my Brothers with my help. Now that they are gone, you are also the only thing I ever created that is powerful enough to become the fabric of the universes. The last and only bond that can stitch them together."

My mind reeled, the weight of his words pounding through my body like the last beat of a dying heart. "So… I was never meant to survive? In the mortal sense?"

Sinivir looked at me for a long time. The hands that had once shattered Creation now hung limply at his side, smooth and young where there had once been a maze of veins. "No. You were never meant to survive within the mortal worlds of Creation."

For a moment, I felt the familiar urge to rage against him, to defy his certainty. Instead, the pressure of Notien's body over my legs began to lessen. The agony in my body was gradually replaced by a sensation like deep water closing over my skin. So, too, did the strength of my heart begin to fade. Along with it, the world around us flickered as more voids of blackened abyss opened in the sky, strips of reality curling away from them.

"But neither was I," Sinivir sighed, lowering his eyes. "Creation should be liberated from the control of *all* Creators."

I wanted to laugh at the irony—my entire existence shaped by a being who now despised his own power. "Then why Creation's War?" My voice cracked, either with pain or frustration, I didn't even know. "Why try to destroy everything you're now trying to protect?"

A small, sad smile curled Sinivir's lips as he lifted his head again. "You, Xiaye, should know all too well what happens to a mind twisted by vengeance." The crimson of his eyes was soft as he spoke, a beg for... forgiveness.

I looked away from him, down to Notien's glazed navy eyes. The air grew thick, the world splintering into impossible, unspeakable colors. Smears of memory whirled their way around my head as I thought I saw a flicker of Notien's smile in her unseeing eyes. The weight of her body was gone, and so too was the beat of my heart. I no longer felt *alive,* in the mortal sense. I was shifting, framing, dissolving into something else. I existed in the same way *genepotentia* did—ever present, ever moving. "What do I do?" I asked quietly. I wasn't sure if I was asking Sinivir, Notien, or, perhaps, whatever else was out there in the Realms that were leaking into each other.

"There is nothing for you to do," Sinivir said. "I've taken care of that. Your power is already being woven into the universes as we speak."

I tried to protest, but the thought dissolved before it could reach my lips. Deep down, I knew he spoke the truth. I could feel the unraveling — the pull of everything I'd been, scattering into the fabric of creation.

When I turned my head, the world tilted. Through the trembling air, Avenlae came into focus, his moonlight eyes fixed on me, wide and unblinking. A tear clung to his cheek, refusing to fall, caught between defiance and surrender. Even as the universe fractured around us, he was still unbearably, beautifully alive.

I reached for him, my hand shaking, finding the hard line of his jaw. His warmth met my palm, and I felt the pulse beneath his skin — the desperate rhythm of someone who still refused to stop fighting.

His lips parted, but no words came. The sound that left him was raw, half a breath, half a prayer. He leaned into my touch as if it anchored him to this world, as if he could keep me here by sheer will.

I wanted to tell him I was ready: that the quiet I felt wasn't fear, but peace. But my chest ached with something heavier than acceptance: the unbearable truth that he wasn't ready to let me go.

The heat of his skin lingered on my fingertips, a tether to a life I was already slipping away from. The more I held on, the more the peace spread through me — slow, consuming, terrifying in its calm — while he trembled under my touch, still breathing, still living for both of us.

"Can I say goodbye?" My voice was so weak, I didn't even know if Sinivir could hear me, if he could answer my plea.

The Creator's eyes moved between us. "I can only give you a moment," he said with a gravity that sounded less like power and more like regret. "My power isn't as strong as it used to be."

A moment. There was so little left. A moment instead of an entire life with the only person I knew how to love unconditionally. The only person who **knew** me. Who knew Xiaye. My throat clenched. "A moment is all I need."

Sinivir nodded, and for the first time since I had come face-to-face with the Fifth Creator, there was no trace of manipulation, no performance, just a simple gesture of assent. Swirling tendrils of his crimson power began to dance around us, transforming the golden grasses of the plains into a lush, emerald forest canopy, the air filled with the scent of leaves and rain. The ground beneath me unfurled into the smooth grey-and-white marbled bark of an ancient tree. Notien's body began to dissolve into the air, like mist in the morning sun, while, in the distance, I could hear the sound of a waterfall. *Avenlae's cave, where he first kissed me.*

But there was one last question I needed answered. "Sinivir," I said, catching his eye as his power began to consume the robes he wore. "What started all of this? What did your Brothers take from you?"

The colors of suns' rise returned above us as the shape of the tree began to solidify, the crimson energy fading into the flames that danced higher up Sinivir's body. His blood-red eyes held me for what felt like an eternity. "Love, Xiaye," Sinivir confessed once his eyes were the only thing left of him in existence. "They took my love."

With the whisper of an exhale, Sinivir was gone, and the sounds of a forest alive with morning light returned. Warmth spread over my skin as the suns shone down on the branch where Avenlae and I crouched, just the two of us. I immediately pulled him close, closer than I ever had before. His arms wrapped around my waist, and he pressed his forehead to mine, eyes searching me with desperate intensity. But I could feel something pulling at me, just slightly like the soft touch of a child.

"Xiaye?" Avenlae's voice was a cracked whisper. "W-what is happening?"

I wanted to tell him that it was okay, that I was there and he was safe. *He's safe.* Suddenly, he clutched at his chest, gasping as his hand clawed at his armor. I reached forward, touching the cool metal of the Creonex against his cheek. He looked up at me, gasping, each breath a ragged plea. "A-are you hurt?" he managed, eyes rimmed with red, pupils blown wide and wild. His hands trembled as he reached up, his fingers tracing the line of my jaw, my cheeks, my neck, as if he needed to memorize every contour.

"It's—" I choked, unable to finish the sentence. I forced a shake of my head. "No, I-I'm not hurt, but I don't have much time."

The relentless tug at my soul grew stronger, and my wings had begun to take on a soft golden glow.

"NO!" Avenlae's cry shattered the air, and his wings flared out behind him, every feather trembling with the effort of holding in the scream that

320

threatened to break him. He grabbed my arm, holding onto me as if his life depended on it. "No, no, no, I *know* what this pain is!"

His words dissolved into sobs, shuddering through his body in great convulsions. I caught his face in my hands, my thumbs sweeping away his tears as they fell, streaming down his cheeks and onto his throat. Avenlae gasped and choked, his breath coming in great, ragged bursts as pain ripped through him.

"I'm sorry," I whispered, my voice breaking, unable to tell him for *what.* I was sorry for *everything,* every small lie, every battle, every fight, every word I said in anger. But most of all, for leaving him. "I-I have to do this."

Tears traced warm paths down his alabaster cheeks as he clenched his eyes shut, muscles tense with another wave of pain. "I cannot lose you!" Avenlae's voice became a strangled shriek as he tried to move closer, his body shuddering with the pain of the *lyceliah* breaking. He buried his face into my neck, his sobs shaking both of us. "Please… d-do not leave me, *le'eseia.* "

My heart fractured. "Av, I don't h-have a choice." And, *finally,* I cried with him. I leaned my head against his, my tears twirling into the strands of his onyx hair, dampening the garnet of the suns' light on his braids. "I'm the only one left with the power to hold together Creation. This is h-how I s-save you."

"Please…" His plea was fragile, a heartbeat slipping away, "I cannot… You are *everything* to me!" His voice cracked, lower now, painfully raw. "If y-you die, I d-die with you. Even if I am s-still breathing."

"P-please, Av, there's still life left for you to live," I whimpered, running my hand over Avenlae's braids, along the feathers of his wings, across his cheek, everywhere I could feel him. Because it was the last time I would know what he felt like. And I moved my eyes over the scar across his face, the scars that carved their way through his tattoos, the tattoos that told the whole story of his life. I saw the silver of his feathers and the beautiful, prismatic chrome of his eyes,

321

those damn moonlight eyes. Because it was the last time I would know what he looked like.

A ragged cry tore itself from his throat, as if ripped out by the very last string of the *lyceliah* tearing. He leaned into me, his strength failing, soft cries shaking his shoulders. "I w-will have loved you f-for forever and it w-wil not h-have been enough," he wept.

"N-no, Av." I raised his eyes to mine, trying to give him a soft smile as my entire body began to brighten with a golden glow, and I felt all that I was slipping away. "You *will* love me, and it will be your love that raises the suns in the morning and hangs the stars in the sky at night."

He shook his head, barely able to speak. "Please do not leave me, Xai. Please."

I sucked in a breath, my glow shining in his eyes. Wrapping both arms around him, I pulled him close with the last of my strength. I pressed my lips to his temple, to the top of his head, to his mouth. It was the taste of salt and sorrow, the metallic tang of fear. I kissed away every last tear, every regret. One last kiss. One last time.

"Live for me," I whispered against his skin. "For all the mornings I won't see. I love you, Av. I always have, and I always will."

As my golden glow swallowed the world around us, I held Avenlae tight, pressing my face in his neck, feeling the warmth of his skin, the beat of his heart, the soft hitch of his breath as he cried one last time.

Silvacastra, the universe, my love, my life, faded to brilliant gold. And I, Xiaye, the Second Creovis, became *everything*.

EPILOGUE

Avenlae fell forward onto his hands, knees digging into the tangled, golden grass, stalks shattering and crumpling beneath him. She was gone. Xiaye was *gone.* As the last pulse of the *lyceliah* ebbed away, so too did his mate, his *le'eseia*, and the last sunrise they would see together. The world became a smear of color and pain, even as the sky returned to blue above him, the suns hanging where they always had been. The planet was intact, but his entire world was shattered.

"Avenlae?" Came Saetyl's shaky voice. He lifted his head, using all the strength he had left, looking at her through the blur of his tears. The gold of Saetyl's irises stood out stark against the bloodshot red of her swollen eyes as she hunched over Notien, her hands a latticework of blood and dirt. "W-where is Xiaye?"

Avenlae tried to speak, but the sounds caught and strangled themselves before they reached his tongue. He could say nothing as another wave of anguish passed over him. He let his head drop, and the tears came in great, wracking shudders. Avenlae's wings fell to either side of him, limp, the life leaking out of him as he realized he could no longer feel Xiaye. He had gotten so used to her presence, something he could always detect in the back of his mind, a reminder that she was *there,* no matter what.

But now, he was alone. The lingering taste of her, the scent of shifting moonsilk, the electric promise of her presence… gone.

Avenlae felt as if he was unraveling, thread by thread, and there was no one left to hold him together.

"Sh-she was just h-here," Saetyl said, cradling Notien's head closer to her, her voice rising and warped in pitch. "I-I do not understand, Xiaye w-was just r-right *here!*" The denial in Saetyl's voice was raw and childlike, naked, and it made Avenlae want to scream.

She still is, Vindicta said, her voice wavering as she lowered her head to rest between Avenlae and Saetyl, a low, mournful whimper deep in her chest. *She is everywhere, now.*

Saetyl's breathing became more erratic as she looked into Vindicta's sorrowful, kaleidoscopic eyes. "W-what do you mean?"

The ultimate sacrifice, Vindicta sighed, *to save Creation. Xiaye is everything that holds our universes together.* There was no pride in her words, and no comfort. Only a dull, senseless ache, and a resignation that made the sky seem even wider and more oppressive.

Avenlae cried uncontrollably, beating his fist against the ground as if he could punish the world for what had been taken from him. Each blow sent a jolt through his body, and he wished it would break him into pieces, let him scatter to dust so he wouldn't have to feel any longer. His spine bucked with the force of his cries, and every breath felt like it was scraped raw against the inside of his ribs. He wanted to scream, to kill something, to disappear, and to do nothing at all. He wanted... he wanted Xiaye. Avenle wanted the one thing he could never have again, the thing that had been torn from his hands at the moment when he thought he had finally, *finally* earned it.

A gentle touch, surprisingly delicate, landed on his shoulder blade, a single tentacle. *Come, now,* Vindicta said, keeping her voice calm and coaxing. *We must return to the tribe, tell them they are now safe.*

"No!" Avenlae heard himself shriek, his voice jagged and heavy with pain. He wrenched himself away from Vindicta, twisting so violently that his wings tangled and he nearly toppled. He glared at her, eyes burning. "I-I cannot leave. She was here. I... I cannot leave here."

Vindicta clicked, moving her snout closer to him. Her eyes, swirling, crystal, and strange, blinked slowly, the corners softening into something like sympathy. ***There is nothing we can do. Staying here won't bring Xiaye back. It won't help you or the tribe.***

He wanted to argue, to shout that she was wrong. But the lie died before it could take shape. He looked down at his hands—splintered with bits of grass and his own blood, trembling, useless—and forced himself to breathe. "They are *her* people," Avenlae spat, wiping angrily at the tears stinging his raw cheeks, even as more welled in their place. "I do not belong to them. I will not go back, now that she..." His voice broke, and he shuddered, the words dissolving into nothing.

"My King," Saetyl said weakly. Avenlae's breath caught, and he forced himself to look at her, how she still curled around Notien's body. "Please. I-I will follow you. I do not h-have anyone else, either, now."

Avenlae looked at Saetyl, really looked at her, and saw what grief had made of her. The proud lines of her face were twisted and stained, her jaw clenched so tightly that the vein there throbbed with every heartbeat. She looked impossibly small, impossibly lost, and he realized that in some cruel way, they were mirrors—broken in different places, but shattered just the same.

He reached for the comfort of anger, but it was already dissipating, the heat leaving behind only a weary, shivering cold. Avenlae wrapped his wings around himself, trying to remember instead what it was like to be more than a scar.

"Please," Saetyl whispered, "just h-help me honor Notien. Then we can d-decide what to do."

Vindicta nudged Avenlae with her snout, her eyes wide. *I will follow you, too. Your pain is not yours alone.*

Avenlae set a hand on Vindicta's snout, then lowered his head down, resting his chest across her scales. She closed her eyes, and a hum reverberated through her chest, a hum that touched his heart, that calmed his pain. As he helped lift Notien's body onto Vindicta's back for transport, he succumbed to a cold numbness. He felt nothing as he helped Saetyl journey back into the forest. Vindicta flared her frill, sending out signals to sense where the tribe was hiding, and began to lead them into the most dense part of the forest, where very little of the suns' light shone through the canopy. Soon, he and Saetyl climbed onto Vindicta's back, too tired to fly and unable to walk well through the underbrush. Avenlae stared at the spines of Vindicta's back that tilted as she limped, getting used to walking with only three legs. Her ribs heaved, a sure sign that she, too, was losing strength, but Avenlae said nothing. He didn't even know what he was supposed to do about it.

It was late in the afternoon before they finally found the tribe, tucked away in a well-hidden cave system. Avenlae wasn't even the one who told them Xiaye, their Queen, was gone, and they had no body to honor. He still couldn't speak. It was the only time he had ever seen, and would ever see, the General shed a tear. The scar across Kaigar's white eye paled as it stretched across his skin, his face crumpling as tears melted across the lines and scars that twisted his expression. Avenlae couldn't even cry with him. He couldn't feel the despair in the cries of his people. He couldn't react.

He attended the Celebration of Passing held for Notien, only because he was expected to. He said nothing, made no show of emotion. The combined tribes still held a massive Celebration of Passing for Xiaye, one that attracted delegations from each of the twenty-five Allied Worlds. Avenlae nodded, shook hands, and bowed to each, as was expected. They all bowed deeply to him, offering support and condolences. He didn't really hear what any of them said. He didn't really care. Only one tear rolled down his cheek at the very end of the Celebration of Passing, and he disappeared into his chambers within the Queen's Nest as soon as it was no longer considered rude for him to leave. But once there, it was too overwhelming. Xiaye's scent was still everywhere in the room. It mingled with the memory of another Queen, a mother. In a sudden fit of rage, Avenlae was throwing things across the room, ripping the bedsheets and blankets, and tearing holes into the wooden walls. It was all just *too much*. No one understood the depth of his pain. No one else was *Y'araye,* and knew what it felt like to have their very *being* ripped from their body when a *lyceliah* broke. And he *hated* it.

In the end, he dragged himself to another room within the Queen's Nest, one meant to serve as the room for Queen Klaecyia when she was alive and came to stay. This became his room, and he never again set foot in the Queen's chambers. Nor did anyone within the Queen's Nest ever speak of how the room had been completely torn apart.

And so, Avenlae became the first Crowned King of the Delfungaye without a Queen.

For a few years, he was simply known as the Silent King. He spoke to no one, besides, perhaps, Vindicta. He appeared only when expected and for exactly as long as expected. The *Hopyroque* and *Fyr'aeset* gradually dispersed back out into the plains and *Fae'oteek* mountains as the horrors of what became known as the Liberation of Creation became something of the past. The pain was fresh, but the danger and fear were gone. Some *Sloviyankae* remained within the *Laizuteek* tribe, having made homes and friends there. The rest migrated with Havyeque back to the Icelands to rebuild what was left of their underground city. Vindicta sent several Voxmor with them to traverse through the abandoned tunnels of Inquiri's hive and help with the rebuilding efforts for as long as needed.

Over time, Saetyl began studying under Kaigar to prepare for her position as General when the time came. She had become as hardened as he after the Liberation of Creation, but, even so, the warriors and trainees whispered that there was still a part of her that was compassionate, if you could find it.

The day Avenlae, Saetyl, and Vindicta returned to the tribe became one of the Delfungaye's most celebrated gatherings every year. The three remained solemn throughout, sitting upon the balcony of the Queen's Nest with their drinks, watching as their people danced, ate, and laughed. They watched with tears in their eyes, but their tears never fell.

Creation seemed to move on. Time continued stubbornly forward, and the Silent King remained, irrevocably, silent. The Delfungaye pulled their involvement in the Allied Worlds back drastically. No one blamed them, really. "Those people have been through more than enough already," citizens of the worlds would say. Trade deals were offered, support was given, but the Silent King never took action on any of it. The Delfungaye people almost seemed to grow autonomous, since they didn't really have much of a king to govern them.

But, as it had happened so many times before, something happened that changed the Silent King.

Avenlae sat upon the highest branch of the Queen's Nest, his silver eyes filled with the deep violets, magentas, and oranges of the suns setting on the horizon. A breeze moved across his feathers—there was a chill to it. *The cold season,* he thought, then immersed himself in numbness once more.

"My King!" came a frantic female voice behind him. Avenlae didn't bother to turn. Just flicked a wing in acknowledgment that he had heard the voice.

"The *Matri Me'liev* requests your presence, Your Majesty."

Avenlae turned his head slightly, thinking. He didn't actually have the energy to see the old woman, and he wasn't interested in another one of her lectures about how he should "learn to let go of his pain".

"Sh-she requests it *now,* M-my King," said the woman, obviously uncomfortable with being so direct with the Silent King. "Just you, Saetyl, and Vindicta. No one else."

That caught his attention. For the first time, something drew a bit of Avenlae out of the Silent King. He frowned, raising himself to his feet and leaping from the branch, gliding straight down to the *Matri Me'liev's* nest. Saetyl was already there, and Vindicta had curled herself up in a corner, trying to appear as small as possible as she took up nearly half of the space.

"Do you know why we're here?" Saetyl asked Avenlae, her brows furrowed and arms crossed over her chest. He shook his head, then looked over at Vindicta, who appeared to shrug. There were wires across the stub where her front left leg had been. The Healers were working tirelessly to build her a prosthetic, but it hadn't quite been perfected yet.

There was a scuffle in the adjacent room, then the *Matri Me'leiv* appeared, her watery navy eyes wide. She carried something in her arms, something wrapped in a soft, white cloth. "It came to us," she said to Saetyl, Vindicta, and Avenlae. "In the night, a star fell from the sky, and it came to us."

Avenlae raised an eyebrow.

"I am sorry, what?" Saetyl scoffed. "We do not have time for spiritual stories."

"I do not lie!" The old woman snapped, holding out the thing in her arms, shaking it slightly in Saetyl's direction. "It *means* something! It is a gift!"

Vindicta raised her snout, sniffing as if she had caught a scent. Then

329

her pupils contracted and she lurched forward, a soft hum in her chest. Avenlae stared at her, feeling a leap in his heart. ***No, it is nothing, you idiot,*** he scolded himself as he sighed and stepped forward. ***Just the ramblings of an old woman***.

But it wasn't.

When Avenlae reached the ***Matri Me'leiv*** and pulled away the cloth, everything he knew changed. Silvacastra seemed to regain its color, and the sounds of the forest alive returned to his ears. His heart thrashed in his chest, and he reached for the bundle, taking it into his arms.

The Silent King found his voice. "She is mine."

For in that bundle was a baby girl, her wisps of hair as white as snow, her feathered wings the very color of porcelain.

And when she opened her eyes, her left was silver as the stars, and her right was as blue as the summer sky.

THE END

Acknowledgments

I was in shock the first time I was writing an acknowledgments page, and this time, I'm simply filled with joy and gratitude.

To my amazing editor — thank you for showing me what I couldn't see. Your insight, honesty, and care have pushed me to grow not just as a writer, but as a storyteller. A "fresh set of eyes" is always needed for any manuscript, and the way you were able to see exactly what I was trying to communicate through my writing was amazing.

To all the new readers who've found their way to my work — I can't begin to express how much your support means. Every message, review, and quiet moment you've spent in these pages has touched my heart more than you'll ever know. Knowing that my words have found a home with you is one of the greatest joys of this journey.

To my incredible beta and ARC readers — thank you for being the first eyes, the first hearts, and the first voices to walk beside me through these worlds. Your excitement, feedback, and love keep the fire alive when doubt tries to settle in.

And to the small independent bookstores that have welcomed my book onto your shelves — you have no idea how much that means. To see my story resting among so many others, supported by people who champion creativity and community, is something I'll never forget. Thank you for believing in indie authors and for keeping the magic of storytelling alive.

About The Author

Willow Grace discovered her passion for creative writing at the age of thirteen, igniting a lifelong love for storytelling that blends the realms of science fiction and fantasy. A proud nerd at heart, she grew up captivated by tales from iconic series such as Star Trek, Lord of the Rings, Harry Potter, Avatar, and The Dark Crystal, which continue to inspire her imaginative worlds. Residing in sunny Florida, Willow cherishes her time away from the keyboard snuggling with her beloved furbabies, all of whom she has lovingly rescued. Alongside her husband, she enjoys spending time outdoors, or building intricate Lego sets, crafting mini dioramas, and playing games—often with him patiently awaiting her discovery of the elusive jump button for her character. Willow's creative endeavors reflect her vibrant personality and her deep connection to the fantastical worlds she loves to explore.